Best Man

CHRIS DELYANI

This is a work of fiction. Names, characters, places, and incidents are either the products of the author's imagination or are used fictitiously. Any resemblance to actual persons, living or dead, is entirely coincidental.

ISBN: 978-1-7918-3515-6

For Dan

CONTENTS

ACKNOWLEDGMENT

The novel you are about to read would not have been possible without the patient guidance of my story editor, Charlotte Cook. The single best thing I did in the writing of this book was to listen to her. My gratitude.

1

OPENING MOVES

Last night I dreamed Jonathan and I zigzagged through a sprawling train station. A shadow chased after us. Marcus. He glided through walls and people, gaining on us with ease. We scrambled to the platform. A huge clock, mounted over the departure board, ticked toward midnight. An old-fashioned black steam train waited, puffing, its doors open. Ice encrusted the platform. White steam swirled around us. The crowd blocked our way. The train faded and receded the harder we ran. Each breath I took felt sharper, icier. My lungs burned with dread.

Then I found myself sitting inside the train, at a passenger window. The train chugged along an ocean cliff. It was daytime now. Sunlight poured in through the window and warmed my arm. Jonathan sat asleep, leaning against my shoulder. The hood of his black sweatshirt hid his face. I looked out the window and down at glistening rocks below, sharp and menacing like broken dragon's teeth. Dizziness overcame me. I focused on the waveless ocean spreading out like porcelain. No birds, no ships, no clouds, no people—nothing but the pallid water and sky merging into a wall of bluish-white. Marcus was out there. I could sense it.

The train picked up speed. The steam engine roared in my ears. The railcar rocked from side to side. I wanted to move, but couldn't. What were we doing here? Where was this train going? Any second, the train could tip over and send us hurtling down the cliff. I turned to Jonathan, his hood ripped off, his face now revealed. But the man next to me wasn't Jonathan. The man was Marcus—a grinning, bright-eyed Marcus.

"Thought you could escape?" His hand came to my throat and squeezed, his eyes a searing blue. "You never will, Frank."

I awoke with a cough and a shudder, my hand to my throat. My bare feet hung off the cushions of the ratty love seat in my sun room. My miniature chess set, the one I'd used to work out a problem last night, sat on a low table in front of me. The Lewis chess pieces sat in their positions, facing off against each other with staring bug eyes. Goose bumps crawled over me even though two blankets and a sheet stuck to me like shrink-wrap against the January cold. I'd hurtled back into the waking world, leaving the phantom of Marcus behind.

Feeble light spilled into the room through the cracks in the blinds. I disentangled myself from my covers, sat up, and put on my glasses. School would be starting in a couple of hours. Had I finished correcting those tests I'd brought home on Thursday? No, wait a second. Today wasn't a school day. Today was Saturday. Today was the day I'd be seeing Jonathan at the San Francisco Ferry Building. I hadn't seen him in six months. Not since my divorce from Ethan. Jonathan had called me out of the blue on Wednesday night, asking if I could see him. No wonder I'd dreamed last night of Marcus chasing me, grabbing me by the throat.

I groped for my wristwatch, taking care not to knock over the chess pieces. What time was it? I brought the watch to my face and squinted. I couldn't make out the numbers. Then my mother's old grandfather clock, which I'd inherited last year after she died, chimed the lonely hours. I listened to the slow, leaden bongs ripple through the downstairs rooms. The clock issued five bongs, then a sixth bong from its oaken heart. I snapped to attention. Six o'clock already? My roommate Julio was usually up at six o'clock on Saturdays. What would he say if he saw his landlord sleeping down here like this? He already must think I was eccentric, maybe even insane. I ached to think he could be right.

I scrambled to stand up, my bare toes touching the freezing floorboards. Into the closet went the sheets and blanket. No time to move the chessboard. I tucked the notebook under my arm and shut the sunroom door behind me. A creak of floor boards above my head froze me in place. Julio's footsteps in his room. I stole up the stairs two at a time and shut myself in my bedroom, taking care not to slam the door. Could Julio have heard me race up the stairs, shut myself in my room? My face flushed as if he had.

Now came the waking nightmare—the thirty minutes I had to wait in this cursed bedroom until Julio left the house. He was only my roommate, a nice guy as far as I could tell, but he felt like an intruder, a stranger who gave me a rent check. I wrapped myself in a bathrobe and assumed my usual position at my writing desk, facing away from my king-sized bed, and closed my eyes.

The plain comforter behind me stretched out in my mind like the ocean in last night's dream. I pictured it as an unbroken field of emptiness that concealed writhing, thrashing memories of what had happened there while I'd been out of the house teaching high school calculus. Ethan and that other man, now his new partner. Their wrestling naked bodies seared across my mind's eye as vividly as ever, the awful image rising up like a sea monster from the depths of last night's dream-ocean. I could never sleep in that bed again.

The pipes groaned in the walls between my bedroom and the bath. Julio was in the shower. I listened and waited. Soon the pipes quieted down. The bathroom fan whirred. Then silence. Julio must be in his bedroom—packing his gym bag, dabbing his short, black hair with gel. What garish color would he wear to teach yoga today—lavender, aqua, apricot-orange? I pictured him as a bright little star moving through the leaden air of this house, oblivious to the sadness that lay like packed asbestos beneath the floorboards, between the cracks in the walls. Thank God he hadn't seen me in the sunroom.

His feet clomped down the stairs. Then the back door opened and slammed shut. I stole to my bedroom window. Under a pale blue sky, the rising sun tinged the housetops pink-orange. Soon Julio came into view. His jaunty step took him down the sidewalk away from the house, his gym bag bouncing on his shoulder. He wore the aqua today. For four months I'd willed myself not to notice Julio's habits—to learn as little about him as possible. It was enough to know he was heading toward the BART station, on his way to San Francisco to teach yoga, and wouldn't come home until around two. The house would be mine until I left to meet Jonathan in San Francisco.

I went downstairs and put on a pot of coffee. The windows above the sink glowed with sunshine—not the sickly, implacable sunlight from last night's dream, but light more suitable to meet old friends. For the umpteenth time I ran in my mind Jonathan's phone call of three nights ago. An edge in his voice led me to think he had important news to confide. Did I dare hope that maybe, after almost twenty years of putting up with Marcus and his abuse, Jonathan had finally had enough? If so, I was ready to rescue him. I could even picture bringing him home with me. Then maybe my house would once again teem with love and good cheer, the very windows shining brighter in the glow of Jonathan's presence. But then I remembered Marcus from last night's dream. *Thought you could escape? You never will, Frank.*

***

Footsteps on the back stairs made me jump. Who could that be? Then the kitchen door swung open, and Julio, out of breath, rushed into the house. He stopped short. His nipple ring showed beneath his tight aqua jacket. I half-turned from him, my insides seizing up, thinking he'd pulled a prank on me.

"Hey, Frank, I had to come back for my—ah, there it is." Julio's eyes lit on his neon-purple iPod on the counter next to the sink. He went over and picked it up. "I can't believe I left it behind."

"Good thing you remembered it," I said, turning my head. If I'd spotted the iPod lying there, then maybe I would've gone upstairs again, to wait for Julio to retrieve it.

He stuffed the iPod into his gym bag, slung the bag over his shoulder, and went to the door. I rose and opened the cabinet where the coffee mugs hung on hooks. I sensed him standing by the door, watching me. I pretended not to notice him, but I couldn't keep the pretense up for long. I turned and looked at him with a frown.

"Sorry." He darted his eyes away and then looked at me again with a half-smile, almost as if he were about to burst out laughing. "I don't think I've seen you wear glasses before."

"Most people don't see these," I said, reaching up and adjusting my square, black-rimmed glasses. "I usually put on my contacts first thing in the morning."

"You look different in them," Julio said in a bright voice that ran like a cheese grater along my nerves. "They make you look—distinguished."

"Oh."

"Gosh," Julio said, hugging his arms to his chest in a mock shiver, "it's not too cold in here for you, is it?"

"I'm leaving the house in a few minutes myself," I said, my body tense. "Besides I like it on the cool side. But you can always turn the heat on when you're here by yourself."

"I know," Julio said, nodding. "I hope you're going out soon. It's warm in the sun today."

"Glad to hear it," I said, turning away from him to end the conversation. Of course it would be warm in the sun. What else would it be?

After Julio left, I went upstairs to shower and change into my contacts. The next hurdle was what to wear. I slipped on a gray T-shirt and an old olive green V-neck to wear over it. Blue jeans instead of the khakis I usually wore to school. I looked myself over in the closet mirror and confirmed I looked ordinary, not tempting, not threatening. A friend and nothing more.

On my way out the door I realized I'd forgotten the chess set on the table in the sunroom. Julio didn't know about the hours I spent working on chess problems. It would mortify me if he knew I did little else with my free time. But I didn't have time to hide the board upstairs or else I'd miss the BART train. So I moved the set to the sunroom's closet shelf, again taking care not to disturb the pieces. Then I made it to the Rockridge BART station in the nick of time. Jonathan, here I come.

***

Two rows of vegetable stalls, crowded with people, lined the gray building stretching out on either side of the Ferry Building's clock tower. I hadn't realized the Ferry Building hosted a farmers' market on Saturday mornings. The setting wasn't nearly as intimate as the one I'd imagined. I peered up and down the Embarcadero trying to look like I belonged here. Then I saw Jonathan. Alone. No Marcus.

His tall, thin frame was bent over a long metal bicycle rack. He was locking up his silver bike, his rolled-up left pant leg revealing a firm, white calf. Of course he'd ride his bike over here. He'd also brought his good camera, wearing it on a shoulder strap. Maybe Jonathan planned to take close-up shots of vegetables for his next collage. Leave it to him to tease out the hidden beauty of beet leaves and Brussels sprouts.

Jonathan rolled down his pant leg, straightened up, and squinted into the crowd, craning his long neck. When he spotted me, his face lit up as if his troubles were over. My insides lit up, thinking my own troubles were over too—or if not over, at least survivable.

"Geez, Frank." Jonathan moved his camera out of the way to give me a badly needed hug. "I'm so glad you could make it. It's been so long. How long's it been anyway?"

"I've been trying to remember myself," I said, although, in fact, I could name the exact day I'd last seen him. "I think it was June, remember? When you guys came to Oakland for a visit right after my mom died?"

"It's been that long?" A look of concern passed over his face. "What a lousy friend I've been."

"No, you haven't." I put on a brave smile. "I haven't exactly been putting myself out there lately."

"We're together now," Jonathan said, his eyes bright. "Maybe we'll have more chances to see each other in the new year."

He clasped my shoulder and smiled, taking in the sight of me. The only difference between today and the day I first met him at the youth group in Santa Cruz twenty-two years ago were crinkle lines in the corners of his soft brown eyes and strands of gray threading through the brown of his short, disheveled hair. We'd both turned forty last year—me in July, him in November. After everything I'd lost in the past year, at least I could say I hadn't lost Jonathan.

"How were your holidays?" Jonathan said, his tone cheerful. "You go down to Santa Cruz?"

"For the long weekend."

"Your sister and dad hanging in there?" Jonathan's expression turned serious.

"I guess so," I said. "They miss my mom."

"I bet, I bet." Jonathan's voice was soft and full of sympathy. "I always liked your mom. Tough and formal, but kind of sweet, you know?"

My mother's last days played out in my mind. Her head had lain like a shriveled apple against the pillows, her ashen face framed by an aureole of dyed reddish-brown hair. Her skin had stretched like rice paper against her high cheekbones. Wendy and I had spent countless hours at her bedside. Once or twice Mom had fluttered her eyelids awake, looked straight at me with watery gray eyes, and then closed them again without recognizing me. The funeral had been a mercy after that.

"At least she's not suffering anymore." I managed to keep a tremor out of my voice. "So, um, you want to go eat breakfast somewhere? Or maybe go inside for a cup of coffee?"

"Coffee?" Jonathan looked up at the Ferry Building. "Sure, let's go inside."

I trailed him through the high archway into the building. People mobbed the shops and stalls, their voices echoing off the high ceilings. Jonathan made his way to the line for coffee, while I staked out seats at a large table near the exit. I used a discarded napkin to wipe the grit off the wooden surface and waited. This was not the cozy coffee shop I'd envisioned. Jonathan made me uneasy besides. He seemed distracted, in a hurry, as if I were only one of his agenda items for a long and busy Saturday. My reasoning mind told me he wouldn't be announcing he was leaving Marcus for good.

Jonathan came to the table, holding two coffees, a small white paper bag, and his camera. He put the camera on the table, sat down, and pulled out two slices of banana bread. For a second I permitted myself to imagine we were a married couple, sharing breakfast on a Saturday morning. If I had started dating Jonathan twenty years ago like I should've, maybe that's the breakfast we'd be having today. And Marcus would mean nothing more to us than one of the blank-faced strangers walking past our table.

"Here," Jonathan said, sliding one of the banana bread slices toward me on a napkin. "They were the last ones left, so I figured I'd take them both."

"Thanks." I pushed in my chair. "So does this mean you don't have time for a real breakfast somewhere?"

"No, sorry." Jonathan shook his head with a regretful look. "Marcus and I are taking the ferry to Sausalito this morning. He's meeting me here in about an hour."

"Oh." I looked down and removed the lid from my coffee.

"I'd forgotten Marcus and I were supposed to meet friends up there today," Jonathan said, his voice dipping. "I thought of calling you to put it off for another week, but then I thought, 'Geez, if I don't see him this weekend, then something else'll come up.' And it's already been too long. How long did you say it's been?"

"June."

"June, geez." Jonathan sighed. "Where does the time go? Marcus and I are so busy on weekends, I feel like I don't have the time anymore even to think."

Jonathan smiled and sipped his coffee. I sensed Jonathan preparing to ask about Ethan and the divorce. With my thumb I traced the base of my left ring finger, where my wedding ring used to be. I'd sold the ring over a year ago, at the tawdriest-looking pawn shop I could find.

"So, um, Ethan. It's all legal?" Jonathan said, looking up. "The papers are signed and filed?"

"Yep, last September," I said, drawing in a long breath.

"What about the house?" Jonathan's look and tone were dead serious. "You keeping it?"

"Trying to," I said in a matter-of-fact tone. "But buying out Ethan wasn't cheap. The house went way up in value since we bought it. If I sell the house I'll have to give him a cut of the proceeds."

"The house isn't too big for you?" Jonathan pulled in his chair and leaned close to me.

"I'm too attached to it." I sipped my coffee. "My dad lent me money. I also signed up to be the chess coach at my high school, so that's a few more dollars. And I'm renting out one of my extra bedrooms."

"Oh," Jonathan said, his voice dropping off. Not even he could put a positive spin on my new living situation.

"I'm not jumping for joy about it either," I said in a rueful tone. "But it was either rent out a room or lose the house."

"Do you like your roommate, at least?"

"I hardly ever see him," I said, grateful to be talking about Julio and not about myself or the house. "He's a yoga instructor. Nice guy. A little loopy, but he cleans up after himself and mostly stays in his room banging away at his laptop. He pays the rent on time. That's what matters."

"For sure," Jonathan said, and nodded.

My watch read a quarter to eleven. Marcus would be here in fifteen minutes, maybe even sooner. I didn't come all the way here to talk about myself.

"How about you?" I said, looking up. "Everything okay? When you called me earlier this week, you gave me the impression you wanted to tell me something."

"Oh!" Jonathan said, sitting up. "Um…yeah."

Then I heard a buzz under the table. Jonathan's cell phone. He scrambled to fish it out of his front pocket. My heart sank.

"He's on his way here," Jonathan said, putting his phone away. "I told him we'd meet him out front. You feel like walking around?"

Not especially, I felt like saying. Instead I popped the last of my banana bread into my mouth and followed Jonathan outside. Not at all what I'd imagined would happen today. In my mind a chessboard spread out in front of me like the dream-ocean. An army of wooden pieces surrounded me, fencing me in place. The next move belonged to Marcus.

***

We didn't have to wait long for him. Even with the crowds thronging the vegetable booths, I had no trouble spotting Marcus coasting to the curb on his cherry-red bike, wearing gold-tinted aviator glasses and a bright yellow track jacket zipped halfway up. He chained his bike and then strode up to us, his broad shoulders pulled back, his muscular chest puffed out, his jacket clinging to him like a second skin. He looked as if he meant to outshine the sun itself.

"Hey, stranger, nice to see you again!" Marcus said, his smile broad and pearly.

"Marcus," I said evenly, shaking his hand. My dislike of him sloshed through me on a wave of nausea.

He wore his light-brown hair short and straight up with gel. Blond highlights speckled the top of each strand. His long, square sideburns were perfectly even, and a small thatch of hair covered the end of his chin. He was a few years older than Jonathan and me, but he could've passed for under forty, maybe even under thirty-five. I remembered my dream, how confidently he'd gripped my throat.

"So," Marcus said beaming, bringing his arm around Jonathan's waist and hooking his finger around the belt strap of Jonathan's blue jeans, "did Jonathan tell you our big news?"

"I was about to tell him," Jonathan said, embarrassed. "But then you called."

"What big news?" I said in as steady a voice as I could manage.

"After all these years of living in sin," Marcus said, squeezing his arm around Jonathan's waist, "we're finally making it official. We're getting married!"

Getting what? The news ripped through my chest like a bullet. Jonathan looked at me with a frozen smile as if hoping for my approval. But what could I approve? What could I even say? And to think I'd been looking forward to this morning, had been clinging to the idea of Jonathan as my salvation, the answer to everything that had gone wrong in my life. All for this.

"Oh—congratulations," I forced myself to say. I looked from one to the other of them, not knowing what to say next. My eyelid twitched. "When's the big day?"

"October," Marcus said, letting go of Jonathan's waist. "We haven't picked the exact date yet."

"And of course you're invited," Jonathan put in, as if to reassure me.

"Sure, sure," I said, feeling for my missing wedding ring with my thumb. "So where are you thinking of having the ceremony? City Hall or something?"

"Actually," Marcus said, smiling at Jonathan, "that's the other part of our news. Have you told him yet, Jonathan?"

"No, not yet," Jonathan said again, his voice trailing off.

"What news?" I said. My body went cold with the same dread I'd felt last night in my dream.

"We're having the ceremony in New York," Marcus said to me, his smile widening to its full wattage. The clock on the Ferry Building read twenty minutes past eleven, but on Marcus's face, the time was high noon. "This time next year we'll be living there."

I looked at Marcus with my mouth open, too stunned to say a word. So not only was Marcus planning to marry Jonathan, he was planning to sweep Jonathan away to the East Coast. And here I'd thought his engagement announcement was checkmate. This was checkmate on top of checkmate.

"So you'll be living right in New York City?" I said, collecting myself. "Manhattan? Brooklyn?"

"Westchester." Marcus pronounced the word as if delivering an extra kick to my stomach. "We're having a house there gutted and refurbished."

"Oh." I did my best to sound interested. "And when will you be moving?"

"We hope by the end of the year." Marcus's face shone with self-satisfaction. "Originally we thought we'd rent it out and move there after we retired. But then we figured, why not move sooner? Besides, our new house is shaping up to be fabulous. We don't have to work that hard anymore either. Even if I want to keep working, my firm's headquarters are in New York. I'm sure I can transfer. And if I can't, I'm sure there are plenty of people in Manhattan who need their money managed."

"Makes sense," I brought myself to say, wondering what it must be like to have the choice to work part-time.

"And I'll find some IT job to keep myself busy," Jonathan said, sounding like he hadn't thought out his future life in New York as thoroughly as Marcus had.

"Or maybe," Marcus said, drawing out the word *maybe*, "you'll use the extra time to develop one of your app games. Or work on your photography. There are millions of things you can take pictures of in New York City."

The edge to Marcus's pleasant tone made me think they'd argued about this. By the look on Jonathan's face I could tell he wanted to stay put. No question Marcus had coerced Jonathan into agreeing to all this. California was all Jonathan knew.

"How's your photography going, by the way?" I said. "That looks like a new camera you're carrying."

"Marcus gave me this for Christmas," Jonathan said in the far-off voice he used when talking about himself and his talents. "I've managed some lucky shots in here and there."

"You should see his latest project," Marcus said, his tone enthusiastic. "He's been taking pictures of martini glasses."

"Martini glasses?" I said. "Like martini glasses in bars?"

"No," Marcus said, beaming, "martini-glass neon signs you see in bar windows. Jonathan started noticing them everywhere we went in the city. So he made a project this past summer of taking as many pictures of them as he could find."

"Nice." I looked at Jonathan, impressed. "That must've been a lot of legwork."

"Marcus drove me everywhere I needed to go," Jonathan said, giving me a bashful smile. "It's not my project. It's our project."

"I'm glad to be a part of it," Marcus said, sounding as if he meant it. "He'll have to show the pictures to you sometime."

"I'd like that," I said to Jonathan. I wished it had been me who'd driven him around last summer.

"The new house is going to have a dark room," Marcus said, grinning. His smile wasn't anywhere as evil as it had been in my dream, but I sensed some gleeful malice behind it. "That's my gift to Jonathan for the cold winters he'll be putting up with."

"Oh, a darkroom," I said to Jonathan in an encouraging tone, not quite understanding why I should be encouraging him. "You've always wanted one of those."

They both looked at me, Marcus beaming, Jonathan with a tight smile. Perhaps they were waiting for me to say something more. Or show more excitement for their grand plans. Instead I glanced up at the Ferry Building clock and wondered how much more of their perfect lives I could take.

***

"So how's everything with you, Frank?" Marcus said. His tone of voice wavered between concern and condescension.

"Fine," I said, slipping my hands into my coat pockets. "The house is fine, school is fine. I'm coaching the chess team this year for extra money."

"Glad to hear it," Marcus said, and hesitated. "And, um—are you seeing anybody?"

"Marcus, geez!" Jonathan said, turning to him.

"What's the big deal?" Marcus shrugged. "You yourself were wondering last night if Frank was seeing someone new."

In that instant, I knew that Marcus and Jonathan were still friends with Ethan, were perhaps "the friends" they would be meeting in Sausalito later on this afternoon. Marcus's words burrowed into my skin, goading me to admit I was alone. I imagined Marcus repeating everything I said to Ethan over drinks. My face burned at the idea of Ethan and his new partner, talking about poor, lonely Frank.

"As a matter of fact," I said boldly, looking at Marcus square in the eye, "I am seeing someone new."

"You are?" Marcus said, giving a start. Then he recovered and flashed a smile. "Good for you, Frank. Anyone we know?"

Ouch. I should've known he'd ask me that. I glanced up at the clock tower, picturing Marcus sitting across from me at a chessboard, confidently putting me in check. How much more time was there before they had to board that ferry? Too much. Quick, Frank. Think of someone you can say you're dating.

"He's—he's a yoga instructor," I blurted out, still looking at the clock.

"Your roommate?" Jonathan said, his eyes widening.

"Yes, my roommate," I said, and looked at Jonathan. My heart raced. "That's how it started anyway. But one thing led to another, and—and here we are."

"Huh," Marcus said, giving me a funny look. "What's his name?"

"Julio." I felt for my missing wedding ring in my coat pocket. Marcus had played me like a chess grandmaster, seizing on my blunder and taking control of the game. And I knew it.

"Julio?" Marcus said staring. "You don't mean Julio Robles, do you?"

"Yes, him," I mumbled, my mouth dry.

"Well, what do you know?" Marcus drew himself up, looking at me up and down as if regarding me with new eyes. "I came from Julio's yoga class this morning."

I shifted from one foot to the other to keep from caving to the sidewalk. I knew Marcus pumped iron. I knew Marcus swam laps. Since when had Marcus taken up yoga classes? Of all the chess blunders I'd ever made, this one was by far the brashest. What had I done?

"He's a great teacher, Julio," Marcus went on. "His class is so fun that I forget how hard he makes us work. He's sweet too. Charismatic. After one of his classes, I feel like I can conquer the world."

"Mm," I said, thinking the last thing the world needed was Marcus conquering it.

"He has a whole following of students, you know," Marcus said casually. "His class is packed every Saturday. I have to go twenty minutes early to find a spot on the floor for my mat."

"Yes, I know he's popular," I said, attempting an insulted tone as if to say of course I knew that. But beneath my flat expression I sensed an army of Lewis chess pieces rising up and looming over me, staring at me with bug eyes. How could I unsay what I'd said about Julio?

"We should have Frank and Julio over for dinner," Marcus said, looking at Jonathan. "Weren't you saying the other day we've never had Frank over to the house? We've been living there for over a year."

"I don't know," Jonathan said sounding worried, and then, in a lighter tone of voice, quipped, "I wouldn't want to subject them to my cooking."

"Don't be ridiculous," Marcus said. "Everyone knows you're a great cook. Everyone but you, that is. You've been talking for months about how we should invite Frank to one of our dinner parties. Why not now?"

"Maybe," Jonathan said, and gave me a timid look. "You think you guys'd be up for dinner at our house?"

"Um." My breath was coming fast. Dinner! "We're at the beginning stages of our relationship. I'm not ready to start introducing him to people."

"Don't be ridiculous," Marcus said, his look and voice exuding false friendliness. "I already know Julio. I'd love to spend time with him outside of yoga class. Jonathan's been talking about having you over for ages. Haven't you, Jonathan?"

"But if you'd rather not," Jonathan said, looking me in the eye.

What pierced my heart was the kindliness bordering on pity in Jonathan's voice. It was as if he knew I'd lied and was throwing me a lifeline. I could almost bear the thought of Marcus knowing I'd lied. But Jonathan? Never.

"Sure, why not," I said.

"You're sure?" Jonathan said, his eyebrows raised and his eyes wide.

"Of course I'm sure." I gave him a tight smile. "You can show me your martini pictures."

"And pictures of our new house," Marcus said. "How does next Saturday sound?"

"Next Saturday, uh—sure, let's do it next Saturday." I rubbed my bare ring finger. "Let us know what you want us to bring."

"Just bring yourselves," Marcus said in a smooth voice, "and we'll take care of the rest."

The smile he gave was exactly as it had been in the train car of last night's dream, radiant, gleeful, triumphant. A smile that could outshine the sun. Marcus hadn't spoken in vain when he boasted of conquering the world. He'd certainly conquered me. I imagined him reaching to grab my throat and holding me fast, leaving me no hope of rescue, no way out.

Rescue did come, though, in the form of the clock tower striking the hour. The ferry had arrived and was loading passengers. I bade Marcus and Jonathan goodbye, told them I'd see them next Saturday, and headed for the BART station. It was a relief to be alone again. But my ears rang with those last words of Marcus's. *We'll take care of the rest.*

Of course he'd take care of the rest. His army was in place, my own king rashly exposed. By this time next week Marcus would discover my lie and deliver a *coup de grâce* more humiliating than any checkmate I'd received at a chessboard. I pictured Julio rushing into the house this morning for his iPod. The way he smiled at me with those large white teeth of his. What would I say to him? How could I even look him in the face? I pictured my mother, her lips pursed in distaste at my blunder. Not since my final days with Ethan had I dreaded going home so much. But I had nowhere else to go.

2

FLAVOR OF THE DAY

What a doofus I was, forgetting my iPod on the kitchen counter this morning. Of course I had to dash home for it. Would that have sucked or what, teaching yoga in a silent room? I'd even stayed up until midnight last night putting together a disco-diva playlist for the class. That's why people come to my classes—they want to start their weekend with some razzle-dazzle to go with their asanas. My students also come to class to look something like me, their hot teacher Julio. I bet I've brought in more business over the years with my abs and my booty than I ever have yammering on about chakras.

I still made it to the Mission in time for class, thank the Holy Virgin. My students dug the old disco songs, some of them even singing along in their twisting crescent lunges. Afterwards I tooled around the Mission and the Castro, wishing I lived nearby. Then, around one o'clock or so, I rode the BART train home—Holy Mother, give me strength—to dull, boring Oakland. Living out here in the boondocks made me feel as if I'd pressed the pause button on my life. What else could I do? Rents in San Francisco had gone berserk. I'd been evicted from my last apartment in the Mission. At least my Mami lives a quick BART ride away in Hayward. She'd beaten a breast cancer scare a few years ago. If I couldn't be closer to the fun, at least I could be closer to her.

I stopped at the window of my favorite ice cream store on my walk home on College Ave. The flavors of the day, scrawled on the front plate glass in splashy red letters, hooked me like they always did. Then Genevieve, the store's owner, caught my eye through the plate glass. Genevieve had become one of my heroes of late: a single woman who ran her own business. She's like Josie and her yoga studio, only way raunchier. I knew I had to go in and give her the lowdown on the hot guy who'd been coming to my classes for the past few months.

"Hey, doll-face!" Genevieve said, holding up her hand like I was a regular at a bar. "What're you having today?"

"Nothing for now," I said, grinning at her. "I'm still working on your honey lavender."

Genevieve was a fiftyish woman with a gravelly voice. Her gimmick was to wear a different-colored wig for each day of the week. Today she wore a long-haired electric-purple wig. I wished I had a gazillion dollars to wear a different-colored pair of yoga pants for each of my classes. Too much of the world looks gray to me, especially in January.

"Gen, honey, you know everything here is my favorite," I said in the flirty tone I liked using on her. "I only came in to tell you about my class."

"He showed up again?" she said, lowering her voice. "Mr. Hot Stuff in the red shorts?"

"Red shorts and not much else," I said. "And get this—he patted me on the shoulder on his way out of class this morning. He never did that before."

"Like a friendly pat?" Genevieve said.

"More like a squeeze," I said with satisfaction. "I can still feel where he squeezed it."

"Way to go," Genevieve said under her breath, looking ready to rip off her wig, close the store early, and head straight home to her boyfriend. "So when're you closing the deal with him?"

"I told you, I can't," I said. I pictured Mr. Hot Stuff standing on his head, his body a redwood tree of hairless muscles, the cut of his abs like grooves in the wood. "Not while he's my student."

"Give me a break," Genevieve said with a wave of her hand. "You're his yoga teacher, not his therapist."

"I don't want trouble with Josie." I glanced down at the ice cream bins and pictured Josie and her beaming freckled face, her glowing skin, her lion's mane of reddish curls. "Josie's like my yoga Mami. And that Saturday morning slot is a moneymaker. I can't risk losing it."

A young mother came to the register with her son. I stepped away to let Genevieve ring them up. A cool feeling prickled across an old scar on my forearm, from a knife wound a bully had given me in high school. The scar never prickled unless I felt excited or in danger—or caught out. But thinking about that guy in my yoga class—sexy and limber—made me think of how much more fun life was in San Francisco compared to here. That guy represented San Francisco in my mind, smiling, gorgeous, a gateway to untold adventures. And all I knew was his first name. Marcus.

***

The house I lived in, around a bend on a dead-end street, was larger than the other houses on my block. I let myself in through the gate. My landlord Frank was in the garden as usual, pruning the rosebushes along the side of the tan stucco house. He looked up startled, as if I'd snuck up on him like some stalker ex-boyfriend. Then he said a quick "Hi" and went back to his pruning. The typical greeting from my landlord. I took in Frank's thin face, his lean frame, his dirty green A's cap that he always wore when he gardened. If Mr. Hot Stuff was what they served up in San Francisco, then my landlord was what they served up here in Oakland—a sad sack poking around in the garden bushes.

I fumbled for my keys, walked up the rest of the stairs, and jabbed the key into the kitchen-door lock. A big yellow envelope sat on the edge of the table. Holy Mother. My massage therapy license. I'd been working and studying for months for that license. Had waited weeks for the thing to come in the mail. Had it finally come?

I dumped my gym bag, plopped down at the table, and ripped open the letter. Inside was a certificate on heavy bond paper. The name JULIO ROBLES was printed in proud bold letters above where it said "Certified Massage Therapist." The paper felt heavy and official between my fingers. The license. I let out an exhale. New license, new business, more income for a new place in San Francisco. In my head Genevieve's gravelly voice rang out, "Way to go!"

I snapped a photo of the certificate with my phone and posted it on Facebook. My phone started pinging right away. Okay. Close the eyes, focus, breathe. Now what? Plan, that's what. First I needed a room to massage my new clients in. I knew exactly the place. Down the hallway, first door on the left. That extra room was half the reason why I chose to ignore Frank's creepiness and move into this strange house. I'd had my eye on that room almost from the day I moved in.

I went to the room and yanked up the blinds. Gorgeous sunshine flooded in. It was still freezing in here. A fake-leather love seat leaned against the wall, a low wooden table sat in front of the love seat, and an old wood-slatted kitchen chair huddled in a corner. Holy Mother, what pathetic furniture. Such a spare contrast to the flea market of a living room next door, weighed down with heavy oak furniture and an ancient piano and a grandfather clock whose chimes made me think of a convict plodding his way to the electric chair. I couldn't do anything about the living room. But this room I could save.

A rectangle of grime framed the dingy wall above the love seat where a picture must've hung. Would it have killed Frank to throw on a coat of paint in this room? I bet Frank would let me paint these walls any shade I wanted, and thank me for it. What colors to choose? Lemon yellow? Pistachio green? Strawberry pink with balsamic swirls? I thought of Genevieve's wigs, her neon-colored ice cream. I could already imagine myself posting photos of the newly painted massage room on my website.

Where would I put my towels and sheets? The room had a closet. I went over and cracked open the closet door. A couple of summer jackets hung on wire hangers. On the shelf above the coatrack, a sheet and a couple of blankets sat in a rumpled mess. Next to them—I rose to my tiptoes—huh? A chessboard? And look at those zombie chess pieces, with their unsmiling faces and round, staring eyes. Even stranger, only a few pieces stood on the board. It was like I'd walked in on someone's game. Frank's game. So Frank was a closet chess player—literally.

But who could Frank be playing chess with? Himself? He must be. I hadn't seen him bring a guest home the whole time I've been living here. And he must've hidden the game in the closet so that I wouldn't see it and ask questions. I know it's terrible to judge—that's not what yoga instructors did—but, holy Virgin, how could I not think this was freaky? My planned new life in San Francisco couldn't come fast enough.

"Looking for something?" Frank's voice cut the silence in two.

I spun around. Frank stood in the doorway with one hand on the doorknob, his other hand clutching his A's cap, his short brown hair stuck to his head. His eyes darted to the closet and then at me as if I'd stumbled across a dead body.

"Oh, uh, no, Frank." I closed the closet door and leaned against it, feeling a zing across my scar. "So is this, like, another bedroom?"

"It has the closet, so it could be." Frank took a careful step into the room as if he were the one trespassing, not me. He had shadows under his watery, greenish-gray eyes. "Right now I use it for extra space."

"Any plans to rent it out?" I glanced around the room, trying not to seem interested in the answer.

"I'm hoping not to." Frank threw a glance at my blue track jacket as if the color would blind him. "I coach my high school's chess team. I work out my chess problems in here."

My phone buzzed against my thigh. More congratulations I was sure, but now wasn't the time for it. I slipped my hand in my rear pocket. Then I looked at Frank. So Frank taught chess to high school students—that wasn't so pathetic after all. And, to be fair, Frank wasn't mean or evil. A little lonesome maybe, but a nice guy at heart. Maybe someone I could sweet-talk into using this room.

"Some good news came in the mail today," I said brightly, holding up the certificate. "The state of California is letting me practice as a massage therapist."

"Oh," Frank said, peering at the certificate with a slight wrinkle of his brow. "I didn't realize you were studying to become one."

"I didn't want to say anything until it came," I said, and gave a modest shrug.

"Sounds exciting," Frank said, his tone not even close to excited. "Congrats."

"Thanks, Frank, I've been working for this for a long time." I took a deep breath. "And so now, um, I was kind of wondering if—maybe—I could use this room to do massages in."

"You want to bring your clients here?" Frank said, blinking and staring.

"Until my business is off the ground," I said in as nonthreatening a tone as I could. "And of course I'll pay you. I don't think I could pay you, um, monthly rent, but I could give you a percentage of my take. How about ten percent? No, let's make it fifteen."

Frank gave a slight shake of his head and looked down at the baseball cap in his hand. His thumb traced the edge of his visor. I held my breath, waiting for him to say something. But he didn't move. The frown and anguish on his face made it clear he didn't like the idea of having strangers clomping through the house. He was probably trying to figure out whether or not he could trust me. A panic rose up from my stomach. If I didn't say something—fast—my dream would be over before it began.

"And I'll paint the room for you," I said, the words rushing out of me.

"You want to paint the room?"

"I love painting rooms," I said, glancing around at the drab walls and picturing them as smooth as orange sherbet. Or lemon sherbet. Or raspberry sherbet. "My Papi used to paint houses, inside and out. I used to go on jobs on him when I was a little kid. I've had eight different addresses in San Francisco. Everywhere I've gone, I've left a trail of color behind me. I'll do a great job for you. You'll see. You'll want me painting all the rooms in your house."

"I will?" Frank said, blinking.

"How about you let me have the room for a couple months," I said, trying to sound reasonable. "If I don't make enough money and you want to rent it out to someone else, then I'll totally understand. Totally. But you don't want another roommate, do you, Frank?"

The stunned look on his face said it all. No, he didn't want another roommate. He probably didn't want me as a roommate either, but if I made a go of the massage business, I'd be moving out too. I gave him a hopeful smile. He walked past me to the window and looked out at the bare-branched trees outside. I thought my heart would stop before he answered. He had to say yes—come on, Frank, say it. I could taste my new business—and my return to San Francisco—as deliciously as Genevieve's honey lavender ice cream.

"I've been trying my hardest not to have to rent this room out." Frank said. He looked at me over his shoulder. "But it'd be nice to make some extra money. Fifteen percent, you said?"

"Yes, Frank," I said widening my smile. "Fifteen percent."

"That's more income than I'm making from this room now," Frank said, speaking more to himself than to me.

"So I can use it?" I said, my heart ready to burst.

"Sure, Julio. Why not," Frank said, his dark expression clearing. He turned to face me. "We can work out the details later."

"Oh, Frank, thank you, thank you." I put a hand to my chest and let go of the breath I'd been holding. "You have no idea how much this means to me."

"Good, glad to hear it," Frank said with a tense, toothless smile, looking like he wasn't sure if he'd done the right thing. Then he bowed his head, slipped his hand into a pocket of his faded blue jeans, and made to leave.

"And if there's something I can do for you," I said, stopping him, "just say the word."

"You don't mean that, Julio." Frank let out a nervous laugh.

"I do mean it, Frank," I said in my most encouraging voice, the voice Josie taught me to use on novice students to keep them coming to class. "If I make a go of this business, my whole life will change. You're giving me the chance to succeed. So if you need help with anything, anything at all, then tell me."

Frank opened his mouth to speak, then didn't. I kept smiling encouragement. An uneasy feeling crept over me. Frank looked like he did need a favor—a favor I might not want to give him.

"Hey, wait a second," I said. "You have something specific in mind, don't you, Frank?"

"Kind of." He seemed short of breath. "But I don't think I can bring myself to ask."

"I don't understand. Why can't you ask?"

"Because," Frank said in a half-sigh, looking up at the ceiling and shaking his head. "I can't."

"Why not?" I said, using my best what's-the-big-deal voice.

"I said a careless thing today." Frank pulled his hand out of his pocket and wiped his forehead. "And now I need help. Your help."

My help? That seemed impossible. What special power did I have? I often told my students I was a diva, but I wasn't Wonder Woman.

"Oh my God, what did you say?" I said frowning, folding my arms in front of me.

"You'll only laugh if I told you," Frank said, his face going from pale to pink.

"Come on, tell me," I said, my voice impatient. "I won't laugh at you. Hand to God."

I held up my hand to show I meant it. Frank looked me up and down. More trust issues. I gave him the nudging smile I'd learned from Josie and now used on my own students, the smile that said I'd be there to catch them if they slipped.

"I found myself in a tight spot earlier today," Frank said, drawing out his syllables and taking a long breath, "and I was feeling, um, cornered. I wound up telling my friends you were, um, my boyfriend. Now we've been invited to their house for dinner. For next Saturday night."

***

Frank's boyfriend? Invited? Next Saturday night? I stared at him. Okay, Frank was right. That really was a dumb thing to say.

"You—you want me to what?" I kept my jaw loose, to keep myself from busting out laughing.

"Remember how I told you I was meeting a friend in San Francisco this morning?" Frank's voice trembled. "I met him at the Ferry Building, and his partner dropped in on us. This partner is someone…well, let's say he's not my favorite person. Anyway, they told me this morning they're engaged. My friend's partner went on and on about their wedding plans. Then he asked me whether I was seeing anybody."

"And you told him you were seeing me?" I said with a gasp.

"My friend's partner was expecting me to say I wasn't seeing anybody." Frank flung his baseball cap onto the chair in the corner. "I couldn't bring myself to say it. I couldn't let him have the satisfaction of knowing I was alone. You were the first person to pop into my head."

"But why does it have to be me?" I brought a hand to my chest. "Can't anyone pretend to be your boyfriend?"

"I wish," Frank said. "But it turns out my friend's partner knows you. He's a student in your yoga class. In fact he came straight from your class this morning to meet us at the Ferry Building. Marcus—Marcus Pierce. Do you know who I'm talking about?"

Did Frank say Marcus? The Marcus in the red shorts? The Marcus I checked out every week? Talked to Genevieve about? Jerked off to now and then? I pictured him in class this morning. The way he squeezed my shoulder on his way out the door after class. The way he walked down the street, looking as good walking away from me as he did walking toward me. Marcus had been following me all day long in my head. Now here was my landlord and housemate Frank Mercer, the last person I'd ever associate with Marcus, saying Marcus's name out loud. The excitement sent a zing across my scar.

"There's only one student in my class whose name is Marcus." I rubbed my chin and looked up at the ceiling, pretending to place the name. "Kind of a tall guy, blondish hair?"

"Yep, that's him," Frank said, his voice dropping. "I didn't even know he did yoga. Otherwise I would've kept my mouth shut. But when I told him I was seeing a yoga instructor he asked a few questions, and now…we're invited to dinner."

My mind turned to Marcus lying face up with his eyes closed on his mat at the end of class. His calm face, his smooth muscles, the line of fuzz leading from his belly button to his waistband. A man engaged to a close friend of my housemate's. Was this the universe's idea of a joke? Of course I wouldn't do it. I was thirty-three years old—way too old for high school pranks. Worse than that, Frank had shattered my Marcus fantasy. How was I supposed to fantasize about a dude who was engaged to someone else? What would I say to Genevieve now?

"I do feel sorry for the mess you're in," I said, speaking slowly. "But I wouldn't feel right about doing this."

Frank leaned against the window frame, ready to sink to the floor if I so much as tapped him on the shoulder. Holy Mother, was he that terrified of Marcus? What had Marcus ever done to Frank?

"For starters, we'd never pull it off," I went on, trying to sound levelheaded. "And even if we did pull it off, I still wouldn't feel right about doing it. I want to live my life authentically. Living an honest life without drama, without keeping secrets. It's what I work on every day. What I teach to my students. What I teach to Marcus. What would Marcus think of me, his instructor, if he found out I was pretending to be someone I wasn't?"

"I suppose you're right," Frank said, his chest deflating.

"So then you understand why I can't do it?" I pictured Josie and thought turning down Frank was what she'd want me to do.

"Of course I understand." Frank's voice was almost like a robot's.

"I'm sorry, Frank," I said.

"No, I'm the one who's sorry." Frank let out a long, shuddering sigh and half-turned from me. "Forget I said anything. I let my pride cloud my judgment this morning. I never should've told them I was dating you. Such a petty, small-minded thing to do."

"What'll you do about next Saturday night?" I said, feeling a stab of compassion for him.

"I haven't thought that far ahead." Frank gave a little shrug. "Maybe they'll forget about the invite."

"But if they remember?" I said. "What then?"

"Then I'll tell them"—Frank looked at me, breaking into a sudden smile—"I'll tell them our romance is over."

"You think they'll buy that?" I doubted if I would buy it.

"They'll have to." Frank's tone was joking, but he sounded as if he was sure they'd never believe it. "I have no other choice."

Frank picked up his A's cap from the chair, put it on, and headed for the door. A knot of guilt tightened in my stomach. I felt as if I'd signed Frank's death warrant. Maybe Josie would've wanted me to say yes to him, to help this poor guy in need. A guy who'd given me the use of his extra bedroom to launch my new business.

"So, um," I said in a cautious voice, "it's still cool for me to use this room for massages?"

"Of course you can," Frank said, turning to me at the door. "Fifteen percent, right?"

"Let's make it twenty," I said before I had a chance to think about what I was saying.

"Sure." Frank smiled, but the dead look in his watery eyes—much like those chess pieces in the closet—made me think no amount of money I offered would ease his worry. "Thanks."

Once he was gone I drew the blinds to the top of the window, letting in more warmth and light. The room seemed as relieved as I was to be rid of Frank. Should I feel guilty for taking this room without giving him what he'd wanted? Hell to the no. I was paying him a fifth of my take. This business had better take off, so I could move out of here pronto. Too many strange people lived in Oakland.

***

Later on I called Dean, my current bed buddy. Most Saturdays I take BART to his apartment in San Francisco to spend the night with him. I couldn't wait to celebrate launching my business but Dean let me down. Dean was happy to hear about the certificate, blah blah blah, but his friend had talked him into spending the weekend in Sacramento. Could I pay him a visit tomorrow? Sure, I said, not telling him how annoyed I felt. What else could I say? If I bitched at him tonight, I wouldn't get laid at all this weekend.

In a couple weeks Dean would be heading to Sicily for nine months, helping to dig up pots or statues or anything else buried in the ground over there. It wasn't too early to start looking for his replacement. So I called my friend Hector. He'd said that he and a few other friends were making their usual Saturday night trek to the dance clubs south of Market in San Francisco. I told him I'd join them there. I took a shower, put on a tight black silk shirt and tight jeans, and hopped on BART.

The big challenge tonight would be not to blow too much money, if I had any hope of launching my business and moving to San Francisco again. I'd stopped drinking a long time ago, so no worries about pissing away fifty bucks or more on cocktails. Paying to come home was another matter. As much as I hated to do it, I'd leave the club at a quarter to midnight to catch the last BART to Oakland. It was either that or hang out until the sun came up. Whatever I did, I'd lay off taking a cab or an Uber home.

But once we made it to the club and I started dancing, I couldn't tear myself away. It was always so easy for me to lose myself in San Francisco, both in time and money. The place was packed with hot sweaty guys. Colored lights swirled around the room. My ears rang and my shirtless body vibrated to the EDM. Why did I have to live on the other side of the bay?

My phone read eleven thirty. The BART train was probably halfway on its journey toward my station. I scanned the dance floor, but I couldn't focus. Too many good-looking guys, too many flavors to choose from. Everyone swirling around me. I wished I could sample a few of them before making my purchase, like Genevieve let me do with her ice cream flavors. Mother of God, why did time have to zip by so fast on a dance floor?

I tapped Hector's shoulder to tell him I had to go, then looked across the half-acre of dance floor and spotted the flashiest flavor in the room. Marcus. He was dancing shirtless near the opposite wall, waving his arms above his head and swiveling his narrow hips. His skin glistened silvery-blue in the flashing strobe lights. A tall, muscular shirtless man with longish, crow-black hair and green-black vine tattoos snaking down his beefy arms danced close to him. His eyes were half-closed as he boogied to Marcus's lead. I stared. Was that Marcus's fiancé, Frank Mercer's best friend? No, it couldn't be.

Then Marcus threw a lazy look over his shoulder and picked me out in the swaying crowd. He turned to face me head-on, his hips moving from side to side. And the look on his face … Holy Mother. I've had enough guys throw me that look to know the porno flick playing in his mind right now, featuring me as the guest star. Then he turned and laid a hand on his partner's tattooed shoulder, leaned in to whisper something into the partner's ear. The partner turned and looked at me. Then they turned to each other and danced as if I wasn't there.

I pulled my phone out of my pocket. Only ten minutes to catch the last BART to Oakland. I thought of Josie and Genevieve and their businesses—no, they wouldn't put their futures on hold for some three-way. What would my Papi say, if he could see me from up in heaven? Marcus and his hunky fiancé could wait. I put on my shirt and made my way through the dancers, out the door, onto the street.

I ran like hell toward Market Street. On Folsom I practically ran out in front of a speeding cab, my arms waving. If I couldn't take the cab all the way home, at least I could take it to the BART station. Then I settled in the nice warm cab. Honestly, how much did I want to take BART home? It'd be a twenty-minute walk from the station to the house. Mami wouldn't like her boy walking the streets at night by himself. How much would it cost to take the cab all the way home, anyway? Thirty, forty bucks? Ah, to hell with it. I'd start saving tomorrow.

On the ride home my mind turned to sad, lonely Frank and the miserable hole he'd dug for himself. How wild would it be if I showed up at Marcus's door pretending to be Frank's boyfriend? Then it dawned on me. How often did Josie say to me that all of us were connected to each other in ways we couldn't understand? Maybe I was destined to be Frank's dinner date next week. I smiled at myself, feeling almost grateful to the universe for keeping Dean in Sacramento.

***

I let myself in through the kitchen door. The house was cold and dark. I slipped off my shoes so Frank wouldn't hear me clomping up the steps. Even through my socks the linoleum floor was ice-cold. I'd have to invest in a space heater if I wanted massage clients.

I stopped short at the foot of stairs. From the half-open door of my soon-to-be massage room came the sound of thin, labored snoring. Had Frank brought a guest home? Someone to play chess with? Or more? Maybe there was such a thing as action in Oakland. I had to see.

I crept to the room's half-open door, still holding my shoes. The blinds were drawn, but enough light came through for me to make out a figure lying on his side on the love seat with his back to me. The man coughed and turned onto his other side, facing me. I gaped. The man wasn't a guest of Frank's. The man was Frank himself.

He'd scrunched himself up in a fetal position, his face deathly white. The sheet and blanket were wound around him as tight as a Tootsie Roll wrapper. His bare feet hung off the sofa cushions. He looked so sad and old, I felt like going over to adjust the blanket to cover his feet. Why was he sleeping down here, instead of upstairs in his own bed? I felt as if I'd stumbled into an ugly secret.

No time to think about that now. I tiptoed up the stairs. The door to Frank's bedroom was shut. Huh. So he was pretending to be inside there. Holy Mother, this was worse than finding that chessboard in the closet.

I had to wonder how long he'd been pulling this charade on me. Maybe as long as I'd been living here. What to make of it? The grandfather clock downstairs pulsed out a lonely one o'clock bong, the leaden sound rippling through the house. I was too exhausted to care. I shut myself up in my room, stripped off my clothes, and fell asleep almost as soon as I crawled under the covers.

***

The next morning I heard the shower running in the bathroom. As usual the pipes whined between the walls like a starving puppy. I blinked and reached for my cell phone. Nine o'clock. I pulled myself out of bed, crept to my door, and opened it. The door to Frank's bedroom was half-open. I crept to the door and peered inside. Hmm. Frank must've snuck into his bedroom before I woke up, and now he was pretending he'd spent the night in there. I hadn't thought how much effort it took to seem normal.

The water in the bathroom stopped. I slipped into my room, my heart pounding, and waited for the sound of Frank going downstairs. Then I pulled on a T-shirt and sweatpants and went downstairs myself. Before going into the kitchen, I peeked inside the massage room. The room looked as abandoned as ever. I went over to the closet and opened the door. No blanket. No sheets. No chessboard. As if what I'd seen last night had never happened. If I had any doubts about what I planned to do this morning, this ended them. My landlord had a secret, and I wanted to know more.

In the kitchen Frank sat in a dark green sweatshirt and gray sweatpants at the table near the door, drinking coffee and reading the newspaper. He didn't look up when I came in. His hair was still wet from his shower. He leaned over the paper and moved his lips while he read. He was only fake-reading the news, I could tell.

I brought my oatmeal and raisins and a bowl out of a cabinet and glanced at Frank for a chance to catch his eye. He kept reading and moving his lips. The strobe lights from last night flashed in my head. Marcus's teeth gleamed in the bluish darkness. I'd stumbled on two mysteries last night, one Marcus's, one Frank's. Okay, Julio, here goes nothing.

"I've changed my mind," I said firmly. "I'll do it."

"Do what?" Frank looked up from his newspaper, his lips parted.

"I said I'll do it," I said again, holding up the teakettle like a weapon. "Dinner next Saturday night. You haven't fessed up to your friends yet, have you?"

"Not yet," Frank said, the corner of his newspaper trembling, "but—"

"Then count me in." I plunked the kettle onto the stove and turned on the pilot full blast.

"You're sure?" Frank drew back and looked at me as if he hadn't heard me right.

"It's the least I can do for you, since you're letting me use the extra room for my business." I turned to close the cabinet door, then poured oatmeal into the bowl. "I was thinking, hey, Frank's a nice guy, he's giving me the use of his third bedroom, wouldn't it be terrible if he had to eat crow? And it's such a small favor. A couple hours around a dinner table. It should be as easy as making this oatmeal."

Frank lowered his newspaper and thought about this, chewing his lip. Then he pulled in his chair and let out a chuckle. I flashed him a smile, picturing Marcus and his fiancé dancing with their shirts off.

"I thought a lot about what you said yesterday," Frank said in a thoughtful tone. "About living life authentically. You were right. I don't think we should do it. Lies lead to lies, which lead to more lies. Nothing good will come if I keep on lying."

In my mind the tattoo vines snaked and glistened in the flashing strobe lights. Then the lights flickered and died. I know I'm a good teacher, but could Frank have picked a worse time to actually listen to—and act on—what I'd said to him yesterday? But of course Frank was right. What would Josie say if she knew I was about to ignore my own teaching, the teaching she'd passed on to me? It was like I was hearing Josie through Frank's mouth.

Then I imagined Marcus smiling at me from across the dance floor. Grinding his hips. Beckoning me toward him. Genevieve flickered in my mind, a devilish smile on her face. Oh, screw the principles. I'd put myself through a lot to reach this decision. I wasn't about to retreat from it now.

"But you can't unsay what you've said," I said, trying to sound concerned. "What good will it do if you told them now you'd lied? I mean, I know it's not good to lie, but sometimes … sometimes a lie is the only choice you have."

"Maybe they won't call," Frank said in a tone of despair, nestling his hands around his coffee cup. "Maybe they'll forget they invited me."

"But if they do," I said, certain they'd call, "then you can count me in."

The teakettle whistled. I moved it to a potholder and turned off the burner, then shook raisins onto my oatmeal. I could practically see Marcus gyrating in front of me, reaching into my pants, while his fiancé ground into me from behind.

Sometimes the universe sent me mixed signals. Like when I was evicted from my last apartment and forced to move to Oakland. Was the universe punishing me for something wrong I'd done in San Francisco? Or had the universe wanted me to live closer to Mami in her old age? I still didn't know. But this time, with Frank, the universe couldn't be clearer. I'd always been intrigued by Marcus, and now here was the universe, handing me an opportunity to spend an evening with him. I couldn't wait.

"All right, let's do it," Frank said with a long exhale. "Let's be boyfriends."

3

RABBIT MEMORIES

Jonathan and Marcus lived on a sleepy street a few blocks uphill from the Castro Muni station, in a mustard-painted, up-and-down condo with balconies on two levels. The place was even larger and more awe-inspiring than I'd imagined it. For months I'd wondered what the inside of the house looked like, had imagined with envy the huge parties Marcus and Jonathan must have thrown for Marcus's A-list friends in the year or so they'd lived here. A bitter taste filled my mouth at the thought that my curiosity would at last be satisfied.

By the time Julio and I climbed the steep stairs in the frigid darkness to their white-painted front door, I needed to put the wine bottle I'd brought onto the welcome mat. I leaned forward with my gloved hands on my bent knees, my throat and lungs burning. All week long I'd been thinking of this dinner as some far-off event that somehow wouldn't happen. Their front door, gleaming in the streetlights, took on an unreal quality, as if I could send my hand through the oak as if through a mirage.

"You okay?" Julio said, putting a hand on my shoulder.

"I'm fine," I muttered, grabbing the bottle and standing up. "I'm more out of shape than I thought."

"We don't have to go through with this," Julio said in a low voice. "I can call them on my cell and say you're sick or something."

"No, we can't," I said. "We've come this far already."

I turned to the door and reached for the buzzer, lit up by the hanging brass lamp above the door. My arm felt heavy, my fingers stiff and frozen. I felt as if I'd electrocute myself as soon as I pressed the button.

"Hey," Julio said, stepping between me and the buzzer. "Look at me first."

I lowered my hand and turned to face him, but I couldn't bear to meet his gaze. My eyes strayed instead to the bouquet of magenta gerbera daisies in his hand. He'd bought the daisies himself earlier today, on a whim, he'd said. He'd had his hair cut today too, shaved close at the side but longer at the top, his sideburns square and neat. The hair was brushed forward and gelled so that it gleamed like jet in the light of the full moon. Julio looked too good to be wasting his time here, helping me execute this charade.

"We're owning this dinner," Julio said in a calm, firm voice. "We have our story down cold. Whatever we haven't rehearsed, we'll make up as we go along. The one thing you can't do is panic. If you panic, they'll notice, and we're done for. Okay?"

I managed a nod. My throat and lungs still burned. But the confidence in Julio's tone made me wonder if maybe we could survive the evening after all.

"I always tell my yoga students if they start to panic in a hard pose, to always return to their breath," Julio said. He used the same serious but friendly tone I sometimes used on my own students. "Deep breaths in, deep breaths out. The feeling will pass. It always does."

"If you say so," I mumbled.

"I know so," Julio said, reaching for the buzzer but with his eyes still on me. "Now let's rock this dinner party. Ready?"

"Ready as I'll ever be," I said. I pictured my mother watching all this with distaste.

"That's the spirit," Julio said with a smile, and he pressed the buzzer.

***

"There you are," Marcus said, opening the door. He stepped outside to wrap Julio in a hug. His teeth and white shirt shone in the moonlight. "I thought I heard voices out here."

"For the lady of the house," Julio said, holding out the daisies with a bat of his long eyelashes.

"The lady is in the kitchen, you bitch," Marcus said, returning Julio's smile and taking the daisies. He looked at me almost as an afterthought. "And Frank. Glad you could make it."

"Glad to be here," I answered in the same flat voice he'd used to address me, presenting him the wine bottle.

Marcus led us inside, with me following Julio, and up a steep set of polished stairs to a cavernous living area that smelled of roasting lamb and garlic. The sparsely furnished room contained a rectangular red couch, a box-shaped black armchair, a drinks cabinet, and a long glass coffee table. On the table a brushed-steel tray held a spread of water crackers and sweating hunks of cheese. A large wooden dining table, painted black, set with gold-trimmed white plates and purple linen place mats, stood near a gas fireplace. Above, a chandelier sprouted crimson glass spikes like a mutant sea urchin. I took in the place and shrank beneath my blue dress shirt. It seemed impossible that a space this large, in a neighborhood as expensive as this one, could be inhabited by only two people.

Marcus put down the wine bottle on an end table, then took our coats and hung them in a closet at the top of the stairs. Originally, Julio had planned to wear nothing but a sheer yellow T-shirt that showed off his nipple ring, so I lent him a plum-colored V-neck sweater. The ring still showed faintly against the thin wool. It struck me that Marcus, as Julio's yoga student, had probably seen that nipple ring many times before, and that no amount of cashmere would erase that image in his mind now. I wished I'd taken on a nerdier roommate, some grad student who wore ill-fitting hand-me-downs and read Milton in his spare time.

Julio sauntered across the room to the sliding glass doors that opened onto a wide balcony. Beyond, the city lights shimmered and winked. I pictured Marcus standing out there on a weeknight, a glass of Scotch in his hand, looking down on the neighborhood like a mob boss.

"Amazing view you have here," Julio said to Marcus.

"You should've come an hour sooner," Marcus said, sweeping a satisfied glance around the room. His chest and arm muscles seemed ready to burst out of what I'd long recognized as his typical Saturday night attire, an untucked white silk dress shirt with a pattern of green and purple zigzags. "We could've watched the sunset from our roof."

"I used to live in a building with a roof deck," Julio said, his face lighting up. "I went up there at six in the morning to practice yoga. I'd do sun salutations right as the sun was coming up."

"Maybe we can spend some time on the roof after dinner," Marcus said. "We can practice moon salutations."

"Only if there's time to practice," Julio said with a little laugh, giving me a nervous smile. "So, um, what's for dinner? It smells amazing."

"Lamb shanks." Marcus glanced at a large doorway on the other side of the dining table. "The food should be almost ready. Come on, Jonathan's been waiting to meet you."

Marcus led us into the small but lavishly appointed kitchen. Jonathan's long back was to us as he stirred a large steel pot at the six-burner stove, steam rising to his face. He turned, put down his spoon, and smiled. My chest expanded. For the first time all week, I was glad Julio had talked me into coming here.

"Frank, hey," Jonathan said, coming up to me and giving me a hug. The warmth of his body, heightened by the steam, melted away the outside cold that still clung to me.

"Great to see you, man," I said, letting go of him and looking at him as if he was the only one in the room.

"And you must be Julio," Jonathan said, turning to Julio.

"I am," Julio said in a bright voice. He stepped around the miniature kitchen island toward Jonathan with his hand out. Both his smile and his eyes were wide, even puzzled, as if he'd been expecting to see someone else.

"Let me put these in some water," Marcus said. He brought out a vase from a cabinet, filled it, and arranged Julio's daisies in them. To Jonathan he said, "Dinner'll be ready soon?"

"Half an hour," Jonathan said with a glance at his pot.

"Good," Marcus said, "then we have time for a drink. I'm making pomegranate martinis tonight."

"None for me, I'm afraid," Julio said in a tone of mock regret. "I retired from drinking a long time ago."

"Frank?" Marcus gave me a glance that said he wouldn't take no for an answer. "A cocktail before dinner?"

"Maybe a glass of water for now," I said, knowing I needed to keep my senses sharp to play chess with Marcus.

"You can't let me drink alone," Marcus said in a friendly but determined voice, "so I'll pour you one anyway."

"Unless you want a beer," Jonathan said, looking over his shoulder at me, his face pink from the boiling water. "I was about to have one myself. My latest obsession is Belgian white ale. You want one, Frank?"

"Sounds great," I said with relief, smiling at Jonathan and not daring a glance at Marcus.

"But if you don't mind," Julio said to Marcus, "maybe a splash of pomegranate juice with some soda water. You can even put it in a martini glass."

"A virgin martini, coming up," Marcus said, smiling at Julio in a way that froze me out.

Jonathan emptied a pot of broccoli into a colander in the sink, then went to the refrigerator and handed me a bottle of ale. I took it and followed everyone with heavy steps into the living area. If my cover with Julio was going to be blown, now would be the time.

Marcus set the vase of daisies on the dining table and then went to the drinks cabinet to make his martini. I sat next to Julio on the red leather couch, closer than I would've in other circumstances, and placed my beer on a brushed-steel coaster, determined to nurse it all evening, my one and only drink of the night. Julio threw me a heightened smile and then mouthed the word "breathe." How Julio could sail through all this without suffocating was beyond me. Maybe I should take up yoga classes myself.

Meanwhile Jonathan plunked himself into the black armchair. One leg draped awkwardly over one of the gleaming steel arms as if he'd never sat there before in his life. He probably hadn't.

"Such an amazing place you have here," Julio said, flashing a smile at Jonathan.

"Thanks," Jonathan said with a careless glance around the room.

I followed Jonathan's glance and tried to imagine what he thought of this museum gallery of a living area. A tender feeling welled up inside me. He belonged in this room about as much as I did. He should be in my own living room, not here. I envisioned playing the piano for him, while he tinkered on one of his games, tapping away on his laptop in my stuffed leather armchair.

"So how long've you guys been living here?" Julio said, snapping me out of the fantasy.

"A while now." Jonathan furrowed his brow. "A few months, maybe. How long's it been, Marcus?"

"How long's it been what?" Marcus called over his shoulder, pouring drinks.

"Since we've been living here," Jonathan called across the room, his voice echoing off the high ceiling.

"About fifteen months," Marcus said, turning around. "We moved in at the beginning of November, year before last."

He walked up to us, holding two brimming martini glasses of dark pink liquid, garnished with a curlicue of lime zest. He set one glass on a silver coaster in front of Julio and then sat down cross-legged on the floor across from us, settling on the gray shag area rug by the coffee table. The drinks looked as artificial as the blond ends of Marcus's spiky hair. Everything here looked fake. Even the view of San Francisco from the windows looked fake. Maybe it wasn't such a bad thing that I'd never been invited here before.

"And I hear you're moving to New York," Julio said perkily to Jonathan. "You must be psyched."

"Yep, psyched," Jonathan said in an upbeat tone that to my ears sounded forced. "We should be moving in by this fall."

"So right after your wedding," Julio said to Jonathan. He folded his hands over his knee.

"That's the plan," Marcus said, cutting off a hunk of cheese and placing it on a cracker. "We hope to move in as soon as we come home from the honeymoon. Every day it seems I'm on the phone with the contractors. This is the last time I ever work with contractors long distance."

"Will the house be ready by then?" I couldn't resist asking.

"It had better be," Marcus said with an edge in his voice, and he crunched down on the cracker. "Come on, boys, you can't let me eat this alone."

I leaned forward and cut a sliver of cheese, busying myself to conceal the quickening of my heart. When Ethan and I had the downstairs bathroom refurbished, the workers told us they could do it in three weeks. Instead, they took three months. How long could a contractor drag out the remodeling of an entire house long distance? I imagined a gutted, windowless mansion in the middle of a frozen landscape, birds nesting in the rafters and snow piling up in the rooms.

"We're looking forward to the change of scenery," Marcus said. "We have all sorts of plans. I'm looking forward to seeing spring in New York again. Plus Jonathan will have plenty of space to keep his bees."

"Bees?" I said, turning to Jonathan. "You keep bees?"

"On the roof." Jonathan glanced up at the ceiling and gave a modest smile. "I gave it a try last summer and found I wasn't bad at it."

"He's fantastic at it," Marcus said, using the same bragging voice he'd used last week when talking about Jonathan's photography. "There's honey in the lamb you're cooking tonight, isn't there?"

"A teaspoon," Jonathan said, the color rising to his face. "I only made six jars."

"With the space we're moving into, Jonathan can start his own honey business," Marcus said. "Jonathan, you think we have time to show them the pictures of the new place before we sit down to dinner?"

"Uh...." Jonathan said. He darted his eyes from Marcus to us.

"How about you show us your martini pictures," I said.

"Martini pictures?" Julio said, turning to me with a puzzled smile.

I told Julio about Jonathan's summer photography project, now and then throwing an encouraging glance over at Jonathan. For the first time tonight I felt more like a friend than a fraud. And I sure as hell would rather look at photos of Jonathan's neon martini signs than Marcus's monument to himself.

"They're upstairs on a flash drive in a drawer full of flash drives," Jonathan said. "It would take me too long to find them now."

"The house pictures are on my laptop in the bedroom," Marcus said, springing up from the floor. "Be right back."

Jonathan pulled himself up from the chair, stretched, and said he needed to finish making dinner. I asked him if he wanted any help in the kitchen, but he said no. My heart sank. So much for the martini pictures. Maybe next time. If there ever was a next time.

***

As soon as we were alone, Julio turned to me with a bright look, as if to say, "I think we're pulling this off great!" I supposed he was right, but still I felt sick at heart—sick to be sitting amid so much excess, sick to watch Jonathan slipping farther away from me, and above all, sick of Marcus, his voice, his smile, his possessiveness. I felt for my missing wedding ring, then reached for my beer and swigged.

A moment later, Marcus came into the room, cradling an open laptop on his beefy forearm. He set the laptop onto the coffee table and sat on the sofa on the other side of Julio. I let my body go numb, my eyes glassy, while Marcus lingered over each photo. He showed us the leafless maples marking the front of the property, the winding creek babbling along the rear of the property, the frost-covered hills framing the horizon. The mansion itself was a yellow-painted brick edifice with black-shuttered windows and two chimneys. The place, when done, would no doubt make the apartment I now sat in look like a fleabag motel. I made a mental note never to visit it.

"Okay, we're ready," Jonathan said, returning to the living area.

We came to the table where a large blue Dutch oven sat on a metal trivet. Jonathan told us to sit anywhere, but of course we let Jonathan and Marcus sit at each head, while Julio and I sat opposite each other. The vase of Julio's gerbera daisies sat between us. Inside the pot, four lamb shanks nestled in a bed of tomatoes and orzo. My stomach rumbled. I was grateful to know that it was Jonathan, not Marcus, who had made this dinner.

Marcus collected our plates from their settings, brought them to the pot, and served us with an olivewood ladle. Jonathan went into the kitchen and returned with a steaming bowl of broccoli, smelling of garlic. I thought of those long-ago dinner parties I'd thrown with Ethan, on the dining table where I worked chess problems, now that Julio had taken over the third bedroom. The china we'd used—blue-trimmed white plates his parents had given us for our wedding—sat imprisoned in the cherrywood china closet. Heaven knew when I'd eat off them again.

For the next few minutes we were busy cutting into our food and thanking Jonathan for making dinner. The conversation died down. I sensed Marcus was waiting for the right moment to interview me and

Julio about our relationship. I was determined to deny him that moment.

"So how long have you been going to Julio's yoga classes?" I said, turning to Marcus.

"Not that long." Marcus looked almost surprised that I addressed a question to him. "It was around the same time I hired the contractors for the New York house. I don't know. Sometime last fall. That sound right, Julio?"

"I remember you at my Halloween class," Julio said with a bright smile. "You wore a Zorro mask to practice."

"I went to your class once," Jonathan said to Julio. "The first time Marcus went, I went too."

"Huh," Julio said. He leaned forward in his chair, apparently trying to place the face. "I don't think I remember you."

"The class was packed," Jonathan said, shaking his head. "And I sucked at it. I've always been more of a gamer than an athlete."

"You were better than you thought you were," Marcus said with a scolding smile. "You didn't give yourself enough of a chance."

"I couldn't do half the poses," Jonathan said to Marcus with a laugh. "I nearly fainted."

"Because," Marcus said across the table to Jonathan, "you didn't hydrate yourself enough before class."

"Yoga's not a contest," Julio said in a diplomatic voice, smiling at Jonathan. "Like what my mentor Josie always tells me, yoga's not about what the person next to you is doing, it's about noticing what you see inside yourself. Without passing judgment. And if you can't do a pose, who cares? You're a diva, not Wonder Woman."

"You gave us that line in class," Jonathan said, smiling.

"It's as true now as it was then," Julio said. "Well, I hope you come to my class again. And you shouldn't feel intimidated by the tough poses. That's what I'm there for. And even if I can't hold you up, all you have to remember is to return to your breath."

Then Julio turned and flashed me a dazzling smile. I unclenched my jaw. How did he know I'd stopped breathing?

"All right, you win," Jonathan said, putting down his fork. "The truth is, I think your Saturday class is too early. I like to sleep in on Saturdays."

"Me too," I mumbled through a mouthful of lamb.

"Julio hasn't converted you to yoga yet?" Marcus said to me in an abrupt tone.

"Not yet." I reached for my wine glass, then drew my hand away. I'd reached for the glass with my left hand—my ring finger hand—and I could swear Marcus had glanced at my missing ring.

"So I have to ask," Julio said, pushing away his empty plate and looking from Jonathan to Marcus. "Where'd you two lovebirds meet?"

"Dance club south of Market," Marcus said, looking across the table at Jonathan, their eyes meeting. "I asked Jonathan to dance. Frank was with him that night. Weren't you, Frank?"

"I was," I said, looking across the table at Julio to avoid Marcus's good-humored smile. "I went to use the rest room. When I came out again Jonathan and Marcus were together in the middle of the dance floor."

"I spotted Jonathan from across the room," Marcus said. "I was here by myself from New York for the weekend, trying to decide if I wanted to move to San Fran. I'd had my eye on Jonathan all night. I had no trouble picking him out in the crowd. He was the tallest, sweetest-looking guy there. So as soon as I saw him standing near the dance floor by himself, I knew I had to go over and ask him to dance."

"How about that, Frank?" Julio said to me with a pleased look. "You took the bathroom trip that changed the course of history."

"That's one way to put it," I said with a chuckle.

I had been living in an apartment in Bernal Heights with two roommates and had been dating Ethan for about a month. Jonathan had recently moved to San Francisco and called me to see if I wanted to go out that Saturday night. Even then, I pictured myself breaking it off with Ethan to be with Jonathan. I'd wanted to confess to Jonathan my feelings for him, but the words stayed stuck in my throat. Then I went to the rest room to brace myself, and ....

"It's so romantic you're still together," Julio said, putting a hand to his chest. "It must've been love at first sight."

"More like lust at first sight," Marcus said with a flare of his eyebrows. "I took Jonathan back to my hotel room."

"Marcus, geez," Jonathan said, turning pink and reaching for his beer.

"Ah, now the dirty truth comes out," Julio said. He pushed in his chair and put his elbows on the table, leaning forward.

"I've never understood the problem," Marcus said, his face shining. "If we'd done it in the bushes, it'd be one thing, but we met in a club. Even if we'd done it in the bushes, who cares? We've been together for eighteen years already."

"Eighteen years?" Julio said openmouthed, putting his hands down on the table. "No way. Me, I'm lucky if I can last with a man longer than eighteen minutes."

My fork slid from my hand and clattered onto my plate.

"Which is why I'm so glad I found Frank here," Julio said beaming at me, letting out a giggle. He pushed the daisies out of the way to reach across the table for my wrist. "I can hardly believe Frank and I have been together four months already. But time moves by more quickly when you're in your thirties, doesn't it?"

"Or Frank here must be doing something right," Jonathan said, turning to me with a smile.

"I try." I pulled my hand away from Julio's grasp and reached for my ice water.

"So you boys were roommates before you started dating," Marcus said, swirling his wine in his glass and throwing a glance at Julio's nipple ring underneath my purple sweater. "That's a bold thing to do."

"Some things can't be helped," I said, repeating a phrase I'd been rehearsing all week in my head.

"But don't you find it awkward, living with Julio and dating him at the same time?" Marcus said, his brow wrinkled.

"Julio's easy to live with," I said, feeding on the confidence my earlier answer had inspired.

"And so's Frank," Julio chimed in. "He's even letting me use the spare bedroom to launch my new massage business. My certificate came in the mail last week."

Nice job, Julio. A slick way to turn the conversation away from us. Both Marcus and Jonathan congratulated Julio and plied him with questions. Apparently this was the first time Marcus had heard Julio's news, or even had known Julio was training to become a massage therapist. I leaned back in my chair and watched my fake boyfriend jabber away. At that moment he almost reminded me of Ethan. Ethan was always better at making small talk than I was.

"Can I help you clear these plates?" I said, turning to Jonathan. From the corner of my eye I noted the wall clock showed exactly nine. The finish line hovered in sight.

"Sure, thanks," Jonathan said with a glance at the empty plates and serving bowls. "I made dessert too. Maybe you can help me bring that out?"

"Let me help too," Julio said, pushing out his chair.

"No, I only need Frank," Jonathan said, with a quickness that took me by surprise. He looked across the table at Marcus. "I have an idea. Maybe you could show Julio the rest of the house while Frank and I bring out dessert."

"What do you say?" Marcus said, turning to Julio after sharing what seemed like a meaningful glance at Jonathan. "Are you up for some moon salutations?"

"If you insist," Julio said, throwing down his napkin on the table and standing up. Then he smiled at me. He'd clearly picked up what I was suspecting too: that Jonathan wanted to speak to me alone. I wondered if Julio had also guessed what Jonathan wanted to talk about. As for me, I had no clue.

***

I brought in the plates from the dining room while Jonathan filled the dishwasher. Then I settled onto a stool by the kitchen island and put a hand to my forehead. Flop sweat. I braced myself for whatever Jonathan might have to say to me.

"Does Julio drink coffee?" Jonathan said, bringing dessert plates and coffee mugs down from a high cabinet shelf.

"Only herbal tea," I said, repeating what I'd rehearsed with Julio earlier. "He tries to avoid caffeine after eight o'clock."

"Geez. I made brownies." Jonathan gave me a troubled look before glancing at a foil-covered tray on the black granite counter. "I made vanilla ice cream to go with it. Maybe Julio can have ice cream."

"Julio loves ice cream," I said, pleased to say something I didn't have to rehearse. "He's always bringing home some stylish flavor or other from this ice cream shop near the house."

"We might have herbal tea in one of those cabinets." Jonathan peeled the foil off the brownie tray and nodded to a tall cabinet near the island. "Would you mind checking?"

"Sure," I said, going to the cabinet.

"He seems nice." Jonathan cut into the brownies with a butter knife. "Julio, that is."

"Yes, he's very nice," I said in a guarded tone. I was on my tiptoes, bringing down an open yellow box of osmanthus tea from the cabinet's top shelf.

"You're happy with him?" Jonathan put down the butter knife to look at me.

"For now," I said, turning to close the cabinet door.

"So you're moving on?" Jonathan gave me a hopeful look.

"Not really," I said, my voice faltering. "I doubt if Julio wants anything serious."

"Still, I'm glad you brought him tonight," Jonathan said. He filled the kettle with water and set it on the stove to heat. "I know you can take care of yourself, but still. I'm glad to know someone's over there in Oakland, you know, to keep an eye on you."

Jonathan nodded and gave me a faint smile. His face looked as fresh as a polished apple. I wasn't sure how much longer I could stand it, with him saying things that struck my heart and then turning around to cut brownies or boil water.

"So I was going through some of my old things," Jonathan said, bringing out a jar of chocolate sauce from a cabinet, "and guess what I came across? The stuffed rabbit from the county fair. Remember the little green rabbit you won for me?"

"Of course I remember," I said, warming to the memory and grateful to be talking about the past and not the present. "I won a blue rabbit for myself. We went with some of the guys at the youth group."

"I remember how you shot all those hoops to win them," Jonathan said, bringing out a small pot and filling it with water, then setting it on the stove. "All of us stared at you, watching you sink one ball after the other. I remember us watching and thinking, who is this guy?"

"A guy who liked to shoot hoops," I said, turning my head and smiling. "I used to drive my mother up the wall. She loved to say I could've become a concert pianist if I didn't spend so much time playing basketball."

"You still play?"

"No, but I should," I said, holding in a sigh. "The basketball hoop is still in the driveway. That was Ethan's present to me when we moved into the house—God, eight years ago now."

"Julio's right, time does slide by faster as you grow older," Jonathan said with a serious look. "I remember that county fair like it was last night. It's all a dream now. Now I'm moving to New York. But we'll still be friends, won't we? After I move?"

"We'll always be friends," I said, with a sinking feeling in my chest.

"Which is why," Jonathan said in an unsure voice, "I was thinking—"

The kettle let out a shrill blast of steam, making both of us jump. Jonathan turned off the burners and took the kettle and pot of water off the stove. He placed the jar of chocolate sauce into the pot of water. Then he looked at me.

"Which is why I was thinking," he said, drawing his words out slowly, "that maybe, if you'd like to, and if it's not too much trouble, you could be, um, the best man at my wedding."

I stared at him. Did I hear Jonathan right? I needed a few moments to let the import, the honor of what he was saying sink in. But then what would I do about Julio?

"Your best man?" I said, my heart pounding. "Me?"

"Why not you?" Jonathan said in a small voice, his face clouding over. "You're my oldest friend."

"But Marcus, last week at the Ferry Building," I said, my mind whirring. "I thought he said the ceremony would be in New York. I don't think I can make a New York trip after the school year starts."

"We changed our minds," Jonathan said stubbornly. "We're having it in San Francisco. It's his dad who wanted us to have it in New York because he lives there. But our friends are here."

"What about Patrick?" I said, and licked my lips. "Wouldn't you rather have him as your best man?"

"He doesn't even know I'm engaged." Jonathan's voice was cold.

"But he's your brother."

"You're more of a brother to me than he ever was," Jonathan said, his tone despondent. "Besides I'd love to have the chance to spend more time with you this summer. We could go pick out tuxes together. Lord knows I'll need help picking one out. What do you say? Will you think about it?"

I glanced up at the stainless steel wall clock with its large black numbers—half past nine—and then at the drip-drip-drip of coffee into the pot. This charade was supposed to end in a half hour or so, not extend into the summer and fall. To say yes to Jonathan's offer would mean to keep pretending to date Julio. As much as it devastated me to do it, I had to say no.

"You don't want me to be your best man, do you?" I shrugged and looked away. "After everything I've been through? What do I know about marriage?"

"It doesn't matter what you know and what you don't know," Jonathan said, his look and voice falling. "You'll be doing it for me."

"But I'm not the guy you think I am," I said, my mind turning to Julio. "There's a reason why we've fallen out of touch these past few months. Most of the time I feel like I'm slogging through mud. I barely have the strength to see anybody or do anything. Sometimes it's all I can manage to make it through the day."

"But what about Julio?" Jonathan said, his eyes wide. "Didn't you say he was helping you to move on?"

"I'm not moving on," I said, looking away from Jonathan. "Julio saw what I was going through and felt sorry for me. He's dating me out of pity."

I put a hand to my throat and felt the rise and fall of my ragged breathing. My chest felt hollow. For the first time all night, I'd said a truth about Julio.

"Julio thinks more of you than that," Jonathan said.

"Maybe so," I said, shaking my head. "But I still can't be your best man. I'm sorry, Jonathan."

My words hung in the air between us. Jonathan drew himself up and bowed his head. I didn't dare look at him. How badly I wanted to give him what he wanted, to turn his frown into a smile. Then Jonathan turned away from me to lift the jar of chocolate sauce out of the hot water and dry it with a tea towel.

"It's okay," Jonathan said with a sigh, and he turned to face me with a brave smile. "At least now I won't be fighting with my brother."

"He'll make a terrific best man," I said in a thick voice.

"I'm sure he will." He had that warm light in his eyes again. "And of course I understand why you don't want to do it. But you're the one I want, Frank. I'm sorry you won't do it."

4

CAUGHT UP IN THE MOMENT

So here I stood guiding Marcus through moon salutations on his roof, while Jonathan had Frank pigeonholed downstairs, talking to him about God knew what. What could Jonathan want? This was like my childhood all over again, my parents and brothers and sisters always keeping me in the dark, telling me I was too young to understand. Whatever. I'd managed to snag what I'd come for—a few minutes alone with Marcus.

What a shock it had been earlier. I'd walked into the kitchen expecting to see Marcus's tatted dancing partner from last week, and instead laid eyes on a tall, skinny guy named Jonathan. Not that Jonathan was a bowser, but I wasn't about to do a three-way with Marcus and *him*. I felt as if the universe had pulled a bait-and-switch on me.

At least Marcus was as hot as ever in his white silk shirt. Wasn't this like a dream, teaching him yoga like this? The full moon looked down on us like some patient goddess. The stars seemed close enough to pluck from the sky. Wouldn't it be amazing to teach all the time up here, sun salutations in the morning, moon salutations at night? But a class with fifty students wouldn't be as fun as giving Marcus this private lesson.

After the moon salutations I stood with Marcus near the roof's edge, looking out on the glittering streets. My lungs filled with cool, cleansing air. I'd never been alone with Marcus before, and it thrilled me. The lights below glittered like the stars above, close enough for me to gather into my arms. I felt like we had all of San Francisco to ourselves. I wished I still lived here.

"So how long've you been doing yoga?" Marcus said.

"Twelve years as a teacher," I said, my body warm from the practice and from the way he'd asked that question. "Practicing for seventeen."

"Your whole life then," Marcus said.

"Half my life, to be exact," I said, nodding and glancing away. "I was sixteen when I started."

"Wow," Marcus said, looking at me up and down. "That's young to start yoga."

"I guess," I half-mumbled, the scar on my forearm prickling. "There was this yoga studio near my high school. I figured going there would keep me out of, you know, trouble. I never thought it would change my life."

"Thanks to that decision, you're changing my life too," Marcus said, the moon lighting up his face and his shirt. "I haven't felt this healthy in years."

Marcus could probably sense I wasn't telling him the whole story. By the way he looked at me, I had to wonder if he could guess at least part of it. But I wasn't about to go there tonight. I'd come here to learn more about Marcus, not for Marcus to learn more about me.

"I saw you last Saturday night," I said in a breezy voice, to switch the subject. "I think that was you I saw on the dance floor."

"Ah, yes," Marcus said, smiling. "I went looking for you later."

"I couldn't stay," I said, sounding as bummed out as I felt. "I had to catch the last train home."

"You poor Cinderella, turning into a pumpkin at midnight," Marcus said. Then he looked at me as if something had struck him. "But you weren't at the club with Frank last week. That's right, you weren't. You were with some guy I didn't recognize."

"That was my friend Hector," I said, letting out a nervous laugh. "My go-to guy when I feel like dancing. Frank would've come with us, but he said he wanted turn in early. He's not much of a dancer, I don't think."

"He's not?" Marcus said, frowning. "He used to love to go dancing with us when he lived in the city."

"Oh, uh, what do you know?" I took a long breath through my nose to slow the sudden rise in my heart rate. "Frank and I go to dinner and movies, stuff like that."

"It's been years since I've gone to a club with him," Marcus said. Either he hadn't noticed my surprise, or he was good at keeping what he noticed to himself. "But you should make him take you dancing sometime. You'd see a whole new side to him."

"Huh," I said, trying to picture a young Frank tearing it up under the strobe lights.

"Of course we were kids then," Marcus said. "And then things changed after Frank moved to Oakland with Ethan."

"Ethan?" I said, my ears pricking up. "Who's Ethan?"

Marcus stared at me, his lips slightly parted. Instinct told me he'd dropped that name on purpose. I'd taught enough classes to know when a student was being less than authentic.

"Who's Ethan?" I said again, more insistent this time.

"Forget I said anything," Marcus said. He brought up his hands and shook his head.

"But I'm Frank's boyfriend," I said in a coaxing voice. "I have a right to know, don't I? So, who was he? Frank's last boyfriend or something?"

"Not Frank's boyfriend, Julio." Marcus leaned toward me, stuffing his hands in his pockets. "Frank's husband. They'd been married for several years. Were divorced last summer. Ethan left him for another man."

Oh. My. God. In all our rehearsing for this dinner, Frank never breathed a word about an ex-husband. A coldness washed through me. Frank's bedroom. Frank's unused bed. The way he tiptoed around me. One more reason why I didn't like going home to Oakland.

"I haven't upset you, have I?" Marcus's voice was cautious.

"Of course you haven't," I said, forcing a smile. "I'm sure Frank didn't tell me anything about it because…because he didn't want to dump all the heavy stuff on me so soon in our relationship."

"Don't tell him I told you," Marcus said, his voice going surprisingly hard. "Okay?"

"I won't, I won't." I tried to sound mature and trustworthy. "When Frank's ready to talk about it, he'll talk about it. Or not talk about it. It's his business if he wants to talk about it—or not. We barely started dating. We're only having fun."

"Good, good," Marcus said, his voice softening. "Frank could use a little fun."

A sweet thing for Marcus to say. Not that I was sure I could believe him. Then again, Marcus and Frank had known each other a long time. What to think? Better to change the subject.

"So I have to ask," I said playfully. "Who was that guy you were dancing with last Saturday? The guy with the snake tats on his arms?"

"My buddy George." A smile spread across Marcus's face. "He was here from Seattle for the weekend. You noticed him, did you?"

"How could I miss him?" I said smiling. "I have to be honest with you, Marcus. I was half-expecting him to see him here tonight. I thought he was your fiancé. Last Saturday night, the two of you looked like you were, you know, a couple."

"What're you driving at, Julio?" Marcus's teeth gleamed like a wolf's in the moonlight.

"Nothing," I said trying to sound innocent, wiping my hands against the back pockets of my blue jeans. "I was only wondering who your friend was."

"I told you, he's my buddy," Marcus said, his voice as soft as silk. "My fuck buddy, if you want to know."

Say what? A thrill ran through me. Although honestly. Of course that's what I expected Marcus to say.

"Jonathan and I have an arrangement," Marcus said, his eyes on me. "If we see a guy we're attracted to and the other guy's interested, we go for it. No questions asked, no explanations given."

"And that works for you?" I said gaping, not sure how I felt about what Marcus had said.

"We're getting married in October, aren't we?" Marcus arched an eyebrow, a satisfied look on his face.

"And what about what's-his-name, what about George?" I couldn't resist saying, my scar feeling like an icicle in the cold night air.

"George has his own partner up in Seattle." An amused look spread across Marcus's face. "Believe me, he doesn't mind."

My mind flipped backward to my early-twenties slut-boy days. How many of the guys I'd slept with had been in committed relationships? All of them? Some of them? Definitely not none of them. I'd never asked questions then. Hadn't cared enough to ask.

"I shouldn't have told you," Marcus said, his tone cool. "I didn't think you'd be a prude about it."

"I'm not a prude," I said. "Believe me, if you knew some of the things I've done in the past, you'd know I'm in no position to judge. Your business is your business. So, um, does Frank know?"

"Jonathan may have told him," Marcus said, giving a slight shrug. "I honestly don't care if Frank knows. Why do you ask?"

"So that I don't say anything to him about it," I said, trying to sound like Frank's concerned boyfriend. "We've never talked about having an open relationship ourselves. I don't think he'd care for it."

"For a guy who's been dating Frank only a few months," Marcus said, the corners of his mouth twitching upward, "you seem to understand Frank to a T."

"So you don't think Frank would approve of, um, your arrangement with Jonathan?" I said.

"Frank doesn't approve of anything I do." Marcus's grim tone sent a chill through me.

"Maybe I should say something to Frank," I said, going into cheerful yoga-instructor mode. "Tell him not to come down so hard on you. Maybe I could change his attitude."

Marcus gave a little smile and turned his head, clearly not believing I could ever change Frank. After all, Marcus and Frank had known each other, and probably been disliking each other, for years. Who did I think I was, sailing into this house—under false pretenses, no less—and offering to make everything all right? I was a diva, not Wonder Woman.

"Let me ask you this, Julio," Marcus said, looking at me square in the face. "How serious are you and Frank, anyway?"

"Serious enough," I said in as light a voice as I could.

"Because I have to ask," Marcus said, looking at me full-on. "Maybe I'm out of line to put this out there, but all the same, I want to put it out there. I hope you won't take it the wrong way."

"Of course I won't," I said automatically.

"You just said my business was my business," Marcus said, his voice as smooth as a fresh batch of Genevieve's ice cream. "I can't help wondering. Are you curious to make it your business too?"

I stared at him, my heart pounding. Marcus's blue eyes glinted in the light of the full moon, the hungry wolf's look on his face again. Did I dare say yes? What would that mean for Jonathan? For Frank? I pictured Genevieve in her store, a flaming-red wig on her head, urging me to do it, doll-face, do it. The sound of footsteps on the balcony below snapped me out of it.

"Marcus?" Jonathan called up.

"You're ready?" Marcus called down to Jonathan, his eyes still locked on me.

"Ready."

"Be right down," Marcus called down. Then he gave me a squeeze on the shoulder and winked. "We'll talk later."

***

I felt a lot warmer in the house after being on the roof. On my way to the dining room my phone buzzed against my thigh. A text. I excused myself, slipped into the bathroom off the hall, and pulled my phone out my front pocket. *Where r u?* was Dean's message. The time on the phone read 9:41. I'd told him last night I'd be at his apartment by nine thirty at the latest. I tapped out the word *soon*, hit send, and slipped the phone in my pocket. The way he put me on hold last week, Dean could wait a few extra minutes tonight, the needy bitch.

I took a leak, washed my hands, splashed water on my face, and walked to the living area. The rest of them were seated, waiting for me. The room was dead quiet. My shoulder was still warm from where Marcus had squeezed it.

"Sorry to make you wait, boys," I said in a pleasant tone, pulling out my chair.

"You and Marcus had a good yoga practice, I hear?" Frank said, looking at me.

"Yes, we did," I said, my smile stretched wide. I felt Marcus's eyes on me. "I've never practiced under a full moon."

"I hope you like osmanthus tea," Jonathan said to me, gesturing toward a little white teapot on a trivet next to my plate. "It's all we could find in the cabinets."

"If it's herbal, it's fine." I plopped myself into my chair across from Frank and reached for the teapot, glad to be busy doing something. "Ooh, and ice cream. Is that homemade?"

"Made it this morning," Jonathan said. "Gave me an excuse to dust off the ice cream maker. Go on, help yourself. There's warm chocolate sauce if you want it."

"Better not," I said, giving Jonathan a smile. "I'm pushing my luck with the ice cream at this hour."

Meanwhile, Marcus picked up the coffee pot, looked Frank in the eye, and asked him in the world's nicest voice if he'd like a cup. I watched Marcus with something like wonder. One minute he's hitting on me on the roof, the next he's offering Frank—my supposed boyfriend—a cup of coffee. I really was an idiot to think I could erase years of bad blood between them.

"I should take a picture of you eating that ice cream," Marcus said a few minutes later, peering over the brim of his coffee cup, "and pass the picture around at next Saturday's class. No one would believe it."

"It's homemade, so I'll make an exception," I said, throwing an appreciative glance at Jonathan. No need to tell Marcus that there was a time in my life when I could've eaten the entire batch—and the chocolate sauce too.

"So," Marcus said, looking across the long table at Jonathan. "Did Frank say he'd do it?"

I let go of my spoon and looked up. Marcus wiped his mouth with his napkin, laid his palms down on either side of his empty dessert plate, and gave Jonathan a smile as if they were the only ones there. First with me on the roof, now with Jonathan at this table—what was Marcus up to? Jonathan glanced at Frank and then gave Marcus a shake of the head. Frank brought his coffee cup to his face. I looked from Jonathan to Frank to Marcus, sensing the energy shift and feeling like the outsider I was.

"Of course I'm flattered Jonathan asked," Frank said, putting down his coffee cup with a clatter. "But the job's more responsibility than I can handle."

"What's more responsibility than you can handle?" I said with a smile, but thinking Frank had better give me a straight answer. "What kind of job are you talking about?"

"It wasn't an accident I asked you up to the roof to practice yoga," Marcus said, his expression flat. "Jonathan wanted to speak to Frank alone. So he could ask Frank to be his best man at our wedding."

I looked down and sank my spoon into the ice cream. Did that mean everything Marcus had said to me on the roof were only words, a trick to stall for time? Then I recalled the look Marcus had given me upstairs. His blue eyes gleaming in the moonlight. Those wolf's teeth. Plus it had to kill him to think that his hot yoga instructor was sharing a bed with his enemy. Marcus would probably love nothing better than to steal me away from Frank. The thought of Marcus doing that was—I had to admit—a huge turn-on.

"Why'd you say no, Frank?" My smile was tight.

"Because I can't," Frank said, a hinting edge in his tone. "You know how busy I am."

I stared at Frank, all the while sensing Marcus's eyes on me. Did I want Marcus's business to be my business, like he'd asked on the roof? A new adventure, right here in San Francisco? If that's what I wanted, then I'd need an excuse to see more of him, outside of yoga class. And here—now—Frank had gift-wrapped that chance and handed it to me on a platter.

"Jonathan's your best friend," I said with as much silver as I could put into my voice. "If it was me, I'd jump at the honor."

"I know. I'm flattered," Frank said. He forced a nervous laugh. "But you know how full my schedule is, with school and the chess team and, um, taking care of the house, that I don't know if I could handle—"

"All week long you've been telling me how good a friend Jonathan has been to you all these years." I leaned in toward him and thought how chess and gardening and housekeeping were so dull, so Oakland. "How much work does it take to be a best man anyway?"

"Not much work at all," Jonathan said, sitting up. "All Frank would have to do is stand next to me. Maybe help me pick out a tux."

The way Jonathan sat there smiling at me, leaning forward with his hands folded on the table, I almost didn't recognize him as the slouchy, fidgety guy from earlier this evening. Huh. So Jonathan knew how to snap out of his funk when he wanted something.

"Sounds reasonable to me," I said in a high voice, flashing a smile at Frank.

"We're also having an engagement party in a few weeks," Jonathan said. "Of course you're invited. We're combining it with a birthday party for Marcus."

"A birthday party." I gave Marcus an impish look, the first time I dared look at him since I sat down. "Twenty-nine again?"

"Har har," Marcus said. "I'll be forty-five."

Forty-what? Marcus was a whopping twelve years older than me? I turned away from Marcus to sip my tea, then glanced across the table at Frank. His face was white, his lips pressed together. He looked at me like I was trying to talk him into jumping off the roof. I didn't understand why. So I'd show up on Frank's arm at the engagement party in a few weeks and maybe at the wedding in October. What was the big deal?

"Looks like we have Julio on board with the idea," Jonathan said to Frank, his voice growing more animated. "Are you sure you can't do it?"

"But you can see Frank isn't comfortable going ahead with it," Marcus said to Jonathan, an edge to his voice. "It isn't fair for you to pressure him like this. Frank, you already said you don't want to do it. You don't, do you?"

He turned and looked squarely at Frank, daring Frank to resist him. Frank seemed to shrink away from Marcus like a cornered rat, his hand closing over his coffee cup. Why did Marcus not want Frank to say yes, anyway? Come on, Frank, don't let Marcus push you around. Say yes, say yes.

"I guess I don't," Frank said in a mumble.

"There, I told you," Marcus said to Jonathan. His tone made it clear he thought the matter settled. "If Frank won't do it, and you don't want to ask Patrick to do it, then you can ask one of my brothers."

"I don't want to ask one of your brothers," Jonathan said. A set look came over his eyes, his mouth. "I want my best man to be someone from my life, not someone from your life."

"Then choose someone from our life," Marcus said, his tone condescending, even nasty. "We have more friends than we can count. What about Ken and Steve? Or Dwayne and Mark? Any of them would be thrilled to be your best man. I don't understand why you have to be like this."

Yikes. This was turning ugly. If Marcus wanted Jonathan to ask someone else, then he shouldn't have talked down to him like that. I looked across at Frank, still looking down at his goddamned plate. Come on, dude—say something!

"Fine, I'll ask Patrick." Jonathan let out a chuckle and gave me a bright look. "So this must be what straight people go through, when they plan their weddings."

"Makes you kind of wish they'd never made it legal," I said in a joking voice.

Marcus reached for the coffee pot and refilled his cup. I looked at Frank on the other side of the table. Frank's shoulders were hunched together, looking like he was sitting on his hands. The silence was enough to make me want to pick myself up and walk out of the room, out of the house, and straight down the hill to Dean's apartment. I patted my front pocket for my smartphone, thinking of the call I'd give him later. It'd be nice to have a San Francisco adventure with Marcus, but not if it meant putting up with this.

But, oh, look at Jonathan, sitting miserable in his chair. Frank looking miserable across the table from me. It seemed so unfair that Frank had turned Jonathan down for my sake. This had nothing to do with Marcus now. What I did next was for Frank and Jonathan.

"Frank," I said, putting down my tea mug, "I think you should be Jonathan's best man."

The look of wide-eyed shock on Frank face—his expression practically screaming, "Have you lost your mind?"—confirmed I hadn't imagined what I'd said, I really had said what I'd said. Jonathan and Marcus stared at me too. They could stare all they wanted. I had no idea what the hell I was doing, but I knew enough to sense this was the right thing to do. Friends helped out friends in this howling bitch of a universe. Josie, Genevieve, and my Mami would all agree.

"Are you're sure there's no one else you want to ask?" Frank said to Jonathan.

"No one more than you, buddy," Jonathan said.

Frank looked speechless at Jonathan. His anguished expression was one I recognized—the same expression he'd given me when I'd asked him if I could use the extra bedroom for my massage business. I could practically hear the gears grinding in his brain, counting the pros and cons. All the while Marcus stared at Frank, willing him to turn down the offer. Don't worry about Marcus, I wanted to say to Frank. If Jonathan means anything to you, you'll say yes.

"Okay, why not," Frank said, and let out a defeated sigh. "Okay, Jonathan, you have yourself a best man."

"You mean it?" Jonathan's eyes were wide as if he didn't dare believe the amazing news.

"Sure," Frank said, choking the word out.

"Thank you so much," Jonathan said, leaping up from his chair. "You have no idea how happy I am to hear that."

Yay Frank! Yay Jonathan! My heart was in such a glow I barely registered the lethal look on Marcus's face. Too bad, Marcus. If Jonathan could let Marcus fool around with other guys, then Marcus could let Jonathan pick his own best man at his own goddamned wedding.

Jonathan walked around the table to Frank and bent down to give him an awkward hug. Frank put his arms around Jonathan's shoulders without standing up. His smile was plastered to his face. Only then it hit me what all this meant, both for him and for me.

"So I guess this means we'll be seeing more of you this summer," Jonathan straightened up. "Both of you."

"Yes," I said, giving Jonathan a polite smile. Then I turned to Marcus and added, "More of you, too."

"Looking forward to it," Marcus said in an equally polite voice. But he wasn't smiling.

***

We said our goodbyes around twenty past ten. Jonathan gave both Frank and me a hug at the top of the stairs. He hugged me the way a close friend would, leaving a warm imprint on my chest. A decent guy, Jonathan. Maybe a little stuck in his own head, but on the whole a decent guy. The sort of guy my Mami would sit down at her kitchen table so she could put some meat on those skinny bones.

Then Marcus led us down the narrow stairs to the front door to let us out. I half-expected him to cop a feel as I walked past him, but he didn't. He didn't even shake our hands, let alone give us a hug. But he did say he was looking forward to seeing us at the engagement-slash-birthday party. He squeezed my shoulder on the way out the door, the way he'd squeezed it on the way out of yoga class last week, on the roof a few minutes ago. My scar prickled in the cold.

Frank and I walked down the hill in silence. The night had grown colder. I sensed Frank was mad at me, so I let my mind wander toward Dean. I pictured Dean sprawled out on his living room couch, as horny as hell, watching a true-crime documentary on TV.

We made it to the bottom of the hill at Market and Castro. The light was red. Frank stood at the curb with his shoulders tense, his hands stuffed into his coat pockets. Time to make a gracious escape.

"My friend lives not far from here, on 14th Street," I said, pretending not to notice how upset Frank was. "See you tomorrow at the house."

"Julio," Frank said rounding on me, his voice furious. "What in the world were you thinking up there?"

I drew in a sharp breath behind my smile, doing my best to look as if I didn't understand what he was talking about. But the accusing look on Frank's face in the light of the streetlamps made it clear he was on to my act. He probably gave the same look to some math student he'd caught cheating on a test.

"I don't know why I said what I said," I said all flirty and sheepish, glancing up the hill to avoid Frank's glare. "Jonathan wanted you to be his best man, and I guess I … I guess I was caught up in the moment."

"Don't you realize what this means?" Frank said, even more enraged. "You and I are going to have to pretend to be boyfriends for the next nine months!"

"Not necessarily," I said in a half-soothing, half-defensive tone, working up the courage to look at him. "We can always stage a breakup before then."

"A breakup?" Frank crossed his arms. "What kind of a breakup? What do you want me to tell them?"

I was about to say *Tell them I cheated on you*, but I caught myself in time. The blood rushed into my face as if I'd said those words. Frank looked different, older and sadder, now that I knew what I knew.

"I don't know," I said, flustered. "Tell them we had a blowout fight or something."

"And then what do I tell them, I've kicked you out of the house?" Frank said. "What'll you tell Marcus in your yoga classes?"

"We can say we had a friendly breakup," I said in a slow and patient voice. "We can always come up with something to explain why we're still living together. I mean, it's none of their business what we do behind closed doors. Or pretend to do behind closed doors. Ex-boyfriends share living quarters all the time. Why can't fake ex-boyfriends?"

"This lie was supposed to last for only one night," Frank said, half-groaning. His eyes were shining, tearing up in the wind. "I don't want to keep on lying to them."

The light blinked green. Frank didn't move to cross the street. He stood at the edge of the curb half turned away from me, his hands in his jacket pockets, staring into the distance with a dazed look on his face. My heart beat faster. Say something, Julio. Say something to make Frank see the good in all this.

"Frank, did you honestly want to turn Jonathan down?" I said in a feeling voice. "You do want to be Jonathan's best man, don't you?"

"Not like this I don't," Frank said bitterly, looking over his shoulder at me.

The light turned red. Cars whooshed in front of us. Frank stood at the edge of the curb, not moving, not breathing. The Josie in me rustled and rose up inside me.

"Let's say I wasn't in the picture," I said in my most persuasive tone. "Let's say, like, Jonathan had called you up one day and asked you to be his best man. You would've said yes, wouldn't you?"

"I don't know," Frank said, looking out onto the cars whooshing in front of us. "I mean, if you put it that way. Probably. Yeah. Sure, I would've said yes."

"Then can't you see why I wanted you to go for it?" I said. "Jonathan is one of your oldest friends. Isn't it an amazing honor he asked you to be his best man? And you were about to turn him down because of me? I'm nothing to you. I'm less than nothing to you. I'm a dude you live with, nothing more. But Jonathan…he'll be your friend for the rest of your life."

"Jonathan and Marcus don't know you're nothing to me," Frank said, turning to face me. "As far as they're concerned, you're my boyfriend. How are we going to manage that?"

"Like we managed it tonight." I dared to give him a little smile. "I thought we made a lovely couple, don't you think?"

"Jonathan won't be my friend for the rest of my life," Frank said, his voice sinking, "if he finds out about this. He'll lose respect for me forever."

"He won't find out," I said, sounding definite. "He'll never find out."

For the next few seconds Frank watched the cars rush past. Marcus's glittering blue eyes flashed in my mind. I blinked in the wind, held my breath, and waited.

"So you don't mind pretending for a little while longer?" Frank said, his tone uncertain.

"Of course I don't mind," I said as reassuringly as I could. "I had fun tonight. It was an adventure. I'm also glad I could be there to talk you into being Jonathan's best man. Who knows? Maybe the universe had wanted me to come along as your date tonight. Because if I weren't around, what would you have done?"

"If you weren't around," Frank said, sounding blue, "I never would've blurted out your name to Jonathan and Marcus last week."

"I'm glad you did," I said nodding, picturing Josie watching all this and saying *you're not a diva, you're Wonder Woman*. "You were meant to be Jonathan's best man. We're totally pulling this off. It'll be easy. Maybe even fun."

"Let's not get ahead of ourselves," Frank muttered. "I'd hardly call tonight fun."

He thanked me for my help tonight, said he'd see me at the house tomorrow, and crossed the street to the Muni station. I pulled out my phone. *B right there*, I merrily typed, and headed toward 14th Street. I'd done my good deed for the day, maybe even for the year, and now I was ready to put Frank, Jonathan, and Marcus into the drawer and focus on the one thing that could make me forget about them. A night in the hay with Dean.

Except I couldn't put them in the drawer. I pictured Frank riding the lonely train to Oakland. Jonathan picking up the dessert plates and fitting them into the dishwasher. Marcus on the roof again with his hands on his hips, looking out onto the glittering San Francisco streets. On a clear night like this, he might even be able to see me all the way from his roof. What would Marcus think if he could see me? Would he think there goes the dippy queen who'd talked Frank into becoming Jonathan's best man? Or would he think there goes the guy I want to cheat on Jonathan with? I walked faster, not daring to look over my shoulder, thinking I'd soon find out.

5

SURPRISE GUESTS

I was on my hands and knees in the garden when the mail lady came, two Saturdays after that awful dinner at Marcus and Jonathan's. I pulled the mail out of the mailbox, and a sturdy cream-colored envelope, addressed to me and Julio, dropped like a dead bird onto the dirt-streaked toes of my tennis shoes. The engagement party invitation. The prospect of that party had by now receded to a back corner in my mind, an event I knew would happen but seemed long distant, like a funeral or a trip to the DMV. But, now, here it was, a lead weight resting on my feet. I picked up the envelope and opened it.

"Can't wait to see you again," Jonathan had scribbled on the invitation in smudged blue ink. The rest of the invitation was all Marcus—raised black script against a white background, art deco edging, a graphic of two clinking champagne glasses fizzing scarlet, heart-shaped bubbles. I pictured Jonathan dashing off his message and sneaking it into the envelope while Marcus wasn't looking.

My mind turned to Julio. He'd come home about ten minutes earlier, walking into the house with his usual jaunty step. For the past two weeks I'd been avoiding him as best I could, thinking if I could put him out of my sight, I could forget what lay in store for us. I slipped the invitation under a flowerpot, thinking I'd retrieve it later.

I needed to think about what I wanted to say to Julio before he saw me with that envelope.

Julio was at the kitchen table when I walked through the back door. His bare feet were propped on a kitchen chair as he tapped on his phone, a glow in his dark eyes. On the table next to him lay a long, narrow cardboard box I'd signed for earlier in the morning, its top ripped open. Business cards for Julio's massage practice most likely. Over the past few weeks I'd signed for all sorts of packages for him—sheets, curtains, a massage table he'd spent half a Sunday assembling himself. I'd been feeling less like his landlord these past couple of weeks and more like his personal assistant.

"Hey, Frank," Julio said looking up, his voice as sunny as the day outside. He put down the phone, sat up in his chair, and reached for the box. "Check it out. I'm ready to launch."

He pulled out a business card, smiled at it, took a picture of it with his phone, and then held it out to me. I took it. Julio's name and phone number, along with the words MASSAGE THERAPIST, shone in hot pink letters against a charcoal background. First Marcus and Jonathan's names on their party invitation, now Julio's name on this business card. All these people with their plans, moving forward with their lives.

"Nice," I said in a pleasant tone, pressing my finger against a sharp corner of the card.

"You don't think the pink is too flashy?" Julio said. An uncharacteristically worried look flitted across his face.

"I don't think so." I dumped today's mail on the table and looked at the card again. "Flashy's a good thing if you want to attract business."

"That's what I thought too," Julio said looking relieved. "And I've always thought pink and gray are a hot combo. Here, take some for your friends."

Julio brought out about a dozen more cards from the box and presented them to me with a magician's flourish. I took them. But so many of my friends had also been Ethan's. I'd lost touch with most of them since the divorce. Maybe I could pass around a few cards at school. But that would mean I'd have colleagues coming to the house. For the first time it sank in that complete strangers would be walking through these doors—my doors—to be massaged by Julio.

From the living room, the grandfather clock rang out the plaintive half hour.

"So I hear Marcus and Jonathan's engagement party is next month," Julio said, looking down at his phone.

At first I thought I hadn't heard him right. Then Julio looked up and flashed me a smile. So much for keeping the invitation a secret from him.

"Yes, next month," I said, trying to match his cool, polite tone. "How'd you know?"

"Marcus told me after class this morning," Julio said. His phone pinged. "He said the invite should be coming any day."

"It came today," I said, my mouth going dry.

"Awesome," Julio said, looking and sounding upbeat. His phone pinged again, and he let out a little laugh. "Sorry about that—I posted a photo of a business card on my Facebook page. So Marcus told me the date, but I didn't have a chance to make a note of it. What day is the party again?"

"March seventeenth," I said.

"Great," Julio said as if he honestly meant it and typed the date into his phone.

"Actually, Julio?" I said carefully. "I was thinking, um, you don't have to go to that party. I can handle it by myself."

"You can?" Julio gave me an incredulous look. "But what about our story?"

"I've been giving this some thought," I said, my finger tracing the edge of a business card. "It's already been a couple weeks since we went to that dinner. It'll be another month until the engagement party. That's plenty of time for me to tell them we've cooled things off."

"But I told Marcus after class today we were looking forward to going," Julio said blinking. "I even told him we wouldn't miss it for the world."

The business cards slipped from my fingers and fluttered to the floor. I bent to pick them off the faded linoleum. I pictured Marcus talking to Julio after yoga class today. Of course he'd make sure I'd take Julio to the party. I knew I mustn't forget who I was dealing with.

"You've already done so much for me," I said, standing up. "What about your real boyfriend? This can't be fair to him."

"Dean's halfway around the world," Julio said, sounding less than sorry about it. "He left for Italy a few days ago to study ancient ruins for his master's degree. I've been thrown over for a bunch of old pots."

"But still," I said, agitated, trying to rearrange the cards into a neat pile in my fumbling hands. "I've imposed on you enough."

"It's fine," Julio said, pulling the box of business cards toward himself like a mother hen gathering her chicks. "Besides, Marcus said I could probably meet new clients at his party, you know, friends who need massages. Rich friends. By the time the party rolls around, the spare room should be painted and ready. I'll be set to put my name out there."

I imagined Julio working Marcus's living area, chatting up Marcus's beautiful, well-heeled friends. In my head pink-and-gray business cards flitted around the apartment like finches, nestling themselves into pockets and purses and wallets, migrating to fashionable addresses all around San Francisco. Soon an army of Marcus's allies would be invading my house, sneering at my scuffed floors and half-empty shelves. And telling Marcus all about it.

"You can't go to the party," I said weakly. "I'm sorry, but you can't."

"But if I bail now," Julio said, his voice falling, "Marcus'll know something's up."

I looked at the ceiling, shaking my head. Fatigue crept into my bones, a wearying sense that Julio wouldn't forgive me if I didn't take him to the party. It showed on his face how badly he wanted to pass out those business cards. When Marcus showed up to Julio's class, wanting to know why Julio hadn't come to the party with me…what then?

"Fine," I said, turning to him. "But we won't stay long."

"Whatever you want," Julio said, looking satisfied. "But in the meantime, maybe allow yourself to look forward to the party. You might even surprise yourself and have some fun."

Fun. What did I know about having fun anymore? I hadn't been to a party since the divorce. Longer, even. But I promised Julio I'd try.

***

About a week before the party I drove to Walnut Creek to buy dark socks. A bright green dress shirt caught my eye. I couldn't resist trying it on. What I saw in the mirror surprised me. I didn't look like a divorced middle-aged math teacher with an unfinished Ph.D. I looked instead like a not-bad-looking guy, reasonably intelligent, with a steady job, a house, and halfway decent dress sense. In a shirt like this, I might have "fun" at the engagement party after all.

Then I peeked at the sales tag. The shirt cost a hundred dollars more than I usually paid for shirts. I couldn't buy it. But then I envisioned the look on Jonathan's face as I walked into his living area. His face lighting up. Picking his way through the crowd to greet me, making a sure path toward me like a hummingbird toward one of the yellow columbines in my back yard. So I held my breath, pulled out my credit card, and charged it. I'd be wearing first-class armor for that party.

The night of the engagement party, we reached Marcus and Jonathan's house at a quarter to nine. Laughter and music came through the closed door. I pressed the buzzer, wondering if anyone would hear it. But in a few moments a smiling and pink-faced Marcus swung open the door. The sight of his flushed face reminded me why I'd avoided calling Jonathan in the six weeks since they'd had us over for dinner.

"Ah, there you are!" Marcus said, taking the bottle of champagne I'd brought and giving Julio and me a bear hug. His breath smelled of alcohol. He never put his arms around me unless he'd had a few. "Jonathan was asking if we'd have to send a search party for you."

"We were stuck in traffic on the bridge," I said, straightening my good wool overcoat. In fact, traffic had been surprisingly light for a Saturday. We'd left the house late on purpose.

"Come on in," Marcus said, opening the door wider. "We've been waiting for you."

Julio and I followed Marcus inside and dumped our coats on a pile in the spare bedroom off the front hall. Then Marcus led us up the stairs, with me going last. I could already feel my body relaxing. I could tell that this would be easier than the dinner party, when Julio and I were the only guests. I took each step slowly, deliberately, not wanting to appear too eager to see Jonathan after six long weeks.

The living area was packed with people I didn't recognize. They stood around talking over each other wearing candy-colored shirts and dresses, posing with green or pink cocktails in martini glasses. A few of them looked and dressed in a less showy way, more like normal people—Jonathan's IT friends, no doubt. I scanned the faces for a glimpse of Jonathan, the friend who'd serve as the ballast in this rollicking sea of unknown faces. Instead my eye landed on a face I recognized only too well. A face I hadn't seen since the day he'd moved out of my house, and out of my life, for good. Ethan.

Yes, Ethan. The man I'd once loved, even married, and now despised with an energy that now heaved up from the pit of my stomach like lava. The man I couldn't bear to think of, let alone look at, without a thousand painful memories rushing into my mind. He stood by the open sliding windows, talking to a tall, skinny man with short rust-colored hair. I recognized him too, from that awful day when I'd walked in on him and Ethan, in my own bedroom, on my own bed, a pair of sea serpents entwined in the throes of passion. Their faces were close together, almost touching in a heart-shaped silhouette. My chest felt ready to cave in.

Then Ethan turned and met my stare. His face seemed to freeze, but then his expression softened. He nodded across the room to me, a faint smile on his face as if he held out hope we might be friends again. Good God. I backed away and fled to the bottom of the stairs, through the door, out into the frigid gray night.

The cold smacked me like a physical blow. For a second I blacked out and grasped the stair railing to keep myself from pitching forward. My mind turned to my dream from a couple of months ago, when I'd imagined Marcus ripping off his hood, grabbing me by the throat. So this was his plan for me tonight. His little surprise. His revenge for my accepting Jonathan's offer to be his best man.

Then a hand seized my arm from behind. I reeled around and came face to face with Julio. My lungs burned with each breath. It hit me that Julio was nothing but a chess piece of Marcus's. My being filled with loathing for him.

"Frank, Frank!" Julio cried, his breath coming fast. "What're you doing?"

"Did Marcus tell you they'd be here?" I said, wheezing. "Did he?"

"What are you talking about?" Julio looked both confused and terrified. "Who's they?"

"You know who I'm talking about," I snapped, wrenching my arm free of his grip. My fancy green shirt clung to my chest like frost.

"My ex is in there. Him and his new partner. Marcus told you everything, didn't he?"

"Your ex?" Julio said after about a second, his eyes blinking. His nipple ring showed ridiculously through his open black silk shirt. "You, um, have an ex?"

"You're lying," I said in disgust, turning away from him. "I can see it on your face."

"Frank," Jonathan called down.

I looked up the stairs. Jonathan stood in the doorway, his body half in shadow. My hands clenched into fists. Jonathan had to know that Ethan would be invited—perhaps even invited him himself—and never told me. I took a step down the stairs, shocked I could be so angry with him.

"Frank, wait," Jonathan said, stepping outside and crossing his arms against the cold. He wore nothing but a dark blue T-shirt and a pair of black jeans. His expression was all remorse. "Please, Frank."

"What's he doing up there?" I said in a half-shout. "Is this some kind of joke?"

"Marcus and Ethan are still friends," Jonathan said, throwing a glance at Julio. Julio stood between us, leaning against the railing and looking from one to the other of us. "They see each other at the gym all the time. We're practically Ethan's neighbors."

"Then couldn't you have warned me he'd be here?" I said, glaring at Jonathan, aware of Julio staring at me.

"I didn't know he was coming," Jonathan said. "He showed up twenty minutes ago."

"I was on the bridge twenty minutes ago." My voice went hoarse in the frigid air. "Why didn't you call or text?"

"I was afraid if I called," Jonathan said in a shrinking voice, "you'd turn around and go home."

Jonathan came down another step to stand next to Julio, an imploring look on his face. Julio was shivering too, hugging his arms in, looking from Jonathan to me as if he didn't know whether to follow me or stay behind. Julio couldn't have known Ethan had been invited to the party. I could at least cling to that.

"If it bothers you that much," Jonathan said, half-turning to the door, "I'll ask Ethan and his friend to leave."

"You might as well let them stay." The shock of seeing Ethan was wearing off, leaving a dull headache. "I only wish I'd known."

"I know. I'm sorry." Jonathan walked down to me and put his hand on my shoulder. "Please. Can't you come in anyway? My mom's upstairs, and she's driving me crazy. Marcus's family is driving me crazy too. I need you up there, buddy. Can't you come up for a few minutes?"

We looked at each other, my eyes tearing in the wind. Julio looked at me as if he was genuinely concerned for me. I felt foolish—ashamed—for rushing out of the house. My mother flickered in my mind, a scolding look on her face. If this were a chess game, she'd be lecturing me, faulting me for losing my cool and retreating instead of facing the enemy with a rational, calculating mind.

And that's what this was—a game. Not a chess game with its rules and elegance, but a game of sucker punches and naked disrespect. Did I want to quit so soon after this game had started? Did I want to let a lesser player win by forfeit? I squared my jaw, tramped up the stairs, and went inside the house.

***

I avoided scanning the living area when I entered again. Still, I couldn't help peeking over at the sliding doors to see if Ethan was still standing there. He wasn't. Meanwhile Marcus stood sipping champagne by the dining table, talking and laughing with a cluster of people. He'd likely seen everything and savored it. I made a point of not looking at him, determined not to let him see me upset.

"Can I bring you guys a drink?" Jonathan said, gesturing to a young waiter mixing drinks behind a table near the TV.

"Ginger ale if you have it," Julio said. He spoke with some cheer to his tone, as if he'd already forgotten the past half hour and itched to pass out business cards.

"Give me whatever he's pouring." I hadn't planned to drink tonight, but my nerves needed soothing. "The green drink or the pink drink, I don't care."

"Stay put." Jonathan patted my shoulder, then picked his way through the crowd toward the waiter.

"Hey, Frank," Julio said, giving me a nervous smile. "Maybe you should take it easy on the booze with your ex here."

"Relax," I said, bristling and thinking again of my mother. She didn't drink and disliked watching her children drink in her presence.

"You were the one who wanted to drive all the way into San Francisco tonight," Julio said in a serious voice, looking me in the eye. "And I don't have a driver's license. So if you're even a little tipsy, we're leaving the car in San Francisco."

"Fine." I reached into my pocket and held out my car keys. "You be the judge if I can drive or not when the time comes."

Julio took the keys and slipped them in his back pocket. I glowered at him. I used to do all the driving with Ethan. Not once did Ethan ever demand the car keys. He'd had no reason to. And it was for Julio's sake that I chose to drive all the way in, so I could take him home sooner. I was beginning to see that having a pretend boyfriend was almost as much trouble as having a real boyfriend—except with no sex to offset the trouble.

A few moments later, Jonathan came up to us with a bottle of ginger ale and a pink cocktail in a martini glass. I sipped it, unable to tell if the bitterness came from the drink or from the taste in my own mouth. I put the glass down, turned away from it, and looked at Julio as if to say, "Happy now?" He looked relieved. I wondered if Julio was a recovering alcoholic.

"Oh hey," Julio said, his face brightening. "Marcus invited a few people I know. From the yoga studio."

"He did," Jonathan said, looking pleased.

"Come on, Frank," Julio said, linking his arm with mine. "Let me introduce you to them."

"Can Frank join you in a few minutes?" Jonathan said, his voice polite. "I'd like him to meet my mom and my in-laws."

"Of course," Julio said, giving Jonathan a smile.

Julio threw me a glance, unhooked his arm from my elbow, and disappeared into the crowd. Only after he was gone did it strike me that my car keys had disappeared into the crowd with him. Like it or not, I was stuck here.

***

Jonathan led me to his mother, a tall, stocky woman in a flowing purple shift and heavy red beads. She was stationed near the drinks table with a pleasant-looking couple who turned out to be Jonathan's cousin and her husband from Pleasanton. I hadn't seen Jonathan's mom since our youth group days. She was friendly enough to me the couple of times I'd seen her in Santa Cruz. This time I sensed tension in her look and manner.

"The best man finally arrives," she said in her throaty voice, holding up her drink as if to toast me. "Jonathan here was beginning to wonder if you'd jilted him."

"Mom," Jonathan said in a warning tone. His cousins looked on nervously.

So Jonathan's mother still hadn't forgiven him for choosing me over his brother Patrick to be the best man. For Jonathan's sake, I knew I had to rise to the challenge. As my dad always taught me in chess, sometimes the best defense was a good offense. In this case, a charm offense.

"The traffic across the bridge was horrible," I said, giving her my first smile of the night. It hurt my face. "But of course I'd never miss this party. Your son … what can I say? He's the best of the best."

"Oh," Jonathan's mother said frowning, looking taken by surprise.

"And I'm happy to see you too again, Emma," I said, proud of myself for remembering her name. "I used to be jealous of Jonathan for having you for a mother."

"Me?" she said, blinking eyelashes heavy with mascara. A jolly if not-quite-believing look spread over her face.

"Of course I did," I said, pressing my advantage. "You were so not like my parents, the boring college professors always in my business about my work and my studies. In those days I secretly wished you were my mother, letting me do as I pleased."

"Be glad you weren't," she deadpanned. "I would've screwed you up too."

"Now, Mom." Jonathan put his arm around her waist. "You did fine."

Jonathan hadn't been lying. He needed me to protect him from his own family as much as I needed him to protect me from Ethan and Marcus. I asked Jonathan and his mother if they'd like me to take their picture with my phone. They gladly took me up on it. I took picture after picture and promptly texted them to Jonathan. The tension eased.

"Where's Patrick?" I whispered to Jonathan when we left them.

"Don't know. Don't care," Jonathan said stiffly. "He's not speaking to me."

"Not speaking to you?" I said, reaching out to put a hand on his arm, then drawing it away. "Because of me?"

"Because he's a lousy brother," Jonathan said with a harshness I hadn't heard often from him. "I don't care if he never speaks to me again. Which is why I'm glad you didn't bail on me tonight. I can live with Patrick not speaking to me but not you, buddy. Not you."

"I'll never do that," I said, and this time I did grasp his arm. "You have my word."

***

Jonathan introduced me to a few of his other friends, people he knew from work, a couple of guys he wrote code with. The normal-dressed people, as I'd suspected earlier. I let myself be led around, smiled and said hello, answered a question here and there. They all seemed decent and genuinely fond of Jonathan. I doubted if Marcus enjoyed their company the way I would if I were Jonathan's fiancé.

Then we made our way over to Marcus, standing with his father and stepmother by the dining table. I'd never met Marcus's father Bill before, a tall, imposing man with a square face and thinning silver hair through which slivers of pink scalp showed. He wore a bright gold tie with a matching gold hankie in the lapel of his gray suit coat, both of which set off the diamond-studded gold of his cufflinks. From his physical resemblance to Marcus and his crushing, I-own-the-world handshake, I knew at once I wouldn't like him. I also shook hands with Bill's second—or possibly third—wife Clarice, a shockingly pretty, shockingly young woman with long, velvety-black hair. Her bosom rose like meringue from the plunging neckline of her sparkly crimson sheath. This was Marcus's stepmother? She seemed too young for someone even Marcus's age.

"So here's my fellow best man," Bill said, sizing me up with bright blue eyes. He regarded his cocktail as if he meant to devour it, martini glass and all, and then downed the green poison in a single swig. "We were talking about who should give the toast tonight."

"I'm giving it, Dad," Marcus said, with the restiveness of someone who'd said it a dozen times already.

"You can't give the toast." Bill's voice was deeper than Marcus's, but the arrogance, the forcefulness, the determination to win were all the same. "It's your birthday. It's your engagement party. One of your best men should be toasting you."

"You don't have to give a toast tonight," Jonathan said to me in an undertone.

"Of course he doesn't have to give a toast," Bill said, throwing me a look as if my presence irked him. "I already said I'm giving it."

"Let's not bother with a toast at all," Marcus said, letting out a sigh. "This is only the engagement party."

"Son, someone has to give a toast tonight," Bill said, and turned to me. "Do you have any experience giving speeches?"

"Years of it," I said, looking at Bill in the eye. "I teach calculus to a classroom of teenagers."

"I used to host banking seminars all over the country," Marcus's dad said, looking unimpressed. "I used to address audiences of four hundred, five hundred people."

"Dad, I'm giving the toast," Marcus said, in a voice that met his father's. "And that's that."

I allowed myself my first direct look at Marcus of the night. Perhaps his agitated look should've brought me a measure of *schadenfreude*, but I couldn't help feeling sorry for him. What if my own dad had been even remotely like Marcus's, a loud, lushy, self-aggrandizing tyrant? Would I have turned into a vindictive bully like Marcus? I shuddered to think I might've.

"I need a glass of water," I said, turning abruptly to Jonathan.

"The bartender can pour you one," Jonathan said, grasping my shoulder to stop me.

"Don't bother," I said.

Before Jonathan had a chance to block my way, I excused myself and headed for the kitchen.

***

The kitchen was empty and much cooler than the living area. I brought a glass down from a cabinet, found some ice in the fridge, filled the glass at the sink, and drank it down in one go. My tongue throbbed. The microwave clock read 9:44. Before we left I'd told Julio we'd leave at eleven o'clock sharp. One hour and sixteen minutes to go.

"You okay?" Jonathan said, appearing in the kitchen doorway.

"Better now." I put the glass on the counter and laid my cold hand on my forehead.

The noise of the party boomed in from the other room. Jonathan moved into the kitchen. I hadn't expected us to be alone like this tonight.

"Is it true what you'd said earlier?" Jonathan said in a quiet but wondering tone. "You secretly wished my mother was your mother?"

"Does that surprise you?" I said, uneasy. "My parents were always so fussy and organized. Your mother…I never knew somebody older who didn't care what anyone thought about how she did things. I had no idea a parent could be someone like your mother."

"That's funny," Jonathan said in a contemplative tone. "I used to wish my mom was more like your parents."

"My parents?" I said surprised.

"I liked spending time with your parents," Jonathan said, sounding embarrassed. "And they loved each other. Didn't they?"

"They did," I said nodding, thinking of my father sitting by my mother's bedside during her final illness, watching her slip away.

"Not like my mom and dad," Jonathan said in a wistful tone. "Passionately in love with each other one day, at each other's throats the next. Coming with my mom to Santa Cruz and leaving my dad and Patrick behind in San Diego was the best thing to happen to me. But there was none of that with your parents. Nothing but peace and quiet and order. Remember the time you had me over for dinner with your family? You played the piano."

The awkwardness at the dinner table that night came to me in a flash. My parents quizzing Jonathan about growing up in San Diego. My mom insisting I play a piece or two for our guest. I'd been more nervous playing for Jonathan than at dozens of recitals and school plays. Then the look of wonder on Jonathan's face when I'd finished. All those lessons, all those grueling hours of practice, had paid off in that one performance.

"Of course I remember," I said softly.

"I think about that night all the time." Jonathan's face shone. "Does your father still have that piano?"

"He shipped it to me last summer," I said, my voice faltering. "Not long after Mom died. That and our grandfather clock. They're heirlooms."

"I'd love to hear you play again sometime," Jonathan said.

"I'm out of practice," I said, turning to refill my glass at the sink. "I haven't played it once since the movers brought it. Every time I look at that piano, I can hear my mother scolding me for letting it collect dust."

"You'll play again," Jonathan said with a gentle smile. "When you're ready. The music lives inside of you."

***

Then Ethan walked into the kitchen. I froze in horror, then turned away. Ethan's bright salmon-colored shirt floated on the edge of my vision. A fresh burst of loathing erupted inside me. But it wasn't only loathing I felt. I felt attraction for him too. Ethan was the last guy I'd slept with. I used to know his body even better than he'd known it himself.

"Jonathan," Ethan said in a quiet, tense voice, "would it be all right if I could speak to Frank alone?"

His shirt, the top two buttons open, tapered down to his slim hips. Even at the age of forty-three, Ethan still had the body to wear a tight shirt. Ethan was a sports therapist and an avid tennis player. The guy he left me for, the guy in the other room, had been one of his patients. I hated myself for picturing Ethan so vividly.

"No, Jonathan, stay," I said wheeling around, keeping my focus on Jonathan's white face.

"Jesus, Frank, do you have to be like this?" Ethan said wincing.

"And if he has anything to say," I said acidly to Jonathan, pointing over to the salmon-colored shirt, "he can say it through our lawyers."

"It's been six months since we made it final," Ethan said, talking to me as if I were a child. "And I'm sorry. I am very, very sorry for all the pain I've caused you. But I was hoping—maybe—we could be friends again. Or at least be civil. My whole family's been asking about you."

"They can call," I said with a glance over my shoulder.

"And also, um." Ethan's voice was trembling. "I also heard about your mother. I wanted to, you know, offer my heartfelt condolences—"

"Oh, you and your condolences!" I turned and jabbed my finger toward his chest, my eyes taking in the full sight of him. "Where were you when she was sick? Where were you when she was dying? She loved you like a son, and you never went to see her. Not once. You don't have the right to talk to me like this. You're nothing to me. You're less than nothing to me. I want you out of my sight."

I spun around and put a hand over my eyes. The voices in the next room seemed to grow louder. Thank God my mother couldn't see me this out of control.

"You can turn around now," Jonathan said in a hushed tone. "He's gone."

"You shouldn't have seen that," I said between gulping breaths, wiping my eyes with the heel of my hand. "But I can't take it, Jonathan. I can't forget what he did. To walk in here and see him with his new husband, and then he wants me to forgive him? To clear his conscience? I can't."

Jonathan put his hand my shoulder and turned me to face him. He placed the half-empty glass of water in my hand and told me to drink some. I drank the whole thing down. My chest burned, but it was a cleansing burn.

"Maybe we could see each other more often," Jonathan said carefully. "Before I move to New York. Would you like that? Maybe meet on Saturdays for breakfast or something."

"Breakfast?" I said with a shrinking feeling inside, remembering that awful morning at the Ferry Building when Marcus had turned up.

"Like how we used to in Santa Cruz," Jonathan said. "We have so little time left as it is, before I move to New York. I usually hang out on Corona Heights on Saturday mornings. Breakfast with you would be more fun. I can maybe take some pictures too. Are you free Saturday mornings?"

"Usually," I said, my heart skipping a beat. "Julio teaches yoga all morning, so I have the day to myself."

"And Marcus will be at Julio's class," Jonathan said, his face breaking into a smile. "So I say we do it. It'll be like the old days."

"Sure."

I recalled my fantasy of a warmly lit coffee shop with lots of dark paneling, Jonathan listening to my troubles with those brown eyes of his. Was Jonathan a wonderful guy or what? In the space of two minutes he'd undone the damage Marcus and Ethan had wreaked on me tonight. He'd made coming to this party worth it. I smiled my first honest smile of the night.

"How about we go up to the roof," Jonathan said, his voice perking up. "You never saw the roof the last time you were here. I downloaded my martini pictures onto a laptop—we can sit on the roof, and I can show them to you. I'm sure no one's up there now."

"Better not," I said, glancing toward the living room doorway. "I can't take you away from your guests."

"I'm over them," Jonathan said in a jaded tone. "This wouldn't be the first time I've played hooky at one of my own parties."

Why not? I followed him into the living area, then sneaked up the stairs, through a spare bedroom, onto a balcony, and up a creaky metal ladder to the roof. Taking in the cold night air did my lungs good. We sat on the gravel, looked out on the city, and talked. I lingered over each and every one of his martini pictures. The sound of the party wafted up to us. With Jonathan by my side, I floated blissfully above it all.

6

FIRST CLIENT

Frank had warned me earlier tonight to be ready to leave Marcus and Jonathan's party at eleven o'clock on the dot. Well, here it was, eleven o'clock on the freaking dot, and Frank was nowhere around. I checked the living area, the kitchen, the balcony—nope, nope, and nope. I still had his car keys. Where could he have gone? And if he didn't show up, who would drive me home?

I went out to the balcony off the living room to take in some fresh air. The vibe was better out here, mainly thanks to Jonathan's Mami and his cousins standing by the railing. Was Jonathan's Mami lit up like a firecracker or what? She spent the next ten minutes trying to talk me into going down to Santa Cruz to give her massages. She was fun to hang with, sort of like Genevieve if Genevieve had grown kids, but I couldn't imagine having her as my own Mami 24/7. She made me think how lucky I was that my own Mami was still alive—as if I needed reminding.

Marcus strode through the sliding glass doors. Even from the other side of the balcony I could tell he was mad. I didn't care. Not after that trick he'd pulled on Frank with Ethan earlier. Then Marcus made straight toward us. I smiled at him, pretending not to notice how pissed off he was. Still my stomach dropped.

"Anyone know where Jonathan is right now?" Marcus said, his smile tight.

What? Jonathan was missing too? A bad feeling stirred inside me. I'd left Frank with Jonathan two hours ago. Maybe they'd gone missing together. Then, all at once, it hit me where they must've gone.

"Maybe the roof?" I said, giving Marcus a weak smile.

Marcus looked up, his body stiffening. His jawline was like a knife blade in the streetlamp light. He gave us a quick nod and excused himself. A cold thrill brushed against the scar on my forearm.

"I hope everything's all right," I said in an innocent voice to Jonathan's Mami.

"Everything's peachy keen," she said with a wave of her hand. She downed her drink and twisted the red beads hanging around her neck, gazing at the sliding glass doors. They were a lot alike, Marcus and Jonathan's Mami. They probably couldn't stand each other.

***

Marcus, Jonathan, and Frank came into the living area about ten minutes later. I went inside and made my way through the crowd toward Frank. He had a lazy smile on his face, like he'd been making out. With Jonathan? On the roof? I couldn't believe Frank had it in him to do such a thing. That smile of his told me that did.

I was about to ask him what he'd been up to when a waiter holding a large silver platter interrupted us with an offer of champagne. I felt my usual sting of temptation, but I turned the waiter down. So did Frank, thank the Holy Mother. Which was worse, Frank making out with Jonathan stone sober, or Frank making out with Jonathan piss-drunk? Neither. Not with Marcus nearby.

Over by the dining table, Marcus stood holding a cordless microphone, tapped it, and made a shushing sound into the mike. The room quieted down. My scar was buzzing now. I felt an awful sensation Marcus was about to call off the engagement and rip Jonathan and Frank a new one, right in front of everybody.

"Jonathan?" Marcus said in almost a purring voice into the mike, nodding to Jonathan a few feet away from him. "Would you mind joining me up here for a moment?"

Jonathan made his way to stand next to Marcus. He was pink-faced and looked like he was holding his breath. I patted Frank's car keys in my back pocket, wishing I could give them to Frank and bail as fast as I could.

"So, as many of you know, I'm celebrating a birthday today," Marcus said, his face shining. "My forty-fifth."

"You old queen!" a guy near the drinks table shouted. Everyone else laughed. I was too nervous to force a laugh myself. Frank kept looking at Marcus with a calm look on his face, as if nothing Marcus could say or do could touch him.

"But thanks to the man standing here," Marcus said, his smile spreading and his voice rising above the laughter, "every day feels like my birthday. And that's why we're gathered here tonight. After all these years, Jonathan is finally making an honest man out of me. We're engaged."

The room erupted into cheers. Marcus hooked his arm around Jonathan's waist, and Jonathan threw the crowd a bashful smile. I counted out a five-second exhale. Okay, so maybe Marcus wasn't about to cause a scene. But if not, then where was he going with this?

"I never would've thought asking you to dance eighteen years ago would lead to this," Marcus said, looking into Jonathan's eyes. "But I'm sure glad it did. I love you, Jonathan. I love you more than I can put into words. You're the best man a guy like me could hope for."

A sigh rippled through the room. Even my own insides went mushy. Who'd a thunk Marcus could crank up the romance? Then I remembered that night with him, up on the roof, and wondered if Marcus really meant what he said, or if he was putting on an act for the crowd.

"Are you two lovebirds gonna kiss or what?" someone shouted from the crowd. This led everyone to chant, "Kiss! Kiss! Kiss!"

Marcus and Jonathan glanced at each other. Jonathan's face went pinker. Marcus pecked Jonathan on the lips and mouthed, "Satisfied?"

"French! It! Up! French! It! Up!" everyone yelled in response.

So Marcus pulled Jonathan close and gave him enough tongue action to spark a live sex show. The crowd cheered. Glasses clinked. Cell phones flashed. By the time Marcus let him go, Jonathan's face was beet red. Marcus licked his lips and gave everyone a triumphant look as if he'd planned that all along. He probably had.

Near the kitchen doorway stood Marcus's Papi and stepmother, watching the happy couple with wide grins. I could tell they'd never witnessed man-on-man lip-lock before. Jonathan's Mami let out a snort, turned away from them, and downed her champagne like a pro. Frank, standing next to me, stood by with a cool, collected look. "Don't buy it folks," he seemed to be saying. "I know better." I burned to know what he knew.

***

The next night, while I was making up a playlist for Saturday's class on my laptop in my room, Marcus called me on my cell. The first time he'd ever called me. I sat up straight in bed at the sound of his deep, ringing voice. Where did he find my phone number?

"I was picking up in the living room this morning," he said in a joshing tone. "I found one of your business cards on the coffee table. My house is littered with them."

"Oh Holy Mother," I said, letting out a groan. "Didn't anyone take a business card home?"

"A few of them might've," Marcus said.

"Sorry I made such a mess." I hid my disappointment with a cheerful voice. "I guess engagement parties aren't a good time to drum up business."

"But you did manage to snag one client," Marcus said, his tone upbeat. "Me. I'm calling to schedule a massage."

Marcus? Here? For a massage? I didn't dare. Frank would wig out if he came home from school to find me rubbing down a naked Marcus. I snapped my laptop shut and pushed it off my lap.

"You're kidding," I said, and forced a laugh.

"Would I be calling you if I was kidding?" Marcus sounded mock offended.

"You want to come all the way to Oakland for a massage?"

"I thought I'd help out a friend," Marcus said. "But if you don't need the business …"

"Of course I'd love the business." I scrambled off the bed and paced the floor. "Uh, when do you want to come over?"

"How about this Thursday," Marcus said. "Thursday's usually my lightest day. Plus I have a client in Orinda I'm seeing in the afternoon. I can see you in the morning, maybe ten o'clock."

"Ten o'clock Thursday works," I said in my most professional-sounding voice.

"And Julio?" Marcus said. "Maybe … don't tell Frank about me coming over."

"Why not?" I said. My scar tingled.

"He might take it the wrong way." Marcus's voice was careful-like. "I hate to ask you to keep secrets from your boyfriend, but, as I'm sure you've noticed, Frank and I aren't the tightest of friends."

"But this is his house."

The other end of the line grew so quiet, I thought we'd been disconnected. I sank down on the edge of my bed and pictured Marcus's face going dark, his jaw like a knife blade again. My scar tingled even more.

"You know, you're right," Marcus said. "I probably shouldn't come. Let's forget I called. I'll see you in yoga class this Saturday."

"No, no," I said. "Come."

"You're sure?" he said.

"My business needs clients," I said point-blank. "Or else I've spent all this money for nothing."

"What about Frank?" Marcus said in a half-warning tone.

"Frank's at school in the mornings," I said. I wasn't sure if I was trying to reassure Marcus or reassure myself. "What he doesn't know won't hurt him."

"It won't cause friction?"

"You're a client," I said in my best what's-the-big-deal voice. "Nothing more, nothing less. If Frank ever finds out—and I doubt he will—that's what I'll tell him."

After the call I tossed the phone onto my desk and lay down on the bed, grasping my forearm with the scar. I thought about Marcus and me on the roof that night. Marcus's ringing speech at the engagement party. The hinting tone he'd used with me now. I still believed Marcus loved Jonathan—honest, I did. But I'd be a chump if I didn't think that maybe, just maybe, Marcus wanted more.

***

On Thursday morning I lay in bed and listened to Frank moving around in the kitchen and bathroom. I didn't climb out of bed until well after he left the house. Even so, I expected Frank to come through the door any second, needing to pick up something he'd forgotten. Marcus was only a client, I'd tell him. Only a client.

Right as the grandfather clock in the living room chimed ten o'clock, the front doorbell rang. I'd never heard the front doorbell ring before, a high-pitched jangle that screwed up the low booms coming out of the grandfather clock. Showtime. I rose from the kitchen chair and walked toward the door, not knowing what to expect.

I couldn't look Marcus in the eye when I opened the door for him. After some chit-chat I led Marcus through the living room to the massage room. He had nice things to say about the paint job, lemon yellow on two walls, cotton candy pink on the third wall, tangerine orange on the wall where my certificate hung. He accepted with a smile my offer to turn on my New Age playlist, downloaded especially for massages. Then I left the room, closed the door behind me, and went into the bathroom to run my hands under warm water. I imagined him undressing and slipping underneath the fresh cotton sheets on the massage table. I pictured Genevieve smiling wickedly at me. A client! I shouted to myself in my head. A client! A client!

He called out to say he was ready. I took a deep breath and went inside. His clothes, all of them, were folded neatly on the couch. He lay face down on the table, the sheet pulled up to right above his waist. His bare shoulders shone like marble in the creamy yellow sunlight coming through my new white curtains. I approached the table like I was approaching an altar.

"Ready?" I said, my hands hovering over his neck muscles.

"Whenever you are," he said calmly.

Thank the Holy Mother he was facing downward and couldn't see how nervous I was. Here went nothing. I rubbed my hands together to warm them some more, then lowered them on either side of Marcus's neck.

His muscles were rock solid. I kneaded his shoulders, then moved on to his deltoids, his rhomboids, his erector spinae. His arms and legs came next. He didn't move or flinch no matter how hard I pressed on him. His physique seemed otherworldly, more cyborg than man. What a great story this would make to tell Genevieve, the next time I went to buy ice cream. But I couldn't tell her. I could never tell her. This adventure had taken a turn for the dangerous.

He didn't make a pass at me. We didn't talk. He might even have dozed off once or twice. Before I knew it, I was finished. Ten minutes later, he was dressed and out of the house, leaving me a check for a hundred dollars. A client, no more, no less. I let out a huge sigh of relief.

Marcus came the following Thursday. Again, nothing happened. He started coming Tuesdays and Thursdays. Still nothing. After about a month Marcus had become a part of my routine—Tuesday massage, Thursday massage, Saturday yoga. I became so used to putting my hands on his half-naked body that I barely felt nervous around him anymore. He even took a stack of my cards to hand out to his East Bay clients.

My new website paid off too. Five weeks into the business I was averaging five, six massages a week. All the while Frank saw nothing, knew nothing, suspected nothing. Everyone was happy. My bank account most of all. I'd be living in San Francisco by this time next year. All thanks to Marcus. What had I been so worried about?

***

Marcus asked me about my scar on a bright Thursday morning at the beginning of May. We were almost at the end of the massage. He lay on his back with his eyes open while I finished up with his shoulders. His eyes landed on the crescent-shaped scar that slashed across my right forearm. I kept massaging him, pretending not to notice he was looking at it. The scar tingled like it had a mind of its own.

"I've noticed that scar in class before," he said. "How'd it happen?"

"You mean this?" I glanced at the scar as if I hadn't seen where he was looking. "High school. Knife fight."

"You were in a knife fight?" Marcus said, his eyes widening.

"With this guy at school," I said, with the offhand tone I used when telling this story. "He'd been pushing me around for weeks. Called me a fat little *maricón*—fag. That's what everyone used to call me then, my older brothers, my classmates, everyone. I was a lot heavier then. A porker. I was an easy target for bullies."

"You used to be overweight?" Marcus said, looking at my trim body and letting out a laugh.

"I used to eat a tone of ice cream as a kid," I said. "Ice cream was my only friend back then. Now I only eat a little. A couple of spoonfuls a day, that's all."

"I never would've guessed," Marcus said.

"I don't talk about it much," I said in a low voice, my mind turning briefly toward those dark days. "Anyway, so this one time at school, this classmate shoved me in the hallway near my locker. I don't know what came over me. I shoved him back—in front of his friends—and told him to go suck his own dick. After school he cornered me in the school parking lot with a knife. His thug friends came to watch him cut me. I'd never been so terrified in my life."

"Jesus." Marcus stared at me. "What did you do?"

"I charged him like a bull," I said, my Spanish accent returning more strongly, a sign I was talking about my past. "Knocked him to the ground. I think he was more shocked than anything else. Then these police officers came in and saved me. Someone must've seen and called 911. I don't know what would've happened to me if they hadn't come running. There was blood everywhere. At first I thought the blood was his. Then I saw it gushing out of my arm."

"And your classmate who attacked you?" Marcus said, darting his eyes at my scar. "What happened to him?"

"Juvie." My deadly tone of voice gave me a chill. "Never saw him again."

The crappiness of those years ran through me like a sword. I pictured that first yoga studio, cool and dimly lit, me and a bunch of smiling older women I knew had never held a switchblade in their lives. I forgot where I was, imagined myself there, not here. Only for a moment, though. Breathe in. Breathe out.

"I started doing yoga after that," I went on in a steadier voice. "The studio was my safe place. Not only from the bullies but from myself."

"So your destiny was hiding in a high school parking lot," Marcus said.

"I never thought of it that way." I loosened my jaw. "But I suppose you're right."

"And your brothers gave you a rough time of it too," Marcus said, his voice soft and curious.

"They did," I said, working my fingers down Marcus's arm. "They're way older than me."

"I have brothers too," Marcus said. "Younger brothers, though."

"I don't blame my brothers anymore for pushing me around," I said, only half-listening to Marcus. I always had trouble listening whenever I talked about my brothers, or about any of my childhood for that matter. "After what they had to go through. They had to run the family after my Papi died. I was only twelve when that happened."

"That's awful." Marcus's voice was sympathetic. "Twelve's too young to lose your dad."

"And it happened so suddenly," I said with a shrug, a burning feeling in my chest. "He fell off a ladder painting a house."

"My God." Marcus turned his head to look at me. "I'm so sorry."

"He'd been drinking, probably," I said, my chest burning that much more. "I don't remember him ever being without a beer or a whiskey in his hand. I don't know if he'd been drinking the day of the accident. Nobody in my family tells me anything. Not even today. They think I can't handle it. Once the youngest, always the youngest."

"And that's why you don't drink yourself?" Marcus said, gazing at me, his voice careful.

"I know I have it in me to become a drunk like my brothers." I laid Marcus's arm on the table. "I've been as drunk as them before. I didn't like it. So no more drinking for me. It's easier that way."

"Good for you," Marcus said, giving an approving nod.

I walked around the table to work his other arm. His eyes were on me. It hit me I'd already finished with this arm, but I kept going. My mind flashed to the time I woke up in bed with this old troll I didn't recognize. Said he'd paid me two hundred dollars to go home with him. To this day I have no idea where I'd met him, or what I'd let him do to me. But then I checked my wallet, and there they were, two crisp hundred-dollar bills. Too late to give him back the money. Never told anyone about it. I wanted to tell Marcus. Wasn't sure I could trust him.

"You want to talk about rough childhoods," Marcus said, and gave me a faint smile. "I testified in open court against my own mother."

"Shut up," I said. I let go of his arm and stared at him.

"She left me no choice," Marcus said. "She'd won custody of me and my two younger brothers. My father was barely at home, and he was cheating on her. Of course the judge sided with Mom. But she was an abusive lush who used to scream at us and leave us alone in the apartment without food in the fridge. I used to deliver newspapers to buy food for me and my brothers."

"Mother of God," I said, my breath rushed. "How old were you?"

"Thirteen," Marcus said, his voice sad. "My brothers were ten and eight. I cooked, I cleaned, I washed clothes. It was an education."

"An education?" I said with heat in my voice. "That's learning the hard way."

"Eventually, I told my dad," Marcus went on. "He dragged my mom to court and won custody of all three of us. Everything hinged on my testimony. She didn't stand a chance."

"And where's your Mami now?" A chill rushed over my scar.

"Now?" Marcus said in a faraway voice. "Shambling around New York somewhere, I imagine. Haven't heard from her for years. I tried to reach out to her while I was in college, but she told me I was no son of hers. Called me a traitor. Told me she should've had an abortion when she had the chance."

"Shame on her," I said. A feeling of disgust swept through me.

"But it's history," Marcus said in a cheerier voice. "And I still have my dad. He drives me up a tree sometimes, but he's good at heart. At least I hope he is. I can't find fault with someone I take after, can I?"

"Your Papi's okay in my book," I said, working on Marcus's forearm. "Maybe he comes on a little strong sometimes."

"Sometimes," Marcus said dryly. Even so, there was love in his voice for his Papi. "He made the mistake of selling his financial advisory business a couple of years ago. Now he has too much pent-up energy. But all in all, he's a decent man."

"My Papi was decent too," I said, feeling guilty for suggesting earlier he was a no-good drunk. "Kindhearted. I was his favorite. He used to take me out for ice cream. I liked going on jobs with him. Thanks to him, I know how to paint a room. Now I have this business. He'd be so proud of me if he could see me today."

I looked at the digital clock on the wooden stool by the door. Eleven past eleven. Thank God, the session was over. If we kept on talking like this, I'd be throwing myself at Marcus. Genevieve flickered in my head again. And here I thought I'd grown so used to kneading his bare flesh.

"Will you look at the time," I said, in a bright, brisk voice. "Looks like I gave you eleven bonus minutes. I'll see you in the kitchen."

***

I switched off the portable radiator and left the room without looking at Marcus. I headed for the kitchen and sat at the table. My tongue had thickened, my eyes stung, my face was hot. I went to the freezer and breathed in the icy air. Out came my half-eaten pint of mint chocolate-chip ice cream. Next appointment in forty-five minutes. Then maybe I should tell Marcus I couldn't schedule a massage for next Tuesday. Feed him some excuse. And keep on finding excuses until Marcus stopped coming here for good.

My cell phone buzzed. Cancellation of my noon appointment. Nothing else going on except a yoga class to teach in Berkeley at three. It was like the universe had cleared my schedule on purpose, to test my will. I pictured myself struggling on a yoga mat and Josie standing beside me, encouraging me to breathe.

Marcus showed up at the kitchen doorway. His muscles were well-defined by his sky-blue V-neck T-shirt. I turned my head, unable to look at him. Never mind that I'd come to know his body as well as my own. I brought out a spoon from a drawer, a bowl from a cabinet. Had to keep the hands busy.

"Ice cream for lunch?" Marcus said smiling.

"One small scoop," I said in a too-high voice. "No more."

I brought out the scoop from a drawer, ran it under the hot water for a few seconds, sank it into the rock-hard ice cream, and plopped a scoop into the bowl. A bite. Creamy mint chocolate-chip coated the inside of my mouth. I felt a miserable craving to eat the rest of the carton, the way I used to when I was a kid.

Marcus's arms wrapped around me before I realized he was coming my way. He held me from behind and planted his lips on the nape of my neck. The spoon slipped from my fingers and clattered into the bowl. Then Marcus turned me around, ground his hips against mine, and kissed me full on. He was every bit as good a kisser as I'd imagined. The salt on his tongue mingled with the sweetness of the ice cream in my mouth. Then he pulled away, leaving a warm, wet imprint on my swollen lips.

"You have no idea how much I've wanted to do that," Marcus said in a half-whisper, his arm wrapped around my waist.

"We can't do this," I stammered, my heart banging against my ribs. "Think of Jonathan. Think of Frank."

"I don't care," Marcus said into my ear, his breath warm against my neck. "I'm tired of fighting this. Why do you think I keep coming here? I can't even look at you anymore without wanting to—Jesus Christ—"

He brought his hands around to the front of my yoga pants, gave me a good grab, and undid the drawstring. My arms felt too weak to stop him. As much as I hated to admit it, that's what I wanted too.

Heavy footsteps on the pavement outside sent a zing of terror through me. I pushed Marcus away, went to the window above the kitchen sink, and raised the blinds an inch. The mailwoman was stuffing envelopes into our mailbox. Not Frank, thank the Holy Virgin. I pictured him hiding in the bushes, waiting, lurking, watching.

"Who was that?" Marcus said, his voice sharp.

"Mail," I said.

"When's your next appointment?" Marcus glanced at the wall clock above the kitchen door.

"Tomorrow morning," I said, realizing too late I shouldn't've said that. "No, wait. I mean…"

I looked at the ice cream carton on the counter. The frost on the side of the carton was melting. The woman standing by my yoga mat wasn't Josie anymore. It was Genevieve, prodding me to do it, doll-face, do it.

"It's because of Jonathan," Marcus said, his voice cool. "Is that it?"

"Jonathan's a good guy," I said in all honesty. "I'm no home wrecker."

"No one's saying you are." Marcus gave a faint smile.

"Then what you said at the engagement party," I said, turning and glaring at him. "About how you loved Jonathan. Was that a lie? A speech to please the crowd?"

"I love Jonathan more than anything," Marcus said patiently. "You want to know why? Because he lets me be who I am. Who I need to be. He doesn't ask questions, doesn't judge. Not a lot of guys are like that."

"Lucky you," I said wincing. "But what about me? I'm supposed to be your side dish before you walk down the aisle?"

"You're no side dish," Marcus said in a calming voice. "You know I'd never think of you that way."

"That's enough," I said, raising my voice. I folded my arms and tried to stand as tall as I could. He was still three or four inches taller than me. "I think it's time you left, Marcus. Session's over."

Marcus gave me a piercing look, held my gaze, and then turned and walked to the door. I stood in the center of the kitchen and watched him. This might be the last time I ever saw Marcus. No way would he keep coming to my Saturday yoga class, not after this. And no way was I going to his wedding with Frank. How could I even look at Frank in the face again?

"I like having you in my life," Marcus said in a low, serious voice, turning to me at the door. "There's a warmth, an aura about you, that I can feel from head to toe. So please don't be offended if—maybe—I can't help wanting more."

"You can't have more," I said in a near-whisper. "Jonathan should be enough for you."

"I told you, he doesn't care," Marcus said in a frustrated tone, holding out his palms.

"And there's Frank too." My breath was shallower than if I was doing one of my toughest balancing poses. "I don't want to run around on Frank."

"Frank," Marcus said, practically spitting his name out. His blue eyes looked even bluer against the paleness of his face. "So you and he are serious."

"Serious enough," I said, feeling myself walking into a trap. "This is his house, his kitchen. He's letting me use that room for massages. Look at you, making the moves on me. Don't you realize where you are?"

Marcus glanced around Frank's outdated kitchen with its plain counters and plainer appliances, the pea-green wooden drawers that ground out sawdust every time I pulled one of them out. The whole room seemed smaller and grimier in the harsh light of Marcus's gaze. I should've offered to paint it.

"Has Frank made you any promises?" Marcus said, his eyes settling on me again.

"Not yet," I said, rattled. "But I'm sure he doesn't want me to fool around with his best friend's fiancé in his own house."

"He doesn't?" Marcus said, sneering. "How do you know he isn't fooling around on you? Do you even know what he's up to when you're not here?"

"You sound jealous of him," I said, daring to provoke him with the j-word.

"Of course I'm jealous of him," Marcus said, his lips parting slightly. "How could I not be? To know what you must be giving him? It's burning me alive. And the couple of times I've seen you interact with Frank, you don't look too close. You were strangers to each other at the engagement party. You working the room with your business cards. Frank up on the roof with Jonathan."

"You had a house full of guests that night," I said, "but you took the time to notice what Frank and I were up to?"

"Honestly," Marcus said in a silky voice, "how much time did I need? I only had to glance at you to know you aren't right for each other. You can't cheat on a boyfriend who's barely even your boyfriend."

He walked up to me, put his hand on my shoulder, and caressed it. I laid a hand on his hand, then lifted my eyes to meet his. Okay, Julio, this was it. Now or never. Did I dare give Marcus what he wanted? Okay, let's face it—did I dare give myself what I wanted too? Marcus was messy, he was bossy, he was even a little scary. But, Mother of God, was Marcus the sexiest guy who'd ever offered himself up to me or what? And it wasn't like Marcus was about to break off his engagement. We could clean out our systems once, then Marcus would marry Jonathan and move to New York. End of story.

"I have a class today at three," I said, my voice all business.

"I'll be out of here long before then," Marcus said, nodding.

"Okay." I focused my eyes on Marcus's chin. "And this is only physical. Nothing else."

"Understood," Marcus said.

"And we're doing this only once," I said, my heart beating faster. "After today, you can't come for a massage again. No yoga classes either. I don't take money from guys I sleep with. Understand?"

"I understand." Marcus drew me into his large, strong arms and ran a knuckle across my nipple ring like someone who'd done that before. "Anything you want, babe."

***

I couldn't describe it in words, not in English or Spanish, what happened after we went up to my room with the ice cream. We threw ourselves into each other, body and soul. Now and then we took turns finishing the ice cream, coating our tongues with it before returning to the job. That's what the experience reminded me of, gorging on a towering bowl of ice cream. Hundreds of flavors heaped high, layers of caramel and marshmallow and chocolate sauce. The same sugar rush. The same sense of feeling hungrier the more I ate.

Then the two of us lay sweating on my double mattress. My sweaty sheets lay rumpled on the floor beside the bed. I still couldn't believe—didn't want to believe—that what we'd done, we'd done. The sugar high was wearing off. Soon I'd feel the crash, the remorse of giving in. Then the craving to do it over. And over and over again.

What kind of trap had I let myself fall into? I ran a finger over my scar and remembered the troll who'd accidentally paid me for sex. The same sense of dread ran over the scar now as it had then. This time, there was no alcohol to blame—or to give up afterwards. I'd walked into this one stone sober.

7

AT THE THRESHOLD

By June I'd come to expect Jonathan's weekly call to make Saturday breakfast plans. He always insisted on bringing his bike over here, instead of me meeting him in San Francisco, saying he needed the change of scenery. Over eggs and bacon or pancakes smothered in blueberries at a greasy-spoon café near Lake Merritt, we talked about our jobs, our families, our old haunts in Santa Cruz. I felt like we were continuing the conversation we'd begun at his engagement party, first in his kitchen, then on his roof. Later we'd walk along the lake and he'd snap pictures, the buildings, the ducks, the play of the sunlight on the water. For two or three hours every Saturday, we were twenty-year-old college kids again.

Late in June Jonathan called to ask if we could do something different on Saturday. Could I meet him in San Francisco instead? The time had come for him to rent a wedding tux.

"Something wrong?" I said, hearing the strain in his tone.

"No, nothing's wrong." Jonathan sounded out of breath. "But time's running short, and I haven't started looking."

"Okay," I said, unconvinced.

Jonathan had no idea where to rent a tux, so I said I'd meet him at Park's, a mom-and-pop suit store a couple blocks off Union Square.

Park's was where Ethan and I had rented tuxes for our own wedding. Our day there used to be one of my happiest memories ever, a memory that had curdled and gone putrid in the heat of my divorce. Jonathan had given me a chance to erase that memory with Ethan, to layer over the old experience with a new one with Jonathan. If Jonathan couldn't set things right, nothing would.

***

The tiny shop was cool and dark. The grubby plate-glass window, blocked by a display of wooden steamer trunks and mannequins in brown tweed suits, let in viscous, sepia-tinted sunlight from the street. A smell of shoe polish and mothballs pervaded the shop, a scent I recognized as soon as it hit my nostrils. An odd and musty place. Even now I couldn't believe I'd once found such joy amid the racks of jackets, vests, ties.

Jonathan drifted among the rows of mannequins, peering up at the tuxes without paying attention to them. His face was pinched and drawn beneath two- or three-day stubble. In his rumpled plaid shirt and raggy jeans, he seemed more like an unwilling usher, the peevish younger brother of the groom, than the groom himself. Still, I wouldn't allow myself to hope that Jonathan's depressed mood was Marcus's doing. I was here to help him buy a tux for his wedding, after all.

"You can't go wrong with black," I said. I gestured toward a mannequin wearing a traditional black tux with satin-edged lapels.

"Marcus owns a black tuxedo," Jonathan said, his tone sullen. "It'd be nice if I could set myself off from him."

"How about white, then?" I turned to an ivory-shaded tux on the mannequin nearest the door.

"That's too different," he said, wincing as if the suit's whiteness would blind him.

"I like this one," I said, and lifted the sleeve of a charcoal-colored tux. "You'd stand out in this."

"That might work." Jonathan looked around the store with a lost, overwhelmed look. "Or not. Why do they have to give us so many choices?"

"There's a suit here with your name on it," I said in a decided voice. "It's only a matter of finding it in the crowd."

Mrs. Park, a short, sixtyish Korean woman in a bright-red silk blouse, came up to us. I remembered liking Mrs. Park the first time I'd met her. She looked precisely the same now, warm, friendly, and eager to find us the right suit. She might even have been wearing the same red blouse.

"How can I help you this morning?" she said in a perfect American accent, her hands folded in front of her.

"We need a tux for my buddy here," I said smiling, trying to match the enthusiasm in her voice. "His wedding's in three months."

"Congratulations," Mrs. Park said, flashing a smile at Jonathan. "Do you see something you'd like to try on?"

"I can't decide," Jonathan said, freezing in the face of Mrs. Park's professional cheer.

"Will the occasion be formal or casual?" Mrs. Park's tone shifted from friendly to professional.

"If we have it in a city hall," Jonathan said, blinking at me, "does that make the occasion formal or casual?"

"You can be as formal or as casual as you want," I said.

"I have suits for all types of weddings." Mrs. Park looked down the row of mannequins as if they were her own male chorus line.

"I don't know anything about weddings," Jonathan said, his narrow chest deflating. "All I know is the guy I'm marrying is wearing a black tux. I need to look as fancy as him, but different."

"We'll let you know when we're ready," I said, trying to be friendly to cover for Jonathan's despondent mood.

Mrs. Park gave me an understanding nod, glanced at Jonathan, and walked to her post behind the counter. God only knew what she thought. I wasn't sure what to think myself.

"That one'll do," Jonathan said in a resigned tone, going to the ivory-colored tuxedo near the door.

The suit did look snazzy, but Jonathan was looking at it as if he'd sooner dump a bucket of ice on himself than try it on. As much as I admired Jonathan—maybe even loved him—I couldn't help feeling frustrated. Why had he suggested shopping for a suit this morning?

"You don't have to commit to a suit today," I said carefully. "Today's only our first day of shopping. We have two months to find a tux."

"The summer will be over before you know it." Jonathan threw a doleful glance around the store. "Besides, if the rest of you are wearing dark tuxes, then I might as well go for the white."

"I'm wearing a tux too?" I said, keeping my voice neutral.

"Marcus's dad picked out tuxes for you and himself." Jonathan cast a disdainful look down the row of mannequins. "He's paying for them both. He wanted Marcus to wear the same tux, but Marcus told him no."

"And our tuxes will be black?" I said, thinking how obnoxious it was—though not unexpected—for Marcus's father to select my tux without consulting me.

"More like a dark gray," Jonathan said almost under his breath, his eyes on the suits. "That's what Marcus told me. I'm sure Marcus's dad would pick out my own tux if I asked him to. But this is my wedding. I want this choice to be my own."

"It should be," I said in an indignant voice.

Jonathan reached into his front pocket, pulled out his cell phone, and checked it. His expression clouded over. He shoved the phone into his pocket and opened the front of the white tux to reveal a plum-colored silk vest and necktie. He must be expecting or at least hoping for a message from Marcus. No doubt about it now: they'd had a serious fight.

"What do you think of the purple?" Jonathan said, trying to seem interested in the vest and tie.

"It goes well with the white."

"White and purple aren't too flashy together?" Jonathan said, turning and looking at me sideways.

"I've always liked purple," I said softly.

Ethan had worn a purple V-neck sweater, maybe a shade more muted than the mannequin vest, on the night I'd met him at a café almost nineteen years ago. If Ethan had worn any other color that cold January night, maybe I wouldn't have smiled at him, encouraging him to sit at my table. Maybe he wouldn't have asked for my phone number after a two-hour conversation. Or taken me to a movie that weekend, reaching out to lay his hand on mine. He'd packed that sweater when he moved out last year.

"Or maybe I could wear it with another vest," Jonathan said. He turned with a dejected look at the rack of vests lining the opposite wall. "Never mind. Purple's as good a color as any."

***

I called Mrs. Park over and told her the groom-to-be would like to try on the white tux with the purple vest. The manager gave a pleased look and led Jonathan to the fitting rooms behind a folding partition at the rear of the store. I leaned against the counter and looked around the empty store. I was free at last to indulge in fond memories.

Ethan and I had made an adventure of it that day, spending all morning trying on the different suits, joking with Mrs. Park, eventually settling on light gray morning suits with tails and black satin edging. We'd bought the suits outright, we liked them so much. Afterwards, we went home and made passionate love until evening. Melvin, our neighbor's gray tabby cat who'd sneaked into the house earlier, appeared in our doorway, staring at us with green, uncomprehending eyes. We'd laughed and laughed, watching the cat watching us. For me, the only happier day had been the wedding day itself.

"What do you think?" Jonathan said. His voice was low and uncertain.

I blinked and turned. Jonathan stood by the cash register looking self-conscious in the ivory tux, Mrs. Park beaming next to him. How could I describe how he looked? The purple vest, dark and brooding against the creamy-white jacket, brought out the warmth in his chocolate-colored eyes. The suit seemed like it was made for him and him only. He glowed. He didn't seem to know how handsome he looked, but that made him look only better. He was every inch the prize I honestly thought he was.

"You don't like it," Jonathan said in a falling voice, apparently mistaking my stare for dislike.

"You look terrific," I said. "You do, Jonathan."

"The white doesn't work," Jonathan said, glancing down at the suit with a look of revulsion. "I can see it on your face. Marcus'll hate it too. I'm taking it off right now."

"No, don't," I said, ready to make a move to stop him. "You took me by surprise, that's all. I've never seen you look so … formal before. Marcus will love it. Any man would."

"Listen to your friend," Mrs. Park said in a friendly whisper.

Jonathan threw us each an uncertain look, then disappeared behind the partition. I shrugged and smiled at Mrs. Park before turning away from her, pretending to examine the vests on the rack. A few minutes later, Jonathan came out in his plaid shirt and jeans, his old self again. I could still see him in the tux, a pulsing white star in the murky light of this shop.

"So you'll rent the suit?" I said hopefully, wishing there was a way I could talk him into trying the suit on again.

"I don't know," Jonathan said, almost petulant, glancing around at the other suits. "Okay, sure."

"I'll need to take your measurements," Mrs. Park said, coming out from behind the counter holding a tape measure. "It'll only take a couple minutes."

She asked Jonathan to hold his arms out to the sides so she could measure his shoulders. Then the front door swung open, and a short, fiftyish man in a dirty linen suit walked in. Mrs. Park told us she'd be with us in a moment and walked over to the new customer. Jonathan brought down his arms, looking dispirited, and then his eye caught a nearby display of black patent leather shoes. The sight of them seemed to strike him with horror.

"If I rent a tux," Jonathan said, turning to me with wide eyes, "will I have to rent shoes to go with it?"

"Unless you already have a pair," I said, uncomfortably aware I wasn't giving the answer Jonathan wanted to hear. "Any kind of black shoes will do. Do you have a pair of black shoes?"

"I don't think so." Jonathan sounded like a little boy who'd forgotten to bring his homework to school. He put a hand to his throat. "I need some air."

In a flash he crossed the room, flung open the front door, and vanished. Sunshine flooded into the store from the gaping doorway. Mrs. Park and the other customer looked up from the counter, their eyes wide. I stared at them, stunned.

"Be right back," I said, and scrambled out the door after Jonathan.

***

I threaded my way down the sidewalk and managed to grab Jonathan's arm at the red light at the corner of Sutter and Stockton, near Union Square. He turned to me with a face I didn't recognize as his. His mouth was open, sucking in breath after breath. Whatever was tormenting him, it had to be more serious, more terrible, than having to buy a tux.

"Jonathan, where are you going?" I was half out of breath, my chest burning.

"I can't, I can't take this," Jonathan said between gulps of breath. "I have to keep moving. I'll be fine. Just go home. I'll call you later."

The light turned green—off he went. I chased him down Stockton Street to Union Square and grabbed his arm at the next red light. He turned and tried to wrench his arm free. I gripped his arm tighter, wondering who this stranger was and what did he do with my friend Jonathan.

"Jonathan, please," I said, half out of breath myself. "You can't take off like this. Whatever it is, you can tell me."

"I don't know what to tell you," Jonathan said, his expression blank and looking at me as if he didn't recognize me. "I don't know why I'm here, I don't know what I'm doing, I don't know, I don't know, I don't know anymore."

"Let's go into Union Square and sit down," I said, using my teacher-voice. "Okay?"

"Whatever." His breath slowed, and he looked at my hand grasping his arm. "You're hurting me."

"Promise you won't run away," I said, determined not to loosen my grip until he promised.

"I won't," he said, his voice eerily rational.

The light turned green. I eased my hold on Jonathan's arm and braced myself for him to take off without me, but he stayed by my side as we crossed the street and went up the short concrete stairs into Union Square. We sat down at a green metal table under an open green umbrella. The day was warm but Jonathan hugged his shoulders as if he'd caught a chill. I figured I'd wait until he'd calmed down before trying to figure out what was troubling him.

Then Jonathan pulled himself up from the chair, patted the front of his jeans, and pulled out a small pill bottle. Anti-anxiety pills—they had to be. The way he fumbled to open the bottle, half-turned from me, I sensed I was the first person to learn about them. I doubted if even Marcus knew about them.

"Let me do it," I said, standing up and holding out my hand.

He looked down at the pill bottle without seeming to hear me. Then he handed the bottle to me without meeting my eye. I peeked at the label before twisting off the lid. My heart sank.

"How long've you been taking these?" I said, looking at the label and then looking at Jonathan.

"A week." Jonathan darted his eyes at the bottle in my hand as if he wanted to snatch them from me.

"I know what these are," I said, holding up the bottle. "I used to have a prescription myself."

"Did they work?" Jonathan said, peering at me ashamed.

"When I let them," I said.

I'd first started taking anti-anxiety pills to survive my Ph.D. orals. Later on, I'd found them forgotten in a bathroom drawer and used them to endure the divorce. In both cases, they'd done little more than postpone the agony. If Jonathan was taking those pills, not only might there not be a wedding day, there might not be a Jonathan.

"I only take them when I need to." Jonathan plopped down and hunched forward with his elbows on his knees, staring down at the sidewalk.

"You'll need something to wash them down with," I said in my best authoritative voice. "I can bring you a bottled water but only if you promise not to run off."

He didn't answer me. His brown eyes, so luminous when he was trying on the tux, looked drained of light, sunken in their sockets. Weariness had overtaken him.

"I promise," he said.

I took the pill bottle with me as insurance. By the time I returned with the water, I was certain I'd find an empty table. But there he was, waiting where I'd left him. He seemed even relieved to see I'd returned. Now was my chance to listen and be a true best friend. When was the last time Marcus had ever listened to him?

"Here you go," I said, setting the pills and the water on the table in front of him.

Then I turned my chair to face him and sat down. Jonathan shook out two small white pills, popped them into his mouth, and took a swig of water. His pill-taking seemed awfully practiced for someone who'd had his prescription filled only last week.

"My bees are gone," Jonathan said in a monotone.

"What do you mean, your bees are gone?"

"Gone as in they flew away." Jonathan swigged some water and nudged away a nosy pigeon with his foot. "Yesterday morning I went up to check on them and found the hive deserted. It's not like they died, or there would've been dead bees everywhere. It seems they found somewhere else they'd rather live."

"And that's why you're upset?" I said.

"Don't you think it's strange they'd abandon me?" Jonathan looked at me with red eyes. "They had a nice space, plenty of water, plenty of trees and flowers for them to explore. I did all I could for them. They still left me. Thousands of them. What did I do? What's wrong with me?"

"Nothing's wrong with you," I said in a consoling voice. "They're insects. You can always start another hive, can't you?"

"And it's not only the bees," Jonathan said, letting out a long, shivering sigh. "Marcus has taken up with someone."

"Taken up with someone?" I said, bristling. "You mean…?"

I couldn't bring myself to finish the question. Jonathan's distressed look answered it for me. I pictured myself standing at the threshold of a door to Jonathan and Marcus's relationship I'd always known existed but never wanted to look at full-on.

"I don't know who the guy is." Jonathan took another swig of the water bottle. "But I know Marcus has been seeing him for a couple months. Maybe even longer."

Jonathan closed his hand over his mouth. Then he wiped his hand across his lips as if to scrub away the filth of what he'd said. I looked away from him, needing to focus on something else while I absorbed this appalling news. A group of teenage girls in short shorts walked past, chatting and giggling. I waited until they left, then turned to Jonathan.

"How can you be so sure?" I said.

"I've been through this enough times to know." Jonathan shrugged and gazed at the people milling around the arts and crafts booths set up near the Victory statue. "He becomes more distant with me. That's how it's been all spring. Doesn't want to do stuff with me anymore. Comes home from work later and later. After I've gone to bed. He creeps into bed next to me thinking I'm asleep. I'm not. I'm lying there staring at the ceiling, imagining where he's gone, who he's been with."

"God."

"And when we're together," Jonathan went on, his eyes large and sad, "he snaps at me for no good reason. The wedding is making things worse. We've argued about what kind of ceremony we want, the people we want to invite, where to have the party afterwards. He's been nagging me about a tux for weeks. Then, last night, he barked at me for leaving a water glass in the kitchen sink. He was so mad about it that he stomped out of the house. It's like he's looking for things to find wrong with me. As if he's trying to make it my fault he's sleeping with another guy. But it's not my fault. Is it?"

"Of course it's not," I said, growing heated. "Did he make it home last night?"

"Eventually," Jonathan said, giving a half-shrug. "He stumbled in stinking of alcohol, then passed out in bed next to me. I lay there with my heart pounding away while he snored and snored. But he woke up at seven thirty as usual and left bright and early for his yoga class. He didn't even look at me when he left the house this morning. As if I was invisible. He hasn't called, hasn't texted, all morning long. For all I know, he's with the other guy right now."

"Good God," I said in shock. "You have to say something to him."

"And say what?" Jonathan said. "Tell him to stop?"

"Yes, Jonathan, yes," I said, wanting to leap out of my chair. "He may think he's some sort of civil rights hero with his worldly notions of modern relationships, but he's only making excuses to cheat on you. And you're letting him."

"It isn't as easy as that," Jonathan said, and bit his lip.

I clenched my jaw and turned my chair to focus my gaze on something, anything, not to blow my cool. My eye landed on the St. Francis Hotel across the square from us. Outside of the hotel's central building, the glass elevators glinted in the sunlight. One of them rose and stopped at the top floor of the hotel. I imagined myself in that elevator, rising high above Union Square. From up there, we probably looked no bigger than a couple of pebbles on the sun-splashed pavement. A new thought brought me down to earth.

"What about HIV?" I said, turning to him and folding my arms. "What about STDs? Aren't you afraid he's going to bring home some nasty germ he's picked up from God knows where?"

"We practice safe sex," Jonathan said, downcast.

"At least he's doing that for you," I said with a snort.

I thought of the countless times I'd had unprotected sex with Ethan while he was sleeping with the other one. The first thing I did when I found out Ethan was cheating on me was schedule blood tests. Negative, thank God.

"Sometimes I wish Marcus would catch something," Jonathan said, squinting into the bright distance. "Not HIV, but something icky that would make him change his ways."

"You want a germ to save your relationship?" I made no effort to hide the antipathy in my voice.

"I know, but I can't help it," Jonathan said. "I work so hard to please him, but he's never satisfied. I feel like no matter what I do, it'll never be enough. I feel like … like I'm groping around in the darkness, searching for the magic door that'll open and lead me into the light."

"Have you told Marcus any of this?" I leaned forward in my chair. "Does he know how you feel?"

"You'd think he could figure it out," Jonathan said in a harsh voice. "Without me having to tell him."

"Jonathan, he's your partner—your fiancé!" I threw a look at the pill bottle on the table. "He should be giving you the red carpet treatment, not turning you into some pill-popping basket case. You deserve better from him. You should demand better from him. He won't stop unless you say something."

"What if he says he doesn't love me enough?" Jonathan said, his eyes flashing and his voice near breaking. "That he'd sooner dump me than give up seeing other people? Then what? He likes sex. I can't change the way he is."

"You're right, you can't change Marcus." I heard the spitefulness in my tone, but I was too angry to care. "But you can change yourself."

Jonathan gave a start as if I'd smacked him. Then he shook his head, turned away, and lifted the water bottle to his lips. My head pounded in the searing sunlight. I fished out my sunglasses from my shirt pocket and put them on. Jonathan put the bottle down without drinking from it and turned to face me. I had no choice but to return his look, half-horrified, half-exhilarated by what I'd said.

"You've never liked Marcus, have you?" Jonathan's eyes held an accusing light, his tone accusing too. "You think I should've left him a long time ago."

"What a thing to ask," I said. I looked away, aware of how unconvincing I sounded.

"You might as well come out and say it." Jonathan's shoulders were hunched and his face was tense and drawn. "Say he's no good. Say you think I should call off the wedding."

"Is that what you want me to say?" I felt the anger flaring up in me again. "You can't call off the wedding unless I say you should? Only you know what's best."

"I don't know what's best," Jonathan said, his voice sad and deflated.

"But you do know." I dragged my chair close to his so our knees almost touched. "Listen to what your heart is telling you. I trust your judgment. If you can look me in the eye and tell me you want to go through with the wedding, then I'll believe you. Okay?"

Jonathan turned and looked at me, his face pale and frightened. I held his gaze and held my breath, honestly not knowing what he'd say or how I'd respond. He'd have a place to stay if he said he wanted to leave Marcus—with me. And then, maybe, I wouldn't have to sneak downstairs every night to sleep on the living room couch.

"I can't do it," Jonathan said in almost a whisper. "Not yet, anyway. Marcus is all I know."

I drew myself up with a buzzing sensation in my hands. Half of me felt proud to be such a supportive friend. The other half wondered if I'd blown my one chance to persuade Jonathan to leave Marcus once and for all. Wherever Marcus was right now, he should be thanking me for the favor I'd done for him. I'd settle for sleeping on the living room couch for a while longer.

"Fine," I said. "But if you want it to work, then you need to talk to Marcus. Before you're married. You don't want to go through a divorce. Take it from me. You don't."

***

We ate lunch at a sub shop on Market Street crowded with tourists. I didn't realize how hungry I was until I started wolfing down my Italian sub. Jonathan ordered a chicken Caesar salad. I kept a watchful eye on him to make sure he ate it, remembering how awful those anxiety pills had been when I didn't take them with food. Was my first hunch right, that Marcus had no idea Jonathan was on those pills? It didn't matter. Even if he did know, he probably wouldn't stop fooling around with other guys.

We left the sub shop and stood at the corner by the BART station. Nearby, a guy in green camouflage pants played classical violin, a tip jar at his feet. The street bustled with cars and shoppers. I wasn't sure if I should take leave of Jonathan so soon after he'd poured out his heart to me. I asked him if maybe he wanted to go one of the department stores nearby, try on more tuxes, but he said no. Even if we parted ways now, I'd be sure to call him later on tonight.

"It's a quarter to one," Jonathan said, consulting the time on his cell phone. "Isn't Julio waiting for you at home?"

"Julio?" It took me a moment to understand what Jonathan meant. "Oh, no. Julio won't be home until later this afternoon."

"So, um, that means you and he still aren't serious?" Jonathan said.

"More or less," I said in an off-handed voice.

"I had a feeling," Jonathan said, and he lowered his eyes. "You never bring him up."

"But Julio's still a sweet guy," I heard myself say. I needed a moment to realize that I'd meant it. "He's helping me through a rough period."

"If Julio isn't home and he doesn't mind you being away," Jonathan said, drawing out those last words, "then maybe you'd like to hang out with me at home today."

The thought of spending the entire day with Jonathan opened up like a fresh rose. Last night I'd told Julio I'd be out all day at a chess tournament, in case my shopping day with Jonathan ran late. If I spent the day at Jonathan's house today, Julio wouldn't notice a thing.

"And do what?" I said. Goosebumps traveled down my arms.

"I don't know," Jonathan said with a shrug. "Anything. We can hang out on the roof like we did at the engagement party. It's nice up there this time of day."

"What about Marcus?" I tried to keep my voice casual. "Won't he be home?"

"Nope." Jonathan pulled his phone out of his pocket, checked it, and put it away. "Still no word from him."

I pictured sitting with Jonathan on his roof, talking about life. My hand reaching out to hold his hand. Leaning in to kiss him. Leading him downstairs to his bedroom. But the fantasy screeched to a stop there. What kind of fiend was I turning into? To sleep with Jonathan in his own bed would make me as despicable as Ethan. I couldn't do something that vile, not even to Marcus. Even to imagine doing it made me feel wretched.

"Nah, I better not," I said. "I have a few things to do around the house before Julio comes home."

"Okay." Was that relief in Jonathan's voice? "Thanks for helping me out today. Say hi to Julio for me."

***

On the train ride home I closed my eyes and let my body cave to exhaustion. Was I right to leave Jonathan by himself this afternoon? Yes, I must be. Jonathan was vulnerable. And on medication. I thanked my parents for teaching me the wisdom to make the right decision for us both.

I let myself into the kitchen. The stove clock read twenty-five past one. My eye caught a familiar-looking pair of gold-tinted aviator glasses sitting on the kitchen table. Wait a minute. Where had I seen those sunglasses before? On Julio? No, he wore a pair of sporty black sunglasses. But if those sunglasses weren't Julio's, then whose were they? And what were they doing on the kitchen table?

I jumped to the sound of voices. Then the house fell silent. Was Julio home already? He usually didn't come home until two. I went to the spare room, now Julio's massage room, and stood in the doorway. The room was empty, the massage table stripped of sheets. Was I hearing things?

From the bottom of the staircase, I heard a voice—no, two voices—coming from above. A moan. Then silence. All at once, I remembered where I'd seen those sunglasses. On Marcus. The morning I'd met him and Jonathan at the Ferry Building. My heart felt like it would stop. Marcus. Upstairs with Julio. Then their voices started up again.

"Tell me," Marcus said, his voice deep and insistent. "Tell me you want it."

"I want it," Julio said.

"Tell me again."

"I want it."

I sidled away from the stairwell to the kitchen, horrified. Ethan all over again. My legs went hollow. My stomach was ready to heave. My entire being trembled with rage. To think I could've gone home with Jonathan today. I could be making love to Jonathan at this very moment, instead of standing here bewildered in my own kitchen, my own house. If only I'd known Marcus had been coming here. If only I'd known that the man Marcus was sleeping with was Julio. Julio, my own fake boyfriend—and now Marcus's all-too-real sex partner. But if Marcus thought this was checkmate, he was wrong. He hadn't even put me into check.

The voices upstairs grew louder, more demanding. I picked up Marcus's sunglasses, regarded them in the sunlight, and placed them on a far corner of the table like a rook or bishop on the enemy side of the board. That should be enough for the lovers upstairs to wonder if I'd walked into the house without their hearing me. Now for my next move—to make a noise they'd hear, then flee. Without a sound I opened the kitchen door and crept outside. Then I closed my eyes, counted to three, and with as much hatred as I could put into a single gesture, I slammed the door behind me. And left.

8

CRUTCHES

Marcus rolled the condom onto himself, a confident smirk on his lips. The steel-blue of his eyes made me think of handcuffs, locking me into place. So risky of me to let Marcus come here on a Saturday afternoon. But I couldn't stop myself. Marcus was like a wildfire out of control. All I could do was watch, terrified that Frank might burst in on us at any moment, but addicted to the flames. The risk of what we were doing made the fire burn that much whiter, that much hotter. I hated myself for the power I'd given Marcus. I hated myself for wanting it, for lacking the will to put out the fire. And then—bang.

"What was that?" I said, bolting up in bed.

"What was what?" Marcus said. He looked around as if hadn't heard anything.

"Kitchen door." I scrambled off the bed. "It slammed."

"I didn't hear anything." Marcus stared at me like no way could I be right.

I went over and half-opened the bedroom door, leaned forward, and listened. No sound. I closed the door, tiptoed to the window, and peeked through a crack in the shade. Nothing but empty sidewalk. I pulled on a T-shirt and a pair of sweatpants, facing away from Marcus. Like having him out of my line of vision would make him disappear.

"Come on, Julio," Marcus said. His tone was impatient. "I'm sure it was nothing but a—"

"Shhhh!" I said, rounding on him.

"You're going down there?" Marcus's mouth was hanging open.

"Frank might be home." I tied the drawstring of the sweatpants.

"And if he is?" Marcus said with a half-sneer.

"Will you keep your voice down?" I said, near panic. "This was a total mistake, me having you over here on a Saturday."

"You seemed happy enough about it an hour ago," Marcus said, stretching out on the bed and throwing a glance at his perfect body.

I turned away, stepped into the hall, and closed the door behind me. My heart beat faster with every step I took down the stairs. In my head I repeated, Frank's not here, Frank's not here. No sound at the bottom of the stairs. I crept to the kitchen doorway, about ten feet away from the stairs. Marcus's sunglasses sat on the table, right there for anyone walking through the door to see. Holy Mother. How could we have been so careless?

My mind flashed to me and Marcus starting in on each other almost as soon as we walked into the house. I'd pulled off Marcus's shades and flung them onto—Mother of God—the middle of the table. The middle! Then what were they doing at the corner of the table? And the way they sat there—neatly folded, the shades facing up, the yellow-tinted lenses parallel to the table edge—made me think of Frank. Who else would've left the sunglasses like that? Everything in this crazy house was neat and organized, from the dishes in the dining room china closet to the coffee mugs hanging off their hooks in the cabinet. Mother of God, Frank had been here. He couldn't have thought of a better way to punish me and Marcus.

No. Wait. I could always be wrong. In fact, I had to be wrong. Frank had told me he'd be out all day for a chess tournament. I wouldn't have let Marcus come here if Frank hadn't told me he wouldn't be home until late. I put a hand to my racing heart and took deep breaths. My monkey mind was playing tricks on me, that was all. I was the one who must've left those shades on the table. In the corner. Neatly folded. The lenses parallel to the table edge. And I hadn't flung them, I'd placed them. Hadn't I?

And what I'd heard wasn't the slam of the kitchen door. It must've been a car backfiring. Or a tree branch hitting the house. Or a meteor. Something else. Anything else. Not Frank. Please, Holy Mother, not Frank.

***

Marcus sat in the bed reclining against the pillows, the rumpled sheets pulled up to his waist. He was using his body to win me over again. That might've worked an hour ago. I admit it—it did work an hour ago. Instead, the stink of my airless room hit my nostrils as if for the first time. My stomach turned. The musty stench held two months' worth of piled-up evil, of the wrongness of letting Marcus guzzle down my energy and my life.

"Do we have company?" Marcus said raising his eyebrows, his voice smug.

"You left these downstairs." I tossed the shades and sent them careening onto the mattress next to him. They didn't land neatly.

"Thanks." Marcus yawned and picked up the sunglasses, stretched, and slid them on. "Told you it was nothing."

"I found them sitting near the corner of the kitchen table," I said, my bare feet planted on the floor. "I'm sure they were on the middle of the table when we came upstairs."

"Guess they weren't," Marcus said with a half-yawn.

"I'm telling you, they were."

"You're being paranoid," Marcus said. His tone was condescending, kind of like how he'd talked to Jonathan, that time they'd had Frank and me over for dinner.

"Then you tell me," I said, raising my voice. "How did the sunglasses move from the middle of the table to the corner of the table?"

"The wind," Marcus said with a shrug.

"Mother of God," I said, "why does everything have to be a joke with you? And will you take those sunglasses off?"

"I'm not joking." Marcus pulled off the sunglasses and leaned forward. The soft afternoon sunlight made shadows on his biceps and forearms. "This is all in your head. There was no one down there, right? Come on, babe. Don't leave me hot and bothered like this."

Did he honestly think I was in the mood for sex now? Especially after he'd put me down like that? Six months of my life with this guy, four months as a friend, two months as a lover, all of it down the drain. I scooped up Marcus's clothes and dumped them onto the mattress by his feet.

"You have no business being here," I said, my voice shaking. "Even if that wasn't Frank, he'll be home any second."

"Is that what you think?" Marcus said with a half-smile, his eyes lighting up. "Do you even know where Frank is right now?"

"Chess tournament," I shot back.

"So that's what he told you," Marcus said, curling his lip. "I'm surprised. A smart guy like Frank, you'd think he would've come up with something more creative."

"What're you talking about?" I said. I couldn't help rising to the bait.

"Hmm." Marcus leaned forward and stroked the thatch of hair on his chin. "Don't you think it's strange he went to a chess tournament in July? Who did he take to this tournament? His students? Isn't school out for summer?"

"It's an adult chess tournament," I said, with no idea if that was true.

"An adult chess tournament," Marcus said in a sneering voice. Even with the shades down, his eyes shone bright and victorious. "We should all have Frank's commitment to excellence."

"Put your clothes on so you can go," I said. I left the bedroom with the door open, hoping some air would come in.

***

I sat at the kitchen table and closed my eyes. The shower roared in the upstairs bathroom, the pipes squealing inside the walls. Marcus was probably jerking off up there. The way I'd walked out on him, he no doubt felt entitled to do that.

My hands felt the itch to be busy. Groceries. Yes, I needed groceries. I opened the fridge and shook my soy milk carton. Half a carton left. One apple and a few soggy cherries in the crisper. Three eggs I'd planned to scramble after Marcus left. I opened a counter drawer, brought out a notepad and pen, sat down at the table. Holy Mother, how could I have ever let Marcus in this house? And in the harsh afternoon light, the truth sank in that taking up with Marcus was one of the dumbest choices I'd ever made. Marcus had to go into the drawer with this notepad, along with all the other guys I wished I'd never slept with. I'd need a bigger drawer for that.

The water stopped. The house went scary-silent. I put down the notebook and pen. Five seconds, inhale. Five seconds, exhale. In a couple minutes Marcus came downstairs all dressed, his sunglasses hanging off the collar of his sky-blue T-shirt. I glanced up at him, then looked down. Even now I had to admit he looked damn fine in that shirt.

"I'll see you Tuesday?" he said, as if nothing had happened.

"Better not," I said, my eyes on the notepad.

I hadn't expected to say that, even less using such a harsh tone. Even without looking at him, I could sense him looking at me square-jawed, his eyes boring into me. On the notepad I wrote MILK.

"So this is it?" Marcus's tone was low and ominous-sounding. "You think you hear a noise in the house, and now we're through?"

"This had to stop sometime," I said, still looking at the notepad. My hand shook so badly that I put down the pen. "Now's as good a time as any."

"Says who?" Marcus said, walking up to me so close that I could smell my peppermint soap on his skin.

"Says me," I said, trying to keep my voice level. "This is messing with my head. I can't take it anymore. I'm sorry, but I can't."

I grabbed the pen and wrote EGGS in shaky handwriting. My mind flashed to every time we'd had sex, each session raunchier than the time before. I hadn't done it like that in years. Who knew when I would have it like that again? Still, I had to let this go.

"If we're nothing to each other anymore," Marcus said, "then that means I can come here for massages and go to your Saturday yoga classes. Right?"

"There are plenty of massage therapists in San Francisco," I said, sitting up straight and grasping the pen more tightly. "And Josie's class comes right after mine."

"For Christ's sake, Julio, will you look at me?" Marcus said, placing his hand down on my hand holding the pen. "Am I so disgusting that you can't even look at me?"

I sucked in a breath and tilted my head upward. Marcus let go of my hand, stood up straight, and folded his arms in front of him, his blue eyes burning. He looked like he meant to stand glaring at me all day. I returned his look with a stony expression, determined not to show the effect he had on me. Now was the time for me to find my inner Josie, the soul's calmness in a tough spot.

"What kind of trouble are you looking for?" My voice came out so severe I almost didn't recognize it as my own. "Your wedding's in a few weeks. That's what you should be paying attention to right now. It's like you're running away from something. Like you're afraid of what's important."

"I'm not afraid of anything," Marcus said, putting his hands on his hips. "What's important is spending time with you."

"You have no future with me," I said, sensing my rough breath. "You never did."

The color left Marcus's face. I'd zombified him. Even I was stunned by what I'd said. But there was no denying the truth of my words. Marcus and I had no future. It really was that simple.

"So this is it," Marcus said in a half-whisper. "It's over."

"It's best that way," I said gently. "Don't you agree?"

"I don't know what's best anymore." He said it in a voice I'd never heard him use before, childlike, maybe even despairing.

"This time next year you'll be in New York," I said, going into Josie-style pep-talk mode. "You'll forget all about me."

Marcus looked at me as if he didn't believe me, then he shuffled toward the kitchen door. My eyes followed him. We'd been lovers these past several weeks, after all. Why not snatch one last glimpse at him?

"Maybe I'll see you in the neighborhood sometime," Marcus said in an I-hope-we-can-still-be-friends voice.

"Maybe." I gave him a quick smile, the kind I hoped said *move it along, Marcus.*

Marcus turned and opened the door. Fresh air flowed in. My lungs expanded again. The first thing I'd do, once he was gone, would be to strip the sheets off my bed. The sooner I rid my bedroom of any trace of Marcus, the better. Even so, I'd still feel him lingering behind, hiding under the bed, behind the closet door, stretched out on the massage table. He'd left his mark in Frank's house.

"Are you in love with Frank?" Marcus said, turning to me.

"In love with Frank?" I should've known Marcus wouldn't leave here without trying to take a piece of me with him. "What kind of a question is that?"

"Because if you aren't," Marcus said, "then there's no reason why this has to end. I won't believe you love Frank unless you look me in the eye and tell me you love him."

"Holy Mother." I rose and glanced over his shoulder at the open door. "What kind of obsession do you have with Frank, anyway?"

"All I want," Marcus said, drawing himself up, "is to hear I meant something to you. That I wasn't some guy you messed with for kicks."

"Of course you meant more to me than that," I said with as much sincerity as I could put into my voice. "Hand to God. I never lie down with a man who means nothing to me."

All right, so maybe that wasn't exactly true. But I had to say something to make him leave, didn't I? Marcus looked over his shoulder and closed the door, blocking it. Fine. Let him have the last word.

"Thanks," Marcus said. "I needed to hear that. You meant more to me too. You're so … in the present. Sometimes, when I'm with, you know, with Jonathan, I feel like he's checked out on me. His mind starts to wander, and I don't know how to reach him. It's so hard to live with a man I can't read."

"You need to have a heart-to-heart with him," I said. I knew this was the obvious advice, even though I'd never taken it myself.

"I've given up trying," Marcus said with a sigh.

"Then try again," I said. "After all, you're planning to share the rest of your life with him."

"Maybe I will," he said, but he didn't sound like he would. He turned to open the door.

"I'll miss you," I said. After the wild ride he'd given me, I figured he deserved to hear that.

"I'll miss you too," Marcus said, turning to face me. He gave a scornful once-over of Frank's drab kitchen. "And so that you know, I have no regrets, no regrets at all about what we did."

"Marcus, please," I said, holding out a hand to stop him from saying more.

"And not that you'll take this advice," Marcus said, "but you should think about putting Frank in your rear-view mirror. I don't know why you're wasting your time with him, here in this old house."

"You don't know Frank," I said, surprised to hear myself say that. "He's not the most exciting guy in the world, but he's decent."

"Sure he's decent," Marcus said with a nod and a grim expression. "If he ever makes it home today, be sure to ask him where he went. Because whatever he was doing, he wasn't playing chess."

"You need to go, Marcus," I said. My voice was weak.

"One last thing," Marcus said, opening the door. "Why do you think I called you this morning, to ask if I could come over? How do you think I knew Frank wouldn't be here? Think about that."

Then he left, slamming the door behind him. I needed a few minutes to feel in my bones he'd really left. I went upstairs and took a long, hot shower. No use. I came out of the bathroom feeling I'd never be clean again.

***

Over the next few days I couldn't bring myself to look Frank in the face. It wasn't hard to steer clear of him, since he left to teach summer school in the morning every day, driving away in his crisp blue shirt and tie. Who said there couldn't be high school chess tournaments in the summer? All the same, I couldn't help wondering where he'd gone last Saturday. Marcus had seemed awfully sure of himself when he'd hinted Frank had lied to me.

I imagined Marcus crashing the Saturday morning yoga class. What would I say, what would I do, if he showed up? The thought ate at me all week long. I almost called Josie Friday night to bail on her, say I had a cold or something. But Josie was my mentor, my third big sister, the woman who'd given me the prime Saturday spot. I owed it to Josie and to my students to teach that class.

I showed up a half hour early to the yoga studio. A few of my diehard students had shown up early, unrolling their mats and filling their water bottles at the drinking fountain. The room slowly filled up. Someone took Marcus's usual spot near the front window. I put on my dubstep playlist, feeling like a doofus for worrying so much.

Then, less than two minutes before I was set to start class, Marcus showed up. My cheery mood deserted me in a heartbeat, my stomach sinking down to my ankles. Our eyes met before he found a place for his mat by the far wall, squeezing between two women I didn't know. He wore his usual red shorts and black tank top. I worked my way down the row of yoga mats opposite him, introducing myself to a couple new students, asking about any injuries. My smile grew tighter the farther I went down the row.

Marcus was next to last in his row. I would've cut him off altogether, but that would look too obvious. The dubstep music and the chit-chat of the other yoga students pounded in my head. I squatted down and leaned toward his ear, my smile as wide as ever. He returned the smile with a half-hopeful, half-challenging look.

"What are you doing here?" My face muscles hurt from all the smiling.

"I have stress." He kept smiling too, but his voice was cutting.

"I told you not to come here."

"Don't talk to me like that," Marcus said, a warning tone behind the smile.

"Marcus, what do you want?" I said standing up, my smile growing as wide as it would go.

"A friend."

"You have tons of other friends." I glanced around the room.

"None like you, babe," he said, reaching up to grab my hand.

"Don't you ever call me that." I was still smiling, but I yanked my hand away with more force than I should've.

"I've had a terrible week," he said in that warning tone again, not pretending to smile anymore. "I have to have you near me."

"Marcus, what kind of trouble do you want here?" Now I wasn't smiling either. "You have a wedding to think about."

"Or not," Marcus said.

"It's off?" I said, my jaw going slack.

"Will you let me stay if I say yes?" His eyes glittered like chips of ice.

He'd argue with me all morning if I let him. I scowled at him and went to the music player to lower the volume. Everyone quieted down. Like it or not, Marcus was staying put. Forget about him for the next ninety minutes, Julio. My students didn't deserve this drama.

I cranked up the heat to ninety degrees, about five degrees higher than usual. Through song after song I put the class through stomach crunches, sun salutations, tree pose, triangle, pyramid, half-moon.

People had to stop in mid-pose, reaching to wipe their faces or take a slug from their water bottles. Not Marcus, of course. He seemed determined to muscle through everything I threw in his way, without seeming to notice I was dedicating this hell of a class to him. Meanwhile, my thoughts came flying at me like glass shards. Wedding off. Marcus here. What now? What next?

"Bring your right foot forward and place it between your hands," I said, after a punishing series of standing poses. The way my voice came out, as smooth as ever, I doubted if anyone other than Marcus could guess the riot going on in my head right now. "Take your back knee down for a lunge. Use a blanket or fold your mat over if you need padding."

My students did as they were told. Several of them wobbled, including Marcus. He held the pose better than most of the class, but his hips were out of alignment. Watching him gave me a feeling of power. Here, Marcus, let me show you and the rest of the class how to do it right. I brought my right foot forward and my left knee down onto the varnished hardwood floor.

Pow. Crunch. My knee exploded. At first I felt no pain, only the sensation of me tipping over onto my side and crumpling into a ball. The room tilted to the left, tilted to the right, and then everything went dark.

***

I opened my eyes to two dozen shocked faces gaping down at me. White-hot flames shot out of my knee. I forgot who I was, where I was. Nothing existed but the pain.

"Everybody stand back!" A familiar voice, full of authority. Marcus.

The circle around me widened. Marcus bent down close to me, put a hand to my cheek. Why was he near me? Where were we anyway? Then it came to me. Saturday morning class. Marcus here. Knee ruined. Sixteen years of yoga down the drain.

"First-aid kit," I gasped. "Closet."

"Someone check the closet," Marcus yelled.

Running footsteps. A door opening and closing. The first aid kit on the floor next to my face. A pair of hands opening the kit. Marcus's hands. The hands he'd put all over me last week. Was that only last week? Marcus brought out a blue vinyl ice pack, slammed it hard against the floor to activate it, and laid it on my knee. The coldness shocked me into an awareness of the mess I'd made.

"You'll be fine," Marcus said in a clinical voice, looking me in the eye. "I'm taking you to the emergency room."

I had barely the strength to nod yes. For all the blazing pain I was in, I had enough sense to notice Marcus in his element. Helping people weaker than himself was what he did. That's why Jonathan stayed with him. Why I needed him now. It was as if he'd come to class meaning to take over like this. Like he'd known all along I'd break my knee. Or like he'd come here on purpose to break it.

"My music player." I felt ready to faint again. "My bag."

"Will someone grab his stuff for him?" Marcus shouted.

Someone scurried away. A strange pair of hands brought my things to Marcus. Then Marcus and another student hoisted me onto my good leg, holding me under each arm. I lowered my left toe to the floor and gasped at the firebomb shooting up my leg. How was I ever going to make it to Marcus's car?

"You're going to be okay," Marcus repeated, softer this time but still sounding as if he was fully in command.

"I need to call Josie," I gasped.

"Don't worry about Josie," Marcus said. "You can talk to her later."

"We can't go anywhere until she comes," I said, feeling ready to fall to the floor again. "I can't leave the studio wide-open."

"I'll talk to her," Marcus said, picking up my gym bag from the floor and taking out my phone. "You dial the number."

I typed in my password, found Josie's number, and handed Marcus the phone. His calm, businesslike voice told Josie about the accident. He shut off the phone and said she'd be here in fifteen minutes. A couple of students said they'd stay behind. Marcus led me out of the studio, propping me up with his arm. My eyelids grew heavy, and my mind wandered away from this place, away from my injured body. I wished I could close my eyes, open them again, and find out I'd turned into someone else. Someone better than I was.

***

Turned out I had a hairline fracture on top of my tibia. The ER doctor hung the X-ray against the fluorescent screen, a pencil line slashing against the glowing white bone. I was lucky, it could've been worse. But I needed surgery. Fucking surgery.

They wheeled me into another room and drew a curtain over my leg. A needle's pinch. The leg went numb. I felt a pressure against my dead leg, a pushing and scraping that made me want to throw up. I closed my eyes and breathed. Five seconds in. Five seconds out. I imagined myself in the yoga studio, with me as both student and instructor. "Notice it, let it pass," I repeated to myself, using the patient, loving voice Josie had taught me. But a yoga pose lasted for only a few seconds. This busted knee would follow me everywhere I went, all day, every day. For how long?

My mind traveled to the first time I'd met Josie at my first teacher training. She was an established forty-year-old yogi. I was a shy twenty-three-year-old still sorting his life out. Her attention and approval were like drugs to me. And this was how I repaid her—by sleeping with one of my own students, betraying everything she'd taught me. She'd never speak to me again.

Nurses finished putting me into the cast. The wall clock read three in the afternoon. I was starving. The last thing I'd eaten was oatmeal and raisins for breakfast. The doctor said I'd be stuck in the cast for at least a month. I was so ashamed, I thought the cast might as well stay on forever.

A physical therapist, an earnest-looking guy who looked about a year out of college, gave me my first-ever pair of crutches and showed me how to use them. After that he wheeled me into the crowded waiting room. Marcus looked up from his magazine and stood, strong as a redwood in his tank top and shorts. He listened to my bad news, then patted me on the shoulder and wheeled me out of the hospital towards his car. He felt like a human version of the cast on my leg. A crippling weight I'd never be rid of.

***

"You can drop me off at the nearest BART station," I said to Marcus, once he'd stowed me into the car.

"I'm driving you home," Marcus said. He settled into the driver's seat and slammed the door.

"You can't park in front of the house." My voice was sharp, but it trembled. "Frank should be home by now."

A snort was Marcus's answer. He sped up Folsom Street, turned onto Eighth, then cut off an SUV to take the ramp toward Oakland. The car pulled forward and zipped across the bridge. If the driver were anyone but Marcus, I'd swear we were headed for a car crash.

Eventually, we made it to Oakland. Marcus parked about a block away from the house, in the shade of a laurel tree. He opened the door for me, helped me out, brought out my crutches. An image of my bed, my warm comfortable bed, swam in my imagination. Mother of God, how was I going to make it up the stairs to my room in these crutches?

"I'll call you later?" Marcus said like some caring boyfriend.

"No," I said, drawing myself up on my crutches.

"Babe, please," Marcus said in a small voice.

"I told you, I'm not your babe," I snapped. "How about leaving me alone for a change? If you had, none of this would've happened."

I pulled away from him, out of the tree shade and into the dazzling sun. I reached for my shades in my gym bag, but my crutch caught where tree roots poked through the concrete. The bag slipped from my shoulder. I pictured the gritty pavement coming up to slap my face. Marcus broke my fall in time.

"Julio, hey, I'm sorry," he said after he'd steadied me, looking into my eyes. "You know I didn't mean for this to happen."

"I'm sure you didn't," I said through my teeth.

"I'll talk to Josie tomorrow and explain," he said. "I'll tell her this was my fault."

"An instructor is responsible for everyone's safety in the studio," I said, repeating what Josie had taught me in teacher training. "It doesn't matter what you tell her. She won't hold you responsible, no matter what you say. This is all on me. Don't call her."

"She'll listen to me, all right," Marcus said. "I'll make her believe me."

"Mother of God, what does it take to make you quit?" I half-shouted, close to tears. "You've done enough."

I kept going and crossed paths with a whitehaired woman in a maroon track suit, leading a fluffy white dog on a leash. How I wanted to be her in that moment, enjoying the afternoon, not a care in the world. I didn't smile at her like I would've if I was by myself.

Then Marcus clapped a hand on my shoulder, forcing me to stop and look at him. No, he'd never quit.

"Wait," he said, out of breath.

"Please, Marcus," I said, wrenching my shoulder away from him. "Please let me be."

"Not like this," Marcus said. "I only came to class this morning because things have been impossible at home. I need you more than you know. You've been on my mind all week long."

"Stop it," I said, trying to work my way around him. "You can't talk to me like this anymore."

Marcus moved in front of me, made me look him in the eye, and planted a tender kiss on me. In my head Josie stood watching me struggle on my yoga mat, balancing on my good leg while my bad leg throbbed with guilt. Couldn't let him do this. Couldn't let him win. I pushed Marcus away so hard I nearly toppled over.

"Leave me alone," I said, furious. "Why won't you listen to me?"

"I had a blowout fight with Jonathan this week," Marcus said. He was breathing hard. "He gave me the silent treatment for three straight days. Then he told me last night he's leaving for Santa Cruz to spend the weekend with his mother. That's where he is right now. His mother hates me. Maybe you saw that at the engagement party. For years she's been trying to talk Jonathan into leaving me."

"So now the truth comes out," I said, glaring at him. "You didn't come to the studio looking for friendship. You came looking for revenge."

"How can you say that?" Marcus said, eyes wide with shock. "I came because I needed a friend. Someone I could talk to. You think I know half the city, but they're false friends. No one I can confide in. Not like what Jonathan has with Frank. But you, Julio, you're different than that—"

"Cut the crap," I said, scowling. "Now how about moving out of my way."

But he didn't move. He kept his eyes on me. I burned to know what Marcus's fight with Jonathan was about, but I wouldn't give him the satisfaction of asking.

"I wouldn't be surprised if Jonathan calls to tell me he's moving home to Santa Cruz," Marcus said. "He's definitely spending next weekend with his mother down there. If I'm free next weekend too, would you consider … keeping me company next weekend?"

"Next weekend?" I said, my mouth falling open. "Are you nuts?"

"I can't be alone in that huge house," Marcus said, shaking his head. "I hear voices echoing off the walls when I'm there alone. But if you stay with me, we can take care of each other. As friends. That's all I want. I promise."

"Thanks a lot, Marcus," I said, sarcastic. "But you don't have to worry about me next weekend. I have Frank to keep me company."

Marcus's expression switched from sympathetic to murderous. I looked away from him and again tried to make my way around him, pretending not to notice the change. He didn't move. If anything, he looked ready to rip away my crutches and knock me to the ground. It was amazing how the mention of Frank's name turned Marcus into a psycho.

"Does Frank even know about the accident yet?" Marcus said in a tone that made my scar tingle. "I don't remember you calling him once. I don't even remember you mentioning his name all day long."

"I called him right before the surgery," I said sounding miffed, although even to my own ears this sounded like a lie.

"On the off-chance life becomes too unbearable with him," Marcus said, his voice cold, "then you know where to find me. Or who knows? Maybe Frank won't be around next weekend. Maybe he'll have another chess tournament to go to. In Santa Cruz."

"And what's that supposed to mean?" I said, gripping my crutches.

"Nothing, nothing." Marcus let out a breath. "All I'm saying is I care for you a lot. I might even care for you more than your boyfriend does. Times like this, you should maybe stop and ask yourself who your real friends are. Call me if you want. I hope you do."

Only after I heard his car drive away did I dare turn around to see if Marcus had gone. What did he mean, a chess tournament in Santa Cruz? Probably nothing. At least I'd stuffed him in the drawer with my other exes—for now. All that was left to do was face Frank. Mother of God, please let Frank not be home. This day had dragged on long enough.

9

STARTER HUSBANDS

I looked up from my chessboard to the sound of trudging, uneven footsteps on the front walk. From where I sat at the dining table, I had a clear view of the large, oaken door in the entrance hall. The lock turned, the door opened, and Julio hobbled into the front hall on crutches. His lower leg was freighted with a cast. I rose from the table, forgetting for the moment that I loathed him.

"What happened?" I said, staring at the cast.

"Slipped in class today," Julio said. His voice was cheerful but strained. "Too much sweat on the floor."

He closed the door with one of his crutches, turned his key in the lock, and let his gym bag drop to the floor. The brightness of his apricot-orange jacket clashed with the dog-tired look on his face. A bubble of compassion for him—a small bubble, but a bubble nonetheless—welled up inside me.

"That must've been quite the slip," I said.

"It looks worse than it is," Julio said, looking down at the cast as if it were a mere nuisance. "They told me I should be out of it in a month."

His face looked drained of energy. How had he made it home from San Francisco? He couldn't have taken BART and then walked from the station to the house. Did he take an Uber? Or did someone drive him? Marcus maybe? But I hadn't heard a car outside.

"Do you need anything?" I said, surprised to hear those words come out of my mouth.

"Not now, thanks," Julio said. He gave me a tight smile and turned toward the living room. "All I want is to go upstairs and lie down."

"I was thinking of ordering some Chinese takeout in a few minutes," I heard myself say. "You interested?"

"That sounds amazing," Julio said, relief spreading across his face. "I haven't eaten since breakfast."

"Let me finish this chess problem," I said, "and I'll order some. Maybe have the food here by six thirty or seven?"

"That sounds amazing," Julio repeated, in a tone of genuine gratitude.

I sat down and looked at my open chess book, then at my board. It was easier for me to focus on this chess problem than figure out how to deal with Julio. But the chess pieces swam in front of me. Something in Julio's tone of voice gave me the sick feeling he'd lied about slipping in class.

"I have money saved," Julio said, blurting the words out.

"Huh?" I said looking up.

"To pay for the takeout," Julio said. He leaned on his crutches by the large doorway between the dining room and the entrance hall. "And pay rent while I'm out of work. I have insurance. In case you thought I couldn't pay rent while I'm out of work."

That had never occurred to me, him not being able to pay rent. It also hadn't occurred to me Julio would be housebound for the foreseeable future. I was used to having the house to myself.

"Okay," I said, pulling in my chair. "I'm sure we can work something out."

Julio pivoted on his crutches and moved into the living room, no doubt intending to cut across the room to the stairwell. I stared and stared at my Lewis chessmen, staring back at me in obstinate refusal to divulge their secrets. About a minute later I looked up. I hadn't heard Julio climb the stairs. The house was never this silent with Julio in the house. I pulled myself up from the chair and headed for the living room, worried about him despite myself.

Julio dozed slouching in the large leather easy chair, his crutches leaning against the arm rest. The cast looked as heavy as an anchor. Seeing him there reminded me of the day the movers delivered the piano and the grandfather clock last summer. It was as if Julio had become another piece of furniture I had no choice but to live with.

I went to the hallway closet, brought out the bedding I'd been using to sleep on the couch myself, and carried it into the living room. My mother came into my mind, watching me with pursed lips, disapproving of the way I was helping someone who'd wronged me. But I knew better than anyone—certainly better than Julio did—that the living room was going to be his bedroom for the next few weeks.

"What're you doing?" Julio said in a slurred voice, snapping awake behind me.

"Fixing your bed." I spread out the sheet onto the leather cushions. "You'll stay down here till your leg's better."

"You don't have to do that," Julio said, yawning and crossing his arms. "I was about to go to my room."

"You can't climb those stairs," I said.

"Sure I can," Julio said, struggling to sit up.

"My ex-husband once twisted his ankle playing tennis," I said. I used the clear, direct voice I used on my students. "And he almost fell trying to go down the stairs. So when I say you can't handle those stairs, I mean it. You can't handle those stairs."

"You don't mind me sleeping down here for the next few weeks?" Julio said.

"Why would I mind?" I finished smoothing out the sheet.

"No reason," Julio said, and shrugged. "Um, thanks for making my bed. I bet I'll be on my feet in no time."

I ordered the Chinese, went into the dining room, and settled in front of my chessboard. The position of the pieces seemed so alien that I could've sworn they'd conspired to move to different squares on their own. Then a thought dawned on me. If Julio would be sleeping on the couch for the next few weeks, where would I sleep?

***

Jonathan called me at home five days later on a chilly Friday night, almost two weeks since our morning at the tux shop. My phone buzzed while I sat at my bedroom desk, deep in a game of online chess against some troll named "Texa$$tud." I grabbed the phone next to my laptop as soon as Jonathan's face popped up on the screen.

"Is this a bad time?" Jonathan said in a hesitant voice.

"Not at all," I said, springing up from my chair to close the bedroom door. Julio was downstairs. "I missed you last weekend. How was Santa Cruz?"

"Not bad," Jonathan said. "My mom was her usual wacky self. Plus Patrick called my mom asking for money again. He wouldn't speak to me on the phone."

"Sorry to hear it," I said. Did Jonathan's mother know about his anxiety pills? Probably not. "Are we still on for breakfast tomorrow?"

"Sure, sure," Jonathan said. "I was also calling to say your tux is ready. Marcus's dad found it at a suit store in Manhattan, but they operate out of San Francisco too. If you call in with your measurements, they should have it ready for you in a couple weeks."

"Sounds good," I said, sitting down in my desk chair again.

"No—wait." Jonathan's voice seemed near breaking. "Maybe you should hold off ordering the suit for now."

Time was running out for me to make a move against Texa$$tud. I moved my black rook to protect my king against Texa$$tud's attacking white pieces. In response, he moved his knight to a choice center square. For a guy with a juvenile name, Texa$$tud knew how to play chess.

"You confronted Marcus, didn't you?" I said, my eyes hurting from the glowing computer screen.

"Um, yeah?" Jonathan's voice rose at the end of the sentence as if unsure the conversation had happened.

"And?" I said to nudge him, my eyes fixed on the ticking chess clock.

"I talked to Marcus like you said I should," Jonathan said in a shrinking tone. "A few nights after we saw each other. I had to work myself up to do it. My chance came at dinnertime. I told him flat out I wanted him to stop seeing other guys."

"How did he respond to that?" I said.

"First, he looked at me surprised," Jonathan said, his voice quivering. "I'd never made a demand on him like that before. Then he leaned forward and put his hand on his chin, you know, like he was thinking about it. He stayed like that for a good five seconds before he shook his head and said he couldn't go along with that. Then he pushed in his chair and started eating again."

"You're kidding," I said.

"I didn't let it drop there," Jonathan went on, sounding more and more upset. "I asked him was it someone in particular he couldn't stop seeing. He kept on eating as if he hadn't heard me. So I asked him again. Then he put down his fork, looked me straight in the eye, and said there was."

A shock ran through me. Julio? My mind zoomed downstairs to Julio sprawled out on the couch. The sounds of Julio and Marcus's lovemaking came to me in all its sickening glory. Who else could it be?

"What did you say to that?" I said calmly.

"I asked Marcus what made this guy so special," Jonathan said, his voice trembling, "he'd be willing to risk throwing away his future with me?"

"Appropriate," I said nodding, my vision going blurry. "And how did Marcus respond?"

"He said he didn't think he was risking anything," Jonathan said in a tone of disbelief. "He said he wasn't doing anything that wasn't part of our so-called arrangement."

"Jesus," I said under my breath.

"So I said if he kept on seeing this guy," Jonathan said, "I'd call off the wedding. And leave him."

"You did?" I said in a low voice, my vision coming into focus again. The chess clock was now at less than a minute. "What did he say to that?"

"He said if that was what I wanted, then he wouldn't stand in my way."

"My God," I said.

"You should've heard the way he said it." Jonathan's voice was dumbfounded. "No emotion. Nothing. I felt like he'd thank me if I walked out on him for good."

Twenty seconds left on the chess clock. I clicked on my knight and guided it over the board. My hand slipped, letting the knight fall in the attack line of Texa$$tud's queen. The queen snapped up the knight in less than ten seconds.

"I haven't even told you the worst part," Jonathan said, his voice small.

"There's more?" My heart shrank in my chest.

"I was so mad at Marcus afterwards, I couldn't even look at him," Jonathan said, speaking rapidly. "I started sleeping in the downstairs guest bedroom, because I couldn't fall asleep with him next to me. That's why I braved a visit to my mother's last weekend. He barely spoke to me when I came home, so I called my mother up again and asked if I could see her this weekend too."

"I will win you will lose HA HA HA." Texa$$tud's blood-red digital letters glowed in the chat box on my screen. I clenched my teeth and rose.

"But then I thought, running away from the problem wasn't the answer." Jonathan sounded as if he was having trouble breathing. "I figured I should sit down with Marcus and hash this out. That's what adults do, right?"

"Of course that's what they do," I said softly. I thought of the yawning, dreadful silences between Ethan and me in those final days before he moved out.

"So I sucked it up and told Marcus last night I'd be staying home this weekend after all," Jonathan said. "That we should talk things over. And he said … he said …"

His voice trailed off. On the laptop screen, Texa$$tud gloated in a stream of capital-lettered gibberish. I sat down and moved my cursor to the RESIGN GAME button. The only thing stopping me from clicking the button was an image of both my parents, watching me with dissatisfied looks. Think, Francis. Think.

"And?" I said.

"Marcus said maybe I should go to Santa Cruz anyway," Jonathan said. "He'd invited a guest to the house for the weekend."

"The other guy?" I said horrified, swiveling away from my laptop screen to face my untouched bed. "Are you telling me Marcus invited the guy he's seeing to your house for the weekend?"

"Yep." Jonathan's voice was so thick that he could barely eke out that one word.

"And Marcus wouldn't cancel his weekend with the other guy," I said, "even though you wanted to stay home?"

"No," Jonathan said, sounding defeated.

"But that's your house," I said, swiveling to face my chess game and staring at my black pieces until they went fuzzy in my vision. "That's your bed."

"The other guy won't sleep in our bed. He'll sleep in the guest bedroom. That's part of the arrangement."

"So Marcus has had other guys in your house before?" I said, aghast.

Silence on the other line. No need for Jonathan to answer. More waves of loathing for Marcus.

"I'm so sorry, Jonathan." I leaned my elbows on the desk. "I should never have put you up to this."

"No, I'm glad you did," Jonathan said with half a sigh. He sounded exhausted. "Like you said, better hash it out now than after we're married. But I don't know what to do next."

"Oh why don't you quit you fuckin nancy faggot." Texa$$tud's comment appeared in the chat box like a bloody gash. I sat up in the chair. Then I pictured Marcus, a smug, smiling Marcus, sitting next to Texa$$tud. Gleefully dictating to Texa$$tud the words to type. Maybe even placing a hand on Texa$$tud's, steering his moves. *Think, Francis, think*, I imagined my mother saying to me in her urgent, imperious voice. My father sat by her side, his eyes glittering encouragement. I scrutinized my position again—and spotted an opening. Not only on the chessboard. With Jonathan too.

"So are you going to your mother's tomorrow?" I reached for my computer mouse.

"It doesn't look like I have a choice," Jonathan said. "God, I hate taking the bus down there so early. I haven't even called my mother to say I'd be staying with her after all."

"Want to come here instead?" I said, clear and confident.

A pause on the other line. In my head Jonathan stood undefended on the king's square, while Marcus dawdled on the far edge of the board, distracted by Julio. I turned my gaze to the other opening, the one on my computer screen. The chess clock had ticked down almost to zero. I lay my cursor on my black queen and sent her hurtling toward Texa$$tud's side of the board, capturing a pawn and attacking both another pawn and his rook. The attacking white pieces were impotent. Texa$$tud could do nothing but watch his position fall apart.

"I don't want to be in the way," Jonathan said.

"You won't be," I said. "Julio's going away this weekend."

"Oh. Where's he going?"

"His mother's," I said, surprised and not displeased with myself for lying so deftly. "He hurt his knee in yoga class last weekend, so he's heading home for some TLC."

"Is he all right?" Jonathan said in a concerned tone that made me want to burst out laughing. If Jonathan only knew.

"Don't worry about Julio," I said lightly, swiveling in the chair from side to side. "The doctor says he'll be on his feet in no time."

"When should I come over?" Jonathan said, sounding nervous.

"Let's say between nine and ten o'clock." I calculated that if Julio was Marcus's other guy, then he'd want to be out of the house bright and early. "I'll text you in the morning."

We ended the call with me telling Jonathan I'd pick him up at the BART station. Now I could devote my full attention to finishing off Texa$$tud. My black queen closed in on his pawn, then his rook. It was checkmate in six moves or less. The chat box filled with line after line of blood-red obscenities. Right before his time ran out, he left the game without resigning. I snapped shut the laptop, picturing myself snapping it shut on Marcus as well as on Texa$$tud.

The next thing I did astonished even me. I went over and sat down at the edge of my bed. After all those months of sleeping on couches—and a week of sleeping in a sleeping bag on the bedroom floor—the bed's firmness took me aback. I ran my hand over the white comforter, letting it sink into the soft, voluptuous cotton. My left ring finger, denuded of its wedding band, looked particularly bare against the white. A feeling of delicious evil surged through me. A feeling to help me accomplish what I planned to do next.

I rose from the bed and went downstairs. Lamplight from the living room spilled into the hallway. Instead of going into the living room, I headed downstairs to the basement to move my clothes from the washer to the dryer. The dryer was full of Julio's laundry, stone cold. I'd forgotten I'd run that load for him two days ago. I emptied the laundry into Julio's yellow rubber laundry basket, moved my own laundry into the dryer, and turned the dryer on. Then I brought the basket upstairs and steeled myself to play the credulous, concerned roommate.

***

Julio was stretched out on the couch, looking haggard in his gray sweat suit and blue terry bathrobe. His hair was growing out and was stuck to his head. On the coffee table lay the torn wrappers of a couple of protein bars—his dinner, no doubt. Lying open on his lap was my father's old hardbound copy of Douglas Hofstadter's *Gödel, Escher, Bach*, a book I'd found in Dad's study when I was twelve. That book had done more to shape my life than any other book. I'd started reading it only to impress my dad, but the book's brilliant musings on the beauty of numbers had inspired me to follow Dad's footsteps in a career in mathematics. That Julio would haul *Gödel, Escher, Bach* down from one of the built-bookshelves next to the fireplace made me want to laugh out loud. If I needed any more evidence to know my roommate had no idea what he was doing, that book was it.

"These were in the dryer," I said, holding up the laundry basket.

"Thanks." Julio looked up from the book with weary, reddish eyes.

"I can fold it for you if you want," I said.

"Nah, leave the basket here," he said, yawning and rubbing the nape of his neck. "I need something to do besides lie here."

Was that guilt I heard in his voice? I set the laundry basket on the floor and sat down at the edge of the leather easy chair. He looked at me, then looked down at the open book in his lap. All week I'd made no attempt to keep him company. He must be wondering what I was doing here now. Good. In life as in chess, it was always smart to keep the opponent guessing.

"How do you like that book?" I said in a friendly tone.

"It's a lot of words," Julio said. He gave me a tight smile. "But I'm tired of staring at my tablet all day."

"That book used to belong to my father," I said. I recalled how I'd settled into Dad's recliner so he could find me immersed in it. "He gave it to me when I declared myself a math major in college."

"Your dad's a math whiz too?"

"He used to teach mathematics to college students." It struck me how little Julio and I knew about each other, even though we'd been living under the same roof for almost a year, and had rehearsed playing fake boyfriends.

"Must be in the genes," Julio said with a bright look.

"I'm adopted," I said, my usual answer for that kind of remark.

"Oh," Julio said, blinking. Then, with a smile, he added, "It was nurture, not nature."

"Something like that," I said with a shrug. "My parents adopted me thinking they couldn't have children. Then my sister Wendy came along. The irony is Wendy hates math."

"I'll take good care of your book," Julio said.

The simple way he'd said it reminded me that Julio was, at heart, a well-meaning guy. Clueless, but well-meaning. What if my hunch was wrong? What if Julio was planning to spend an innocent weekend on the couch, plowing through *Gödel, Escher, Bach*? And if so, how would I manage both Julio and Jonathan in the house tomorrow?

"You're not going too stir-crazy," I said gingerly, "spending all your time at home?"

"Not too much," Julio said with what sounded like forced cheer. But then he sagged his shoulders, smiled, and added, "Maybe a little."

"If you're craving some fresh air," I said in as level a tone I could manage, my face growing warm, "I could take you out for a drive tomorrow. They say it'll be a hot day."

"Oh! Uh, thanks, Frank," Julio said, looking startled at me before switching to a smile. "But I'm going to a friend's house in San Francisco tomorrow morning."

"I see," I said, looking straight at Julio. "Is your friend coming over here to pick you up?"

"No, I'm taking BART," Julio said, letting out a mock sigh. "My friend lives near the BART station."

"I'll drive you to the station," I said, thinking that would help drive home the guilt Julio must be feeling.

"I can take a Lyft or an Uber," Julio said, his smile widening.

"It's no trouble for me to drive you," I said.

Beneath Julio's smile I sensed his mind working, looking for a way to extricate himself. I blinked and gave him a pretend-puzzled look. He'd make a horrible chess player, Julio.

"If you don't mind then," Julio said, conceding. "Thanks, Frank."

"My pleasure." I rose from the chair, walked over to the laundry basket, and picked it up. "And it's no trouble for me to fold these clothes for you. I'll leave them in the massage room."

"Great, thanks." Julio looked up at the ceiling, his hands lying flat on the open pages of the book, his face growing long. "Man, is it even worth it for me to go away this weekend? All the way on BART to San Francisco tomorrow, and all the way home again on Sunday. I don't even know why I said yes. Maybe I should call my friend and bail."

I froze at the doorway with the laundry basket. My fantasy of greeting Jonathan at the door tomorrow morning gave way to the thought of receiving a call from Jonathan and hearing Marcus's "guest" had canceled on him. Maybe that was for the best.

"If you don't feel up to going…" I said, turning to face him, letting my words die on the air.

"But I already said I'd go." Julio winced. "It's too late to back out."

"You're injured," I said in a reasonable tone. "I'm sure your friend would understand if you called and cancelled."

"I said I'd go, so I'm going." Julio looked down at the Hofstadter book, his expression troubled.

Now was my chance to talk Julio out of it. That would be the upstanding thing to do, not only for Julio's sake, but for Jonathan's sake. Maybe even for my own sake. On the other hand, who'd instigated this crisis? Marcus. If Marcus could sleep around on Jonathan, why couldn't Jonathan sleep around on Marcus? With me?

"So then I'll drive you to the BART station?" I said, my voice cool. "Say, about a quarter to nine?"

"Quarter to nine sounds great," Julio said with a half-smile, looking up from the book.

I left the room and hurried upstairs, not wanting to give Julio the chance to change his mind. A quick text to Jonathan to say I'd pick him up at the BART station, any time after nine. Jonathan's reply: *see u then.* A thrill went up and down my body. I was beating Marcus at his own game.

***

The next morning I helped Julio into my car, stowed his bag and crutches in the trunk, and drove him to the Rockridge BART station. I insisted on parking and walking Julio to the station entrance with his bag, my body tense with the thought he'd change his mind. Instead he thanked me, slung his bag over his shoulder, hobbled his way to the escalator, and rode up to the station. A huge feeling of relief flooded through me. I was halfway to checkmate.

About a minute later I heard the roar of not one but two trains, one inbound and one outbound, on the elevated track above my head. My heart rate quickened. If Jonathan happened to be riding the train coming from San Francisco, would he run into Julio on the platform?

In a few moments a tall, gangly figure in an arctic-blue plaid shirt hanging loosely off his shoulders appeared at the top of the escalator. Jonathan. I hesitated before I called out his name, wanting to savor this sublime moment of taking in the sight of him before he noticed me.

"Hey, buddy," I said, breaking the spell.

Jonathan's face lit up as soon as he turned and saw me. But his lips were pale, his eye sockets had bluish rings, and he looked as if he hadn't shaved in a week. It was as if he'd aged ten years in the two short weeks since I'd seen him at the tux shop. I wanted to rush up to him and pull him close. The poor guy deserved to be treated better. I could only hope he'd let me.

***

We said little to each other on the drive to the house. I fought the urge to ask him if he'd seen Julio on the platform. Probably not, or Jonathan would have said something. I kept my eyes on the road, driving more carefully than usual, trying not to glance over at Jonathan in the seat next to me, his shoulders hunched, his bag wedged between his knees. So long as Jonathan was safe this weekend, I'd be happy.

Once in the house I told Jonathan to make himself comfortable in the living room while I finished cleaning the breakfast dishes in the sink. I could've waited until later to clean them, but I needed to settle my nerves. He was here, actually here. Once finished, I drew myself up and walked into the living room, armed with the toothbrush and toothpaste I'd bought on an emergency trip to the supermarket first thing this morning, before Julio was up. The windows and floorboards shone brighter in the glow of Jonathan's presence, the way I'd always imagined it.

"These are for you," I said, holding up the toothbrush and toothpaste. "In case you forgot to pack them."

"I remembered." Jonathan sat slumped in the middle of the couch with his knees wide apart, his arms folded in front of him, his hands buried in his armpits. "But thanks."

"You okay?" I said.

"I'm better now I'm here," Jonathan said. Then he sucked in a breath, unzipped for the log-shaped gym bag next to him, and brought out a stuffed green rabbit, about the size of a newborn kitten. "Remember this?"

The rabbit I'd won for him shooting hoops at the carnival all those years ago. The rabbit's cheap fur, once a bright peppermint green, was matted and faded. One of its felt eyes hung half torn off, and a long ear bent over like a broken reed. The rabbit could've been Jonathan himself, ruined from years of neglect.

"Of course I remember," I said, my voice near breaking.

"I was going through some old boxes a few days ago and found it." Jonathan's innocent tone was enough to break my heart in two. "I couldn't bear to leave it behind."

That did it. I strode over to the French windows and drew the blinds. The room sank into yellow-brown darkness. Then I turned to face Jonathan. I never felt more deeply for him than then. Without taking my eyes off him, I walked up to him and pushed one end of the coffee table away from the couch. Jonathan's watched me, frozen in place. Then I knelt down on the floor between Jonathan's knees, put my arms around him, looked at him, and kissed him with a passion twenty years in the making. Jonathan resisted at first, but only for a moment. The wait was worth it.

I unbuttoned Jonathan's shirt. But by the time I'd made it to his belt buckle, he pushed me away, nearly knocking me to the floor. He leaped up from the couch and paced the room, his hand at his throat.

"Mistake," Jonathan said between gasps. "This. Was. A mistake."

He pivoted and made a step toward his bag on the couch. I scrambled to my feet and blocked his way, my lips warm and swollen. Now was not the time for Jonathan—or me, for that matter—to grow a conscience.

"You can't leave me like this, Jonathan," I said, holding my hands out. "No, you can't. Please."

"But what we're doing is wrong," Jonathan said with a pained look. "I can't take you away from Julio."

"Julio means nothing to me," I said, unsure if I'd break out into a laugh or a sob. "Absolutely nothing."

Jonathan tried to step around me to make a lunge at his bag, but I stepped in his way and put my arms around his waist. Then I brought him close to me, grinding our hips together. We were both hard. I remembered how I'd walked out of the men's room on that distant night, to find Jonathan in more or less the same position with Marcus on the dance floor. How stunned and cheated I'd felt, the searing resentment that had inundated me from the very first moment I'd first laid eyes on Marcus. This was a payback two decades in the making.

"Don't pretend you didn't want this when you came here," I said in almost a whisper, trying to meet his gaze. "Why did you come here if you didn't?"

"I don't know," he said.

"I want you so bad, Jonathan," I said. I pictured my knight leapfrogging to the center of the board, putting the helpless white king in check. "I've wanted you for years. From our first days at the group. Practically from the first moment I laid eyes on you."

"Don't talk like that," Jonathan said, halfheartedly nudging me away.

The room grew brighter and hotter. The sun must've emerged from the tree line across the street. The grandfather clock read almost ten o'clock. Only an hour since I'd driven Julio to the station. I felt myself so close, so tantalizingly close, to checkmate.

"You were different from everyone I'd ever known," I said, cupping Jonathan's soft cheek with my palm. "Me, this nerdy math student living with my boring, repressed mom and dad, and you riding around Santa Cruz taking pictures, not caring about a thing. I always felt like I belonged in the world when I was with you. That's how I want to feel again, Jonathan. All the time."

"I never knew you'd felt that way," Jonathan said.

"Of course you didn't," I said. "I've always been good about not expressing how I feel. My parents had taught me well. Then you started dating Marcus, and I fell in love with Ethan. The months turned into years. I used to think it was supposed to work out that way. But lately I'd begun to think maybe you and I were meant to be together. As if Marcus and Ethan were a couple of starter husbands, preparing us for each other."

Jonathan looked at me as if he didn't know who I was anymore. I wasn't sure I knew either. Shame flooded through me. What a fool I was to bring Jonathan here and lay my soul bare for him, only for him to turn away. Twenty years of friendship, undone in the space of an hour. My gambit had failed. Time to click the resign button on this unwinnable game. I went over and picked up the green stuffed rabbit and put it in Jonathan's gym bag, then zipped the gym bag up tight.

"You were right," I said, too mortified to look at him. "You shouldn't have come here."

"What?" Jonathan said, startled.

"I've lured you into my house, trying to break you and Marcus up," I said. "What kind of lowdown scum does that? I don't deserve to be your friend. I don't even deserve to be in the same room as you. You'd better go now, before we do something we regret."

I held out the bag, still unable to look at him. Maybe I'd tackle a note or two on the piano after he was gone. A peaceful weekend by myself. Then I felt the pressure of his hand on my wrist, forcing me to look him straight in the eye. Oh, God.

"Put the bag down," Jonathan said, in a low but assured tone that made me hard again.

The bag slipped from my numb fingers and thudded to the floor. Jonathan was looking at me with a desire I'd never seen on him before. I watched him, feeling stunned, knowing that whatever happened next, it would be out of my control.

"You're not a lowdown scum," Jonathan said, his voice soft and breathy. "You're kind, you're decent, you're loyal. You're the most terrific person I've ever known."

His foot nudged away the bag between us. Then he kissed me. For a man who seemed so mellow, Jonathan's kiss was like that of twenty men. So incredibly different from the kiss I'd given him a few minutes ago. His nervousness, his resistance felt like things of the distant past. My body went slack and leaned in toward him, my body against his wiry frame. No more struggle, no more words.

I had nowhere else to make love to Jonathan, except on the bed in my bedroom, under the brand-new, never-used sheets I'd bought to replace the ones Ethan had long ago defiled. I couldn't believe it. The bed Ethan had used to cheat on me would now be the bed I'd use to steal Jonathan away from Marcus. No—"steal" was the wrong word.

I was merely taking what should've been mine in the first place. The time had come to set things right. The smooth white comforter beckoned me. I took Jonathan by the hand and led him upstairs to the dream-ocean.

10

SPIDERWEB

I leaned on my crutches on the platform. My skin itched under my cast. A minute went by. Two minutes. Five. It was like the universe had held up the train on purpose. I pictured Josie's smiling freckled face, encouraging me to turn around. But before I could fish out my phone to text Marcus I was bailing, the train screeched into the station. The train doors opened like welcoming arms. I hesitated. No one was making me board the train. Deep in my heart, I knew what I was doing was wrong. Turn around, turn around.

Then the past five days in Frank's house crashed down on me. The sagging couch. The stifling heat. The tick-tick-tick of the grandfather clock. Worst of all, Frank's caretaking. Bringing me meals, buying me groceries, changing my sheets, towels, pillowcases. All the while he barely spoke to me, barely even looked at me. It was like he'd meant to put me in his debt. As if he knew about me and Marcus. That banging noise I'd heard while I was upstairs with Marcus two weeks ago went off in my head again, making the skin under my cast crawl. I couldn't take it anymore. I couldn't face another day of torturing myself—does Frank know, does Frank not know—with Frank inside the house, quietly doing chores for me. Not on a hot weekend like this.

I stuffed the phone into my pocket, boarded the train, and plopped into a seat by the door. The eastbound train whooshed in on the opposite side of the platform. The doors opened and let a few people out. My eye landed on a lanky guy in a blue plaid shirt walking toward the escalators. A log-shaped gym bag hung over his shoulder. From behind he sort of looked like Jonathan. He had the same funny duck-walk too. But that couldn't be Jonathan, could it? I mean, Marcus had told me Jonathan was seeing his Mami in Santa Cruz for the weekend. What would Jonathan be doing in Oakland?

But I knew the answer to that question right off. Frank. Frank, of course. I'd thought he'd acted weird last night, asking me about my plans for the weekend. He'd all but stuffed me into the car to drive me to the BART station this morning. He was probably waiting at the curb for Jonathan right now, with the car still running. Holy Mother, what a douchebag. I never would've thought Frank could be such a sneaky little bitch.

Wait. No. What if the man in the blue plaid shirt wasn't Jonathan? I'd only seen the guy from behind. Only one way to know for sure. I struggled to hoist myself off the seat, grab my crutches, reach down for my bag. The train doors closed before I could rise to my feet. I was trapped. Then a sigh of brakes, a grinding of wheels, and off the train went. I sank back in my seat and let the train pull me away from Frank's house, away from my troubles there, and toward my own uncertain adventure.

***

"Any trouble making your way here?" Marcus said. He turned the key in the ignition of his Beemer.

"No, no trouble. The train was a couple minutes late."

"And Frank?" Marcus glanced into his side-view mirror.

"I told him I was meeting a friend in the city." I hoped my tone made clear I didn't want to talk about Frank.

"You don't like lying to Frank, do you?" Marcus said, more as a statement than as a question.

"I don't like lying to anybody." My jaw tightened.

"Hey, forget I said anything about Frank," Marcus said, caving for a change. "I want you to have a good weekend."

He pulled the car onto 16th Street, then took a sharp left onto Mission, cutting in front of an oncoming car. Thank the Holy Mother I was only spending the weekend with him. What must it be like to live with him all the time?

"So Jonathan's in Santa Cruz," I said.

"That's what he told me," Marcus said, a slight edge to his voice.

"And Jonathan'll be coming home tomorrow?"

"Probably." Marcus looked out the windshield, one hand on the steering wheel, the other grabbing the stick shift as if he meant to snap it in two. "He didn't say."

"Early or late?"

"I said I don't know, Julio," Marcus said sharply, his look hardening into a glare. "We haven't spoken to each other in two days."

"Sorry," I mumbled, thinking I'd leave the house tomorrow at the crack of dawn. But what if I went home to find Jonathan and Frank holding hands at the kitchen table? Or worse?

"Let's enjoy today," Marcus said a moment later, in a nicer tone of voice. "I want to stay present."

"Fine," I said. My insides squirmed at the way he'd turned my own teaching against me. "But we're only friends this weekend. Friends and nothing more."

"Yes, you've established that," Marcus said. He let out a sigh.

At the house Marcus helped me out of the car with my bag and crutches. Climbing the stairs to the front door on crutches was a total bitch. But the house was cool inside. I'd also be sleeping in the guest bedroom, thank the Holy Virgin, right inside the front door. A vase of red tulips sat on the sleek white dresser. A plush white bathrobe hung on a hook on the bathroom door. I wondered how many other guys had worn that robe.

"You've eaten breakfast?" Marcus said.

"Yep, before I left," I said, glad I'd scarfed down a bowl of oatmeal first thing this morning. The less Marcus did for me this weekend, the less obligation I'd feel for him.

"And you've been sleeping okay in that cast?" Marcus said.

"Okay enough," I said, using two hands to heave my leg onto the bed. "My knee isn't giving me any problem. It's my lower back that's sore. I've been sleeping on the living room couch all week."

As soon as those words tumbled out of my mouth, I knew I'd blown it. The surprise on Marcus's face said it all. *Guess that means you and Frank aren't sleeping together.*

"I see," Marcus said, blinking slowly. "Why don't you rest up. I thought we could drive to Marin. Should be a hot one today."

His eyes flickered in the cool green light, then he left the room and pulled the door shut. Thank the Holy Virgin, Marcus had thought of something for us to do that didn't involve us spending the day indoors. He was right about the weather too. Barely ten o'clock and already the air promised to be scorching. A day like today on Frank's couch would've been murder.

***

At Tomales Bay, way north of the Golden Gate Bridge, we stopped along the road for oysters in a small, wood-framed restaurant. I still felt guilty about spending this time with Marcus. But in the middle of sunshine and fresh air, I was glad I'd come.

Later on we drove to Muir Woods. My heart swelled at the prehistoric redwoods, roots dripping with yellow-green moss. The high branches blotted out the sun and tore the sky into rags. My ears pricked to a fly's buzz, a babbling creek, the *whit-whit-whit* of some bird high above us. Then my eye caught a humongous silver spiderweb gleaming in a tree hollow, the spider glinting in the web's center like a gold nugget. Alluring but dangerous, like the man hiking the trail next to me. I mustn't forget who'd brought me here.

Two thin redwoods stood across one of the trail paths. One tree leaned against the other, half its roots sticking out of the ground. The second tree had stopped the first one's fall. Looking at the two trees, the one supporting the other, made me think of me and Marcus. He was my redwood today. But maybe I was the stronger tree, not him. After all, I wasn't the one whose fiancé might be cheating on him.

Maybe I should tell Marcus what I'd seen on the BART platform this morning. Now was probably my best chance to say something. But what good would telling him do? I wasn't even sure the guy on the platform had been Jonathan. Besides, I was mixed up enough in Marcus's business—and had a cast on my leg to show for it. I turned up my face to the sky-rags, letting my lungs fill with cool, calming air.

***

We made it home to his place at around six thirty. He suggested we order a pizza. I was glad he didn't want to walk down to the Castro for dinner. Someone might see us there.

So we camped out in his living room, me on the couch and him in the easy chair, eating pizza and watching a slasher movie on the flat screen. Hiking, pizza, movie. How first-datey. I couldn't remember the last time I'd spent a whole day with a guy like this and not ended up having sex with him.

It seemed a lot later when the movie finished, but the wall clock said only a couple minutes before ten. A silence settled over us. All of a sudden, the place seemed too big. I hauled myself up from the couch, yawned, and told him I was turning in.

Once downstairs I brushed my teeth, stripped down to my smiley-face boxers, and slipped into bed. After a week camped out on that pancake griddle of a couch, I felt like I was resting on a cloud. The only thing that nagged me was the thought of Marcus rolling around with other guys here. He must've, the dog.

In a few minutes Marcus's footsteps came down the stairs on sly wolf's feet. I had barely time to switch on the bedside lamp when the door creaked open. Marcus stood in the doorway like a football player ready to tackle, a wild, red-eyed look on his face. Holy Mother. I should've barricaded the door.

"We have to talk," Marcus said, shutting the door behind him.

My travel pajamas lay in a heap at the foot of the bed. For the first time in my life, I wished I looked less hot in my boxers. I sat up, reached down, and untangled the pajama top from the pile, making sure the bedsheet covered my lap.

"I can't sleep," Marcus said with a desperate look.

"Marcus, please," I said. I fumbled to slip first one arm, then another arm into the pajama top.

"I can never sleep in my bed alone," Marcus said, his voice full of anguish. "I'm not used to it. Can I please sleep down here? I won't touch you, I promise."

"Dude," I said, and yanked the sheet up more. "Do you honestly expect me to believe you?"

"You have my word of honor," Marcus said, slapping a hand on his chest. "And I'll be out of here first thing in the morning. I swear.

Please, Julio. I've been sleeping by myself in this huge house for three nights running. I've had barely three hours of sleep each night. There's nothing worse than sleeping alone."

"Mother of God," I said with a groan, putting a hand to my aching eyes. "Fine. Have it your way. You want to sleep down here, go ahead and sleep down here. Because I'm going home now."

I made to hop around the bed to collect my crutches and the rest of my things by the dresser. Who cared if he saw me in my boxers? And who cared what was waiting for me when I reached home tonight? But Marcus walked up and grabbed my arm to stop me. I let out a cry and wrenched my arm free. Marcus stood by the corner of the bed, blocking my path to the dresser. His boozy breath stung my nostrils. My stomach turned. I don't think I ever saw him as clearly as I did right then.

"Move out of the way." I was trembling.

"Not until you hear me out," he said, folding his arms.

"You're wasted," I said in my angriest voice. "You're nothing but trouble, and drunk besides. I wish you'd never come to my yoga class. I wish I'd never laid eyes on you."

On the other side of the bed, my bag and my crutches called out to me. Marcus stared at me with a smirk and glimmering eyes. I knew he'd tackle me if I made the slightest move toward them. My foot in the cast sank into the carpet and took root there.

"I called Jonathan's mother this morning," Marcus said in a fake conversational voice. "Right before I came to pick you up. I asked her to tell Jonathan to call me when he showed up at her house. She said he'd called her to say he'd changed his mind. He wouldn't be seeing her this weekend."

"So?" I said with attitude, but I had to glancing away.

"If he didn't go to Santa Cruz," Marcus said, leaning forward with his upper lip curled, "where do you think he went?"

"Like I'm supposed to know?" I said.

"What, didn't your dear Frank tell you?" Marcus said, his tone half honey, half poison.

"What does Frank have to do with this?" I shook with anger.

"If Jonathan didn't take refuge at his mother's today"—the threat in Marcus's voice came through loud and clear—"then who else could he have turned to in his hour of need? Who was there to rescue him?"

The blue sky, the oysters, the redwoods—all of it was sucked into the fire pit of Marcus's raging jealousy. He was too ugly to look at. My eyes darted toward the drooping red tulips on the dresser. So beautiful, so innocent, so out of place in this dungeon of a room.

"Go upstairs," I said, sputtering. "Go upstairs and sober up. You're scaring me."

"Frank's been lusting after Jonathan for years." Marcus forced a little smile, but his face was deathly white. "He doesn't think I know, but I see it on his face. Every time he looks at Jonathan. That's why I didn't want him to be Jonathan's best man. I knew he'd work his way between us."

"And that's why you flirted with me on your roof that night," I said, the truth sinking into my bones. "Why you signed on for those massages. You didn't care about me. You only wanted to stick it to Frank."

"I cared for you more than Frank ever did." Marcus straightened up and gave me a grim look, his mouth set and his eyes blood-red. "Or ever will. Sorry to break this to you, sweetheart. Frank doesn't love you. It's Jonathan he loves. So if you think I used you, Frank's been using you worse. The man's a chess pro. He knows a good pawn when he sees one."

"You monster." I turned my head to keep him from seeing my burning face. "I'm ashamed to say I know you."

Forget about my brothers or that ratfucker who tried to slice me up in high school—Marcus was worse, far worse than that sorry crew put together. How could I ever have talked to Genevieve about this guy like he was some kind of god? Or thought that he was the best San Francisco had to offer? I turned and lunged for the door, not caring about my bag or my crutches. Then I lost my balance, and Marcus moved in front of me and put his arms around me to steady me. Holy Mother, even now I needed Marcus.

"I do care about you," he said in a severe tone. His burning gaze bore into me. "Don't you ever say I didn't."

"You're hurting me," I said, using what was left of my strength in a pointless effort to push him away. "Let me go."

"Look me in the eye, and tell me I don't care about you," Marcus said, grabbing me by both shoulders and pulling me in.

"Okay, okay, you care about me," I cried near panic. "Now let go of me. Let go of me right now!"

Which he did, lovingly. He looked spent. Maybe even sorry. I grasped the edge of the nightstand to keep from toppling over, then hopped my way to the bed and sat down, breathing hard. Marcus came over and settled onto the edge of the bed next to me, letting out a long, deflating breath. The path around the bed to my stuff was clear now. But I was too dead tired, too depressed to move.

"Jonathan and I should never have gotten engaged," Marcus said. His voice was tinged with sadness. "We were doing fine as boyfriends."

"Then whose idea was it to have a wedding?" I made sure to put scorn in my voice.

"Mine." Marcus let out half a sigh. "All the ideas in my relationship are mine."

"But Jonathan went along with it," I said, annoyed. "You didn't put a gun to his head, did you?"

"I didn't have to." Marcus let out another sigh. "Jonathan always goes along with everything I say. He'd said yes to the wedding as if I'd suggested we go away for the weekend. Same thing when I said we should move to New York. And when I said I wanted to open up the relationship, five years ago now. 'Sure, fine, whatever you want.' I didn't even want to have an open relationship. But Jonathan didn't even blink. If anything, he seemed relieved."

"Relieved?" I said. "What do you mean, relieved?"

"Relieved he didn't have to have sex with me so much." Marcus rose and paced the carpet in front of me. "He never seemed to want it. I always felt like he was going along with it, you know? Like sex was distracting him from taking photographs or writing code for one of his app games. If he didn't let me fool around with other guys, then we definitely would've broken up. I'm living with the one gay guy in San Francisco who doesn't seem to enjoy having sex."

The walls of the room seemed to be closing in on me. The tulips seemed to droop even more. I turned my gaze on a framed photograph of the Eiffel Tower next to the door, wishing myself in Paris or any other place than here. Maybe even Sicily with Dean. Right now it felt like I'd be stuck in this room forever.

"But now I'm beginning to wonder," Marcus said, jutting out his jaw and massaging his chin beard. "Maybe Jonathan had never wanted to have sex not because he didn't want to have sex, but because he didn't want to have sex with me. Maybe he's finally sleeping with the guy he's been wanting to sleep with all these years."

"You don't know where Jonathan is right now." My thoughts returned to the guy on the BART platform this morning. "He could be anywhere."

"Maybe." Marcus sat down next to me again, hunched over, and leaned his forearms on his thighs, looking at his spread-out palms. "You think you'll ever settle down, Julio?"

"I don't know," I said, wondering where that question came from. "Maybe. I'm only thirty-three."

"I was twenty-seven when I met Jonathan," Marcus said in a faraway tone. "Until then I'd always thought I'd be single my whole life. I never thought we'd last longer than a year, let alone eighteen years. But here we are."

A vision flickered in my mind of a young Marcus and a young Jonathan on the dance floor. Their eyes bright and full of promise. I glanced away from Marcus, my heart in my throat. If I ever needed proof of why I'd never settle down with anybody, he was sitting next to me right now. Not that I'd mind settling down with some halfway decent guy, if such a guy existed. The problem was, he didn't.

"I've been thinking about us a lot lately," Marcus said in a thick voice. "You're easy to talk to, fun to be with, great in bed. I wouldn't need to have an open relationship with you. Do you think, maybe, I could be the right person for you?"

"Not when you're drunk," I said. The blood rushed to my face.

"I'm scared," Marcus said in a simple, boyish tone. "I'm scared of what the future holds for me. But when I think of you, I can't help wondering if—maybe—we'd all be better off if Jonathan really did leave me for Frank."

He leaned over and laid his hand on my bare thigh. The booze on his breath made me want to puke. I pushed his arm off my thigh and forced my way to stand, leaning hard against the nightstand. This had gone on long enough.

"Marcus, you don't even know what you're saying," I said in a disgusted tone. "It's time you went to bed."

"Julio, please," Marcus said, looking up at me with a wide-eyed anxious look.

"I mean it," I said. "Please. It's late. You've had too much to drink. You shouldn't be saying things you might regret tomorrow morning."

He gave me a look of sorrow, as if I'd maimed him. Then he lifted himself off the bed. First I thought he was going to pass out on the carpet. Then I thought he was going to say something, find some other excuse to stay. Instead he gave me a sad nod, went to the door, threw one last look at me, and left.

What if Marcus hadn't been such a lush right now? Would I have pushed him away so easily? What he'd said made sense, sort of. After all, if Jonathan left Marcus to shack up with Frank, then what was to stop me from shacking up with Marcus? Josie's studio was a twenty-minute walk from here. I could give private yoga lessons on the roof. This very bedroom could become my massage room. I pictured my prana flowing into every corner of the house. Clubs, shows, friends—all of it would be nearby. San Francisco seemed to call to me like a display of Genevieve's ice cream, an endless row of flavors and colors.

I knew I couldn't say yes. Not until I knew what was going on between Jonathan and Frank. And not until Marcus lost the stink of hooch on his breath. Marcus could offer me the city on a platter, and still I wouldn't take it. No way was I living with a drunk.

***

I opened my eyes in the morning to the sound of the front door opening and slamming shut. The room blazed with morning sun. Right then I realized—way too late—I'd forgotten to set the alarm on my cell phone. Most shocking of all, Marcus was asleep in bed with me, turned on his side to face me. He must've snuck into the bed in the middle of the night. Mother of God. I should've known better than to think he'd honor my wish to sleep alone.

Marcus opened his eyes the same time I did. His wide-eyed look proved I hadn't imagined the sound of the front door. The footsteps went up the stairs. Marcus swore under his breath, slipped naked out of bed, and pulled on his silver basketball shorts lying on the floor. He grabbed the white robe on the bathroom door hook and shrugged it on. The footsteps clomped above our heads now. Marcus turned to me at the bedroom door and put a finger to his lips. This wasn't the confident Marcus giving orders and whisking me off to the emergency room. His white face told me we were in real, honest-to-God trouble. He opened the door a crack, listened, and slipped out of the room.

I dashed out of bed, struggled into my clothes, crammed my stuff into my bag. O most holy Virgin in heaven, please let me leave this house unseen. I hobbled to the door and opened it a crack. No sound but my heart pounding in my ears. The bolted front door was barely five feet away from where I stood. Did I dare make a dash for it?

Two raised voices sounded above my head. No trouble making out Jonathan and Marcus. Their voices grew closer, booming down to me from the top of the stairs. My heart was beating so fast that I thought it would stop. Their footsteps clomped straight toward me. I shut the door and leaned my whole body against it, squinching my eyes shut and clenching my teeth. Then I slid to the carpet. I was trapped.

"So he's here?" Jonathan's voice was high and furious.

"No—don't!" Marcus said in a half-command, half-plea.

The doorknob above my head turned and jiggled. Then pounding and kicking against the door. The kicks sent shock waves through me. Mother of God. I couldn't believe that this was me, that I was huddled on the floor like this.

"Open up, you son of a bitch!" Jonathan shouted. "Open up where I can see you!"

My muscles locked in place. I glimpsed the tulips in the vase across the room, their heads bowed low. Inhale five seconds, exhale five seconds. Focus on the tulips instead of Jonathan on the other side of the door. Such a gorgeous shade of red, those petals. I imagined the petals multiplying all over the carpet and myself falling into them, the red swallowing me up in a whirlpool and sucking me through a portal to my old bedroom in Hayward. *You're checking out* is what Josie would tell me now. She'd be right. Except this was no yoga pose. No breathing my way out of this one.

Jonathan kept pounding against the door, the doorknob jiggling frantically above my head. I curled up into a ball, leaned against the door, and prayed. My scar burned as if it had split open again. If the Holy Virgin helped me escape this torture cell without Jonathan seeing me, I promised Her I'd never, ever do a bad thing again. A scuffle against the door. The pounding stopped. Marcus must've come between Jonathan and the door. A promising sign. I knew from experience how well Marcus could stand in someone's way.

"Please, Jonathan, you don't need to go in there," Marcus said in a clear voice from outside the door. "You'll only make things worse."

"Why do you have to bring them here?" Jonathan said, half-shouting, half-begging. "Why do you have to bring the trash into the house?"

"Please, you have to listen to me," Marcus said in a shushing voice. "Nothing happened."

"Then why couldn't I stay here this weekend?" Jonathan shouted, sounding like he was unleashing all the anger he'd pent up over God knew how many years. "What kind of idiot do you take me for? You were down there with him when I came in! I'm so sick of you. You and your lies. I can't take it anymore. I'm leaving."

I heard the *thunk* of the bolt turning in the front door. Another scuffle. Oh Holy Mother, Marcus must be trying to stop Jonathan from leaving. Which meant Marcus wasn't guarding the bedroom door. I lay down on my side and stretched out on the carpet along the door. Mother of God, look at the level I'd sunk to. If Mami and Josie could see me, they'd turn their heads in shame. And Frank? What would he say? Would he be happy to watch me brought low like this? To hear Jonathan let rip at Marcus? He probably would. After all, Frank was half the reason why I'd agreed to spend the weekend here.

"Let me go, you bastard," Jonathan said in a strangled sob. "I've had enough of you, you liar, you fake, I hate you, I hate you, I hate you—"

"Now you listen to me here." Marcus put sternness in each of his words. "I know I've been a lot of things to you, but I've never lied to you. I never have and I never will."

Dead silence. It was probably dawning on Jonathan that Marcus had maybe told the truth. Which didn't make Marcus honest, in my opinion. I closed my eyes, thinking I'd be lying on this carpet, blocking this door, until the time came for me to meet my maker.

"And what about you, Jonathan?" Marcus said, his voice accusing. "Where'd you spend last night?"

"None of your damned business," Jonathan said.

"Did you go see Frank?" The threat in Marcus's tone made my blood freeze. "If you tell me you slept with Frank last night, I swear to God I'll kill him. I'll drive over there and rip his heart out."

"You have some nerve," Jonathan said. His voice seethed with contempt. "Asking me where I went last night. I wouldn't have had to go anywhere if you hadn't kicked me out for that slut behind the door."

More pushing and shoving, this time closer to the bedroom door. A fist pounding above my head. I pictured tears streaming out of Jonathan's red eyes. Marcus restraining him. My heart thumped through the back of my ribcage against the door. My eyes focused on the tulips. Holy Mother. An awful truth dawned on me. I deserved to be curled up on the carpet like this. If I hadn't had the affair with Marcus, none of this would be happening. I'd never been so terrified—or ashamed—in my life. I now understood what it meant to stay present, to notice the bad as well as the good.

"Fine then," Marcus said. "You want to leave me, then there's the door. But if you go, you'll be throwing away everything we've built together. What'll come and take its place? Do you even know?"

I pictured Jonathan at the front door, his hand on the doorknob. Then I pictured myself standing in Jonathan's shoes. Come on, Jonathan—walk out the door. I wanted him to show me it was possible for someone to walk away from Marcus. Plus Jonathan had Frank to go to. Frank would never jerk Jonathan around the way Marcus was jerking him around now.

But even from behind this door, I could tell Jonathan was staying put. Marcus had broken Jonathan's spirit a long time ago, the same way he'd caused me to break my knee in class. Now Jonathan needed Marcus the same way I'd needed Marcus this weekend. No untangling from his spiderweb.

"I love you, Jonathan," Marcus went on, his tone softening. "And I swear to you, on my life and soul, I didn't do anything with anybody this weekend. If anything, having you away this weekend made me realize—you're the one I want."

My mouth fell open.

"But you were in that room," Jonathan said in a halting voice, "when I came home."

"To sleep," Marcus said, sounding as sincere as I'd ever heard him. "I'd thought you'd left me. You know how I don't like sleeping in the big bed upstairs without you. Come on, babe, you have to believe me. You know I'm not lying to you."

"Why do you do this to me?" Jonathan sounded exhausted.

"I know," Marcus said, his voice close to breaking. "I'm so sorry, babe."

Their voices went muffled. Marcus must've put his arms around Jonathan and was now crying on Jonathan's shoulder. A lump of disgust settled in my stomach. Less than twelve hours ago Marcus was talking about wanting a fresh start with me. Now he was recommitting himself to Jonathan? So it really was the booze talking last night.

Their murmuring voices faded upstairs. In a few moments, no doubt, they'd be having the makeup sex session of their lives. I hoped Jonathan had taken a shower before he left Frank's house. And I sure as fuck hoped Marcus had forgotten his threat to rip out Frank's heart.

I grabbed my stuff and made my escape. Limped and stumbled down the hill as fast as I could without sticking my crutches into some crack in the pavement. My lungs were burning by the time I reached the bottom of the hill. What a purgatory this weekend was. But a necessary one. I remembered the pounds I'd shed as a teenager, how my new, strong body had emerged from those layers of flab. This was the same thing. I'd shed a part of myself in Marcus's house—a part I didn't need—and now I felt lighter for it. My worst mistake was now behind me. A mistake I vowed on Papi's soul never to repeat.

About an hour later, on the BART ride home to Oakland, my cell phone pinged. A one-word text from Marcus. *Sorry.*

Leave me alone, I texted him. *You creep.*

11

CAT AND MOUSE

I dreamed about the black train again last night, the night I slept with Jonathan. This time the train didn't steam along a cliff overlooking the ocean. Instead, it roared full-speed along the white, frozen surface of the ocean itself. The wheels shot sparks in grooves carved into the ice. We rushed headlong with purpose, as if the train consciously knew its destination. What the destination was, I had no idea. I didn't care. To know I was headed toward somewhere definite—with Jonathan—was enough to satisfy me.

Jonathan sat beside me, as he had in the last dream. I sensed his body next to mine even though I was looking out the window at the ice. A funny notion crept over me. So long as I kept my head turned away from Jonathan, he'd remain sitting there. But if I turned to look at him, he'd vanish. Eerie. My first sense this dream was taking me somewhere I didn't want to go.

I kept my gaze out the window on the blinding ice. Nothing out there but a perpetual field of white. My eyes hurt. But what was that warm feeling on my face and arms? The sun? It couldn't be. Sunlight would melt the ice. Any moment now, the ice would crumble. And everything—the train, me, Jonathan—would plunge into the frigid depths.

The train rumbled and shook. Cracks in the ice zigzagged outside the window. The front of the train pitched forward in slow motion. My stomach pitched forward with it. If I didn't do something now to save me and Jonathan, we'd drown. I threw my arm across the seat to grab his arm—and grabbed only air.

My eyes snapped open. The shattered ice had become the rumpled bedspread and my newly christened sheets. The warmth on my face and arms was the sunlight seeping into my bedroom through the drawn shade. And the hand I'd flung out clutched the abandoned space where Jonathan had lain. Jonathan was gone? Why hadn't he woken me up? How could I not have noticed?

The sheets on Jonathan's side of the bed were as cold as my skin. He must've left at least an hour ago, maybe even longer. The nightstand clock read 8:41. The last time I'd slept this late was, was… God, I couldn't remember. My arms and legs felt heavy. My eyelids too. Such a long time since I'd slept in an actual bed, a warm body next to mine. Jonathan's warm body. I hadn't dreamed that part. I'd accomplished what I'd set out to do.

***

I scrambled out of bed and into some clothes, then drove downtown and lingered over breakfast until eleven. Still too early to go home and face Julio. Plus Jonathan should be calling me on my cell at any minute. I didn't want to take the call where Julio might hear us. I drove over to Lake Merritt and hiked the three-and-a-half-mile paved path around the sprawling lake.

Gulls circled overhead, ducks and geese waddled along the grass, cormorants and even a pelican or two sunned themselves on the docks. Watching the birds helped my nerves. Couples in kayaks and paddleboats glided past along the silvery-blue water. What a difference between this placid urban lake, surrounded by buildings on all sides, and the frozen dream-ocean from last night. I imagined myself sharing a kayak with Jonathan, basking in the sun. We'd be safe here.

By two o'clock, my cell phone still hadn't rung. My legs and back had grown sore and stiff from walking. I couldn't wander around the lake forever. Julio must be home by now. Time to go and deal with him.

I entered the house to the faint sound of remixed tango music wafting down from his bedroom. He'd managed to climb those stairs for the first time since his accident, no doubt at some risk. Julio probably hadn't wanted to see me any more than I'd wanted to see him. God, this was Ethan all over again, this feeling of foreboding in my own house. And if my current situation with Julio was anything like my former situation with Ethan, then I could be certain this runaway train was headed toward disaster.

***

I spent the rest of the afternoon weeding the garden. Still no call or text from Jonathan. Then I went inside through the kitchen door and stopped short at the sight of Julio leaning on a single crutch by the stove, stirring a pot of something with his free hand. His face was drawn, his eyes dull. He didn't look up when I came in. He must've had a tough weekend with Marcus. I took some satisfaction in that.

"Hey," I said, glancing at the pot. "You must be feeling better if you're cooking for yourself."

"Yes." Julio looked up and smiled. "Much better."

"And I see you made it up the stairs," I said, keeping my tone as cool as possible.

"They weren't as tricky as I thought." Julio voice had a touch of false bravery.

"So then you'll be sleeping in your own bed tonight?" I said, imagining sleeping in the living room again. Could I stand another night on the couch? Or could I manage another night in my own bed, now that I'd shared it with Jonathan?

"If I don't," Julio said, throwing me a quick smile, "I can still manage to make the bed down here."

He half-turned from me, pivoting on his crutch. I walked past him to the hall doorway and glanced at him over my shoulder. The corners of Julio's mouth were drawn slightly downward. For the first time, he looked like a man closer to thirty-five than to thirty. Marcus must've drained him dry over the past day and a half. I burned to know what had happened between them.

***

From that day onward, I took my phone everywhere I went. The phone stayed within easy reach on my desk, on my nightstand, on the bathroom sink while I showered and shaved. Night after night I lay in my huge bed imagining Jonathan lying next to me, thinking about our Saturday together, wondering what he was doing, what he was thinking. But he neither called nor texted. The knot in my chest tightened with each passing day.

Meanwhile, Julio moved around the house with more and more dexterity. Most afternoons I came home from teaching summer classes to find him giving some client a massage. He still needed my help bringing his laundry up and down the basement stairs, but otherwise he could maneuver around the kitchen—and apparently his massage table—on one crutch. His mood seemed altogether lighter, as if he'd unburdened himself of a crushing weight. Was Marcus the crushing weight? And if so, did that mean Marcus and Jonathan had reconciled?

My answer came on a sunny Friday afternoon in mid-August, three weeks and six days since my night of passion with Jonathan. I walked in the door after teaching summer school to find the mail in a neat pile at the edge of the table. Concealed at the bottom of the pile was a heavy, cream-colored envelope addressed to me "and guest" from Jonathan and Marcus. My breath deserted me. The knotted ball of anger and sorrow, lodged in my chest for weeks now, shifted and rumbled. Jonathan had finally delivered his answer, as clearly as if he'd called me.

My fingers ripped open the envelope with a tearing sound that seemed to rip into my chest. I didn't have time to hope I was mistaken. There it was in gleaming silver script, my very own invitation to witness "the marriage of Jonathan Butler and Marcus Pierce at San Francisco City Hall." The linoleum seemed to crack under me like the ice in the dream-ocean. I sank trembling into a chair.

Voices drifted toward me from the massage room. The kitchen clock read a few minutes past four. Julio must be finishing up with a client, probably his last of the day. How did Julio react when he saw this invitation? With anger? With shock? With relief? Or perhaps he hadn't reacted. Perhaps he'd known the invitation was on its way. One thing was certain: I wasn't about to let him pretend the invitation had never arrived.

"Same time next week, Genevieve?" Julio's cheerful voice rang out from the front hall. A woman's husky voice assured him she'd be here. Another successful Friday for Julio.

The front door opened, the front door closed, and then the house fell silent. I rose from the chair, my messenger bag still slung over my shoulder. It probably wasn't a good idea, confronting Julio while the knot of anger squeezed in my chest. But I wanted answers. I wanted them now.

"Hey, Julio," I called out, my voice echoing through the house.

Julio appeared at the doorway to the dining room, leaning on one crutch, giving me a half-smile as if he knew why I'd summoned him but was pretending to be clueless. I couldn't wait to wipe the smile off his face.

"Oh—hi!" Julio said with forced cheerfulness. "What up?"

"It's official," I said, holding out the invitation, my eyes locked on his.

"What's official?" Julio's eyes darted to the envelope.

"The wedding." I swallowed the anger rising up to my throat. "Jonathan and Marcus."

"Oh," Julio said, perking up. "Cool!"

Julio seemed to want to pivot on his crutch and flee, but then he hobbled over to the counter by the fridge and pulled out a drawer where I kept tea towels and pads of paper. He brought out a pad of paper and a pen. I unslung my messenger bag and watched him. The knot in my chest grew tighter and tighter.

"So have they told you when you'll be out of that cast?" I said, going for politeness to calm my buzzing nerves.

"Two weeks from Monday." Julio put down the pen and paper and gave me a satisfied look. "My doctor said she never saw anyone heal so quickly."

"Oh good." I made no effort at sincerity. "So then you'll be teaching yoga again soon."

"First Saturday in September," Julio said, his eyes and voice bright. "If everything goes well. It should."

He threw a look at his cast, flashed another smile at me, and turned to work on his list. Julio and his lists. Always making plans.

"I wonder how the house in New York is coming along," I said, more to myself than to Julio. "I wonder if it's not ready in time."

"They'll make it there sooner or later," Julio said, and he let out a forced sigh as if he'd be sorry to see them go.

"Has Marcus told you anything about it?" I tossed the invitation onto the table. It landed with a thud.

"No." Julio looked up. "Why would he?"

"Because," I said, my pounding heart pressing against the constricting knot of anger in my chest, "he's your student in yoga class."

"Marcus doesn't come to my class anymore," Julio said in an airy but not altogether pleasant tone. "I haven't seen him since before I hurt my knee."

"Oh." My mind seized on this as proof that Marcus and Julio had broken things off.

"What about Jonathan?" Julio said. "Has Jonathan said anything to you?"

"I haven't heard from Jonathan in over a month," I said.

The kitchen felt unbearably hot. The sun sliced through the drawn blinds over the sink, lighting the white enamel tiles into a glaring orange. Julio pivoted on his crutch to open the refrigerator, a set, stubborn look on his face. The little bastard—he'd made that crack about Jonathan on purpose. But I wasn't through with him yet. I went over to the wildlife wall calendar next to the kitchen door.

"The wedding is the second Friday in October." I held up the calendar page. "It's at three in the afternoon. You don't teach classes on Friday afternoons, right? If you do, then you'll have to cancel them."

"Um, you're right, I don't teach Friday classes," Julio said, drawing his words out. He closed the refrigerator door. "About that, Frank."

"About what?" I said, letting go of the calendar page. I made sure the coldness in my tone came across clearly.

"I was thinking," Julio said, "do you need me to go to the wedding with you? With my injury and Marcus not coming to my class anymore, um, like, I'm sure they've forgotten me by now. I'm sure you could totally tell them we've broken up, and they won't think anything of it."

Julio gave me a guilty half-smile. My body went rigid. Of course Julio wouldn't want to go the wedding. But if I had to stand by and watch Jonathan marry Marcus, why shouldn't Julio have to stand by and watch Marcus marry Jonathan?

"It's a wedding," I said testily. "A big one. All you'd have to do is show up."

"But I have nothing to wear," Julio said in almost a whine. "I only have my tux from my senior prom. It has to be four sizes too big for me. It's pink besides. Hot pink. How would you like that? Me showing up at Marcus and Jonathan's wedding in a hot pink suit?"

"You and Marcus are friends." I put a special emphasis—but not the slightest amount of authenticity—in the word *friends*. "I'm sure he'll be disappointed if you don't go to his wedding. It's no accident there's an 'and guest' on the invitation."

"We're not close friends," Julio said snippily. "He'll barely notice I'm missing."

He ripped off the sheet of paper from the pad, dropped the pad into the drawer, and banged the drawer shut as if to end the subject. I picked up my bag, slung it over my shoulder, and walked past him to the hallway door. What a craven liar Julio was. Here he was, daring me to accept his lie. And here I was, walking away from him in my own kitchen, forcing myself to swallow the lie whole. Was I going to let him get away with this? Was I?

"I don't know if what you're saying sits well with me," I said, turning to look at him, my hands clasped behind my back. "You promised you'd go to that wedding with me."

"Holy Mother," Julio said. "You're beginning to sound like a real boyfriend."

"You promised you'd go," I said in an chiding voice. "We had a deal."

"The deal," Julio said, leaning forward on his crutch, "was I could have the third room if I went to that dinner with you in January. I didn't say anything about going to the wedding."

"You were the one who opened your big mouth at that dinner," I said, returning his glare. "You were the one who talked me into becoming Jonathan's best man. Why'd you do that? Was it for my sake? Or for yours?"

"Fine, Frank," Julio said, his tone like a resentful teenager. "If I don't go to the wedding, then I'll pay more for the use of the third bedroom. How much more do you want for it? Give me a number."

"Twenty-five percent," I said, spitting out the first number I could think of.

"Done," Julio said, his tone harsh with triumph. Then he picked up his shopping list, folded it in half, and slipped it into the side pocket of his black pants. "We're even."

"No!" I shouted. "I want 35 percent! Thirty-five percent more!"

"But you said—never mind, forget it," Julio said, his voice shaking. "You want 35 percent for your room, you can have your 35 percent. I'll still have plenty left over so I can start looking for a new place before the end of the year. There has to be better place for me than this—this crummy house."

My heart pounded, my eyes burned. Julio pivoted on his crutch and yanked open the freezer door. I turned, adjusted my bag strap, and stalked out of the kitchen. I started up the stairs then stopped, my hand still gripping the railing. The nerve of him, talking to me like that. Who owned this crummy house? Who gave him that extra room?

My grip on the railing loosened. The messenger bag slid off my shoulder and thudded to the floor. I took slow, deliberate steps to the kitchen doorway. Julio leaned on his crutch by the open freezer door with an open pint of ice cream, pistachio-green foaming like toothpaste in a corner of his mouth.

"What do you want me to tell Marcus and Jonathan?" I said, keeping my voice as level as I could. "They're bound to ask about you. If I show up to the wedding by myself."

"You went to college, make something up," Julio said in a don't-bother-me tone. "Tell them we broke up. That we were never right for each other. That's pretty much the truth, isn't it?"

The knotted ball of anger in my chest burst. Hot rage flooded through me. I stalked up to Julio, slammed the freezer door shut, ripped the spoon out of his hand, and hurled it careening against the wall.

"Or how about I tell them you cheated on me with Marcus!" I shouted into Julio's shocked face. "And that you were too much of a coward to show up at his lover's own wedding. Now that would be the truth!"

I ripped the pint carton out of Julio's hands and hurled that across the room. Pale green ice cream exploded against the wall behind the kitchen table. Now I knew what the knot of anger looked like—a sickening, gooey splatter of pistachio-green.

"So, how was your weekend with Marcus a few weeks ago?" I snapped, turning to face Julio full-on. "Did you two boys have fun? Did he make you feel like the luckiest guy in the world?"

"Honestly," Julio said terrified, his crutch tipping over and banging to the floor. He gripped the counter edge to keep himself up. "I have no idea what you're talking about—"

"Knock it off," I said, my breath coming fast, "you know damn well what I'm talking about. The weekend you told me you were visiting a friend in the city. Who were you visiting? Can you look me in the eye and tell me you weren't seeing Marcus?"

"It's none—none of your business." Julio turned his head and looked up at the cabinet, breathing hard with his mouth half-open.

"You liar, you snake, you deceiving bag of scum," I said, too angry to control the words coming out of my mouth. "So much for living your life authentically, huh? Is this what you teach your yoga students? How to fake it? How to hide from the truth?"

"All right, all right," Julio said turning to me with red eyes, his voice and face hard with contempt. "You want authenticity? Fine. Yes. Yes, I slept with Marcus. Happy now?"

I blinked and put a hand to my heaving, burning lungs. The crater in my chest cracked open like the ice in the dream-ocean, a maw of dark, freezing water. First blue water. Then black water. Down and down I went.

"I don't know why you're so mad I slept with Marcus," Julio said in a caustic voice, his knuckles white at the edge of the counter. "Or that I went to see Marcus that weekend. You wanted me to see Marcus, didn't you?"

"What're you talking about?" I said through clenched teeth.

"Now look who's hiding from the truth," Julio said, sneering. "You wanted me to come between Jonathan and Marcus. You wanted Jonathan to be left all lonely and upset that weekend, desperately needing his best friend Frank to save him. Huh? Isn't that what you were gunning for all this time?"

My body went numb as if the icy ocean-water had soaked through my clothes to my skin. I gripped the back of a kitchen chair to steady myself. To think we'd degenerated to this. Lies lead to lies that lead to lies.

"So then you know," I said in a dull tone.

"I saw Jonathan on the BART platform that morning." Julio's high-pitched voice bounced off the walls. "The morning you dropped me off. I only saw him from behind, but that had to be him, I'm sure of it. So did you hit the jackpot, Frank? Did you score?"

I let go of the chair back and shifted my gaze to the floor. No point in lying to Julio anymore. I should've known I couldn't force Julio to spill everything without spilling everything myself.

"Yes," I said, looking up ashamed.

"Nice job," Julio said, his tone cutting. "You steered me out of the house to nail Jonathan that weekend. Hell, you didn't even have to make two trips to the BART station to do it. You didn't even have to turn off the car."

"Jonathan wouldn't have had to come here," I said, "if you hadn't made plans to see Marcus over there."

"You knew where I was going," Julio said bitterly. "You could've stopped me."

"And so that makes it my fault," I said, flaring up again. "You made the choice to see Marcus, but it was my responsibility to stop you? What are you, a little kid? You need someone to stop you from making a mistake?"

"You could've saved us both from making a mistake," Julio said, his voice stubborn. "But you didn't want that. You wanted Jonathan to yourself."

"Don't you pin this one on me," I said. "You and Marcus were the ones who started this cat-and-mouse game. I never would've had a chance with Jonathan if Marcus hadn't started up with you first."

"Oh, yeah?" Julio said, his back as stiff as his crutch. "And whose idea was it to tell Jonathan and Marcus you and I were boyfriends? If you'd been straight with them from the beginning, none of this would've happened. This whole mess starts with you, not me. You."

"Of course, it starts with me," I said, slapping my thigh with my hand. "I lied to them seven months ago, so that makes everything my fault. But why stop there? Why don't you say it's my fault for trusting you in the first place? For thinking you were on my side? You'd think by now I'd have learned not to trust anybody anymore."

Julio opened his mouth, but no sound came out, as if he'd suddenly gagged on something. I turned to face him and straightened myself up to my full height. Julio was showing skill in this chess game, but the truth—a piece more potent than any rook or queen—still sat on my side of the board.

"Let me ask you this," I said, my sharp voice piercing the stale air. "I know Marcus told you Ethan had cheated on me with another man. But did he tell you how I found out? No, he couldn't have. I've never told anyone how I'd found out. Not even Jonathan."

"I don't want to hear it, okay?" Julio said. "I never meant to hurt you—I mean, this whole thing started by accident—"

"An accident, was it?" I said, my voice full of contempt. "That's how Ethan had put it to me too. It was an accident I'd come home early from school one afternoon to find Ethan and the other guy having sex in my bedroom, in my bed—"

"Stop it," Julio said, his voice rising.

"—the same exact way I found out about you and Marcus," I went on, talking fast to keep Julio from cutting me off again. "I walked through the kitchen door and heard noises coming from upstairs. At first I thought I wasn't hearing right. I thought maybe Ethan was watching a porno online or something. But then I started climbing the stairs and realized that was Ethan's voice I was hearing—Ethan's and another man's. Even then I wasn't sure what I was hearing. So I walked up to the door…"

"Holy Mother," Julio said, turning his head.

"And there they were," I said, my voice wobbling. "Completely naked. The sheets ripped off the bed. I thought I'd kill them both."

"I said stop, Frank," Julio said, looking up at the ceiling.

"So you'll have to forgive me for not barging in on you and Marcus a few weeks ago," I pressed on. "I've witnessed enough cheating in my own house."

"You and I aren't even boyfriends," Julio said.

"But Marcus thought you and I were boyfriends." My voice was steady, but grim. "That's what makes it cheating. He wouldn't have homed in on you if he didn't think you were mine. That's what aroused him. And you fell for it. How was he, anyway? Was he worth it?"

For the next few seconds, Julio said nothing. His head was half-turned from me, bowed in shame. I felt for my missing wedding ring, remembering how I'd nearly broken my finger pulling it off on the day I'd caught Ethan upstairs.

"No, he wasn't worth it," Julio said, his expression half-pained, half-pleading. "Not even close. You were right about Marcus. He's unclean. I've paid such a price for letting him into my life, and now, and now … all I want is to move on. I can't tell you how sorry I am."

I picked up the crutch from the floor and leaned it against the refrigerator, the last of my anger finally dying out. The gold script on the wedding invitation caught the sunlight trickling into the room. I went over and raised the blinds over the sink. The crumpled ice cream carton lay like a dead rat on the floor. I picked it up and threw it into the garbage. Then I brought out a sponge and went over to the greenish splash mark on the wall. The stain probably wouldn't come out.

"I know you're sorry," I said, wiping the stain. "I'm sorry too."

"Hand to God, Frank," Julio said, and he held up his hand as if giving an oath. "I can't believe I ever thought—I mean, Marcus is not a nice guy. He's not even that good-looking. And frankly he's too old—"

"Stop it," I said, and I tossed the sponge into the sink. "There's no undoing what's done. I won't make you go to the wedding. I also don't want 35 percent for the extra room. Keep your money. Save it for your next apartment. San Francisco is where you belong. This house really is a crummy place for you to live."

Fatigue filled the space where the anger had once festered. As horrible as that fight with Julio was, at least the truth was out. Jonathan would marry Marcus. Julio would move to San Francisco. Me, I'd eke out a living here alone. At last I knew where the steam train was headed—to the same place where I'd begun. I took some paper towels, cleaned up the spilled ice cream on the floor, and left the kitchen.

***

At the bottom of the stairs I picked up my messenger bag and plodded up to my room, shutting the door behind me. Was I still Jonathan's best man? I imagined myself being fitted for that tux, paying for the rental, and showing up at City Hall to find Jonathan's brother wearing the same tux, standing next to Jonathan in my place. No. Impossible. Jonathan would've had the decency to tell me if I was off best-man duty.

I still had to know. I fished out my phone from my bag, sank into my desk chair, and found Jonathan's number. I didn't expect Jonathan to respond to my message, but still I had to try. He couldn't have thought he could pop that invitation in the mail and not hear from me.

Invite came today, I tapped into the phone. *I'll go rent the tux.*

The heavy phone slid from my fingers to the desk. I swiveled around to face the bed. Not even with Jonathan had I slept well in that bed. But tonight I'd sleep well. The anger living inside me was gone. All that remained was the aching realization that Jonathan had drifted past my reach, the well-protected king behind Marcus's taunting army.

"Hey, Frank," Julio said, tapping on the other side of the door. "Can I talk to you?"

"Go away," I said wearily.

The door creaked open. Julio flicked on the overhead light. Only then I realized how darkness had shrouded the room, how long I must've been sitting slumped in the chair. Hunger gnawed at my stomach. I looked up at Julio blinking, too exhausted to move a muscle, let alone rise from the chair.

"You left this downstairs," Julio said, holding out the invitation.

"Thanks," I deadpanned.

Julio took a careful step into the room and laid the invitation on the desk, next to my phone. The sight of it sent a pain up my side. Why did Julio feel it necessary to bring it up here? I'd wait for him to leave, then rip it into a million pieces.

"You weren't expecting the invitation to come today, were you?" Julio said, his voice sympathetic.

"No," I said. "I'd even let myself think it might never come."

"Maybe, Frank," Julio said cautiously. He licked his lips. "Maybe you should start thinking about letting Jonathan go."

I gazed at the elegant gold script of the invitation. Easy for Julio to tell me to let go of Jonathan. Julio had no friendships that went back that far.

"You knew the invitation was coming," I said, looking up at Julio. "Didn't you?"

"Not really," Julio said with a shrug. He looked down at the carpet.

"But you'd guessed," I said. "You knew Marcus and Jonathan were going to patch things up."

"More or less," Julio said in a shaky voice. "Marcus loves Jonathan. Sex is only physical for him. He'll never give Jonathan up, not for my sake or for anyone else's. I know it seems hard to believe, but in his own way, Jonathan means more to Marcus than anyone else in the world."

"Me too," I said snorting, turning away from him.

"But Jonathan's not yours," Julio said. "You'll only make yourself sick chasing after some guy you can't have. There are other guys out there. Lots of other guys. With Jonathan out of the picture, maybe you'll notice them."

I let Julio's words sink in. In my head the field of ice stretched as far as ever, but what was that shadow moving across the sky? A gull? A cormorant? A beacon of hope for sure.

"I suppose you're right," I said, my voice low and thoughtful. "Thanks for saying that. And I'm sorry for yelling at you downstairs. Those were some ugly things I said."

"Sure thing," Julio said with a faint smile. "I'm sorry for what I said too. You're a good guy, you know."

I shut the door after Julio left, feeling better than I'd thought possible when I first laid eyes on the wedding invitation. Even after everything he'd put me through, I'd still miss Julio, his energy, his optimism. Maybe he was right about the other man in the crowd, hiding in Jonathan's long shadow.

Then my cell phone buzzed. I jumped. My mind must be playing tricks on me. The phone buzzed again. A scream of gulls in my head. Cracks zigzagged across the ice. I lifted the heavy phone and shuddered at Jonathan's glowing text.

im in SCruz this wknd – come & ill explain –

12

MISSING

Okay. So that was no fun. I couldn't decide which was worse, being stuck in Marcus's bedroom last week or Frank reaming me out last night. But at least Frank and I had everything out in the open. Now it was time to take the whole lesson, put everything in the drawer, and move on to the next lesson. Mother of God, who was I kidding? The past week was one of the worst of my life. And I deserved every second of it.

Forget about sleeping. My mind roiled with pictures of Frank walking in on his ex and his ex's new partner. In Frank's own bedroom besides. Then for Frank to walk into the house to hear me and Marcus. No two ways about it—I'd been an asshat. I suppose I should count myself lucky that moving Marcus's sunglasses to the corner of the kitchen table was all Frank had done that afternoon. If it was me, I'd've set the house on fire.

No undoing all that now. In a few weeks it wouldn't matter. Once my cast came off, I'd be out of the house more often. Not only that, an instructor friend of mine had called me about a week ago, saying she was thinking of opening her own studio near Lake Merritt. A studio with not-crazy-expensive apartments to rent right above the studio. I could already picture myself living there come first of the year. Operating my massage business upstairs from her, teaching classes four times a week. It wasn't San Francisco, but it was close.

I still had to face Frank in the morning. How could I look him in the eye again? I fell asleep with no clue on how to handle it, and opened my eyes at the crack of dawn feeling just as clueless. Maybe I should haul myself out of bed now before Frank woke up, and be out of the house before Frank came downstairs. But where could I go this early in the morning? In a cast to boot?

Then I heard careful-sounding noises coming from downstairs. I blinked and sat up. Frank, up already? My nightstand clock read 6:38. Frank was never moving around the kitchen this early on a Saturday morning. He must've had a sleepless night like I'd had. I pulled my sheet up to my chin and closed my eyes. No point in facing my shame any sooner than I had to.

The shutting of the kitchen door snapped me awake again. Footsteps in the driveway. A car starting outside my window. I pulled myself out of bed and hobbled to the window to see Frank's Volvo pull out of the driveway and drive off. My nightstand clock read 6:51. I stood and stared, my body frozen at the idea that Frank had left the house so early. Where could he be going at this time of the morning?

Frank must've had the same idea I'd had, to make a run for it while the house was still quiet. Fine by me. He'd saved me the trouble of having to do it myself. Which was Frank's way, come to think of it. Always thinking one step ahead of everyone else. One step ahead of me, at least.

I made my way downstairs and put on some oatmeal. My yoga class would be starting in an hour and a half without me. The house felt bigger and quieter without Frank here. I wondered if he felt the same way when I wasn't around.

I still wanted to put off seeing him for as long as possible. Wherever he went, he'd probably be home sometime later this morning. No point in leaving the house now. But what if Frank had taken the car to pick up a quart of milk or something and would be walking through the door any minute? No, no way. Frank wouldn't've bolted the house so early for a freaking quart of milk.

Lucky for me, I already had plans this morning. I was meeting my buddy Hector in the Castro for lunch. Until now I was a little pissed off at Hector for not wanting to meet me here in Oakland—all my San Francisco friends thought Oakland was a million miles away. And I was the one in a cast! But now I was glad for it. A good excuse to duck out early and stay away from the house all morning, in San Francisco.

Frank wasn't in the garden when I came home in the afternoon. No car in the driveway either. I let myself into the house—nope, nobody. My now-dry breakfast dishes sat in the drainer, exactly as I'd left them. Maybe Frank had come and gone? But nothing in the kitchen seemed out of place. My oatmeal bowl hadn't been strategically moved a few inches like that last time with Marcus's aviator sunglasses.

What was I supposed to do now? Sit around the house and wait for Frank to come home? Then I remembered Mami. Mami, of course. Who else could I call up at the last minute to see if I could stay over for the night? And as always she was happy to hear from me and said sure, come on down. But she sounded concerned. Everything all right? she asked. Yes, Mami, everything was all right. How did Mamis pick up on these things?

I threw a few things together in a bag and headed to the BART station. Take that, Frank. If you could ditch this house for the weekend, then so could I. I'd take my time coming home tomorrow morning, too. Frank had to be home by then. Good. Let him be the one to wonder what had happened to me.

***

My blood went cold even before I walked through the kitchen door at eleven o'clock on Sunday morning. Frank's car still wasn't in the driveway. I let myself into the house. Everything in the kitchen was exactly as I'd left it. Even the kitchen chair I'd purposely pulled out at an angle hadn't been pushed in again. I called out Frank's name. My voice died in the air. So Frank not only wasn't here, he hadn't come home all day yesterday.

I pulled out the chair all the way, sank into it, and looked up at the green stain on the kitchen wall where my pistachio ice cream had gone splat. Mother of God. Where was Frank? He'd been so pissed off yesterday. I don't remember anyone letting fly at me like that before. The thing that killed me was I'd had it coming. That stain had no right to be there. This kitchen was miserable enough.

What should I do? The last time I saw Frank was over twenty-four hours ago. Should I call the police? No, that would be paranoid. No way could I call the police without calling Frank on his cell phone first. Maybe shoot Frank a text? But that would look like I was checking up on him. Was worried about him, which I was, of course. Frank didn't need to know that.

To hell with calling Frank. Wherever Frank was, he was probably still in one piece. He must've spent the night at a friend's house or maybe down in Santa Cruz with his folks. And he hadn't felt the need to tell me because—duh—I wasn't part of his life. Not after what had happened on Friday. The man owed me nothing.

Once I moved to the apartment above my friend's studio in Lake Merritt, he'd forget me as much as I planned to forget him. Once I made the big move home to San Francisco—where I belonged—I'd think of Frank as a hazy fantasy from my past. But could I do that? After everything we'd been through this year? After what Frank had said and done in this very kitchen? Frank might fall out of my life, but no, he'd always stake a place in my memory. He was a decent guy whose trust I'd thrown to the ground and stomped all over. And how many guys that I've met could I say were decent? In his own way, Frank had left a mark on me as permanent as the pistachio ice cream on the wall up there. I might even remember him more fondly than I ever would Marcus.

I pulled myself up, left the house, and hauled myself on the crutches to Genevieve's. Genevieve wasn't in the store today. I'd forgotten she had an assistant now, a young woman with thick glasses and pink highlights in her hair, kind of like a Genevieve-in-training, to take over on Sundays. Eh, who cared? It wasn't as if I could tell Genevieve about what happened. She didn't even know I'd slept with Marcus. I'd long ago lied to her and said the hot guy in the red shorts had stopped come to my class. Still, it would've been nice to see her smile and not judge me.

I spent the whole day tooling up and down College Avenue, errands, window shopping, a cup of tea at a café. Thank the Holy Virgin the weather was so nice. I also couldn't help noticing how well I managed on the crutches. My knee felt great under the cast. All the while my mind kept turning to Frank's house, wondering if Frank had come home. I was determined to stay out as long as possible. Give him the time he needed to return.

At six o'clock I headed home with a small bag of groceries. No car in the driveway. No Frank in the house. Madre de Dios. What was

Frank trying to do to me? To think I'd been worried how I'd face him again. I never thought I'd be worried I might never see him again.

***

Frank finally came home at a few minutes past eight. I was stretched out on my bed, skimming through that math book I'd pulled off the living room shelf, when I heard his car pulling into the driveway outside my window. Thank the Holy Mother. The bitch decided to show his face after all.

Even so, my body stiffened to the sound of Frank's footsteps coming up the stairs. What should I do? Go to the bedroom door and greet him? Say hi like he hadn't freaked me out all weekend? Give him shit for leaving me to worry about him for almost two straight days? No, forget it. The easiest thing would be for me to stay put. Frank had no right to know how much he'd set my nerves on edge.

I listened to the water running in the bathroom, the pipes creaking in the walls. Then I heard his bedroom door close. My thoughts turned again to the fight we'd had on Friday afternoon. It must've killed him to tell me about walking in on his ex. Yet he'd told me. The first person he'd ever told.

I closed my eyes and imagined Frank as a brand-new student in my yoga class. He wouldn't be the first student to walk into the studio feeling shivery and vulnerable from some trauma or other. I pictured myself going to Frank and giving him extra attention, adjusting his poses, keeping an eye on his balance, using my most concerned voice to ask him if he was okay. Frank would hiss at me if I pulled that on him now. Still it was worth a try. I reached for my crutches, pulled myself up from my bed, and hobbled out of my bedroom and toward Frank's closed bedroom door. No sound coming from the other side of it, but the light was still on. Okay, Julio, here went nothing.

"Frank?" I said, tapping on the door. "Frank, can I come in?"

A pause, then Frank's faint voice. I couldn't tell if he said yes or no. Probably yes. He would've shouted if he'd said no. Not that it mattered. I was going in no matter what.

I opened the door a crack to find an unsmiling Frank hunched over his desk with his laptop open, the screen throwing a sickly blue light on his face. The bags under his eyes and the downturned corners of his mouth made me think Frank hadn't slept in two days straight. He threw me a glance, then moved his mouse and clicked.

"Frank," I said licking my lips, my voice coming out croaky, "I just wanted to tell you again how sorry I am about, you know, what I did."

Frank straightened up and sucked a big breath through his nostrils, but he didn't turn to me or say a word. I'd made his breathing worse, not better. Not a good start to the yoga practice.

"And I also want to thank you," I said, my voice rising a little.

He moved his hand off his mouse and looked at me, surprised. I hadn't expected to say those words myself. But it was true. If Frank couldn't bear to accept my apology, maybe he could accept my gratitude.

"Thank me for what?" Frank said, looking at me bleary-eyed.

"For walking in on me and Marcus," I said in a low, clear voice. "I broke it off with him soon after you left the house. I'd wanted so bad to break it off with him before, but I couldn't find a way to do it. So thanks. You gave me the strength I needed to stop something I never should've started."

"But you spent the weekend with him," Frank said in a dull tone. "Why?"

"Escape," I said, in a stronger voice than I probably should've used. "I'd broken my knee and was stuck on the couch downstairs. Deep down I knew you knew something was wrong. Marcus offered me the extra bedroom, and I took it. It was never more than that. Hand to God."

Frank turned his head and looked up at the ceiling, his eyes narrow and his lips pressed together. He still wanted to hate me, I could tell. But at least he now knew he'd been the reason why Marcus and I weren't sleeping together anymore.

"What's done is done." He looked at me. "And if you mean what you say, then I'm glad I could help."

"You helped. I swear." I ventured a smile and then turned to leave the room. "Oh, and Frank?"

"Yes, Julio?" Frank said, reaching for his mouse again.

"The next time you leave the house for the weekend," I said in my most diplomatic voice, "maybe you could, like, tell me you'll be gone? And give me an idea when you might be home? I didn't know what had happened to you. I was worried all weekend."

"I see," Frank said, frowning. "Okay. I promise."

"Thanks," I said, and left the bedroom.

Then I shut myself in my own room and sat down at the edge of the bed, caressing my scar. My heart was still pounding from what I'd said. But my whole chest felt lighter. If Frank could be brutally honest with me on Friday, then I could be brutally honest with him. I could only hope that Frank would accept my words as sincere. He really did deserve better.

13

ESCAPE PLAN

Meeting Jonathan on Santa Cruz pier, where we'd used to hang out as college kids, had been my idea. The weather had been postcard-perfect that Saturday afternoon, or so it seemed now in my memory. Anglers threw out their lines, while sea lions splashed in the water below. There must've been wrinkles on the ocean surface, but my memory had smoothed out the water into waveless azure porcelain, as far as I could see. The reality of that paltry half hour with Jonathan was a cruel travesty of all my dreams and memories.

For the next few days I could think of nothing else. No matter where I was—at school, in the car, lying awake in bed at four a.m.—the scene uncoiled like a sea serpent from the depths of the dream-ocean, coiling itself around my brain and squeezing out any other thoughts. I felt as if I was stumbling through a fog that seemed only to thicken as the wall clock in my head ticked the lonely minutes toward Jonathan's wedding.

I'd pleaded with him to call it off. No matter what I said, my weak words had fluttered like bits of paper over the pier's edge, dissolving into the cold salt water. All Jonathan would say, in a dull robot's voice, was he'd changed his mind. That he and Marcus had talked things over and decided to go ahead with the wedding. If anything they were closer than they had been at their engagement in January. He added he'd understand if I wanted to drop out of the wedding party. I refused. I told him I had to watch them exchange vows before I could believe their marriage was true.

Then there was Julio. I couldn't help thinking about what he'd said to me on the Sunday evening when I'd returned home from Santa Cruz. His tone of concern when he asked me not to leave the house for the weekend without telling him where I was going. I thought I could handle it better if the concern was fake, but Julio had sounded as if he'd genuinely been worried about me. Maybe everything I'd told him in the kitchen had sunk into that air head of his. I'd been a teacher for too long not to recognize when a teenager had finally learned his lesson.

No matter. Once Julio moved to a new place, he wouldn't have to fret over my comings and goings. I also wouldn't have to worry about walking in on him having sex with anyone else. Doubtless Julio wanted the same things for himself. This reminded me so much of my final weeks with Ethan in the house. First tension, then silence.

That whole weekend left me determined to make a change in my life. A change of scenery, maybe. If Marcus and Jonathan could build a new house for themselves in New York, and Julio could launch a brand-new business for himself in my house, why couldn't I shake things up for myself? I hadn't met this year's incoming class of students, but no doubt they'd be another batch of rich kids who saw me less as a mentor and more as a stepping stone to bigger and better things. The sort of teacher they'd recall in twenty or thirty years and think, "Whatever happened to that guy?" Maybe it was time to resign this chess game—a game I was clearly losing—and start a new one somewhere else.

Julio's pink-and-gray business cards flitted around in my head like finches, nestling themselves in pockets and purses. What if those finches carried resumes in their beaks, seeds for them to sow in a new city, a new home? I was suffocating under the weight of my mortgage, let alone from the memories crawling like termites in the crevices of that house. Why not move somewhere smaller and cheaper? Why not start over again?

I wouldn't tell Jonathan where I was going. I could change addresses after the wedding, and be long gone by the time he ever thought to call me again. I had to do something to prepare for the awful aftermath of Jonathan's wedding. Sitting there and taking it was not an option.

The next night I holed myself up in my room and called up my résumé on my laptop. The last time I'd consulted it was over five years ago, the résumé I'd used to land the job I now had. A little editing, a hastily written cover letter, and I was ready to change my career path. I looked up every business contact I could find, entered them onto labels, and printed them out, twenty-six labels in all. I was done by midnight. Twenty-six envelopes, twenty-six opportunities. Résumés would be traveling as far as Denver and San Diego, Seattle and Portland. Why not? Nothing was left for me here.

My heart went hollow as soon I dropped the envelopes into the mailbox on my drive to work. Of course not one of those finches would drop a seed on fertile soil. The people reading those cover letters would sense the desperation in my cover letter and slip the résumé into a file that would never be opened again. Even if they did like the résumé, what were the chances a school would be looking for a math teacher at this time of the year? Close to zero.

And once Jonathan moved to New York with Marcus, what would be the point of moving? If I couldn't leave Jonathan first, then there was no point in leaving. I could see the future spreading out in a desolate frozen sea, Jonathan gone, Julio gone, and me grinding my wheels into the ice as I'd been these past two years, same job, same house, same everything.

***

In a few days I received an email from Marcus's father, telling me my tux had been ordered and was now waiting for me at an exclusive men's store near Union Square in San Francisco. No doubt about it—the wedding was on. I couldn't help wonder if this email was a coincidence, or if Jonathan or Marcus had had a hand in sending it to me.

The next Saturday morning I took BART to Union Square to pick up my rental suit. The dark gray suit befit the tastes of a vulgarian like Marcus's father—wide lapels, black-pearl buttons, and black velvet trimming as crisp as a hundred-dollar bill. Way more elaborate, more outlandish, than the suit I'd worn to my own wedding. Perhaps this tux would outshine the wedding outfits awaiting their moment in Marcus and Jonathan's own closet. Could Marcus's father be so childish, so clueless, so divinely narcissistic to upstage the grooms at their own wedding? The answer seemed as glaring as those black-pearl buttons.

I figured I might as well try on the suit before I left the store. The pants were too tight in the waist. My mind traveled to the neglected basketball hoop in my driveway, the expired gym membership card in the top drawer of my desk. I sensed my body slipping away from me as inevitably as Jonathan had slipped away from me.

The tailor said he'd need an hour or so to fix the pants. What should I do with myself in the meantime? Camp out in Union Square and watch the glass elevators at the St. Francis Hotel? I remembered how I'd talked down Jonathan from his panic attack. That morning probably represented my best chance to steal Jonathan from Marcus. An open line to checkmate I'd let pass. On the other hand, who was to say the outcome would have been any different? Jonathan had been no more prepared to leave Marcus on the morning we'd shopped for tuxes than he'd been last week in Santa Cruz. Perhaps this game had never been winnable.

I realized now was as good a time as any to buy Marcus and Jonathan a wedding present. Why not? Their cupboards and shelves were already crammed with more beautiful things than their eyes could behold, but I couldn't show up to their wedding empty-handed. Besides, shopping for a gift had to be a better way to kill an hour than sitting on some bench in Union Square, chewing over the might-have-beens.

I went into a department store across the street and took the escalator to the housewares section. Shelves of serving bowls and candlesticks and tinted crystal vases sparkled at me, gaudy useless objects that would soon be packed away and flown thousands of miles to a mansion in Westchester County, New York. Which of these items would I choose to contribute to the galaxy of their possessions? A devious feeling came over me, a selfish desire to give them something Jonathan and Marcus—or at least Jonathan—would have no choice but to make room for.

I settled on a circular brass desk clock that also served as a paperweight. The way the clock sat on the shelf, carving a modest but dignified circle among larger and bossier desk clocks, made me think of Jonathan. Or at least the Jonathan I thought I knew, the Jonathan I'd known from my days in Santa Cruz. But the only clock left was the one on display, and the clock had a flaw, a minuscule scratch near its base. I decided to buy it anyway. By the time either Jonathan or Marcus noticed the scratch I'd be long vanished from their lives. Even if they did notice, maybe they'd deem the scratch as a symbol of my relationship to them. A shiny surface concealing the flaws.

The saleswoman wrapped the clock in pink tissue paper, nestled it in a cream-white box, measured out a length of crimson ribbon, and tied the box up in a graceful bow. I pictured Jonathan opening the box, folding back the delicate pink tissue. Maybe the clock would make him think of the time we could've had together. Or maybe he'd stow it away, like the stuffed green rabbit I'd once won for him, and forget it existed. What did it matter now? I tucked the gift under my arm and headed for the tailor's.

The suit still wasn't ready. So I sat in a chair and waited for another fifteen minutes until the tailor brought the suit out on a plastic hanger, mummified in sheets of plastic. I reached for my wallet to pay for it, but the tailor told me it was already paid for, by a Mr. William Pierce. I slung the suit over my shoulder, too worn out to be insulted, and took BART to Oakland.

My car was parked at Rockridge Station. I stowed the clock and the suit in the trunk and drove home. Would Julio be home at this hour? I couldn't let him see me enter the house holding a rental tux and a tastefully wrapped wedding gift in my hands. So I left the stuff in the trunk, and walked into the house to the sound of electronic tango music wafting from upstairs. My hunch was right.

I wound up leaving the gift and tux in the car for another two days. Julio spent more time at home than I'd realized. His cast was to blame. But it wouldn't be long before Julio would shed that cocoon. Then he'd transform into a butterfly in his bright aqua jacket, flitting here and there, teaching classes, going to parties, staying out late with his San Francisco friends. I could revert to my old self again. Right where I'd started.

But not quite where I'd started. Something had shifted. What? Then it hit me. The fight with Julio in the kitchen. Me unleashing all my pent-up rage. Then seeing Jonathan in Santa Cruz. Telling Jonathan of my love for him in the most feeling language I could summon. I knew I was walking away from this empty-handed, my king lying face down on the chessboard. But at least I could say I'd been honest.

A couple of days later Jonathan sent me his first text since Santa Cruz. *Wedding still on for 10/12 3 pm, pix at main staircase 2:30.* Cold, clinical, businesslike. His way of saying he wanted no trouble from me. Jonathan was ashamed we'd slept together. The only thing keeping him from ejecting me from the wedding party, in all likelihood, was fear of causing a scandal. He didn't have to worry. As much as I wanted to shake sense into my best friend, I knew I couldn't. Not at the wedding, not anywhere else.

14

REQUEST

I kissed the crutches and that dumb cast goodbye at the end of August. The knee felt creaky when I bent it, but at least it bent. I developed a habit of caressing the smooth skin of my calf. This was like a rebirth, with me taking my first baby steps in the world.

Later that night, I called Josie to say I could teach the next Saturday class—the first Saturday of September. Her ecstatic tone brought tears to my eyes. I didn't deserve to hear her go on about how happy she was I could teach again. But what could I do? Tell Josie I'd been a scumbag? For the sake of the universe, I needed to pretend to be a better person than I was.

I posted a photo of my healed leg—still a nice-looking leg, and shaved besides—on Facebook, with a message saying I'd be teaching the next Saturday class. My phone pinged with congrats within seconds. An hour later over fifty people had responded. No word from Marcus, though.

As Saturday morning approached I couldn't shake the feeling Marcus would still show up and find some way to turn my world upside down. I wouldn't let him. I couldn't let him. That class was my life. And my life belonged to me.

***

My scar tingled as soon as I walked into the yoga studio. Students surrounded me, hugging me and saying how great it was to see me again. No Marcus. So far, so good. More students filed into the studio. Still no Marcus. Ten minutes to class. Eight. Six. Marcus was cutting it close if he planned to crash my coming-home party. Would he slip in at the last second? It almost didn't matter. In a class as crowded as this one, I'd have no trouble pretending he wasn't there.

Then the studio door opened—and in walked Jonathan. Our eyes locked. My bad knee nearly buckled. Still, something told me Jonathan had no idea I'd been the guy quaking behind his spare bedroom door two months ago. Whatever Jonathan wanted this morning, a smackdown wasn't it.

Jonathan wore a rumpled white undershirt and a pair of dirty gray sweatpants. He crept his way around the students who were already seated, looking for somewhere to put down his gym bag and unroll his mat. Or should I say Marcus's mat. Yes, that was Marcus's black mat. Then he turned to me with a hopeless expression, looking like the kid in the cafeteria on his first day at a new school, not knowing where to sit. I walked over to Jonathan with my biggest smile and welcomed him to my class. A couple of my regulars shifted their mats at my request to make room for "my friend Jonathan." My stomach went sick for playing this sham.

I taught an easier class than usual, keeping an eye on Jonathan. Luckily for me, Jonathan needed my help. I spent more time adjusting his posture than I did any other of my students. Once I put a hand to his back and felt his heart knocking against his ribs. A pang of guilt shot through me. This was partly my fault, to make his heart suffer like this.

***

After class I stood outside the open front door to see my students out. Jonathan was nowhere around. Had he slipped out early? Then the restroom door at the back of the studio opened and out he came, his hair wet. He'd changed out of his sweaty gym clothes and into a long-sleeved olive green shirt and blue jeans. My scar buzzed as he walked up to me.

"Great class," I said to him through a fake smile.

"I sucked," Jonathan said.

"You did fine, Jonathan." I patted his shoulder. "You're a diva, not Wonder Woman."

"Marcus told me you'd hurt your knee," Jonathan said in a half-serious, half-hopeful voice. "You better?"

"More or less," I said, and looked down with pride at my knee.

"Good," Jonathan said, letting out a long exhale. "I'm so glad to hear it. Marcus'll be glad to hear it too."

So Marcus hadn't told Jonathan I was the other woman. Thank the Holy Virgin. Then what was Jonathan doing here this morning? Without Marcus? Using Marcus's yoga mat? He sure as fuck didn't come here for the exercise.

"So, um," I said, trying to sound all casual. "What's Marcus up to this morning?"

"He's in Las Vegas," Jonathan said offhandedly, slinging Marcus's rolled-up mat over his shoulder. "His brothers are meeting him there for his bachelor party."

"Oh." I thought I'd never let Marcus go to Vegas without slapping a tracking bracelet on him first.

"So, um," Jonathan said in a lowered voice, his eyes darting at the students walking past us into the studio. "Would you happen to be free for a few minutes to talk?"

"About what?" My scar felt suddenly cold.

"I don't want to talk here." Jonathan looked up and down the street, the buildings like dirty shadows against the gray sky. "I could take you to breakfast or something. Are you hungry? The car's parked about a block from here."

"I'm meeting a friend in Oakland for lunch," I said, grabbing the first lie that popped into my head.

"I only need five minutes." Jonathan's tone was polite, but it carried a whiff that he hadn't bought my story.

"Gosh," I said, pulling my turned-off cell phone out of my track jacket, "and he's texting me now, asking me if I could make it sooner."

"Julio, please," Jonathan said, grasping my forearm, right over my scar, with an urgent look on his face. "I need to talk to you."

I slipped the phone in my front pants pocket, feeling like a doofus. It wouldn't be fair for me to beg out of talking to him.

Besides, I was curious to know what he needed to tell me. Something about Marcus maybe?

"I can't leave till Josie shows up," I said, darting my eyes into the studio. "After that we can go."

"I won't take up too much of your time." Jonathan let go of my arm. "I promise."

My stomach felt like it was about to crumple like a paper bag. Mother of God, did I have to go through with this? Then it hit me that talking to Jonathan was as much a part of my healing process as dealing with those crutches. And, after all, I really had been a louse to him, nearly busting up his relationship to Marcus. The least I owed him was five minutes of my time. I smiled and told him why not.

***

Josie walked around the corner in her usual black top and purple tights. Soon she was beaming in front of me, giving me a hug and asking me how the class went. I told her great and introduced her to "my friend Jonathan." They had more in common than they realized, those two. Both were innocent people I'd deceived.

Jonathan's car was about a block and a half away from the studio. The doctor had told me to take it easy for the first couple weeks, so I used the metal cane she'd given me to make the walk. Dread filled me at the sight of Marcus's black BMW. How could I not remember the last time I'd slid into the front passenger seat on that blazing Saturday morning in July, with Marcus at the wheel? At least I'd graduated from crutches to a cane.

Jonathan settled himself behind the driver's seat and pulled out. I thought we'd take forever to merge into the traffic on 16th Street. The way Jonathan leaned on the gas and then slammed on the brake, I could tell he must let Marcus do the driving. Boy, Jonathan must've really wanted to talk to me if he'd taken the trouble to drive all the way down the hill to the studio.

"I have an idea," Jonathan said at a stop light, looking up at the craggy hill looming above Castro Street. "You ever go up to Corona Heights?"

"Once or twice," I said, leaning forward to peer through the front windshield at the hill. "I don't think my knee can handle the climb to the top."

"We don't have to climb to the summit," Jonathan said, his voice all lively as if that's where he'd meant to take me all along. "We can park at the children's museum. There's a park and plenty of places to sit and watch the city. You mind?"

"If you don't mind driving me down to the BART station later," I said, patting my knee.

"Of course I don't mind," Jonathan said, jerking the car forward when the light turned green. "And I'll make sure you make it home in time."

"Make it home in time?" I said, blinking. "Home in time for what?"

"Didn't you say you were meeting a friend in Oakland for lunch?" Jonathan said, throwing me a glance.

"Right, right," I said, feeling like a doofus again. "Eh, don't worry about my friend. If we run late, I'll text him."

We drove up the hill in silence. Hmm. What if Jonathan did know I was the guy Marcus had been sleeping with this past summer? What if he was waiting to pull me aside before he lit into me? Nah, I couldn't picture Jonathan going apeshit. He'd probably settle for saying how disappointed he was. Maybe even shed a tear or two. My scar buzzed away. I couldn't decide which would be worse, Jonathan shouting at me or Jonathan speaking to me in a low, hurt voice.

Still, whatever Jonathan had to say, I knew I had to listen to it. If an apology was what he wanted, then an apology was what I'd give him. It seemed not nearly enough to make up for the wrong I'd done him.

***

Jonathan parked near the entrance of the one-story children's museum. Then, at his suggestion, we walked around the museum and to a low, backless concrete bench overlooking the city. The streets and buildings sprawled in front of us. An amazing view, even on a day as overcast as this one. Then I thought of the price Jonathan had paid to live so near all this beauty. I'd never trade places with Jonathan.

"I love coming up here," Jonathan said, and took a long breath. "I come here to remind myself how lucky I am. God, I wish I could feel more grateful. You know what I mean?"

"Gratitude is what I teach," I said with a half-sigh. "Or used to teach. When I'm not blowing out my knee."

Jonathan rose from the bench and walked up to the chest-high chain-link fence that separated us from the sheer drop to the public tennis courts below. On one of the courts, a guy played fetch with a bounding golden retriever. I sat and watched Jonathan while the cold air made the scar on my forearm sing.

"I used to come here every Saturday morning," Jonathan said, turning to me, "when Marcus was at your class. I pretended to be asleep until he left. Then I'd scoot out of bed and come here and take pictures. I've never shown him the pictures I've taken. I like having this secret place from him, a place I can call my own."

"We all need a place like that," I said.

A group of parrots squawked over our heads, soaring over the swaying cypress and eucalyptus trees. A nearby crow let out a *caw-caw-caw*. Meanwhile, on the tennis court, the man threw a red rubber ball over the head of the panting dog. The dog raced for it and scooped it up, the ball letting out a circus clown's wheeze. Must be nice to be a dog, to have no better care in the world than to chase a rubber ball.

"I wanted to say I'm sorry," Jonathan said, and he sat down next to me with a sigh.

"You're sorry?" I said, blinking. "Sorry for what?"

"You don't have to pretend not to know, Julio," Jonathan said in a small voice. "I know you know what I'm talking about."

He pulled himself up and looked down at his hands in his lap. Guilt was written all over his face. I leaned away from him and stared. He'd brought me up here to apologize? Mother of God, what in the world for?

"I don't know what you're talking about, Jonathan," I said, wondering if Jonathan might be joking. "Hand to God, I don't."

"Please, Julio," Jonathan said, half-turning from me and putting a hand to his forehead. "Don't make me have to say it out loud. You know what I did."

The parrots swooped chattering above our heads again, making Jonathan jump up from the bench. Poor Jonathan—some crime haunted him, whatever he thought he'd done. I wished there was some way I could tell him that whatever he'd done to me couldn't be a gazillionth as crappy as what I'd done to him.

"It was me, Julio," Jonathan said turning around to face me, his voice shaking. "With Frank that weekend. I'm the reason why Frank broke up with you."

I sucked in my lower lip, fighting an attack of laughter. Or was it an attack of sobs? My mind flashed to that awful Sunday morning, trembling behind the bedroom door while Jonathan pounded away at it, Marcus blocking the way. It should be me confessing to him, not him confessing to me.

"I'd never done anything like that before," Jonathan said, putting a hand to his chest. "But Marcus was seeing someone else that weekend, and I was angry. I wanted revenge. So I picked up the phone and called Frank—and he invited me over. He said you were seeing your mother in San Leandro."

"Hayward," I said.

"At the time I'd managed to convince myself I only wanted Frank's friendship," Jonathan said, the words coming out in a rush, "but I can't lie to myself anymore. I used him. He's my best friend in the world, and I used him."

"But Frank was the one who invited you," I said, going for a reasonable tone. "Plus you must've been feeling vulnerable. Is it possible Frank was, um, using you too?"

"Not like I used him," Jonathan said, shaking his head. "I called him on purpose so he'd invite me over. Deep down I knew he'd do anything for me, but I wouldn't admit it. Not even to myself. Geez, I'm such a lowlife. But I wasn't thinking straight. I was too carried away. Too focused on me and my problems, my situation, my wedding—"

Jonathan turned away from me with his arms folded and his shoulders hunched, shivering in the sharp breeze. I scrambled up from the bench, ignoring the twinge in my knee, and went over to him. Even so, I couldn't shake the feeling that Jonathan was being less than straight with me. If Jonathan felt guilty for using Frank, then why was he apologizing to me instead? And being such a drama queen about it? My scar buzzed. This was beginning to remind me of Marcus and his sob story of his tough childhood, an attempt to tug at my heart strings.

"It's all right, it's all right." I yanked down the sleeve of my jacket. "Hey, how about you turn around so I can look at you."

Jonathan stopped shivering, stood motionless, and then turned to face me, still not looking me in the eye. His blank expression looked as if I'd shaken him awake from a nightmare. I saw a chance to redeem myself. If I could make Jonathan feel better now, then maybe I could forgive myself for sleeping with Marcus.

"You didn't break me and Frank up," I said with conviction. "You didn't, I promise. We were never anything more than…a couple of roommates who happened to sleep together. That's all it was. Hand to God."

"Frank told me more or less the same thing," Jonathan said in a gloomy tone. He turned to look into the gray distance. "Otherwise I never would've—I mean, I never would've even thought to, you know, do what I did."

"You don't have to explain yourself," I said all generous-like and yoga teacher-y, my best impersonation of Josie. "And you can't change the past. All you can do is notice it, learn from it, let it go, and move on."

"Maybe I should," Jonathan said, peering at me. "But I'd still feel a lot better, um, if you'd consider giving it another shot with Frank."

"I don't know," I said cautiously, my hand diving into my pocket for my cell phone. Who was I thinking I could call? My imaginary lunch date? Frank?

"But Frank has so much love to give," Jonathan said, his tone heartfelt. "He was devoted to Ethan too. He was so devastated when Ethan left him. You saw that yourself at my engagement party."

A jet roared above our heads, a gray needle tracing a white line across the clearing sky. I imagined myself way up there in that plane now, happily traveling far away from Corona Heights. I clutched my cell phone even tighter. But then a funny thing happened. The fantasy shut off in my head almost as fast as it had turned on. It hit me I didn't want to flee on a jet plane. I pictured Josie in front of me, telling me this was what being present meant.

"I know," I said, letting go of the cell phone and bringing my hand out of my pocket. "I remember."

"You were the first person Frank started seeing after his divorce," Jonathan said, his voice solemn. "When he told me he was seeing you, I was so relieved. He did say it wasn't serious between the two of you, but still I felt good he was finally, you know, taking an interest in other guys. All I've wanted is for Frank to move on with his life."

"But Frank wants to move on with you," I said gently. "He thinks you're the way forward. I was never more than a placeholder to him."

"Is that what he told you?" Jonathan said, his voice going wobbly.

"He didn't have to tell me," I said. "Even when we were together, I always had the feeling he had someone else in mind. Then when I saw you guys together, you know, the time you invited us over for dinner, I could tell you and he shared a special bond."

"I don't know what to do," Jonathan said, sighing and looking anguished. "I've already tried to reason with him. But he won't listen."

"So then you've talked to Frank recently?" I said, and stiffened. I remembered the weekend of my fight with Frank, the weekend he'd disappeared.

"We met in Santa Cruz a couple weeks ago," Jonathan said, shifting from foot to foot. "A few days after we mailed out the wedding invitations. I had a feeling, um, Frank wouldn't be happy to receive it. So coward that I am, I went down to spend the weekend with my mother. Then Frank sent me a text message, something about renting a tux. I could tell how much he must've been hurting. I knew I couldn't hide from him. So I told him where I was."

So Frank had sauntered off to Santa Cruz that weekend. No wonder he hadn't told me where he was going. What a doofus I was.

"So, um, what'd you say to him?" I said, bracing myself for the worst.

"I said Marcus and I had talked things over and patched things up," Jonathan said in almost a frightened tone, as if he thought I'd scold him for his decision. "And that our relationship was worth saving."

Jonathan and Marcus shouting on the other side of the bedroom door came to me again. Was that Jonathan's idea of talking it over? Of saving their relationship? What was he trying to save?

"And?" I said, as if I couldn't already tell the answer by the sickly look on Jonathan's face.

"He said he wasn't sure if he could accept that," Jonathan said, his jaw tensing, his face coloring. "He said he loved me more than he'd ever loved anyone. Including Ethan. He said when we—when we spent the night together, you know, at his house—he said he thought his ordeal with Ethan had begun to make sense. As if he was meant to break up with Ethan, to make room for me. He said I was the most genuine person he'd ever met."

My mind flashed again to Frank and me in the kitchen. Frank looking me in the eye and opening up to me about Ethan. It sounded like Frank had done the same thing with Jonathan in Santa Cruz. Showed his heart, went for broke, told Jonathan everything that had been bottled up inside him. No longer the secretive Frank I'd come to know, but a man unafraid to let it all hang out. I wasn't the only one who'd recently broken free of a cast.

"Holy Mother," I said under my breath. "How'd you answer that?"

"I said I was sorry, but I couldn't leave Marcus." Jonathan gave me a defensive look. "We've been through so much together, Marcus and I. He's the one who keeps me sane when my family is driving me crazy. The one who drove me around the city last summer so I could take photos of neon martini glasses. Frank doesn't understand he's only been fantasizing about me all these years. He's never had to live with me. Marcus has. He knows how to make it work. I can't throw all that away, Julio. He's all I've ever known."

"And what did Frank say?" I wasn't sure if I wanted to know the answer.

"He said he'd never believe I was happy with Marcus," Jonathan said. "He said he could give me a better life than Marcus. It's like he has this ideal image of me, an image that isn't real. I wish there was a way I could make him understand. And that's why I thought—maybe—if you forgave him, he'd start putting things into perspective again."

I looked out onto the city, imagining Frank making his case to Jonathan on the Santa Cruz pier. Then my mind turned to Marcus. The way Marcus had threatened Jonathan to keep Jonathan from walking out. Frank had used the truth to win over Jonathan, while Marcus had used lies and bullying and manipulation. Frank was right. Jonathan would be better off, way better off, if he left Marcus for Frank. But Jonathan didn't have the guts to pull away from Marcus's orbit. Maybe Jonathan deserved Marcus after all.

"It's not a question of me forgiving him, Jonathan," I said, drawing my words out slowly. "The truth is Frank loves you. I can't change that."

"Then, um," Jonathan said, his voice going thin, "maybe can you consider, um, going to the wedding with him anyway? I'm afraid of what he might do if you don't."

"What do you think he'll do?" I said.

"Raise an objection," Jonathan said, his lips white. "Before we say our vows."

"Come off it," I said wincing. "If he couldn't talk you out of it in Santa Cruz, do you honestly think he'd try to do it at your wedding ceremony?"

"Still," Jonathan said, giving me a pleading look, "I'd feel better if someone was by his side."

Holy Virgin in heaven. So this was Jonathan's plan. What Jonathan had wanted to worm out of me. Why he'd sweated through my class. The sneaky bitch. Jonathan was less innocent than I'd thought. He really did deserve Marcus.

***

"I obviously don't know Frank as well as you do," I said slowly. "But I do know Frank's an adult. He's classy too. He never made a move with you until you gave him the signal. I think you standing in front of the JP with Marcus would be enough for Frank to keep his shit together."

"Is that what you think?" Jonathan said, raising his eyebrows. "You saw how mad he was at the engagement party in March. You should've seen him shout at Ethan later on in the kitchen that night. Frank may seem like a mild-mannered guy, but when he's mad, he's frightening."

My scar felt cold. I licked my lips. In my head a blob of Genevieve's pistachio-hazelnut ice cream hummed across the kitchen and splashed against the kitchen wall. Yes, Jonathan, I think I had an idea of what Frank could be like when he was mad. But I also remembered how he'd cleaned up the mess afterwards. He'd apologized too. Jonathan had to know Frank never lost his cool unless he'd been blindsided. Frank would never go to Jonathan's wedding on purpose to make a scene.

"Frank's a class act," I said, my cane wobbling under my grip. "He'd never ruin your wedding."

"I wish I could be sure," Jonathan said shaking his head, his eyes on the ground.

I clenched my teeth. Okay, Jonathan was turning into as much of a jerk as the piece of work he was engaged to. Breathe, Julio, breathe. There had to be a way to stay out of this cesspool.

"Then can't you, like, tell Frank he's out of the wedding?" I heard the impatience in my tone. "Don't you have your brother you can still ask?"

"I can't ask my brother," Jonathan said in a half-groan. "If there's anyone in the world more likely than Frank to cause a scene at my wedding, it's my brother Patrick."

"Then blow off having a best man altogether," I said, growing even more annoyed at Jonathan and his spinelessness. "This is your wedding. Who says you have to have a best man?"

"Because Marcus's father is Marcus's best man." A worried look came over Jonathan's face. "It would look funny if I don't have my own best man. And if Frank drops out of the wedding now…then Marcus will know why. I can't let that happen. Marcus already suspects I slept with Frank this summer. I swore to him on my life I hadn't. If Marcus finds out the truth, I can't say what he'll do to Frank."

I let out a long breath and leaned on my cane. Marcus's voice on the other side of the door, vowing to rip out Frank's heart, shuddered through me. Holy Mother. And Jonathan? He was almost as bad. He'd strung Frank along—used him—and then dumped him. Now he wanted Frank to show up as best man to his wedding and pretend like nothing had happened, or else Marcus might kick the crap out of him. This whole thing reeked.

"Sorry, Jonathan," I said in a careful voice that hid my anger. "I wouldn't make any difference by going to the wedding. I might even make things worse."

"It's only for one day, Julio." Jonathan's eyes darted over his shoulder as if he thought Marcus was spying on us from the roof of their house with binoculars. "All you'd have to do is stand by Frank's side and make sure he behaves himself. You could pretend to be his boyfriend for the day. Nothing more."

I looked away from him, holding in a groan. A pretend boyfriend for the day. Where had I heard that before? This must be the universe's way of pranking me, daring me to make the same decision that had sent this boulder of shit rolling downhill in the first place.

"I don't like pretending," I said, feeling like a fraud. "Authenticity is what I teach, Jonathan. What you're asking me to do…goes against everything I believe in."

"But what about compassion?" Jonathan said, his voice almost like a child's. "Compassion was what you taught this morning too, wasn't it? Maybe this is one way you can show compassion for Frank. He needs your compassion, Julio. He deserves your compassion."

I looked up at the sky, shaking my head. The sun had burned away the clouds by now, leaving a clear, bluish-white sky. I pictured Frank at the house. The frustration he must be feeling right now for losing Jonathan to a lesser man. What a coward Jonathan was for sticking with Marcus over him. But hadn't I made the same choice? Pretended to be Frank's boyfriend, while sleeping with Marcus for real? Didn't I owe Frank something for the wrong I'd done him too?

"It's a five-minute ceremony at City Hall," Jonathan said, apparently taking courage from my silence. "A big party at the house afterwards. It's the ceremony I'm worried about. The rest should be easy."

I looked at Jonathan and let out a sigh. Such a beautiful boyish face. He must've been a cutie when Frank had first laid eyes on him in Santa Cruz. The sort of face Frank might risk everything for. But Jonathan wasn't worth it. No man was. Still, if I could help Frank stop clinging to the fantasy of Jonathan, then, maybe, I could put this episode of my life behind me.

"I suppose it couldn't hurt if I went," I said. "I do care about Frank, even though, you know—we're not together."

"Then you'll come?" Jonathan said, his eyes brightening.

"I have to convince Frank to take me," I said. "No guarantees there."

"I'm sure you'll think of something," Jonathan said with relief in his tone, breaking into a smile. "I know you can. Thanks, Julio."

"Sure thing," I said, realizing I had no choice but to go through with it now. But how to tell Frank without letting on that Jonathan and I had talked?

***

I found Frank on his hands and knees in the front garden. He was too absorbed in what he was doing to look up. For the first time I saw how graceful the succulents along the side of the house looked. Maybe this was why he struggled to maintain this huge house, for the sake of tending these plants. That Frank would strive to make something grow here—at a house where his own husband had cheated on him—spoke volumes about his character. His desire to persist. How Jonathan had managed to look Frank in the eye and refuse him, I had no idea.

I slipped inside the house, not wanting to make Frank self-conscious at the sight of me. Upstairs in my room I dug out my pink prom tuxedo from the closet. I'd lied to Frank about it being four sizes too big. I'd had it altered a couple years ago to wear to a Halloween party as part of a lion tamer costume, with the guy I was seeing in the costume of a submissive lion. Could the suit help me tame the wedding? I sure as hell hoped it would. The problem was, Frank was no submissive lion. He wasn't an idiot, either. If I wanted to pull this off, I'd have to find a way to outsmart him.

Could I ask him flat out to take me to the wedding? Say I'd changed my mind about going? Nah, he'd only ask questions. Maybe surprise Frank at City Hall on the day of the wedding? Pretend I'd been planning to go all along? No, he'd have enough stress on the wedding day. Still, I liked the idea of surprising him. The less time Frank had to think, the less time he'd have to figure out what I was up to.

Then it hit me. I'd catch Frank on his way out the door to the wedding. I'd clear my schedule, park myself near the door at around the time he'd have to leave for City Hall, and then offer to go with him, pretending like I had nothing better to do. Could I pull that off? It would be risky to leave it to the last minute. But that seemed like my best shot. Okay, I had a plan. I'd do it not for Jonathan, but for Frank. Poor guy. He really didn't deserve to go through that horror-show wedding alone.

15

LAST-MINUTE JITTERS

The summer days melted like ice floes in my dream-ocean, inching ever closer to Jonathan's wedding day. I imagined frigid water rising above my knees, hips, shoulders. Then boom—the day was here. My eyes snapped open in the morning at 7:28, two minutes before my alarm clock was set to ring.

Sunshine streamed into the bedroom. The room's close air promised a hot October day. Julio was already making noises downstairs. He was up earlier than I would've thought for a Friday morning. Massage clients must be coming first thing. Good. The more appointments Julio had, the better chance I could slip out of the house without him seeing me.

Julio's first client rang the doorbell at nine o'clock. I slipped out of bed, went downstairs, made some coffee and a bagel, and brought everything up to my room. I played three concurrent games of online chess while I ate. My plan was leave the house no later than eleven thirty. Julio would probably leave the house before then for lunch. I'd still have plenty of time to make it to City Hall for the ceremony at three.

Eleven o'clock came. Julio was still working on a client. Around eleven twenty I made a ham and cheese sandwich and brought it upstairs. Took a quick shower. The tux came out of the closet at twenty-five minutes to noon. I shrugged on the shirt and realized the shirt required cufflinks. Another irritant.

I rooted through my sock drawer and disinterred the box that held my one pair of cufflinks. They were sterling silver squares my dad had given me at my high school graduation, telling me in his deep bass voice that cufflinks were the *sine qua non* of a true gentleman. The last time I'd worn them was at my own wedding. Like the last time, I had no trouble fastening the right cufflink, but putting on the left cufflink proved impossible. Ethan had helped me out then. Today I had nobody. The bedside clock read 11:46. This cufflink was going to make me late.

I tucked the wrapped gift under my arm and went downstairs. If I left for City Hall right now, I could show up early and have someone in the county clerk's office help me with the cufflink. Not ideal, but at least the job would be done before the wedding party arrived.

The sound of a spoon scraping against a bowl stopped me at the bottom of the stairwell. Julio was in the kitchen? What the heck? Was he planning to leave the house at all on this golden October day? Worse, my car keys lay in their usual spot in one of the kitchen drawers. I'd meant to bring them up with me earlier. My mother came to mind, shaking her head. No choice now but to reveal myself to Julio in my suit. At least he could help with the cufflink.

***

The spoon slipped from Julio's fingers and clattered into his bowl of lentils as soon as I stepped into the kitchen. I set the wedding gift on the counter and walked up to him without looking him in the eye. Even so, the impressed look on Julio's face was impossible to miss.

"Would you mind helping me with this?" I said, holding out the cufflink.

"Uh," Julio said gaping, pushing the bowl away. "No problem."

I pulled out a chair, plopped down across the table from him, and laid my wrist palm up on the table. My eyes swept the kitchen, looking anywhere than at Julio working on my cufflink. His hands were soft and warm.

"There," Julio said in a pleased voice. He gave the fastened cufflink a little pat.

"Thanks." I drew my hand away from him and held up my wrist, the cufflink cinched in place. My palm felt warm in the spot where he'd touched it.

"I hope I did that right," Julio said.

"Nope, it's good," I said, and gave him a quick smile. "Thanks again."

I felt his large dark eyes on me as I pulled myself up from the chair and went over to the counter to collect the wedding gift. Julio was standing up when I turned around again, looking at me up and down. He was wearing his usual massage therapist's outfit, tight black pants and a tight black T-shirt, his nipple ring as pronounced as ever. My eyes darted away from him.

"You look amazing," Julio said. His voice was simple and direct.

"Thanks," I said, glancing down as if I were noticing the tuxedo only now. I adjusted the gift under my arm and headed for the back door.

"So, um," Julio said, stopping me from leaving, "today's the day, huh? Marcus and Jonathan's wedding?"

"Yep," I said.

"I could go with you if you want," Julio said in a half-tentative, half-eager tone.

I let go of the doorknob and turned all the way around to look at him. Julio's smile broadened. Something shifted inside me, a sense that Julio's offer sounded less spontaneous than he'd wanted it to seem.

"You're not serious," I said, forcing a little laugh.

"It's a gorgeous day for a wedding," Julio said. He glanced over at the drawn blinds above the sink, glowing white in the sun. "And look at you in your tux. You don't want to face the universe alone dressed like that, do you?"

"That's nice of you," I said half-turning. "But I'm already running late."

"I can be ready in five minutes flat," Julio said.

"Five minutes?" I said staring at him. "How? Do you even have anything to wear?"

"My old prom tux," Julio said with a satisfied look. "The pink one."

"I thought you said that tux didn't fit you," I said, my eyes narrowing.

"I thought so too," Julio said. "But I tried it on for kicks the other day. Guess what? It fits perfectly."

"But—don't you have massage clients coming this afternoon?" I said.

"Not today," Julio said grinning, sliding his hands in his pockets and rocking on his heels. "Business has been so good, I thought I'd start the weekend early."

I set the gift on the table and looked hard at Julio. His face was clean-shaven. He'd had a recent haircut too, with the same square sideburns he'd sported the night of our first dinner at Jonathan and Marcus's house. A prom tux that fit, no massage clients, a fresh haircut, a shave. I visualized Julio writing out one of his lists, a series of tasks to cross off before parking himself in a kitchen chair and pretending he'd forgotten that today was Jonathan's wedding.

"Nice haircut," I said, in the pleasant but cutting tone I often used on students I knew were lying to me.

"Um, thanks," Julio said, putting a hand to the nape of his neck. "I could probably grow it out longer, but I can't stand the way it itches around my ears."

"And that's lucky about your prom tux," I said. "What made you try it on the other day? A sudden urge to relive high school?"

"I don't know, I felt like it," Julio said. He let out a nervous laugh.

"You were planning this all along," I said coldly, dropping all pretenses. "Weren't you? You were waiting here on purpose to catch me on my way out the door."

"Hey, hey, now that's not true," Julio said, holding out his palms. "I only thought you might want some company. You know, at Marcus and Jonathan's wedding."

"You're lying to me," I said, my heart beating faster. "Someone put you up to this. Who was it? Marcus?"

"No, not Marcus," Julio said, and he let out a long breath. "Jonathan. He showed up at the yoga studio one morning. Told me all about your trip to Santa Cruz."

"And he talked you into pulling this stunt?" I said, my jaw going slack.

"He wants you to be happy." Julio took a sharp intake of breath and glanced away from me.

"My God," I said, my voice low and shocked. "Jonathan wants you to keep an eye on me today. He thinks I'm planning to ruin the wedding."

"You're not, are you?" Julio said with a tense look.

"I'd never do anything like that," I said, hoping I sounded as offended as I felt. "And I don't need a chaperone."

"Of course you don't." Julio's voice hovered between placating and worried. "But I don't like the idea of you going by yourself. I don't mind, Frank. I can pretend to be your boyfriend for one more day."

"I don't need a pretend boyfriend today," I said, a lump growing in my throat. "I'm tired of pretending."

I turned to pick up the gift, but a constriction in my chest made me reach for my throat with one hand and the back of a kitchen chair with another. The next thing I knew, Julio was standing behind me, draping his arm around my shoulder. My mind traveled to the last time he'd laid a hand on me, at Marcus and Jonathan's front door on the night of that first dinner. For someone who could be such an airhead, Julio knew the meaning of an act of kindness.

"What if we didn't pretend?" Julio said in a low voice in my ear. "What if we made it real?"

What was Julio talking about? Make what real? I looked at him. He returned the look with an intensity I hadn't seen in a man's eyes for a long time. I had barely time to realize what Julio meant to do when he put a hand on my cheek, leaned in, and planted his lips on mine.

This couldn't be happening. A warped fantasy, a dream. I imagined watching this scene from a distance, the frozen dream-ocean melting and inching above our knees, hips, shoulders. Except this wasn't a dream. Ice wasn't cracking beneath my feet. No. This was my kitchen. The sunshine blazed in. And here I stood in a thousand-dollar tux, kissing a yoga instructor who happened to be my roommate.

***

I pushed Julio away from me and turned from him, wiping my swollen lips with the back of my hand. As Julio would say, that kiss was amazing. Too amazing to be true, perhaps. All Julio had proved was his prowess as a kisser. His precious lies hadn't succeeded into letting me take him to the wedding, so he'd resorted to kissing me instead. No doubt Julio had pulled that on countless men before. I knew when I was being patronized.

"I don't need this," I said between my teeth.

"You don't need what?" Julio said between hard breaths.

"Your pity!" I said, rounding on him.

"That wasn't pity," Julio said, a shocked look on his face. "That was, um, I don't know. But I think you're right about Jonathan. He's about to make the worst mistake of his life today. Choosing Marcus over you. You're ten times the man Marcus is. Or ever will be. Take it from me, Frank. I've been with Marcus. I know."

The buzzing of my phone against my thigh stopped me from answering him. I half-turned and pried my phone from out of my front pocket. Jonathan's name and face glowed on the screen. A phone call, not a text. What could Jonathan want now? Did he think I was going to be late? I put the phone to my ear, prepared to tell him I'd be there. But in my heart of hearts I knew I'd rather stay here with Julio.

***

"Frank, thank God you're there." Jonathan's voice on the other side of the line was high-pitched and panicky.

"What's wrong, Jonathan?" I said, looking Julio in the eye and making sure I'd said "Jonathan" nice and clear.

"Marcus has gone missing," Jonathan said. His voice was close to breaking.

"Missing?" I said, half-turning from Julio. "What do you mean, missing?"

"Missing as in we had a fight last night," Jonathan said in a desperate half-shout, "and he hasn't come home since. I've called, I've texted, he won't answer me. I have no idea where he is. Frank, what am I going to do?"

"Don't panic," I said, and looked at the digital clock on the stove. 12:26. "He can't stay missing forever."

The doorbell rang. I turned and traded looks with Julio. The horror-struck look on Julio's face told me he was thinking the same thing I was. Marcus wasn't missing. He was here, at my own front door.

"Frank?" Jonathan said. "Frank, are you still there?"

The doorbell rang again. Julio went to the window, raised the blinds a little, peered outside, then turned to face me, his face ashen, his hand at his heart. If I had any hope that it was someone else at the door, the look on Julio's face disabused it.

"Jonathan, Marcus is here," I said in a calm but firm tone, gazing into Julio's eyes. "He's ringing my doorbell now."

"He's what?" Jonathan said, his breath coming fast through the phone. "Oh, God. Oh, my God."

"And I think we can still make it to City Hall in time for the wedding," I said, talking over him. "Are you dressed?"

"Am I dressed?" Jonathan said, sounding flabbergasted. "Of course I'm not dressed. I'm not going to City Hall today. And you can't open the door for him."

"Why not?" I said, leaning against the counter for support. "The fight you had last night—it wasn't about me, was it?"

"Don't open the door, Frank," Jonathan said, his tone half-begging.

Another ring of the doorbell. A pounding at the door. Julio jumped, then turned and looked at me. But my gaze had strayed above Julio's shoulder to the glowing white blinds above the sink. I visualized my Lewis chess pieces against the blinds, the position treacherous but not impossible to navigate. Would I be doing what I planned to do now, had Julio not kissed me a couple of minutes ago? I wanted to think I would.

"Take it from someone who's been through this," I said, maintaining my tone of reason. "This is nothing but last-minute wedding jitters. There's still plenty of time for Marcus to make it to City Hall. So be dressed and ready to meet us at the bottom of the main staircase. The same goes for your family. Marcus's family too. Everything's going to be all right, okay? I'll see you at City Hall."

***

Another blast of the doorbell. Julio stood between me and the doorway to the dining room as if to block my path. The look on his face was one of alarm. A shiver went through me. I was more determined than ever to face my enemy head-on.

"I'm calling 911," Julio said, reaching for his phone on the counter.

"No, you're not," I said, making to walk around him to the doorway to the dining room. "I'm letting Marcus in."

"You can't," Julio said, putting his hands on my shoulders. "I once heard Marcus say if he ever found out you and Jonathan had slept together, he'd—he'd rip your heart out."

"Julio," I said, putting my hands around his waist, "Marcus isn't ripping out anyone's heart today. I'm taking him to City Hall to marry Jonathan."

"You can't open the door," Julio said, shaking his head. "I won't let you."

"I'll be fine," I said. "I promise. Now go upstairs and put on that pink suit of yours."

"You want me to leave you down here alone with him?" Julio said, aghast. "Forget it."

"There's no time," I said.

A set look came over Julio's face. The doorbell rang again. Then Julio stepped away from me and turned out his forearm to reveal a long, crescent-shaped scar. It was smooth and shiny, slightly raised from his tawny skin like an embossment. I'd noticed Julio's scar before, but never this close. Scary-looking, but beautiful in its way. Kind of like how this whole crazy morning was playing out.

"You see this?" Julio said, his voice low. "A guy twice my size tried to knife me in high school. I charged and knocked him to the ground. Marcus knows I can do the same thing to him. So the second you think you need help, you give me a holler. I'll come down here and pin that ratfucker down so you can kick the shit right out of him."

"It won't come to that," I said, my face flushing.

Who was this man, this roommate I called Julio? First he's locking lips me, now he's offering to help me in a brawl? And his language was nothing my mother would ever approve of. She'd never approve of a nipple ring either. But she'd approve of me opening the door to Marcus. She'd see Marcus as a sort of chess piece, and my situation as a matter of moving the piece from my front door to City Hall. It wouldn't be easy. But it could be done.

***

Julio gave me one last lingering look and left the kitchen. Marcus pounded at the door. Panic swept through me. Oh God, what was I doing? What was I thinking? Then I thought of Julio's scar and his promise. The fierce way he swore. Yes. I could do this.

"Coming," I called out in a clear voice, loud enough for Julio to hear me from upstairs.

The house fell silent. I walked through the dining room to the front door, taking each step slowly and deliberately. My lips were still warm from Julio's lips. This was my house, my chessboard. I promised myself I wouldn't forget that.

"Frank, let me in," Marcus said, his voice hard and forceful through the oaken door. "I can hear you in there."

I hooked the chain to the door before unbolting it and opening it a crack. Marcus's face was pale and pinched, the bags under his eyes tinged brownish-purple, his arms folded in as if he were freezing in the scorching white heat. His yellow track jacket and loose gray sweatpants looked like they'd been slept in. His hair was freshly shorn and highlighted, no doubt for the wedding, but the rest of him looked ready to explode at the nudge of a finger. This was a Marcus I'd never seen before, a Marcus disfigured and ravaged by jealousy. As much as I loathed him, I couldn't help feeling partially responsible.

"Marcus," I said in a flat tone, looking at him up and down, "what brings you here?"

"I need to talk to you," Marcus said.

"We're supposed to be at City Hall in an hour and a half," I said, using my authoritative teacher's voice.

"I need to talk to you first."

"What about?" I said. I tightened the grip on the doorknob.

"Let me in and I'll tell you."

I took in a breath and opened the door. Marcus stopped short and stared at me in the tux his father had selected for me. Perhaps it was dawning on him that only one of us was dressed for this battle. I threw back my shoulders and stepped aside to let him in.

Marcus moved into the living room before I had a chance to shut the door. I went to the doorway and watched him. He stood in the middle of the room with his hands on his hips, taking in the piano, the couch, the grandfather clock. I knew he was trying to make me feel like the house belonged to him, not to me. It really was pathetic, to witness his feeble attempt to claim territory—my territory—in that grimy yellow track suit, with those ridiculous blond highlights in his hair.

"Is he here?" Marcus said, turning to face me with bloodshot eyes.

"Is who here, Marcus?" I said coldly. "Julio?"

"Not Julio," Marcus said. A look of sheer hatred flickered in his red eyes. "Jonathan."

"Jonathan?" I said. "What would Jonathan be doing here?"

"You tell me, Frank," Marcus said sarcastically. "Maybe it's because he has a tendency to come crying to you when he and I have a blowout."

"Jonathan's the one looking for you," I said. "He called me right before you rang the doorbell. Do you think I'd be wearing this tux if he was here? Honestly, Marcus, if you're looking for Jonathan, maybe you should look for him at home."

"I didn't come here looking for him," Marcus said, his eyes fixed on me. "I only wanted to make sure he wasn't here. The one I came for is you."

"Here I am," I said, squaring my shoulders. "Now what do you want?"

Julio had to be listening to all this. He was probably ready to rush into the living room at any moment. No, Frank. No. You don't need knight's odds to beat Marcus. My heart pounded. I didn't dare blink.

"So did you do it?" Marcus said in a low, murderous tone.

"Do what?" I gave Marcus a blank stare.

"What you've wanted to do for years," Marcus said, his eyes flashing.

"It's a quarter to one," I said in an irritated voice, throwing a look at the grandfather clock. "You're about to miss your own wedding."

"Then tell me what I need to know." Marcus's mouth was a grim, flat line. "Did Jonathan finally give you what you've been after all this time?"

Marcus looked like he wanted to beat me to a pulp. And would beat Julio to a pulp too, once he found Julio hiding upstairs. My body trembled for both myself and Julio.

"And if I said yes?" I said, working up a challenge in my tone.

"So then you did do it," Marcus said, his face going red. "You and your high and mighty notions of fidelity. But it didn't work. Jonathan didn't leave me for you. And you know why? I'm the one who knows him. I'm the one who's been taking care of him all these years."

"Right, taking care of him," I said, a thrill running through me like an electric pulse. "The way you treat him, he'd be better off with anyone but you."

Marcus bared his teeth and lunged. Two hundred pounds of solid muscle hurtling my way. I let out a cry and flung out my hands to stop this screaming locomotive. My hands locked with his. My teeth clenched. I poured all my strength into my hands and pushed against Marcus, looking into his bloodshot eyes. Was I going to let him win? Was I? I pushed against him even harder. Then I remembered what Julio had said in the kitchen earlier. I was ten times the man Marcus was. Ten times. I shoved Marcus so hard away from me that he fell to the floor on his rear. He could've been a life-size enemy king piece, tipped on its side in defeat. I stood over him like the victor I was, breathing hard.

"Who the fuck do you think you are," I shouted at him, "coming in here and pushing me around? This is my house, Marcus. Mine. You come after me again, and I'll bash your fucking face in. Now pick your sorry ass up and pull yourself the fuck together."

Marcus scrambled on his rear away from me, not taking his eyes off me, and made his way onto the couch. His face was as white as his eyes were red. He looked small, weak, insignificant. Meanwhile, my ribcage vibrated from what I'd said. In ten seconds I'd dropped more f-bombs than I'd dropped in the past ten years. But I felt rejuvenated. Euphoric, even. Swearing was way better therapy than anti-anxiety pills. I'd learned something new from Julio.

"You want to know about me and Jonathan?" I said, planting my hands on my hips. "Two hours before your fucking wedding, do you really want to hear the truth?"

"Jonathan wouldn't tell me last night," Marcus said, his upper lip curled. "You might as well tell me now."

"Fine," I said, bracing myself in case Marcus charged at me again. "Yes. Yes, I slept with Jonathan this summer. He came here, and I slept with him. I have you to thank for it."

"Me?" Marcus said.

"Yes, you," I said in disgust. "Jonathan came to me because you were screwing around on him. And who were you screwing around with this summer? Would you care to enlighten me?"

Marcus leaned back on the couch and folded his arms, turning his head away from me and sticking out his jaw. His eyes roamed the room like a petulant teenager. I may've physically knocked him to the floor a couple minutes ago, but that was nothing compared to what I planned to pummel him with now.

"With Julio," I said, leaning toward him. "Isn't that right? Upstairs in his bedroom, in this very house?"

"Julio said you and he weren't serious," Marcus said. He threw me a contemptuous, sideways look.

"I don't care what he said," I said sourly. "What I care about is why you did it. Of all the guys you could've gone after, you chose Julio. Don't try to tell me it was his idea to go after you. No, Marcus, this was your project, your adventure. Why did you do it? Was it for the pleasure of sleeping with Julio in my own house? Or were you jealous I had what you wanted?"

"Right, jealous of you," Marcus said, letting out a snort and rising from the couch. "Who could be jealous of you? You're a high school math teacher with no husband and an unfinished Ph.D. You're a nothing."

"And you're worse than nothing, you deranged monster," I shot back. "Let me ask you this. Why did you confront Jonathan with this last night? Why not sooner? No, don't answer. I already know. Because you're not man enough to commit yourself to him. You're bailing at the last second and using me as an escape hatch. Fine. Blame me all you want. But we both know the truth. You can call me a nothing all you want to. I'd sooner be nothing than a coward."

"I hate your guts," Marcus said, jabbing his finger at me, "and I never want to see you again."

Marcus crossed the room and went into the front hallway, not looking at me as he stalked past. I followed him. He fumbled to unbolt and open the door. He clearly had no idea where he planned to go next. My heart throbbed with a surprising pang of compassion for him. I knew what it felt like to be cheated on, after all. My thoughts flew to Jonathan, waiting for Marcus in his tux at San Francisco City Hall. For Jonathan's sake, I knew I had to say something to keep Marcus from walking out of here.

"And you want to know what the kicker is?" I called out. "Julio was never my boyfriend."

Marcus froze in the doorway. Then he turned and stepped into the house with a look of total disbelief. I felt a lightness in my chest, a sense that the lie that had gripped me all these months was about to loosen its talons and fly away. The lie had tangled up all our lives long enough.

"What did you say?" Marcus said, gaping.

"Julio was never my boyfriend." I felt a childish pleasure delivering this news. "We've been faking it all along."

"You're kidding," Marcus said with a slight shake of his head.

"You were such a smug little prick that day at the Ferry Building," I said, feeling a jolt at the use of the word *prick*. "The smug look on your face when you asked if I was seeing someone new. So I made up that story. Julio wasn't kidding when he told you he and I weren't serious."

"Good God," Marcus said, his expression a mixture of wonder and contempt. "So you're a liar too. You're a nothing and pathetic besides."

"And you're not pathetic?" I said, pointing a finger at him. "You thought Julio was my boyfriend, so you went chasing after him. If you hadn't gone running after Julio, Jonathan would never have come running to me. Now look at you, a jealous wreck two hours before your own wedding. This whole thing is your fault, your doing. If you'd learned to be happy with Jonathan, none of this would've happened."

"I never wanted Jonathan to pick you as his best man," Marcus said, a sullen look on his face. "I knew you'd be trouble."

"I wasn't the trouble, Marcus," I said, glowering at him. "You were. You might as well have driven Jonathan over here and delivered him to me yourself. I have to wonder if that's what you'd wanted all along. If you can't go through with the wedding, then don't go through with it. But don't do it by picking fights with Jonathan and pinning the blame on me."

The grandfather clock chimed one o'clock. Marcus looked over my shoulder at the clock, then gave me a shamefaced look. For all his power, Marcus was no better equipped to handle life's challenges than a child. He certainly wasn't equipped to handle what I'd said to him. What would he do now?

"I only wanted to know," Marcus muttered, breathing hard through his teeth. "Jonathan wouldn't tell me. He never tells me anything."

"Now you know," I said, lowering my voice. "He's still a great guy. You couldn't hope for better. You know that as well as I do. Come on, Marcus. Is this wedding on or not?"

Marcus looked down at his feet, a set look on his face, his jaw jutting out. Exhilaration rushed through me. Had I saved this wedding after all?

"I want to marry Jonathan," Marcus said, looking up at me. "Yes, I do. But I can't go through with it unless you promise me one thing."

"I'm listening," I said.

"You can't see Jonathan again," Marcus said in a grave tone. "For as long as you live."

I looked at him. So this would be our deal, the concession I'd have to make to salvage this wedding. My first days with Jonathan in Santa Cruz came to me, one image after another. Sitting in a circle at the youth group. Hanging out at the Santa Cruz pier. Winning him the rabbit at the carnival. My oldest and closest friend.

Then my mind traveled upstairs to Julio. How warm his lips had felt against mine. That kiss wasn't nearly enough to make me forget twenty years of friendship with Jonathan, but it had given me a glimpse of my future. A new life awaited me after today's wedding. As for Jonathan—he was never mine to begin with. If I finally let Jonathan go, then maybe I could feel free myself.

"Okay," I said, speaking slowly. "But you have to promise me something in return."

"What?" Marcus said warily.

"No more fooling around," I said, my voice low and unyielding. "If I find out you've cheated on Jonathan even once, I'm moving in on him. I'll make him forget you so fast, he won't even remember your name. So what do you say, Marcus? Do we have a deal?"

I held out my hand. Marcus looked at the hand stonefaced, then gripped it as if he meant to crush it. I gripped right back, looking Marcus in the eye, thankful my dad had taught me how to do a proper handshake when I was thirteen. My last deal with Marcus. I could only hope he'd honor it.

***

The clock chimed a quarter past one. If we hurried we could still make the appointment with the JP. I talked Marcus into giving me his car keys—deeming him too upset to drive—and then shooed him out of the house, saying I'd be out in five minutes. Relief washed over me as soon as I shut the door. The enemy had retreated, and I was still in one piece.

I went into the kitchen and collected my cell phone and the wedding gift. Then Julio appeared in the kitchen doorway in his old prom suit. He hadn't been exaggerating when he'd said the tux was pink. He looked like a giant stick of cotton candy—or should I say like a flamingo or some rare exotic bird, a species unto himself. Yet Julio managed to pull the look off. He radiated a zany confidence I wished I had myself sometimes. I couldn't help smiling.

"Frank," he said, coming up and putting his arms around me. "Thank the Holy Virgin you're all right."

"You heard all that?" I said, letting my body go weak against his.

"Enough of it," Julio said. He looked and sounded distressed. His Spanish accent was stronger than usual. "I was this close to coming down. But then I heard you shouting at Marcus. I could tell you owned him. You were amazing."

"I felt you with me," I said, and laid my hand on his cheek. "You gave me the courage to fight him."

"When we come home tonight," Julio said, his tone low and serious, "we're celebrating."

"But we're roommates," I managed to stammer out. "You pay me rent, for God's sake. Wouldn't that be a mistake?"

"We've been making mistakes all year long," Julio said, a wicked gleam in his eye. "What's one more?"

I pulled him close and kissed him. If only I could take him upstairs now, instead of wasting my time playing the part of Jonathan's best man. Who said a math teacher couldn't be the lover of a man with a nipple ring?

16

TOAST

I followed Frank out the front door with Frank's wedding gift wedged in the crook of my arm. Frank marched straight toward Marcus's black Beemer, not looking left or right. No time to stop and catch my breath. Fine by me. So long as I kept moving, I wouldn't have to worry about answering the questions buzzing in my head. This morning with Frank had turned me upside down.

I stopped cold at the sight of Marcus leaning against his car, arms crossed and shoulders hunched. His eyes were hidden behind those ridiculous gold-tinted aviator glasses. Between the sunglasses and the faded yellow track jacket and those screaming blond highlights, he looked like a piece of tarnished gold. Fool's gold. This was the guy I used to brag about to Genevieve? The guy I'd slept with this summer?

Frank aimed Marcus's keys at the car without breaking his stride or looking at Marcus, and unlocked it. Marcus opened the passenger door and climbed in, then gave the door a good slam to close it. Frank sat down behind the steering wheel, while I settled into the back seat with the gift. I never thought I'd see the inside of this car again, let alone with Frank behind the wheel. To look at the two of them, Frank in the tux, Marcus in those sweat clothes, I would've thought it was Frank, not Marcus, on his way to marry Jonathan.

On the freeway Frank weaved through heavy traffic, one hand gripping the wheel, the other hand gripping the stick shift like he was manning the Space Shuttle. Meanwhile Marcus pushed in his sunglasses and slouched in his seat like a kid in a squad car on his way to juvie. I shoved my hand into my pocket for my cell phone, then realized I'd left it on my bureau. Eh, good place for it.

***

We reached Marcus's house at a couple minutes past two. Frank pulled up behind one of two plain white minivans filling up the driveway. Were those moving vans? What, did Jonathan find the good sense to take a hike than marry his no-good boyfriend? I felt a lift in my heart.

"The caterers," Marcus said in a half-groan. "I forgot about them."

"Good." Frank said. He pulled up behind one of the vans. "You think you can change and be down here in twenty minutes?"

"Do I have a choice?" Marcus said.

"Now you listen." Frank glared at Marcus. "You can waste your time making snide remarks, or you can go upstairs and make yourself presentable. This is your wedding."

Marcus threw him a scowl, opened the door, and hauled himself out of the car, again slamming the door behind him. This had to be killing him, the way Frank was bossing him around. But what could he do?

We watched Marcus plod up the stairs and into the house. Frank pulled out his phone and started texting. In a few minutes Marcus plodded down the stairs in his tux. He settled into the passenger seat and slammed his door shut. His untied bow tie was wrapped around his hand like a bandage. He'd shaved, thank the Holy Mother. But his eyes were still bloodshot, and his tightly pressed lips plainly showed how pissed off he was. He looked like he was on his way to his criminal sentencing, not his own freaking wedding.

"You spoke with Jonathan?" Frank said, reaching for the key in the ignition.

"Ten minutes ago." Marcus lowered the car's sun visor and draped the bow tie around his neck. "The whole family's at City Hall. Here, take this—it's my wedding ring. Jonathan forgot it."

Marcus pulled a small white box from the inside of his tux jacket and flung it onto Frank's lap. Then he leaned toward the visor mirror and worked on his tie while Frank drove. The great gilded dome of

City Hall loomed in front of us. The clock on the dash read seven to three. We'd be a few minutes late, but no big deal. So Frank had made the wedding happen. I wondered if my kiss had something to do with it.

***

We trudged up the stairs and into City Hall. Jonathan and the two families were waiting in the huge marble-floored area on the other side of the metal detectors. Jonathan and his Mami and a rat-faced guy who was probably Jonathan's brother, plus Marcus's Papi and dishy step-Mami and what was probably Marcus's two brothers and their dishy wives. As soon as we made it through the metal detectors, Jonathan walked straight up to Marcus, put his arms around him, and kissed him. People around us—total strangers—stopped to notice the guy in the white tux and the guy in the black tux making out. Then everyone started applauding. What was I supposed to do, stand there with my hands in my pockets? So I started clapping too. Then the rest of the wedding party joined in, Jonathan's mother and brother, Marcus's father and brother and wives. Even Frank clapped for them. Holy Mother in heaven. We were rooting for an aircraft going down in flames.

Jonathan and Marcus exchanged their vows in the rotunda, at the top of the main staircase. The wedding itself couldn't have lasted longer than five minutes. Still, I could barely keep my lunch down, listening to Jonathan and Marcus repeat the justice's yip-yap about love and devotion and commitment. Frank handed Marcus's ring to Jonathan like he was supposed to, and then the JP pronounced Jonathan and Marcus lawfully wedded husbands. More kissing. More clapping. More barf.

***

All I wanted afterwards was to go straight home. Screw the reception. Frank could manage on his own. Frenching him at the house felt like it happened a hundred years ago. Better to stuff the whole incident into the drawer and pretend it never happened. I was sure Frank would want that as well.

The photographer took some pictures of the happy couple and their families, and then we walked out of City Hall, blinking in the sunshine. Jonathan and Marcus were holding hands. Passing cars honked their congratulations to us. Sacred Mother in heaven, couldn't these people give it a rest?

Frank went over to Marcus, exchanged a few words, and then handed Marcus the keys to his car. It looked like Marcus and Jonathan would be driving Jonathan's Mami and brother to the house, leaving us without a ride. Cool. My escape would be easier. I patted my front pocket for my cell phone, remembered I didn't have it, then slipped on my sunglasses, turning over in my mind the best way to tell Frank I wanted to bail on the reception.

"So what's the plan now?" I said to Frank once we were alone on the front steps of City Hall.

"The party at the house starts at five thirty," Frank said with a half-yawn. "I told Marcus and Jonathan we'd take Muni there."

"So, um, Frank," I said, my voice tense, "about what happened at the house earlier—"

"You don't have to say any more," Frank said looking embarrassed, holding up the palms of his hands. "It was scary back there. Stressful. We weren't thinking."

"So then you understand?" I asked in a hopeful tone.

"Of course I understand," Frank said, patting me on the shoulder. "And you don't have to come to the reception either. I think I can handle it from here."

"What?" I said startled. "Are you sure?"

"No, you've done enough," Frank said, shaking his head. "Both at the house and here at the wedding. I'm not sure I would've done—you know—what I did, if I didn't know you were upstairs. There's nothing left for you to do now. Besides Marcus will probably blab to everyone we aren't boyfriends. It'll look absurd, you showing up on my arm."

I pictured us in that huge living room, the snob crowd staring and snickering. I hadn't thought of it that way. My role as Frank's fake boyfriend was officially done with. I didn't like the idea of Frank facing the firing squad alone.

"How do you think Jonathan's going to take it," I said in an uncertain tone, "when he finds out you'd lied to him about me?"

"If I'm lucky, I won't have to." Frank yawned and stretched his arms toward the sun. "He's about to have more guests in his house than he had for his engagement party. I won't stay long. I'll probably leave after I give the toast."

"The toast?" I said, pulling off my sunglasses. "You're giving the toast?"

"Marcus asked me about it now, when I gave him the car keys," Frank said. "I asked him if he was sure, and he said yes. His father must be a real attention hog if Marcus trusts me to pull off that speech."

"What're you going to say?" I said, staring at him.

"I haven't the faintest idea," Frank said smiling, his tone light. "Something will come to me on the train ride over. It'll have to. Where are you going now? Home?"

"I guess," I said, putting a hand to my forehead. "I can at least walk with you to the station."

We walked across the plaza to the Civic Center station and took the down escalator. People walking by stared at our tuxes, but my mind was on Frank. Frank giving the toast without me there to support him didn't sit well with me. But it wasn't only that. Something else Frank had said had unsettled me. What?

"So I'll see you at the house tomorrow?" Frank said at the turnstiles.

"Tomorrow afternoon as usual," I said in a vague tone, my thoughts all cloudy. "I have my class to teach in the morning."

"Great," Frank said, and patted me one more time on the shoulder. "Thanks again for coming with me today. I don't think I could've done it without you."

He walked through the turnstile and down the stairs to the Muni platform that would take him to the Castro. Then I turned to walk toward the BART turnstiles that would take me to dull, boring Oakland. I fed my card into the turnstile and went into the BART station. Then, halfway down the escalator, I realized what Frank had said to unsettle me so much. Frank had said Marcus and Jonathan's house would be more crowded today than it had been for their engagement party. Who'd been waiting for Frank at the engagement party in March? Frank's ex. Which meant Frank's ex would be going to the wedding reception. Holy Mother. I couldn't let Frank walk into the same trap alone.

***

I turned and ran up the down escalator like a salmon swimming against the current. Through the BART turnstiles, over to the Muni turnstiles, and downstairs to the Muni platform. A Muni train roared into the station right as I made it down the stairs. My bad knee throbbed, but I ran and ran. In my head I heard Josie's voice telling me I'd make it if I put my mind to it. A huge crowd of commuters piled into the train on the far end of the platform. Frank had to be in the crowd somewhere. I thanked the Holy Virgin for making Muni such a shitty train system.

Everyone had boarded by the time I made it panting to the train. People looked at my pink suit, then at me. They could kiss my ass as far as I cared. Where was Frank? I made my way through the crowd, wondering what I'd do if he wasn't here. But there he was at the other end of the subway car, staring off into space. Thank the Holy Mother.

I swayed and wobbled my way through the crowd toward Frank, taking care not to put too much pressure on my leg. My knee throbbed even worse now. Six weeks of physical therapy down the drain. All worth it.

"Hey, you," I said gasping for breath, grabbing Frank's forearm and trying not to wince from the pain in my knee. "Going my way?"

"Julio," Frank said, his eyes widening. "What are you doing here?"

"I don't want you walking into that house alone," I said, dropping the flirty pretense from my voice. "Ethan's going to be there."

"Yes, I know," Frank said, wrinkling his eyebrows at me. "He was invited to the engagement party. I'm sure he'll be at the wedding reception."

"So then you know," I said, grasping the support pole with both hands as the train screeched into the next station. "I thought you'd forgotten."

"No, I didn't forget," Frank said, and then he let out a little laugh. "But it's nice of you to turn around and find me."

"So then you don't mind seeing Ethan alone today?" I said, remembering how violently Frank had freaked out the last time he'd laid eyes on his ex.

"I'm not jumping for joy about it," Frank said, shrugging and looking down at the floor with a thoughtful expression. "But Ethan was my husband. He once meant the world to me. I can't avoid him forever. And at least I know he'll be there."

"Okay," I said. I hung onto the pole as the train jolted us forward. "So, uh, it sounds like you have the situation under control. I might as well turn around and go home."

"Unless you'd like to come," Frank said, giving me a little smile.

"Are you sure?" I said.

"You came this far," Frank said, looking at me up and down, "Besides, where else are you going to go dressed in a pink tux? The circus? The circus is where I'm headed, at Frank and Jonathan's house."

I let out a laugh. What a doofus I was, rushing across the train station to save Frank. I'd forgotten Frank was the stronger one today. Way stronger than I'd given him credit for. Maybe even the strongest one all along.

***

I took it easy climbing the hill to Marcus and Jonathan's house, then up the steep flight of stairs to the front door. A young black-haired woman in a black waitress uniform opened the door for us. At the top of the stairs another waitress stood holding a tray of glasses of white wine. I begged off as usual, but then so did Frank. Huh. If there was anyone who deserved a stiff one today, it was him. Maybe he thought he'd need to stay stone sober to give the toast and stare down his ex-husband besides.

Jonathan and Marcus and their families were out on the balcony. My eye immediately landed on Marcus by the railing, looking onto the city in silence. If I didn't know better, I might almost feel drawn to the guy, all brooding and handsome in his tux. Of course I did know better. So I stood off to the side, well outside Marcus's orbit, and regarded Marcus with wiser eyes—Frank's eyes, maybe—and saw a tired-looking man who'd managed to stumble his way into middle age without knowing the first damned thing about himself.

Jonathan came straight up to us to give us both a hug. His tie was undone, his hair tousled. He wore a look of smiling relief. Marcus couldn't have told Jonathan about Frank and me yet. Or Jonathan didn't care even if he did know the truth.

We made our rounds of the rest of the family, Jonathan's Mami and brother, Marcus's Papi and step-Mami and their families. I was glad to watch Jonathan's Mami give Frank a warm clasp of the hand, and even the brother—Patrick I think his name was—had a couple nice words to say. Then, of course, there was Marcus's Papi and his runway model of a wife. I could picture her walking out on him one of these days, taking half of everything he owned. The way she looked, she could probably sell tickets to her divorce court hearings.

"I can still give the toast," Marcus's Papi said, turning to Frank. "If you don't want to."

"Dad, please," Marcus called over to us from the railing, annoyance in his voice.

"Come on, son, I'm only trying to help," Marcus's Papi said. "Your friend's had a busy day today."

"No, I'm feeling up for it," Frank said, giving Marcus's Papi a polite but bold smile. "In fact, it would be my pleasure."

"I didn't say it wouldn't be a pleasure," Marcus's Papi said, looking put off. "I'm only saying I can step in if you don't want to do it."

"But I do want to do it," Frank said, his smile broadening, looking at Marcus's Papi full in the face. "Marcus asked me to. This is his wedding day. If we can't give your son what he wants today, then when can we ever give him what he wants?"

The balcony went dead silent. The scar on my forearm zinged. Holy Mother. Frank crossing swords with Marcus earlier today must've given him the brass balls to stick it to Marcus's Papi now. Marcus's Papi clearly wasn't used to having it stuck to him. He looked at Frank as if he wanted to chuck him over the side of the balcony. Everyone stared at them. My own breath left me.

"I love your dress, Mrs. Butler," I said, feeling giddy, turning to Jonathan's Mami.

"Call me Emma," Jonathan's Mami said, downing the last of her white wine, "and thanks for noticing."

The doorbell rang faintly from inside the house. The first guests must be coming. I kept chatting with Jonathan's Mami, not daring to look over at Frank. I'd already put the brakes on going any farther with him. Still, the way he'd stood up to Marcus's Papi was as sexy as fuck. Way sexier than anything Marcus had ever done in yoga class. Or in my bedroom.

***

Jonathan and Marcus went into the house to greet their first guests. Frank and I hung out on the balcony with the rest of the family while the room inside filled up. Around five-thirty Frank turned to me and said he should probably go inside to give the toast. My scar was still zinging as I followed him into the house. I didn't understand why I was so nervous. It wasn't me giving the toast, after all. And who was standing right in the middle of the room? Ethan and his partner. Barf. Honestly, what did that other guy have over Frank?

A team of waiters and waitresses moved through the crowd with trays of empty champagne glasses. A few minutes later, another team of waiters and waitresses moved through the crowd with champagne bottles, filling everyone's glass. The biggest yoga class I ever taught was about sixty people. There had to be twice as many people in this room now. What would I say if I had to give this toast? And to Marcus and Jonathan besides? I closed my hand over my forearm, my scar going cold.

Frank stood in the middle of the room and tapped on his champagne glass with a spoon. A hush fell over the crowd. Marcus led Jonathan by the hand to stand near Frank. I stood a few feet away behind them, ready to hustle Frank out the door at the first sign of weirdness. In my head I heard Josie telling me to breathe. Still I held my breath.

"So let me tell you how I met Marcus Pierce," Frank said in a crystal-clear but confiding voice. "It was almost nineteen years ago, a Saturday night in July, at a dance club that no longer exists. I'd gone dancing there with my best friend Jonathan Butler, who'd come up from Santa Cruz to spend the weekend in my hole of an apartment."

The story came back to me. Marcus had given his side of the story the night they'd had us over. I leaned forward, anxious to hear how Frank would spin it.

"Jonathan and I had been standing by the dance floor," Frank went on, taking in the crowd with a smile, "and then I told him I needed to step to the restroom. I must've been in there for about three minutes. When I came out, what did I see? Jonathan dancing with a stranger, this tall good-looking guy from out of town. Marcus. I remember not thinking much of it at the time. A one-night stand at most."

Laughter rippled through the crowd. Frank's smile widened. But underneath the smile I sensed a tremor. My mind's eye saw how things must've played out that night. Frank had probably wanted Jonathan for himself, but couldn't work up the courage to say so. He'd gone to the restroom to pull himself together. Maybe practiced in the mirror what he wanted to say to Jonathan. Then walked out to find Marcus had beaten him to it. I traced my thumb against my scar.

"But that's not what happened, is it?" Frank said, smiling over at Marcus and Jonathan. "That night on the dance floor turned into a date, the date turned into two dates, then three dates, then four. Weeks turned into months. Months turned into years. Now here we all are, a lifetime of people they've come to know on their journey together, here to congratulate them on their special day."

Frank seemed to grow taller as he spoke. I could feel his prana touching everyone here. He owned the room, even Marcus and his Papi. But the crowd here couldn't understand—the way I understood—the meaning behind Frank's words. He was preparing to give up Jonathan. His quest was over.

"I didn't realize then what a privilege it was for me to be there that first night," Frank said, turning to face Marcus and Jonathan. "To witness the start of your journey together. To watch your love grow stronger and deeper with each passing year. To both of you, two of my oldest friends in the world, I wish you the happiest of marriages, and the best of all possible things."

A sigh and a cheer from the crowd. Everyone clinked and sipped. I watched Frank from halfway across the room, feeling stunned. It struck me that Frank had finally realized he hadn't been in love with Jonathan all these years. He'd been in love with the thought of what might've been. And instead of crying over it, he'd reshaped his history with Jonathan into that gorgeous toast. He was a true best man.

Frank put down his champagne glass and scanned the crowd. Who was Frank looking for? Then his eyes landed on me. A look of relief spread across his face. It was like he knew I was the only one who'd understood what he'd meant in that toast. Now he was heading my way, looking for approval. Holy Mother.

"You were amazing," I said to him, clasping his forearm.

"Thanks," Frank said, his voice shaking.

"But I have to ask," I said lowering my voice, moving in close to him. "You know those two are a train wreck. How could you have gone on about their love like that?"

"Because I need to believe they love each other," Frank said. "Everyone here needs to believe that. If people can't believe in love at a wedding, then when are they ever going to believe it? Life is scary enough as it is. We all have to believe in love. Don't we?"

He looked at me as if he was terrified I might tell him he was wrong. I looked at him and thought, who is this guy? Frank had walked in on his husband having sex with another man. He'd lost his closest friend to Marcus. If there was anyone in the world who'd be justified in never believing in love again, it was Frank. But not only did he still believe in love, he wanted other people to believe in love too. He made me almost want to believe in love myself. I fought the urge to kiss him.

"You're a good man, Frank Mercer," I said in a firm voice, squeezing his forearm. "And you did a good thing. Now how about we blow this joint."

"I need to talk to Ethan," Frank said, glancing around the room. "I want to apologize for how I'd acted at the engagement party."

"Okay," I said in a more serious tone.

"I won't be long, though," Frank said. "Do you mind waiting for a couple of minutes?"

"I'll be by the front stairs," I said, and left him so he could look for Ethan.

Yeesh. This felt like the last party, when I'd left Frank to fend for himself while I went and passed out those business cards. Was it right for me to let him out of my sight? Maybe I should make sure Frank didn't cause a scene. But that would mean I didn't trust Frank to do the right thing. And Frank had been doing and saying the right things all day.

***

I waited near the top of the front steps, smiling and nodding to total strangers. Five minutes went by. Then ten. I craned my neck for a glimpse of Frank. No spotting him in the thick crowd. A strong urge to use the bathroom came over me. I hadn't gone all day. Come on, Frank, where did you go?

I peered down the stairs and remembered the bedroom off the front hall. The bedroom I'd slept in, the weekend I'd spent with Marcus. No one here probably knew about the bathroom down there. Would it be okay if I sneaked down there to take a leak? Eh, why not.

I stole down the stairs to the bedroom. Someone was already in the bathroom, but at least there wasn't a line. I took in the bedspread, the framed picture of the Eiffel Tower on the wall. The tulips were gone, of course, but the plain glass vase that had held them still sat on the bureau. I never would've guessed that the next time I'd step into this room would be on Marcus and Jonathan's wedding day.

The toilet flushed, the door opened, and out came Marcus, his bow tie still tied. We stared at each other, frozen. He looked as blown away as I was that the two of us had found ourselves alone in this very bedroom again.

"Hey," he said, his voice stiff.

"Hey," I answered.

"Having a good time?" Marcus said, giving me a tight half-smile.

"A blast," I said, darting my eyes over his shoulders at the bathroom. "Actually Frank and I were thinking of leaving."

"But it's early," Marcus said, wrinkling his brow. "We're about to serve the food."

"Frank's tired." In fact, I had no idea if Frank was tired or not. "It's been, um, a long day."

"You can say that again," Marcus said, and nodded.

Marcus filled up the bathroom door like a linebacker, his body half in shadow, the white shirt of his tux picking up the last of the sunlight. I could barely see his face in the fading light, but his blue eyes glinted. My scar went cold again. I looked over his shoulder into the bathroom, hoping he'd take the hint to move out of the way. Nothing doing. What was it with Marcus and doorways? Why did he always have to stand in them, not letting me pass through?

"Um, nice to see you again," I said, half turning to the door and thinking I'd use a bathroom upstairs.

"So you and Frank were never boyfriends," Marcus said in a matter-of-fact tone.

"No, not really." I looked away from him, my breath going shallow.

"You sure had me fooled," Marcus said, his face showing no emotion. "The way you acted guilty, all those times we were together. Making me think you were cheating on Frank."

"Dude, it's late," I said, peeking over his shoulder into the bathroom. "Are you going to let me take a leak or not?"

"Only tell me this," Marcus said, of course not even close to moving out of the way. "Why'd you go along with it? What was in it for you?"

My mind turned toward Marcus in yoga class, doing headstands in his red shorts. Marcus dancing with the guy with the snaking vine tattoos. Marcus flirting with me on his roof. Offering me a home in this very house, right in the middle of my beloved San Francisco. Wisps of vapor now. No more real than Frank's fantasies of Jonathan. But they were the reason why I'd gone along with Frank's scheme. Of course I wasn't about to tell Marcus any of this. He didn't deserve the satisfaction of knowing.

"I did it because Frank is good and decent," I said with confidence. "Because he needed my support. Too bad he couldn't count on that from his own friends."

I turned and made for the bedroom door. Time to put Marcus in the drawer, lock it up and throw away the key. I pictured myself in the ice cream store describing this scene to Genevieve—my last Marcus story—and Genevieve nodding and telling me I'd done the right thing. Even she had to know that talking sex was easier than having sex.

"I was thinking of going to your yoga classes again," Marcus called out, stopping me at the door.

"Holy Mother," I said, turning to face him again. "Have you lost your mind?"

"Why not?" Marcus said, his voice all huffy. "I've been out of practice. I was thinking I could start up again as soon as Jonathan and I come home from our honeymoon."

"What about New York?" I said, without even trying to sound polite about it. "When are you and Jonathan moving?"

"The work on the house is nowhere close to done," Marcus said, his voice flat. "Jonathan's not keen on spending cold winters there. When it's finished, we'll decide."

"Whether you stay or whether you go," I said coldly, glancing at my knee, "I don't want you coming to my class."

"Then how about a massage?" Marcus said smirking, a knowing light in his eyes.

"Marcus, in case you've forgotten," I said, not bothering to hide my feelings of total contempt. "Today is your wedding day."

"So?" Marcus said shrugging. "What does that change?"

I shrank away from Marcus, horrified. So this whole day was for show. What would Frank say if he heard Marcus now?

"Marcus," I said, leaning forward so he could see the hatred in my eyes, "I wish you and Jonathan the best of all possible things."

I left the bedroom and slammed the door behind me. Forget about locking Marcus in the drawer—this was more like kicking him to the curb with the empty bottles. I rushed up the stairs, feeling my body moving further away from Marcus and his gravitational pull. Frank's toast rang in my mind. His need to believe in love. The reason why he'd saved this wedding. I couldn't let Frank know what Marcus had said. Never, never, never.

***

I raced upstairs, used the bathroom down the hall, and went into the living area to look for Frank. No time to hesitate, to write a list of all the things that might go wrong. All I knew was I needed to speak to Frank.

Frank was standing near the sliding doors, chatting with Ethan. Ethan's partner stood a little off to the side, looking like a third wheel. I worked my way through the crowd, not taking my eyes off Frank. Maybe I should've stood by and waited until he was done talking with Ethan. Too bad.

"So, Frank," I said in a playful voice, sliding my arm around Frank's waist, "aren't you going to introduce me to your friends?"

"I, uh, was waiting for you to show," Frank said turning pink, looking at me with a smile and a pair of wide eyes. "Julio, this is, um, Ethan."

What can I say about Frank's ex-husband? Not much, except to say he seemed like an okay enough guy. I also let myself be introduced to the ex's new husband. He seemed okay too, as far as homewreckers went. A few minutes of chitchat, and then Ethan and the new husband moved off. Frank turned to me and gave me a puzzled look. My heart burned with feeling for him.

"Do you remember that Sunday morning last January?" I said in a shaking voice. "When I said I was willing to come here for dinner with Jonathan and Marcus? Do you remember what you said to me?"

"No," Frank said, looking confused. "What did I say?"

"You said, let's be boyfriends," I said, and I kissed him. "I say let's do it. Let's do it, Frank. Let's be boyfriends."

17

ROLLING FORWARD

Last night I dreamed Jonathan slipped into my room in his ivory-white tux. His face and eyes shone in the soft light of the nightstand lamp. I sat up in the bed, alone and naked, while Jonathan locked his eyes on me and stripped off his tux, letting it drop to the floor where my gray tux lay in a heap. I opened my mouth to ask him why he'd come, but the words stayed stuck in my throat.

No. Wait. Yesterday was Jonathan's wedding. I'd driven Marcus to City Hall. Handed Marcus the ring to put on Jonathan's finger. Given a toast. Had a word with Ethan. Then, later, I'd gone home with—and slept with—Julio. Yes, Julio. My dark gray tux had fallen to the bedroom floor and mingled not with Jonathan's white tux, but with Julio's pink one. Pink and gray, Julio's hot combo. The image of Jonathan flickered and faded, and I opened my eyes to mellow autumn sunshine peeking through the blinds.

***

My tux lay in a heap on the floor. Julio's tux was gone. Julio himself was gone. A feeling of disquiet settled into my bones. Julio must've woken up at dawn, realized what he'd done, and fled. I should probably count myself lucky he'd given me the one night.

I pulled on a pair of boxer shorts, wrapped myself in my bathrobe, and went into the hallway. Julio's door was open. I crept to his doorway and peered inside. The room was empty, the bed unslept in, the pink tux nowhere in sight. My copy of *Gödel, Escher, Bach* sat on his bureau. I went downstairs to the kitchen. Julio's blue ceramic bowl and the little blue pot he used to make his oatmeal sat drying on the rack next to the sink. Then it struck me. Today was Saturday, the morning of Julio's yoga class in San Francisco. After yesterday's drama I'd lost track of the day of the week.

All the same, the day would arrive when I'd wake up in the morning and find Julio gone for good. The way he'd been toiling at his business all summer, he'd surely saved enough money to move into a new place. Julio's life, like time itself, never seemed to stop rolling forward. With Jonathan and Marcus's wedding finally past, it was high time for me to do the same.

***

After breakfast I changed into a tank top and shorts, brought up my old basketball from the basement, went out to the driveway, and for the rest of the morning shot hoops on the basketball hoop Ethan had long ago given me. My aim was awful for the first half hour or so, but eventually I found my groove. My mind couldn't help but wander to the time I'd shot hoops to win Jonathan and me those silly stuffed rabbits. What was Jonathan doing right now, the morning of his first full day of marriage to Marcus? The answer hit me with the speed of the sunlight warming my face. I didn't care.

By noon the sun had grown too hot. I went inside, took a shower, ate some lunch. The afternoon spread out in front of me. What next? What other areas of my life had I been neglecting for Jonathan's sake? The answer came in the form of an itching in my palms and fingers. An itching to play Mom's piano again. The last time I'd played that piano was the day after Mom's funeral. My hands had shaken so badly I could barely manage more than a few bars of her favorite Mozart sonata. For months that piano had sat in a corner of my living room, dormant, silent, reproachful, my fingers growing heavy even when I dusted it. But today my fingers felt light. The piano deserved to be played.

I went into the living room and opened the French windows a crack. From the piano bench I pulled out Bach's Piano Concerto Number One, one of the first pieces I'd performed in public, at age twelve. This was the very sheet music I'd used at that performance, the pages now soft like linen and tinged yellow. I settled myself on the bench, opened the piano, and arranged the music in front of me.

An excitement rippled through me as if that long-ago audience were sitting in the living room now. In my mind the audience held its breath to see if I could pull it off. My parents and Wendy sat in the front row. I pictured Jonathan and Marcus sitting in a row behind my parents, Marcus bored and fidgeting, Jonathan sitting up with a worried look on his face. My mind conjured Julio by the door, ready to slip out as soon as one of his friends pinged him on his phone.

I did a simple scale. The sound of the notes set my heart to beating. I followed the sheet music for the first few bars. The notes came to me as if they'd been imprisoned in my hands. I closed my eyes and kept playing. The music flowed out of my hands and into the poor neglected piano, the notes floating in my mind like bubbles. This was the sweet vibration I'd foolishly imagined Jonathan would bring to this house on the bright January morning I'd gone to meet him at the Ferry Building. The house didn't need him after all.

I opened my eyes and watched myself working the keys as if my fingers belonged to someone else. In a rosy flash of remembrance I recalled how these very fingers had worked over Julio last night, in the silver light of the streetlamp outside my window. If male anatomies were pianos, then his was a Steinway, an instrument I approached last night with a reverence verging on awe. I recalled how I'd reflexively felt for my wedding ring before reminding myself I was no longer married. After what Julio had given me last night, I could almost bless Ethan for leaving me.

***

Eventually my fingers went numb. The music slowed to a trickle. I couldn't expect to connect with Julio like that again. Julio would never have slept with me if he hadn't thought he'd be moving out of the house—out of my life—sooner rather than later. The bubbles I'd imagined floating around the room popped one by one into nothingness. The silence that remained felt like a physical blow to my chest. An omen of the loneliness awaiting me.

"Hey, why'd you stop?" Julio said in a soft voice.

I gave a start and looked up. Julio stood in the hall doorway in his aqua track jacket, his yoga mat and gym bag slung over his shoulder. I rubbed my sweaty palms together, wondering how much of my performance he'd witnessed before my mind strayed to the sad thought of one day parting with him.

"I didn't hear you come in," I said, letting out a nervous laugh.

"So you do play this piano," Julio said, coming up to me with a smile spreading across his face. "I always wondered."

"I've been out of practice for a while," I said. I ran a finger over the keys. "It used to belong to my mother's grandfather. My mother told me it came across the country on a train after the Civil War. She sent me to piano lessons at the age of six."

"Sounds like the lessons took," Julio said in an admiring tone. He put down his stuff and sat down on the arm of the leather chair to face me. "So who were you playing? Like, Beethoven or something?"

"Bach," I said, folding my hands in my lap. "The same Bach in the book you borrowed from me. *Gödel, Escher, Bach*. How do you like that book, by the way?"

"Oh, uh," Julio said, turning his head and letting out a laugh. "It's not exactly beach reading."

"To say the least," I said, and chuckled. "I only started reading it myself because it was my dad's favorite book when I was growing up. I must've been about nine years old when I took the book down from Dad's shelf. He never looked so pleased. The things we do to impress our parents, huh?"

"I'm glad my Papi was a painter," Julio said. "Painting a room is easier than reading that book."

"Not for me it isn't," I said, looking around the living room's dirty beige walls. "And for what it's worth, I managed to plow through about a hundred or so pages of *Gödel, Escher, Bach* before I gave up on it. I'm good at math, not great at math. I see that now."

Those long hours of me working and studying toward the elusive Ph.D. unraveled into a heap of tangled thread. If I hadn't sunk so much of my time and energy into that fruitless quest, Ethan might never have found the other man. The lesson I'd learned was far tougher than math.

"I'd love to hear you play some more," Julio said warmly, his eyes glowing.

"Maybe some other time," I said, stretching out my arms. "I've been at it for over an hour."

I rose from the bench and went to the French doors. I could feel Julio's eyes on me even with my back turned to him. A strong desire to be Julio's lover again came over me.

"Did I wake you this morning?" Julio said.

"No," I said, glancing at him over my shoulder. "Not at all."

"Good. You were dead to the world."

"I know," I said, shutting the French doors and turning to face him. "I haven't slept so deeply since—since—"

I was about to add *since the divorce*, but I caught myself. How tiresome that phrase was. How useless and counterproductive to divide my life by events that no longer mattered.

"What are you up to tonight?" Julio said.

"I haven't thought about it," I said.

"Good," Julio said, and he smiled.

"Aren't you seeing your friends in San Francisco tonight?" I said. "You always see your friends in San Francisco on Saturday nights."

"Not tonight," Julio said with a shrug and a smile.

"You cancelled your plans?" I brought my hand to my chest. "For me?"

"Does that surprise you?" Julio rose from the chair arm and walked up to me.

"I can't believe we're doing this," I said. "I can't make sense of it."

"Neither can I," Julio said, "but you don't have to make sense of it. This isn't some book from your Papi's shelf, some geometry or chess problem you'll be tested on. It's you plus me, Frank. The math is simple."

Less than five minutes later I was upstairs with Julio, playing an encore of last night's concert. The emotions weren't as intense as they'd been last night, but in a way that made it better. This time I had enough presence of mind to pay attention to the notes. The music came straight from my heart.

Julio slept with me every night afterwards. We made love every three or four nights. He stopped going to San Francisco on Saturday nights, while I let tests and homework assignments pile up, uncorrected. It felt like living with Ethan again, in those heady days when I first moved in with him and we both felt as if we were the only people in the world. I no longer felt for my wedding ring. I'd kicked that habit for good.

The honeymoon wouldn't last, I knew. I didn't dare ask Julio how his apartment search was going, but no doubt the day would come when he'd sit me down to tell me he'd found a place in San Francisco. He could be out as soon as the end of November. That still gave me a few more sublime weeks of sleeping with him. I knew I should be grateful. Still, I'd be a lot more grateful if I could hang on to him for a month or two longer.

***

One day late in October, while I read the newspaper alone in the teacher's lounge at lunch, my phone buzzed with a call from my good friend Diana, an art teacher and colleague who'd moved up to Portland to teach at a small private school. I'd sent her a resume in August and never heard from her. She wouldn't be calling me unless she meant to talk about a job opportunity. The finches I'd set free in August had dropped a seed on fertile soil after all.

Sure enough, Diana told me her school was desperate to find a new Advanced Placement calculus teacher to start in January. The old teacher was moving east to take care of a sick parent, and had given sudden notice to leave at the end of December. Would I consider moving to Portland? My first thought was of course I couldn't move to Portland. What about my family? My house? Julio?

Still, I called Diana and told her I'd be happy to give the school a phone interview, thinking the school would never call. Two hours later someone from the school called me and arranged a telephone interview in the morning. My heart raced. I knew it was only a job interview, but already I could picture myself receiving an offer. This was happening too fast. I felt invigorated and terrified.

I walked through the kitchen door at four o'clock. I'd fallen into the habit of having sex with Julio on a Thursday afternoon like this one. His last client of the day had usually left by now, and we both still liked being together while the sun still shone.

Julio came in from the hallway in his black massage clothes. If I weren't so excited and distracted about my phone interview tomorrow morning, I might've noticed the look of worry on his face.

As it was I figured the less time we spent talking, the less chance I'd have to tell Julio about my interview.

"Good day?" I said, going up to him.

"Maybe, um, let's not today," Julio said, turning from me.

"Hey, hey now, Julio," I said putting my hand on his shoulder. "What's wrong?"

"I had a good lead on an apartment," he said, looking up at me, "and now it looks like it won't happen. This friend of mine, she was talking of opening a yoga studio in downtown Oakland and having me as a sort of live-in instructor and massage therapist above the studio. Now she's telling me she can't pull the money together and some restaurant is moving into the building instead."

"I'm sorry," I said, and then felt a pang about tomorrow's phone interview. "You'll find somewhere else, I'm sure."

"But that place was perfect." Julio turned and leaned his hands against the counter. "It was the right amount of space. Not too pricey either. Do you have any idea how much apartments are going for nowadays? I can barely afford Oakland, let alone San Francisco."

"It's okay," I said, putting my arm around him again, rubbing my hand between his shoulder blades. "There are other places, Julio. Something will come along."

"I suppose," he said, his shoulders trembling.

He seemed close to breaking down in tears. I knew the market for apartments was obscene, but it wasn't hopeless. There had to be something else, something far worse than losing an apartment to make Julio this upset.

"Julio?" I said. "What else is going on?"

"My sister called," Julio said, his face red and splotchy. "Mami's breast cancer is back."

"Breast cancer," I said in horror, holding him close to me. Before now I hadn't known anything about his mother or her cancer. "I'm so sorry, Julio."

He buried his face into my chest. I don't know how long we stood together like that. His body felt limp against mine.

"But there's still hope, right?" I said in a near-whisper into Julio's ear. "Can't she go into treatment?"

"That's what they're saying," Julio said, his voice uncharacteristically lacking in hope.

"She recovered before, didn't she?" I said, putting force into my tone. "If she beat it the first time, then she can beat it again."

"You must've been talking with Mami," Julio said. "That's exactly how she put it to me on the phone. She's upbeat. But she went through hell with the radiation five years ago. This time she'll probably have to have a full mastectomy, plus chemo."

"Women have mastectomies all the time," I said in a reassuring voice, thankful I'd never known anyone who'd gone through one before. "If your mother's strong like you, then she'll pull through it."

"I like to think I'm her son," Julio said, sounding desolate.

"She's beating the cancer," I said firmly, and kissed him on the cheek, "When are you going down to see her?"

"Saturday morning after class," Julio said, a dullness in his voice.

"Why not now?" I looked Julio in the eye. "I'll drive you."

"You don't have to do that," Julio said with a pained look.

"But she needs you now," I said.

"I know she needs me now," Julio said, looking away from me. "But my sisters will be over at Mami's for supper tonight."

"Your mother needs you now," I repeated, grasping his hand. "Give me ten minutes to change. I'll drive you down, and then I can come later to pick you up."

"No. You'll have to stay for supper," Julio said, his voice resigned. "Mami would never let you drive away without feeding you."

"Your mother's been diagnosed with cancer," I said incredulously, "and she's planning to cook tonight?"

"If Mami can't cook," Julio said with a shake of his head, "then she might as well let the cancer take over."

Julio pulled out his phone and dialed. I waved my arms, signaling to him he didn't need to invite me over, but he turned away from me as if I were no longer in the room. In a moment he was talking in rapid Spanish into the phone. I leaned against the counter. It had to be my luck I'd be having dinner with Julio's mother and sisters on the eve of a life-altering job interview. All the same, a thrill ran through me—against my will—at the thought of meeting Julio's family.

"It's settled," Julio said, putting his phone onto the counter. "You're coming."

"You didn't have to do that." My face grew warm.

"What's the matter?" Julio said with a glimmer in his eye, his Spanish accent thicker than usual. "Afraid to meet my Mami?"

"No, of course not," I said, turning out my palms, "but—but—"

"But what?" Julio said, his playful tone returning again. "Come on, Frank, don't be shy. I want you to meet her. She's always asking when am I going to bring a man home to meet her. I know she'll like you. Plus she's an amazing cook. I hope you had a light lunch today."

My mind turned to Portland. I only had an interview tomorrow. A phone interview at that. I couldn't shake the feeling the job would be perfect for me, and I'd be offered it. What would I do about Julio then?

"All right," I said, breaking into a smile. "Let me change."

***

I smelled the beans as soon as we walked in the door of Julio's one-family stucco house in Hayward. Julio's mother was a small woman with dark skin and large dark eyes like Julio's. Julio teared up as he gave her a big hug, but she was having none of it. A small, tough woman. Kind of like my own mother, only a better cook, probably.

"I told you," Julio's mother said, patting his shoulder as if he were the one with the cancer. "Everything's gonna be okay."

"You say that," Julio said, wiping his eyes, "but how do you know?"

"I know," she said firmly. "Ah, Julio, you and your crying. Now come in and eat."

She let go of Julio and turned to me, clasping my outstretched hand with both of her own. I could already tell what my role would be tonight—the guy who'd keep Julio from breaking down. I thanked her for inviting me on such short notice. My own mother would never have let me do that with one of my own friends.

Julio's older sisters, busy at the counters, took a moment to greet me. They were making rice and beans and pork to go with the stack of fried corn cakes, or *arepas*, that Julio told me he used to eat almost daily in this house. I could see why Julio's mother had no problem with Julio bringing home a guest on short notice. They'd made enough to feed twice as many of us.

"Now you know why I was so fat as a kid," Julio joked to me in an undertone.

The five of us squeezed around Julio's mother's kitchen table—smaller than my own kitchen table—eating pork and beans over fried corn cakes. They talked nonstop and laughed at my lame attempts at Spanish. I'd always been terrible at learning languages, a grievous disappointment for my mother, who'd sent me to French lessons every Thursday night for six years. But by dinner's end Julio and his sisters had taught me a few phrases. I enjoyed being the student for once.

I ate way more than I'd meant to. Such a difference from my own family's dinners of the last few years, the unbearable silences punctuated by a "please pass the salt" or maybe a "so, Frank, how's the thesis coming?" Not one word about Julio's mother's cancer. It was as if the cancer sat at the table as an uninvited guest, and we were doing what we could to snub it. A wonderful night all around, made even more wonderful because I hadn't planned or foreseen any of it.

***

The next morning I called the school in Portland from my car in the school parking lot. Diana had apparently told them I was the smartest guy on my own high school's faculty and good with teenagers besides. I came away from the interview with a strong sense that not only was I their best choice to replace their departing math teacher, but perhaps their only choice. I suppose I should've known this would happen, after my wonderful dinner last night with Julio and his family.

At the end of the interview, the head of the math department asked if I could come to Portland to talk to them in person. The department head said he and the school principal would be delighted to meet me on a Saturday and show me the school. How about next weekend? I could fly up on Friday night and be home on Sunday afternoon, all at the school's expense, without missing a day of work. I heard myself saying yes before it sank in what that yes might mean for me and Julio. But how could I not go? It wasn't as if Julio had said he wanted to spend the rest of his life with me. Julio himself would want me to go for it.

Luckily for me, I didn't have to do much talking when I walked into the house in the afternoon. Julio was already in the kitchen waiting for me, ready to make up for our lost session of the previous afternoon. We went straight upstairs and didn't finish until the streetlamps glowed in the darkness outside. Afterwards, while we held each other in the soft light from my bedside lamp, Julio told me about a Halloween party his friend Joseph was throwing next Saturday in San Francisco. He said he'd seen Batman and Robin costumes online. Would I like to be Batman to his Robin? Or vice versa? I lay in bed, the sick feeling coming into my heart again. The time to tell him had arrived.

"I wish I could," I said, staring up at the ceiling. "But I'm going away next weekend."

"To Santa Cruz?" Julio said, turning on his side to look at me. His skin glowed like caramel in the lamplight.

"No," I said, trying to control the quiver in my voice. "To Portland."

"Portland?" Julio said frowning. "Like Portland, Oregon?"

"Yep," I said, biting my lower lip.

"What's up there?" Julio said. He sat up in bed and looked at me.

"A school," I said, my breath coming faster. "I'm interviewing for a teaching job up there."

Julio blinked slowly, his face empty of expression, and then he slid his eyes away from me. My heart hammered away. If only he'd say something, anything, to let me know what he might be feeling now. I hadn't expected to stun him into silence.

"So you're thinking of moving to Portland," Julio said, his voice calm and low.

"There's this job up there," I said, speaking rapidly. "My friend called me out of the blue to ask if I wanted it. I figured it couldn't hurt to check it out."

"Huh," Julio said tonelessly. "I didn't know you were looking."

"I wasn't," I said. "But the opportunity came my way."

"And the house?" Julio said, running his hand down the side of my arm. "What'll you do about the house?"

"I don't know. Sell it, I guess."

"I thought you loved this house," Julio said. He sounded more concerned about my own welfare than his.

"I thought I did too," I said, glancing around the room I'd called my bedroom for over ten years. "The house had felt like the only thing I had left after Ethan walked out. That, and Jonathan's friendship. But now I have to wonder what I'm clinging to here. This place is more than I need and more trouble than it's worth. Like Jonathan was more trouble than he was worth. I think it's time I let the place go."

"Makes sense," Julio said softly. "I'll miss you."

I supposed I shouldn't be surprised he'd say that. Of course Julio wouldn't think to come with me to Portland. His family, friends, and job were all here. We'd been together for too short a time. I wasn't sure myself if I wanted him with me. Even so, I felt a pang in my side. Giving up the house would be nothing compared to giving up these fine autumn days with Julio.

"I probably wouldn't put the house on the market until at least January," I said, looking him in the eyes again. "After I moved out. So you'd have plenty of time to hunt for a new place for yourself. Of course you can stay here after I move out."

"It'd be lonely here without you," Julio said, giving me a half-smile.

"Ah, you won't be here for long," I said in a reassuring tone. "I bet you'll be gone before I move out myself."

"Is that why you applied for that job in Portland?" Julio said. "Were you afraid I'd leave you first?"

A burning sensation came into my chest. I pulled the covers up to my neck, knowing I couldn't lie to him. A direct question deserved a direct answer.

"The house felt so empty when Ethan moved out," I said, looking up at the ceiling. "That was the worst part of the divorce. I made sure to be out on the day he left for good. His house keys were sitting on the kitchen table when I walked through the kitchen door. That's when it sank in he was gone. I know it's not the same with you. But all the same, I don't think I could walk into an empty house with your keys sitting on the kitchen table."

Julio turned on his side and hugged me close. My heart felt emptied-out. I'd never told that story, not even to Jonathan. To say the words now felt like liberation. I turned to him and let his warm body press into mine.

"If they offer you the job in Portland," Julio said in a murmur, "then I think you should take it."

"I don't know if I even want it," I said.

"Then find another one up there," Julio said in a nudging tone, the tone of someone who thought little of obstacles such as a broken heart. "You're smart and nice to look at. That's enough to take you places anywhere. And if you do move to Portland, I want you to promise me something."

"Promise you what?" I said, half-anxious about what Julio might have in mind for me.

"I want you to whore around with lots of guys up there," Julio said in a definite voice. "Be slutty. I know you have it in you. You need to spread your love around before you settle down with someone new."

"If I settle down with someone new," I said.

"You'll settle down," Julio said, nodding and narrowing his eyes at me. "You keep a good house."

"You're something else, Julio," I said, letting out a soft laugh.

We ate dinner at a Burmese restaurant in Berkeley. On the way home we picked up a pint of chocolate ice cream at Genevieve's, Julio's favorite place. She was locking up the store when we reached it, but all Julio had to do was tap on the glass for her face to brighten and let us in. Julio introduced me to her as his roommate, but by the way she looked at me, her eyes as bright as her cherry-red wig, I could tell Julio had been talking to her about me. That was enough to set my heart glowing.

Later on, as we settled down to go to sleep, I thought that if I was offered the job in Portland, I'd take it as a sign my adventure with Julio was meant to end. Then I'd take the lessons I'd learned from Julio and put them to good use in Portland. How exciting would that be?

And yet the way Julio's warm body pressed against mine, fitting the contours of my body, made me think the adventure wasn't over yet. However Julio and I were meant to end, it wasn't meant to end this soon. I fell asleep thinking I wouldn't land that job.

18

PARTING

Frank's plane ticket to Portland was for early evening next Friday, the first weekend of November. He'd packed his suitcase on Thursday night and left it by the kitchen door so he could leave almost as soon as he came home from school the next day. Looking at the suitcase by the door all Friday reminded me of the sucky weekend I'd have without him, and the suckier weeks I'd have if he moved away. Even the thought of moving to San Francisco couldn't keep me from thinking I'd have a hard time replacing Frank.

I was tidying up the massage room when Frank came home from school on Friday afternoon. As soon as I heard the door I went straight to greet Frank with a hug and a kiss. Of course I didn't want him to wish he didn't have to head to the airport right now, but I couldn't help myself. His ride to the airport came sooner than I wanted. The sound of the car driving away left a hollow feeling in my chest.

That night my cell phone buzzed. My ex-flame Dean had returned to San Francisco, home from his wanderings in Sicily. His voice sounded tired but hint-y—the voice of a guy who hadn't had a decent lay in months. If Dean had come home a few weeks sooner, I would've given him the time of his life. October with Frank had changed everything.

Dean wanted to know if I was free to meet him tomorrow night for dinner. Maybe somewhere in the Mission? He said he lived there with three other grad students in a tiny apartment off 24th Street.

Dean didn't come out and say he wanted sex, but that had to be what he wanted. I might even want it for myself, maybe, once Frank moved to Portland.

***

The next night I went to one of my favorite Salvadoran restaurants in the Mission with Dean. Over *pupusas* Dean told me about his studies and the Sicilian heat, his fellow archaeologists, the locals he'd met, and the few days he'd spent in Rome and Florence on his break. Dean's months in Italy had done him good. It hit me that Dean was a younger, less refined version of Frank.

Dean and I left the restaurant to a cold and clear night. The wind had picked up. The BART station was a half block away. I checked my phone for the time. Only 8:47. My heart sank. I didn't want to go home with Dean, but the thought of entering that huge house in Oakland with Frank not there—and not expected home until Sunday night—was enough to slow down my pace.

"You want to come over and see my new apartment?" Dean said innocently enough, zipping up his dark blue fleece jacket. "If we're lucky, we might even have the place to ourselves."

"Can't," I said, the word coming out like a cough. "I'm teaching a class in Berkeley in the morning."

"That's never stopped you in the past," Dean said, putting his hand on my arm.

"Sorry, Dean," I said trying to laugh it off, and drew my arm away. "Not tonight."

"Hey, wait a minute," Dean said with a look of surprise. "Are you involved with someone?"

"Kind of," I said, looking away from him and slipping my hand into my pocket to grab my cell phone. Wouldn't it be nice if Frank surprised me with a phone call now?

"What do you mean, kind of?" Dean said, an amused look behind his gold-rimmed glasses. "You're either seeing someone or you aren't."

"Okay, okay," I said, my face growing warm in the bitter wind. "I'm seeing someone."

"You are," Dean said in a sinking voice. "How long have you been seeing him?"

"A while," I said, glancing at the BART sign halfway down the street. "But we didn't start doing anything about it until last month."

"Last month?" Dean said, stopping and staring at me. "And you're already that serious?"

"It's serious enough," I said with an edge in my tone.

Dean looked at me with a curious half-smile, as if he didn't know who I was anymore. The bitch. Like it was Dean's business to second-guess why I didn't want to go home with him.

"Who is he?" Dean said. His voice was low but still held a hint of disbelief.

"He, uh," I said, already sensing how Dean would react, "it's Frank. Frank Mercer. The guy I'm sharing a house with."

"The math teacher?" Dean said, looking like I'd grown a second head.

"What's wrong with dating a math teacher?" I turned to look him square in the face. "He used to be a grad student too."

"Nothing's wrong with dating a math teacher," Dean said, flustered. "But I thought you told me he was strange."

"He isn't," I said. "I misjudged him."

We walked in silence to the BART station, both of us looking straight ahead. I didn't have to look at Dean to sense his frustration. Tough titty. Honestly, did Dean think I'd be waiting for him after all this time? Then it hit me. Of course he'd think that. Why would he think anything else? Dean had known me as someone who liked to have sex, not as someone who might develop feelings for another man. I'd matured more than I realized.

"Where's Frank now?" Dean said timidly.

"Oregon," I said, letting out a hard breath through my nose. "He has a job interview up there."

"He's moving?" Dean said turning to me, a hopeful rise in his voice.

"Maybe." My jaw went tense.

"When?"

The tone in Dean's voice was unmistakable. I pictured Dean heading straight home and marking Frank's moving date on his calendar.

"I'm not sure," I said, my voice raspy in the wind. "He's not sure if he wants to move up there."

The cold crept under my jacket collar. For all I knew, Frank was sitting in some bar now chatting up some hottie, already making a network of potential boyfriends for himself. He'd be within his rights. But in my heart I knew Frank would never even think of doing such a thing. I pictured him walking into the house with me and Marcus upstairs. He'd be crushed if he found out I'd slept with Dean.

"So if your housemate moves to Oregon," Dean said, drawing his words out, "then maybe you and I could start seeing each other again?"

"I don't know, Dean." I kept my eyes trained on the glowing white fluorescent lights of the BART station. "I haven't thought that far ahead."

"Man, Julio," Dean said, looking and sounding surprised, "sounds like you've fallen hard for this math teacher."

"No, I haven't fallen for the math teacher," I said rounding on Dean, losing patience. "But I like him. I don't want to run around on him."

"Of course." Dean blinked at me in shock. "All I'm saying is I want to be next in line."

"Will you knock it off?" I said, feeling an anger I hadn't felt since Marcus's wedding, when he'd hit on me outside his guest bathroom. "There are other guys out there for you to date."

"Okay, okay," Dean said, drawing back. He stared at me in silence, then leaned forward and stunned me with a peck on the cheek. "But I hope you let me into your life again. I've been thinking about you a lot."

Dean patted me on the shoulder, gave me a look full of meaning, and walked off into the night. Holy Mother, six months in Sicily had instilled some serious Marcus into Dean. I hurried downstairs to the train station, my mind blurring with images of me and Dean together, then of me and Frank together. Dean had nothing on Frank, and I knew it. Frank had better not be chatting up some hottie right now.

***

Frank didn't come until after eleven on Sunday night. His plane was late. I snapped awake to the sound of a car door slamming outside my window without realizing I'd dozed off with the lamp on.

Footsteps came up the steps, then the kitchen door opened and closed. I hauled myself up in bed, relief flooding my veins. To hell with not wanting to act boyfriend-y. Two days of not having Frank around made me see how I'd stumbled ass-backwards into being Frank's boyfriend. I wondered if Frank saw it that way too.

He showed up at my bedroom doorway looking pale and watery-eyed. His expression looked exactly like it had on that January afternoon all those months ago, the time he'd asked me to pretend to be his boyfriend. Scared, confused, not sure how I'd react. My heart melted. So he did miss me this weekend.

"There you are," I said, leaping up from bed, putting my arms around him and breathing in the cold air that lingered on his coat. "I thought you'd never make it."

"The plane sat on the runway for an hour," Frank said, sounding exhausted. "I couldn't even send a text."

"It doesn't matter," I said, thanking the Holy Mother I hadn't gone home with Dean last night. "And, um, how'd the interview go?"

"They liked me," Frank said. "And I liked them. It's a beautiful school. They have a grand piano in their auditorium."

"They offered you the job?" I said, my breath leaving me.

"I'll hear from them Tuesday," Frank said, looking down at the floor. "I don't want to talk about it now."

I sat with him in the kitchen while he ate the broccoli beef I'd brought home earlier from our favorite Chinese restaurant. As dog-tired as I'd felt before he'd come home, now I was wide awake. It was enough for me to sit there and watch Frank chew. Mother of God, listen to me. What would I watch him do next? Take out his contact lenses?

Afterwards I went upstairs with him thinking he wouldn't want sex, not this late at night and with school the next morning. But Holy Mother, did he ever. By the way he did it, I could tell he hadn't relieved any pressure in Portland. I couldn't believe I once thought I'd be comparing future lovers against Marcus for years to come. A few wrestling matches with Frank, and now I missed Marcus about as much as I missed drinking. Frank had helped me kick my latest bad habit to the curb.

***

All day Tuesday I massaged my clients and repeated the mantra that I wanted Frank to land that job. A new job, a new place, maybe even a new boyfriend—Frank deserved all those things and then some. Still I'd miss him. Holy Virgin in heaven. It was supposed to be me moving out on him, not him moving out on me.

The kitchen door slammed at a quarter to five, a half hour later than usual. Then he showed up in the doorway to the massage room. He was smiling, but his face was pale and tense. The sheet I was folding went limp in my hands. Even before he opened his mouth to speak, I knew what he needed to hear from me. My permission.

"You got the job," I said, looking straight into his eyes.

"Gee, Julio," Frank said, his face turning pink, "is it that obvious?"

Then he burst out laughing, and I laughed too. I dropped the sheets onto the massage table and went up to him to hold him tight. I couldn't let this be about me. If Frank could be classy enough to let Jonathan go, then I could be classy enough to let Frank go.

For the rest of the day I put on a show of being happy for Frank. To keep myself from losing it, I made sure Frank did all the talking. I asked him a million questions about his plans. The school wanted him to start right after New Year's, giving Frank a few weeks to break the news to his family, pack his things, and put the house on the market. It also meant two more months I could keep on sleeping with him, bringing our affair to a tidy three months. My history with Frank wouldn't be as solid as the eight months I'd had with Dean, but at least it was one more month than I'd stuck it out with Marcus. So there.

***

The next day Frank brought home a stack of brand-new cardboard boxes. He spent an hour or two each night in the basement, sorting through his stuff, and came to bed too exhausted for sex. Strange to say, I didn't crave sex. To lie next to Frank with his arm lying heavy on my chest was plenty. Maybe I was feeling tired too, after this long and crazy year.

Box after box of things Frank didn't need came up from the basement. Frank's Mami's wedding dishes came down from the china closet and into boxes too. Frank had talked of holding a yard sale, but eventually he started driving everything to Goodwill. The house grew larger and sadder. Holy Mother, would this place feel lonely once Frank moved away or what?

On the Sunday after Thanksgiving I came home from a long weekend taking care of Mami to the sound of recorded classical music drifting in from the living room. Good, Frank must be home from his own weekend with his Papi and sister down in Santa Cruz. He'd promised me a real date this weekend. I planned to make him stick to his promise. After a stressful November—Frank with his packing, me with Mami recovering from her surgery—we both could use the release.

I slung my weekend bag over my shoulder and followed the sound of the classical music to the living room. Frank was kneeling by the built-in bookshelves in his blue plaid work shirt and gardening jeans, placing his books into a moving box. He gave me a nervous "hi" when I walked into the room. I had the sense he'd been doing something besides packing books before I came home.

The only other box in the room was a gleaming-white cardboard box on the coffee table, about the size of a couple reams of paper. Not a moving box. The lid was crooked too, as if Frank had closed it in a hurry. What was in that box? What had Frank been up to? I knew better by now than to ask Frank straight out. Better to pretend I didn't notice the white box, and then tease the truth out of him.

"Look at you, Mr. Busybody," I said in a half-cheerful, half-suggestive tone. The grandfather clock read ten minutes to five. "Ready for a break?"

"Let me finish packing this box," Frank said, giving me a little smile and then reaching for a handful of books.

"You know I don't like waiting," I said with playful strictness. I put down my weekend bag and plopped down in the leather easy chair.

"Yes, Julio," Frank said, a hint of sadness in his voice. "I know."

He pulled down a few books from the shelf and fitted them into the moving box. The clock now read five minutes to five. He was acting as if I was his brand-new housemate again, not his lover who knew him and cared about him more than he probably realized. I glanced at the white box on the coffee table.

"I still have your book," I said, trying to sound more clueless than I was. "I was hoping to finish it before you left, but I don't think I can. You want me to bring it down for you?"

"No, hang on to it," Frank said, sounding distracted. "You can bring it when you come for a visit."

"A visit?" I said, a smile spreading across my face. "When am I visiting?"

"As soon as I'm settled," Frank said, and threw me a smile.

I'd never been to Portland before. I once dated a guy from there, though. He said it was like San Francisco, only colder and rainier and had more trees and fewer people. If Oakland was more of a ghost town than San Fran, Portland must be like living in the sticks. All the same, the thought of visiting Frank there gave my heart a lift.

"Do you have to pack now?" I said, sitting up and glancing at the clock. "You have another month to put those books away."

"That's less time than you think," Frank said, looking over his shoulder at me. "I have people telling me they want to see me one last time before I go. Nothing like moving away to make a guy popular, right? And maybe visit your mom again. How's she doing, by the way?"

"Her first chemo treatment is Thursday," I said, realizing how Frank was trying to change the subject. "She recovered from surgery way better than anyone expected. I told her I'd see her Wednesday night for supper. She says you're invited too."

"I'd love that," Frank said, his voice and eyes gentle, his sincerity hitting me to the core.

Frank went over to his music player on the mantel and turned off the classical music. The clock chimed five. My eyes strayed to the gleaming white box on the coffee table. Frank saw that I saw. An uncomfortable silence settled between us. Maybe I didn't want to know what was in the box after all.

"Those are my wedding photos," Frank said, letting out a sigh. "We'd hired a professional photographer to mingle with the crowd and take candids. I stowed the pictures in that box, along with a few other mementos from the wedding. I meant to make an album out of them, but I never did, and then…you know what happened next."

Frank went over and plopped onto the couch. The box he'd been packing was only half-filled with books. I stood motionless and watched him, not knowing if he wanted me to join him or not.

"Well," Frank said, sounding defeated, "come on over and have a look at them."

"Nah, let's go out," I said, hesitating. I didn't want to go through those pictures if it meant stressing Frank out. "I'm hungry."

"It's barely past five," Frank said. "Come on, Julio, I'd like you to see them. Maybe you can help me decide which ones to keep and which ones to throw away."

I went over, sat next to him, and kissed him on the cheek, thinking I'd breeze through the pictures and wrap it up by five thirty. Then the funniest feeling came over me. A feeling that here was Frank, this guy who'd be boarding a plane and flying out of my life in a few weeks, and here was me, about to be shown his old wedding photos. What was going on here? The old me would've been striving to know Frank less, not to know Frank more. Ah, to hell with it. I lifted the lid of the box.

***

Extra wedding invitations sat at the top of the pile. They were pale green with gold trim, shamrocks glittering in the lower left-hand corner, and Frank and Ethan's names glowing in gold letters. Below the invitations was a stack of wedding cards from Frank and Ethan's family and friends. I flipped through pictures of valentine hearts and interlocking wedding rings and grooms holding hands on wedding cakes. Frank prompted me to open a few of them. "Love always!" "So happy for you!" "May you have many joyous years together!" A lump grew in my throat. I couldn't imagine what it must have felt for Frank to go through these cards again.

"Garbage," I said, holding up the cards and tossing them on the coffee table next to the box, away from Frank's reach. "All of it."

"I know," Frank said, looking and sounding embarrassed. "Go on."

At the bottom of the box sat an open manila envelope, ragged at the corners. I took out the envelope and pulled out the photographs inside. Frank and Ethan posed in fancy gray suits with black edging, beaming by the pink rosebushes outside the French windows. Frank's face was healthier-looking, the look in his eyes more youthful. More pictures of Frank and Ethan showed them holding hands, cutting the cake, fixing each other's bow ties. The most natural-looking photo was of the two of them talking to each other by the tall wooden fence, looking wiped out but happy. An intimate, unguarded moment. I saw the relationship Frank and Ethan must've had, the many moments they must've shared, before everything went down the shitter.

"Those are a no-brainer," Frank said, ripping those photos out of my hand and placing them face down on the coffee table. "I'm shredding those."

"Ethan shouldn't have left you," I said.

"I was a different person then too," Frank said, turning his head. "It wasn't all Ethan's fault."

"Oh yes, it was." I neatened the stack of photos on my lap, not wanting to hear him protest. "You never would've fooled around on him."

The next photo was of Frank smiling between a tall, gray-haired man and a straight-backed woman with dyed reddish brown hair and a queenly expression. Frank's Mami and Papi. A tough-looking pair, those two. I could easily picture them putting Frank through his paces when he was a kid.

"My wedding was the last time my mom was well," Frank said, his voice all melancholy. "Before the Alzheimer's took over."

"She's lovely," I said, wishing I could've met her.

"If there was one good thing about her losing her memory," Frank said in a voice thick with emotion, "is she never knew what I went through with Ethan. Right up until the end she would ask about him. She'd approved of Ethan. Both my parents did. I think they always thought I needed someone to take care of me."

"You have to keep that picture," I said.

Frank smiled at me and nodded his agreement. I flipped through more pictures. Frank with his Mami, his Papi, his sister, his friends. He'd had more friends than I'd realized. Frank said he'd lost touch with most of them during the divorce. Any pictures with Ethan went face-down onto the pile headed for the shredder. Any with Frank, or Frank with a friend or relative, went right-side up on the keep pile. Far more went onto the shredder pile. That Ethan sure was a camera whore.

"You still haven't seen the best pictures," Frank said, sucking in a breath.

"What pictures are those?" I said.

"Which ones do you think?" Frank said, giving me a faint smile. "Jonathan and Marcus, of course."

I braced myself to come face to face with Marcus again. There he was with Jonathan, standing by Frank's tallest pink rosebush. Marcus looked as sunny as ever in a peacock-blue silk shirt under a white sport jacket, while Jonathan was his usual laid-back self in a pale green aloha shirt. Marcus's face was younger and thinner, his shirt catching the blue in his eyes. Marcus's arm was hooked around Jonathan's waist. My scar buzzed. Marcus had managed to come between Frank and me—literally.

"Shred that picture," I said in a dull tone to Frank, and pointed at Marcus's face. "You don't need memories of either of them."

"I guess not," Frank said. "It's a nice picture, though."

And now for the last picture. Frank and Jonathan alone, talking by the fence. Their faces close to each other, Jonathan leaning into something Frank was saying. Another tender, unguarded moment the photographer had caught. My heart dropped. In this one image I glimpsed the future Frank must've imagined for himself and Jonathan. A future he must've felt he could touch, as real as the memory captured in this photo.

"You can't keep this one," I said boldly. The photo trembled in my hand.

"You don't think so?" Frank said, turning to me with a searching look.

"He burned you, Frank," I said with a stony look down at Jonathan. "He's no friend of yours."

"But I'll never see him again," Frank said in a despairing tone. "Wouldn't it be cruel of me to send a twenty-year friendship through the shredder?"

"He strung you along for twenty years," I said, my voice rising. "You call that friendship?"

The grandfather clock chimed six. My stomach growled. Time to put these pictures in the drawer and focus on our date. I went upstairs and took a shower, leaving Frank alone to linger over his precious pictures. I figured whatever photos Frank took up to Portland would sit in that box on a closet shelf or something for another few years. How Frank would even think of keeping that picture of himself and Jonathan was beyond me. Would he have any pictures of me when he moved away?

The next morning, after Frank left for school, I slipped into the living room and stared at the short "keep" photo pile and taller "shred" photo pile sitting on the coffee table. The top photo of each pile was face down. I hesitated. I had no right to peek, but I had to know what Frank had decided. I walked up to the "keep" pile and turned over the top photo. And there stood Frank and Jonathan, talking by the fence.

***

December slid past even faster than November had. Every other night, it seemed, Frank was going to dinner with some old friend he hadn't seen in months. He always invited me to go with him, but I told him no, he didn't need me hanging around him while he relived his past. I sure didn't need to watch his friends tell him how much they'd miss him. Watching him go would be hard enough as it was.

At the end of the month Frank drove down to Santa Cruz to spend Christmas with his Papi and sister. They both supported his move to Portland, Frank told me. Meanwhile I spent the holiday at Mami's. It wasn't much of a Christmas. The chemo had made her so sick she spent most of the day sleeping. I didn't tell Frank about it afterwards. I only told him she was fighting hard, and the doctors were happy with her progress. Frank didn't need to hear about Mami's troubles. My troubles.

The weekend between Christmas and New Year's, movers came and packed Frank's stuff to drive to Portland. The house had always seemed big to me, but now, with most of the rooms abandoned, it seemed gigantic. A sharp-faced Realtor had already come to see the place and said she could find a buyer for it within days. I prayed to the Holy Virgin I could find a new place for myself soon. But with hardly anyone moving in the winter and rents skyrocketing all over the place, I resigned myself to having to stick it out in Frank's empty house at least through January. San Francisco felt as far away as China, and Portland even further.

Frank's bed headed up to Portland that weekend too. No choice for the next few days but for us to share my double bed. It had to have crossed Frank's mind that here was where Marcus and I had been together, but he never said a word about it. Whether he felt icky about it or proud he'd taken Marcus's place, I had no way of knowing. Marcus was the one person in our past we could never talk about. The one person whose memory would always come between us.

***

Frank's plane ticket to Portland was a couple nights after New Year's. I insisted on riding with him in the cab to the Oakland airport. Frank was so preoccupied with his luggage that he didn't pay attention to the messenger bag I'd slung over my shoulder and brought with me. In the bag was a final piece of business I had with Frank, one last item I had to check off my list.

The terminal was half-empty. My chest tightened as we checked his bag and made our way toward the security line. I felt dazed and helpless.

"Good luck, Frank," I said, giving him a hug and squeezing my eyes shut. "Not that you'll need it. You're gonna kick ass up there. I know it."

"Thank you," Frank whispered in my ear. "I'll never forget what you've done for me. I've never had someone like you in my life. I'll never, ever forget you."

"And before I forget," I said, sounding as if this thought only now had crossed my mind, "here's this."

I unslung my messenger bag, opened it, and pulled out *Gödel, Escher, Bach*. Frank gaped at the book in my hands, his face going white. He had to know if he didn't take the book from me now, he'd never see it again.

"But you can bring it up when you come visit," Frank said stammering. "I thought that's what we'd agreed."

"I know," I said in a voice I hoped sounded final, "but who knows when I'll make it up to Portland? I'd hate for you to lose something your Papi gave you."

Frank looked at me, then his eyes went over to my now-empty messenger bag hanging off my shoulder. For a second I thought he'd insist I hang onto the book. Instead, he pulled the book out of my hands and tucked it under his arm.

"But you'll come and see me sometime?" Frank said, looking into my eyes. "In the spring, maybe?"

"Sure I will," I said smiling, thinking that by spring Frank would have found new friends and probably a new boyfriend. "Hand to God."

"Oh, Julio," Frank said wrapping his arms around me. "I hope I'm doing the right thing."

"You are," I said, near tears myself. "Now go."

Frank let me go and looked at me, smiling. Then he turned and stood in the short line for the TSA agent. I could've turned and left the airport then, but I hung back and watched him move forward in the line. The agent waved him through. I kept my eyes on him, thinking what a wonderful thing it would be if he'd turn around to look at me.

And then Frank turned. At first he didn't see me. His brow furrowed, as if he thought I'd already sashayed off and forgotten him. So I raised my arm and held it there until he spotted me. His look of relief felt like a blessing from the universe. Frank waved at me, smiling, and then he bowed his head, turned, and moved out of my line of vision toward the metal detectors. Holy Mother, so he really did turn to look for me. He'd read my mind. What would Frank have thought if he'd turned around to see that I'd gone?

I didn't start heading for the exit until I felt sure Frank had moved well past the metal detectors. The large glass doors of the exit slid open. Cold, drizzly air hit my face and burned my lungs. It felt like a chilly reality that smacked me awake from that amazing goodbye with Frank.

The burning in my chest didn't stop even after I'd regained my breath. The drizzle felt like pinpricks against my face. I put a hand to my chest, hurried into the airport again, and sank onto the ledge of an unused baggage carousel. A miserable Uber ride to a three-quarters-empty house was all I had lined up for the rest of the night. I'd head home after this burning in my chest stopped. But it didn't stop. The sensation seemed familiar. What was going on here?

Then I remembered. My chest had burned like this when Papi died. His funeral mass. His burial. The terrible weeks that followed, as the truth sank in that the universe had swallowed up Papi forever. Frank hadn't died, but the universe had claimed him all the same. Again I faced an unknown future. Again I'd lost someone I loved.

19

ENDGAME

I was three weeks into my new life in Portland. The cold, the rain, even the heavy, churning clouds didn't bother me. Instead, I imagined Julio looking around and saying, "How can I brighten this? What colors can I add?" Soon enough, colors met me everywhere I went. A woman's crimson head scarf. A pair of hot pink rain boots. The city lights shining like gold coins beneath the silvery surface of the Willamette River. I strung up pink star-shaped lights along the balcony railing of my temporary furnished apartment. A necklace of light to defy the gloom.

During my unpacking I came across my Lewis Chessmen. No need to hide them in a closet now. I found the right place to put them, on a table near the window. But the way White and Black squared off against each other unsettled me. I rearranged the pieces so that White alternated squares with Black, the two armies knitted together to create a peaceful whole. So long as I could look at the chess set and not think of it as war, I knew I'd be all right in Portland.

***

My chance to call Julio came in late January. I needed to tell him I'd be putting the house on the market in a few weeks. The Realtor had asked me to be there for a walk-through before she listed it. I planned to fly down on a Friday night after school, meet with the Realtor early Saturday afternoon, and then drive to Santa Cruz to spend the night with Dad and Wendy. With luck, Julio would be coming home from his yoga class right as I finished the walk-through with the Realtor.

My heart raced as I dialed him on my cell. It was only a phone call, I reminded myself. Julio might even have a new boyfriend by now. The way Julio kept busy, he probably wouldn't even answer. He didn't. I left him a voicemail, keeping my tone cool and friendly.

Julio called me later that night, a few minutes before nine o'clock, while I lay on the couch skimming through Dad's old copy of *Gödel, Escher, Bach.* He sounded glad to hear from me, but his voice betrayed no wistfulness, no hint he'd missed me the way I'd been missing him. He had news for me too. He was moving in with his mother at the end of January. So much for seeing the Realtor with Julio still living in the house.

"I'll find a place after she's better," Julio said in his usual chatty tone. "It'll be my chance to take care of her for a change."

"Makes sense," I said, masking my disappointment with a neutral voice. "If I don't see you at the house, then maybe I could meet you for coffee or something."

"Oh, um," Julio said. "We'll see. I've been busy with classes and massages and stuff. It sounds like you won't be down here for long."

"No," I said, trying to sound as if I didn't care one way or the other. "No, I guess I won't."

That night I dreamed I was paddling a kayak in the middle of Lake Merritt in Oakland on a warm summer's day. Gulls circled overhead, ducks and geese glided past. I remembered how I'd once fantasized about rowing that lake with Jonathan. But the other man in the kayak in this dream, sitting in front in his aqua track jacket, was Julio. His feet were propped up on the side of the kayak, letting me do the work. I rowed faster to compensate. No use. The boat turned in circles like the screeching gulls overhead, until my eyes blinked open to the wan light of winter.

***

A few days later I came home from the gym, half-expecting to find a voice message on my smartphone from a guy who worked at the library where I taught disadvantaged kids arithmetic on Wednesday afternoons. We'd gone on a couple of dates, no big deal. A phone message was waiting for me when I reached home, all right, but from a San Francisco number. I'd erased the contact information long ago, but I knew the number as well as my own. Jonathan's number.

"Hey, Frank," Jonathan said in the voicemail, his tone as laid-back as ever. "Long time, no talk. Call me when you can."

I'd be lying if I said I'd banished all thoughts of Jonathan since his wedding. Every now and then a funny feeling would steal over me, a vague wondering of what Jonathan might be doing at any given moment. I settled myself on my living-room couch, took a breath, and called the number.

"Frank, there you are," Jonathan said, his tone happy and excited. "How've you been, my friend?"

"Pretty good," I said. My insides stiffened by his use of the word *friend*. "Have you settled in New York yet?"

"New York?" Jonathan said in a blank voice. "Oh, right—New York. Nah, the move's on hold for good. We decided to stick it out in San Francisco after all."

"Good for you." I wondered if Marcus knew Jonathan was talking to me. "You wouldn't have liked those brutal winters."

"I wouldn't have," Jonathan said, sounding relieved. "But I hear you're the one who's moved to a new climate. To Portland. Is that true?"

"Yep," I said, putting a hand to the nape of my neck and massaging it the way Julio had taught me. "I'd been meaning to let you know I'd moved, but I've been so busy with my new job and settling down here that I didn't—um—"

"You don't have to explain," Jonathan said. "But I'm sorry I didn't say goodbye to you in person."

"So, um," I said, "how'd you find out I'd moved?"

"Julio told me."

"He did?" I stood up and went over to the chess set by the window.

"At the yoga studio." Jonathan sounded mildly surprised, as if he'd assumed I'd known this all along. "I went to his class on purpose last weekend to ask where I could find you. I'd tried you on your old phone, but it was disconnected."

"I see," I said, more to myself than to Jonathan.

"So I've been thinking," Jonathan said lowering his voice, "I've never been to Portland before, and I haven't seen you since the wedding. So, um, I was thinking maybe, um, I could fly up to see you one of these weekends."

I started separating the white chess pieces from the black. A white knight slipped from my fingers and landed on the edge of the board. The knight's bug eyes stared up at me. I righted the piece and glanced out the window as if Marcus were watching me from the rain-soaked street below, stonefaced, unblinking, his eyes flashing with a yearning for revenge.

"Uh," I said, unable to keep panic out of my voice.

"Maybe even next weekend," Jonathan said.

"You want to come up next weekend?" I turned away from the chessboard.

"I know it's short notice," Jonathan said with a strange urgency, "but would you mind? I have a new job that's driving me crazy. I need a break."

"But, um, what about Marcus?" I said. "If you're so busy at your new job, won't he mind if you spend your one free weekend with me in Portland?"

"He won't mind," Jonathan said with assurance. "Me visiting you in Portland is his idea."

"It is?" I looked out the window and imagined seeing Marcus again, only this time he was nodding and smiling, encouraging me. "Are you sure?"

"Positive," Jonathan said, his voice dropping like a lead weight. "Listen, Frank, Marcus told me all about, you know, about the deal you cut with him. But that's dead. When Marcus told me what you'd agreed on, I—I thought I was going to lose it on him. He had no right to force you into agreeing to that. You're my friend."

"I said what I had to say," I said, putting a hand to my forehead. "Or else there wouldn't have been a wedding."

"Listen, it's all in the past," Jonathan said. "So what do you say? Can I come up?"

I closed my eyes and imagined Jonathan spending the weekend with me. Having him in the apartment was a nonstarter. I didn't even like the idea of Jonathan staying at a nearby hotel. But something must've happened between Marcus and Jonathan since the wedding. I had to know.

"Tell you what," I said, letting out a long exhale. "I'm coming down to Oakland in a couple of weeks to meet my real estate agent. I won't have much time, but I could see you Saturday morning before I do the walk-through with her. I could meet you at the Ferry Building, at the Saturday farmers' market, like we did last year. Would that work for you?"

Silence. My heart thumped against my ribcage. Clearly Jonathan had wanted more. No doubt he thought I'd give him more, as the friend who not too long ago would've given him anything.

"Sure, okay." Jonathan's voice was grudging. "Give me a call when you come."

"See you soon," I said, making a stab at cheerfulness.

That night I dreamed Jonathan and I were hurrying through the old-fashioned train station again. The clock in the middle of the station looked like the Ferry Building clock tower, ticking toward ten in the morning. We were running even though I knew we had no need to run. Marcus wasn't chasing us. No ice on the platform, no crowds blocking our way. The station was as empty as a chessboard in the endgame.

We boarded an empty train with its doors agape, its engine sighing up puffs of steam. No one to take our tickets. No other passengers in the car. The overhead compartments gaped wide open, eerily bare of luggage. Perhaps we'd boarded too early. I wondered when this train might be leaving. And then it dawned on me. The train would never pull out the station. It would sit here forever belching steam, its wheels locked in place, its doors wide open, its seats free of anyone with anywhere to go. I woke up thinking a journey with Jonathan wasn't a journey to nowhere. It was a journey that never began.

***

I flew to Oakland on a Friday after school, picked up a rental car, and drove to the motel near the airport where I'd be spending the night. The thought crossed my mind to call or text Julio, but decided against it. It was already pushing eleven o'clock by the time I reached the motel. It wasn't as if Julio could squeeze me into his schedule tomorrow morning. After all, Julio had a yoga class to teach. I went to bed but couldn't sleep.

Julio had to be wondering if Jonathan had ever called me, and what might've come of it. What if Julio was waiting for my phone call, to let him know what I'd decided? I shot up in bed. Hey, wait a minute. When did Julio teach his yoga class on Saturday mornings?

I scrambled out of bed, found my phone, and searched Julio's name and "yoga instructor" online. I clicked the link to Julio's website. His smiling face glowed in the darkness of the motel room. Did he publish his schedule of classes? Yes, right there. I clicked the banner. His class in the Mission would be starting tomorrow at eight thirty sharp. Plenty of time for me to speak to him before I left for the Ferry Building. The morning light couldn't come soon enough.

***

I made it to the yoga studio a few minutes before eight. The door to the yoga studio was locked. What now? My eye caught a coffee shop across the street with a large plate-glass window that faced the studio. I crossed the street and entered the coffee shop, bought myself a coffee and blueberry muffin, and parked myself on a stool by the window. I thought I'd miss him if I so much as blinked.

In a few minutes a tall woman with long red hair tied into a ponytail unlocked the yoga studio door and went in. Then she opened the door wide and put down the door's kickstand. A trickle of students, mostly women—no Marcus, thank God—went into the studio. Soon my eye caught something bright and blue on the sidewalk across the street. The aqua track jacket. Julio. He had his hands in his pockets and large white earphones wrapped around his ears, walking along with his jaunty step. A wave of joy and relief surged through my body. As Julio himself would say, thank the Holy Mother.

Julio disappeared into the studio right as I put down my coffee cup and left the shop. No time to lose. I'd have barely five minutes with him before his class started. I rushed across the street and into the studio. Five minutes would still be worth it, if Julio responded the way I wanted him to.

The heads of at least two dozen yoga students looked up at me as I walked in. The red-haired woman with the ponytail gave me a curious smile from her post at the register. Then a door at the other end of the studio opened, and out came Julio in a pink tank top and the dark gray yoga pants I'd given him for Christmas. He stopped short when he saw me. Then he smiled and walked up and gave me a tighter hug than I'd expected. It felt like sinking into a warm bath, having his arms enfold me again.

"I know you don't have a lot of time," I said, "but I thought I'd swing by and say hello."

"I'm glad you did," Julio said beaming. "This must be the weekend of your walk-through."

"It's this afternoon," I said in a rushed voice. "She's coming to the house at one."

"Good," Julio said in a polite tone that discouraged me. "You must be glad to be letting go of the house."

"I am." I gave him a faint smile. "So, um, if you're free later today, I could see you for an hour or so before I leave for Santa Cruz."

"Ouch," Julio said with his voice dropping. "I wish I could. But I, um, I'm supposed to be somewhere this afternoon. I could maybe see you later?"

"I'll be in Santa Cruz," I said, keeping the disappointment out of my voice. "If your plans change, give me a shout. Or come on over to Oakland if it's not too late. You know where I'll be at one."

"Maybe," Julio said, and then his expression brightened. "You know, I'm free for a few minutes right after class. Can you be here at, like, ten?"

"I can't." The color rose to my face. "I'm meeting Jonathan."

"I see," Julio said, clearly disappointed. "So he did call you."

"Um, he did," I said, darting my eyes to my watch. "He wanted to visit me in Portland, but I told him I couldn't. So I'm meeting him for a few minutes at the Ferry Building this morning, and then, um, that'll be it."

"What about that deal you made with Marcus?" Julio said. His expression was dark.

"He had a change of heart," I said with a shrug. "I'll find out more in ninety minutes."

"You be careful with Jonathan," Julio said, giving me a grave look. "Don't forget what he did to you."

"I won't," I said softly, glancing over Julio's shoulder at his students on their mats. They had quieted down and were watching Julio, no doubt waiting for class to start. "I haven't forgotten."

***

I arrived at the Ferry Building at exactly ten o'clock. Jonathan was already waiting for me under the clock tower, his hands in his pockets. He'd probably stationed himself there well in advance, for once taking the trouble to be on time. And Marcus was nowhere in sight.

My heart beat faster as Jonathan spotted me and smiled. My breath had left me by the time he came up and hugged me. Not as tight a grip as Julio had given me, but enough to feel Jonathan's warmth, his softness. I imagined Julio watching me and shaking his head.

"You look great," Jonathan said.

"Thanks," I said, too flustered to respond in kind.

From the wrinkles around his eyes and his general air of exhaustion I sensed Jonathan must've rolled out of bed and onto his bicycle to ride over here. His hair was grayer, but his cropped-close haircut and longish sideburns—a new style for him—made him look as boyish as ever. After twenty-plus years of looking at Jonathan in plaid shirts and faded Levi's, I couldn't help noticing his crimson T-shirt, his shiny silver belt buckle, his purple suede sneakers peeking out from the artfully frayed cuffs of his blue jeans. Jonathan must've looked at himself in the mirror one morning and realized he should probably stop dressing like a college undergrad. About time.

"Want some coffee?" I said, recalling how we'd gone into the Ferry Building for coffee last year.

"Actually, Frank," Jonathan said with a glance at the rows of busy market stalls, "I was thinking we could take a walk somewhere. Away from this crowd, you know? Maybe one of the piers. Unless you haven't had breakfast yet."

"No, I've eaten." I wondered where Jonathan was headed with all this. "Sure. Let's take a walk."

We walked along the Embarcadero toward the long wood-planked pedestrian pier about a quarter-mile away from the Ferry Building. The day was clear but windy. An uneasy feeling settled inside me the further we walked away from the farmers' market crowd. Fewer people meant less protection.

"So, Portland, huh?" Jonathan said, turning to me. "You like it up there?"

"So far," I said, looking straight ahead. "Nice people, less crowded. Cheaper. I'm enjoying building a new life for myself up there."

"But Portland's so different," Jonathan said, a note of wonder in his voice. "Had you ever been to Portland before you moved there?"

"No," I said, and shrugged. To hear him, I'd moved to a Tibetan monastery instead of the Pacific Northwest. "But I'd heard good things about it, and the job opportunity was great. So I thought why not give it a go."

We turned onto the pedestrian pier, a long, wide boardwalk flanked on either side by black-painted electric lamps, made to look like old-fashioned gas lamps. The boardwalk stretched out in front of us, then seemed to disappear into the jade-colored bay. Benches were placed between the electric lamps, but I didn't suggest we sit on one of them. Not yet. We'd sit as soon as Jonathan turned this conversation personal.

"I had no idea you were moving away," Jonathan said, as if deep down he knew he had something to do with this upheaval in my life.

"I didn't expect it to happen either," I said evenly. "But it did."

"Good for you," Jonathan said, and his smile tightened. "You wanted to make a change, and you went ahead and made it. That took courage."

A year ago I might've felt flattered, honored even, to hear Jonathan praise me for my "courage." Instead I heard Julio's voice in my head: *You be careful with Jonathan, Frank*. Perhaps that was the real reason why I'd gone to Julio's yoga class this morning. To hear Julio give me that advice in his own words, in his own voice.

"So you're not moving to New York," I said, thinking it would be rude not to ask about it. "What about that house you were building?"

"We sold the property to a couple of obscenely rich gay guys." Jonathan's tone was indifferent, as if he wouldn't have cared if the earth had split open and ingested the house intact. "There's lots of obscenely rich gay guys in New York."

"Huh," I said, and wondered how much wealth one would have to amass to qualify as "obscenely rich" in Jonathan's estimation. "And so you're here in San Francisco to stay?"

"For now." Jonathan turned and leaned against the pier's metal railing to give a contemplative look at the shimmering skyline that ringed the Embarcadero. "I started a new job soon after we came home from our honeymoon. A dream job. Or what I thought was a dream job."

"A job," I said frowning. "What kind?"

"Gaming company," Jonathan said absently, tilting up his chin to take in the clear blue sky above the buildings. "A startup. They liked one of the games I'd been working on so much they bought it and offered me a job."

"You're kidding," I said gaping.

"I think I might've told you about the game," Jonathan said, looking and sounding embarrassed, even apologetic. "You know, the one about the lobster who shoots baskets, and he has to worry about lobster traps and being eaten by sharks?"

"That game?" I said, flabbergasted. "Can I download it now on my phone?"

"Look it up," Jonathan said with a shrug.

I pulled out my phone and found the app. A grinning blue cartoon lobster balanced a spinning basketball at the tip of his claw. Goofy, likable, original. A crustacean version of Jonathan. I pressed the download button and imagined thousands of people around the world doing the same.

"But my bosses think they own me," Jonathan went on, his voice hurried. "They've been working me into the ground. Seventy-hour weeks. Eighty-hour weeks sometimes. It's barely been three months with them, and already I feel like I'm breaking apart."

"Ouch," I slipped my phone in my pocket and thanked heaven for my vanilla teaching job.

"I've been thinking of quitting altogether," Jonathan said, his tone harsh. "Tell those immature brats to take their job and shove it. It wouldn't be the first time someone's quit after barely three months there. What do you think? Do you think I'd be foolish to do that?"

"If you think you're breaking apart," I said, "then at least you should be thinking about your options."

"And I don't even need the money." Jonathan bit his lip and looked down at the boardwalk. "The game royalties are paying me more than enough. I thought I'd have more independence, not less, if I earned my own money instead of, you know, relying on Marcus all the time. But I feel as trapped as ever. Hey, would you mind if we sat down?"

"Oh, um," I said, glancing around. No more stalling—the time had come. "Sure, why not."

We sat on a bench with a view of the piers and the Bay Bridge. The hazy Oakland skyline glinted in the sunlight across the bay. Nearby, an old man in a floppy white porkpie hat tended to three different fishing rods leaning against the metal railing. I burned to know the time, but the Ferry Building clock tower was blocked by the *San Francisco Belle*, a huge white-painted riverboat that looked like a many-tiered wedding cake floating in the water. It seemed eerily fitting that I might be late for my walk-through on account of Jonathan and whatever he'd worked himself up to say to me.

"Then there's Marcus," Jonathan said, looking out on the water.

"What about him?" I sat up with my hands on my knees, making sure to keep a few inches of distance between myself and Jonathan.

"What do you think?" Jonathan turned and looked straight at me. "Marcus is Marcus. He'll never change."

Then Jonathan laid a hand on my arm. I sprang up from the bench. As shocked as I was, I couldn't help thinking of the different reaction I would've had if Jonathan had laid his hand on my arm on that Saturday morning a year ago. I had nothing but time on my hands then. But today, I had a real estate agent to meet at one o'clock and a family to see in the afternoon. As Julio might put it, I didn't have time for this bullshit.

"Jonathan," I said, glancing at the wedding-cake riverboat and thinking bitterly of my toast at their wedding reception, "what are you and Marcus up to?"

"Marcus knows I missed you." Jonathan lowered his eyes. "He knows I won't forgive him if he doesn't let you be in my life again."

"But he knows what we did last summer," I said in a half-whisper, throwing a glance at the old man. "I told him the day of your wedding."

"I know," Jonathan said. "He told me."

"So Marcus is condoning this?" I said, feeling exhausted all of a sudden.

"Marcus wants me to be happy," Jonathan said with a half-sigh, and then rose from the bench to face me. "He wants to save our marriage."

"So Marcus wants us to sleep together in order to save your marriage." I glanced at the old man again before I realized I didn't care if he heard us or not. "He encouraged you to invite yourself to Portland so you could sleep with me. Do you have any idea how depraved that is?"

"It's not, it's not," Jonathan said, looking at me square in the face. "Marcus said he'd sooner lose me than see me be unhappy. If that's not love, then I don't know what is."

"If that's not love"—what nonsense. And they needed me to make their marriage work? I turned and looked at the *San Francisco Belle*, wishing the wedding cake would sink so I could see the time on the clock tower.

"You leave me out it," I said. "If you want your marriage to work, then you and Marcus can go work on it yourselves."

"I'm sorry, Frank." Jonathan's lips barely moved when he spoke. "I'm sorry I said anything."

"Okay, okay, let's forget this happened." I pulled out my phone. "And if you don't mind, I need to leave for Oakland. The Realtor's waiting for me."

We walked in silence to the BART station. I kept my eyes fixed on the pavement. Poor Jonathan. If only someone nicer had approached him on that long-ago night at the dance club. Anyone even remotely nicer than Marcus would've made Jonathan a better man than the man he was today. All those years I'd thought I'd ruined my best chance at happiness by never opening up to him. It never occurred to me—until now—that I'd blown it for both of us.

***

My Realtor Amanda stood outside the front door waiting for me at exactly one o'clock. I couldn't believe I'd once thought I needed to hang onto this house—with Jonathan, no less—to make my life complete. Such a strange experience, to walk through the empty, echoing rooms and realize this would be the last time I walked through them.

At around two o'clock Amanda left the house to meet another client. Nothing left to do but lock the front door on the way out, drop the key in the strongbox hanging off the front doorknob. Amanda would take care of the rest. It was still too early to leave for Santa Cruz. So I walked through the empty rooms again. The walls of Julio's massage room were as bright and cheerful as ever. I hoped the new owners wouldn't repaint them.

Then someone knocked hard on the front door. The knocking sounded that much louder, that much more urgent, with all the rooms empty. It wouldn't be Amanda, since she could let herself in with her own key. Holy smokes. What if it was Julio? What if he'd cancelled his plans to see me?

"One second," I called out happily.

I unbolted and swung open the door. But the person standing at the doorway wasn't Julio. The person standing at the doorway—with a wide-eyed, tormented look on his face—was Jonathan. I could only stare at him, my heart shriveling to the size of a prune.

"I need to talk to you," Jonathan said, and walked past me into the house.

"Jonathan," I said, my hand still gripping the knob of the half-open door, "what are you doing here?"

"I want to go to Portland with you." Jonathan's strong, determined voice resounded through the empty space.

"What?" I said.

"My mind is made up," Jonathan said, his chest going up and down. "I'm leaving Marcus."

"What are you talking about?" I said, inwardly cursing myself for not checking to see who it was before opening the door.

Jonathan walked up to me, grabbed me by the shoulders, and pushed me against the front door, slamming it shut. Then he planted one of the deepest, most passionate, most desperate kisses I've ever been given. I closed my eyes and forgot who I was. No pushing him away, either. Jonathan had real strength, when it occurred to him to use it.

"That's what I'm talking about," Jonathan said, his hard breaths warm against my face. "Now do you understand?"

"Jonathan, you don't know what you're doing," I said, wriggling my way out of his grasp. "You need to go right now."

"Listen to me," Jonathan said, stepping between me and the door. "I can't take it with Marcus anymore. If you want to play for keeps, then I'm yours for keeps. Isn't that what you've wanted all along?"

I turned away from him and put my hands on my hips, still breathing hard. Jonathan had finally done what I'd hoped against hope he'd do last year—leave Marcus and come live with me. Except—

"You're too late," I said, my heart beating faster. "I'm in love with Julio Robles."

There. I'd said it. Something I couldn't bring myself to say for months now, not even to myself. Something I should've said to Julio at the yoga studio this morning, instead of slinking off to meet Jonathan. But the words were out. I wouldn't unsay them even if I could.

"You're kidding," Jonathan said, his mouth open. "Marcus told me the whole thing between you and Julio was a lie."

"The lie is now the truth," I said with an expanding feeling in my chest. "I don't expect you to understand it. But believe me when I tell you I love Julio. He's the reason why we can't be together. Not now. Not in six months. Not ever."

For the next few seconds we stared at each other. Jonathan looked at me as if he no longer recognized me. I almost had to wonder if I'd said what I'd said. But I had.

"I see," Jonathan said, with a chastened purse of his lips. "I guess there's nothing left to say."

"You're right, there isn't," I said. "Now if you'll excuse me, I'm leaving for Santa Cruz in a little while and I'd like some time alone in the house before I go. You could think about leaving Marcus anyway. He's a selfish no-good jerk. You know that as well as I do. If you want any hope of happiness, then leaving him is what you'll do."

***

The house felt larger and more silent after Jonathan left. I pictured Julio rushing down the stairs in his pink-flamingo tux, coming to congratulate me for dismissing Jonathan for good. His spirit had certainly hovered above my head, watching with satisfaction as I closed the door for good on Jonathan.

I walked around the house. The kitchen wall still showed a pale green stain where I'd thrown Julio's pistachio ice cream. I went upstairs and turned on the shower to listen to the pipes groan. What a relief it was, to think those pipes would soon be someone else's problem. Then I went downstairs to Julio's massage room and lingered at the doorway, taking in the brightly colored walls. I pulled out my phone, walked to the center of the room, and snapped picture after picture, from each of the corners, from the door, from the window. My heart sank at my careless failure to take a single photo of Julio while we were together.

Would it be selfish of me to call Julio now? Open up my heart to him, tell him how I felt? My mind turned to this morning with Julio at the yoga studio. It seemed only logical, only natural, for me to take that step, so soon after I'd said the words out loud.

But, no, I couldn't do it. I sure couldn't expect Julio to abandon his life down here—his friends, his massage practice, his mother with Stage Three breast cancer—to join me in rain-soaked Portland. Besides, he'd all but said this morning he'd moved on to someone else. That's the news he would've given me if I'd broken down and declared my love to him this morning. He probably wouldn't even answer the phone if I called him now.

I could still text Julio, though. He'd looked so reproving—so like my mother—when I'd told him this morning I was meeting Jonathan. Wouldn't he like to know how I'd handled it? I couldn't leave for Portland with him thinking I hadn't learned my lesson.

At the house, I typed. *Just sent Jonathan away. Was wrong to see him. Thought you should know.*

The phone buzzed against my thigh. For a moment I thought it was my mind playing tricks on me. Then it buzzed again. I pulled out the phone. Julio's name glowed at me. His message made my heart skip a beat.

Open the door.

I had barely time to ask him what door he meant when a second message popped up on my screen. A photo. My front door from the outside. I sucked in a breath. He'd come here after all. I slipped the phone in my pocket, went to the front door, and grasped the knob.

How could I describe in mere words, the emotions flooding through me when I swung open the door? To behold Julio in his aqua jacket, a shy look on his face? He must've been walking up to the house when he received it. So he would've journeyed all the way here whether I'd texted him or not.

"I thought you had plans today," I said, half out of breath.

"I bailed." Julio's eyes glowed. "So are you going to let me in? Or do I have stand out here all day?"

I stepped out of the way and let Julio walk into the house. He moved with a stateliness I'd never seen in him before. No jaunty step. The silence in the house reminded me of the silence in his yoga studio this morning. He seemed older, more content with himself.

"So Jonathan was here a few minutes ago," Julio said, turning around to face me.

"He followed me here from the Ferry Building," I said, nodding. "I kicked him out."

"Good," Julio said, giving me a satisfied smile. "You saved me the trouble of having to do it myself."

"Is that why you came?" I said with a smile of my own. "To save me from Jonathan?"

"I had no idea he'd be here," Julio said. "The one I came for was you."

He walked up and put his arms around my waist, looking at me with a calm light in his eyes. My heart pounded away. Even with my arms wrapped around him, I still wasn't sure this wasn't one of my dreams. Any second now, a train whistle would blow and I'd snap my eyes awake to find myself on the ratty love seat. But my eyes were open. This was real.

"I was such a doofus this morning." Julio shook his head and glanced away. "Pretending like I haven't been missing you since the day you left. I was only being jealous. I thought Jonathan had snapped you up for sure."

"Jonathan wanted to snap me up," I said, breathing in Julio's warmth, "but I wouldn't let him. I told him someone else had hold of my heart. He's holding it right now."

"You can't mean that," Julio said. "I've been so awful to you."

"Awful?" I said. "How have you been awful?"

"You know what I mean," Julio said, his voice dropping to almost a whisper. "Marcus."

"Him?" I said with contempt. "I don't care about your past with him. He can't touch either of us now."

Julio squeezed me tighter, his cheek pressed against my chest. I kept my eyes open to make sure I wasn't dreaming. I wasn't.

"I want to come with you to Santa Cruz today," Julio said, his voice half-muffled against my chest.

"What?" I let go of him and looked at him.

"I want to go with you to Santa Cruz," he repeated, looking up at me wide-eyed. "Would you mind?"

"Mind?" I said, astonished at what he'd said. "I'd love to introduce you to Dad and Wendy. Unless you have a class to teach. Or your mother to take care of."

"I have one class tomorrow night," Julio said smiling, "but that's it. My sisters are ten minutes away if Mami needs help."

"Good," I said, already looking forward to introducing Julio to Dad and Wendy.

"And," Julio said, putting his arms around my waist again, "maybe, um, I could join you for more than Santa Cruz."

I blinked at him, not sure if I'd heard him right. His intense look told me I had. He'd suggested what I hadn't dared to suggest myself.

"You mean Portland?" I said, my body going slack against his.

"A part of me went with you when you boarded that plane last month," Julio said, his voice trembling. "I can't watch you leave again."

"But what about San Francisco?" I said. "All you ever talked about was how much you wanted to live in San Francisco again. Do you want to give that up?"

"San Francisco can take care of itself," Julio said, giving a slight shrug. "What does San Francisco matter if you're not around? I belong wherever you are, Frank. I love you too."

And there they were: the words I'd longed to hear from Jonathan, the man I'd loved last year, coming instead from Julio, the man I loved today. In my head a field of ice broke apart and melted, leaving behind a warm, tranquil sea. He'd said what I'd barely let myself hope he'd say.

"And your mother?" I said, thinking Julio could stay down here as long as he needed for her sake. "Won't she be upset if I take you away from her?"

"Are you kidding?" Julio said. "She was upset I let you slip away in the first place. 'Give him a call already,' she keeps telling me. 'What are you wasting your time for, moping around your old mother's house like this?'"

"So she's better?" I said, excited.

"She's tired a lot, but better," Julio said, breaking into a smile. "So much better she nags me about you."

"Ah, moms," I said, and I let out a laugh at the thought of Julio's mother, sick with cancer, reserving enough strength to give Julio a hard time about me. Julio had clearly inherited his big heart from her. "She can visit us once she's better. But how about I take you to see her now. I want to thank her in person. Then we can drive to Santa Cruz."

I locked up the house, gave it one last look, and then we pulled onto the freeway heading south. The blunder I thought I'd made last year, telling Marcus and Jonathan I had a boyfriend named Julio, turned out to be the move of a grandmaster. I pressed down on the gas, squeezed Julio's hand, and smiled. Julio was nothing like any other man I'd brought home to meet my family, but already I could tell Wendy and Dad would like him. So would Mom, if she were alive. I pictured her watching me from afar, a formal but pleased expression on her face, looking gratified to know that after so many missteps, so many false paths, her son had at last found his way to checkmate, and captured his best man.

ABOUT THE AUTHOR

Chris Delyani is the author of *The Love Thing* (2009) and *You Are Here* (2012). He lives in Oakland, California.

www.chrisdelyani.com
Twitter: @chrisdelyani

Made in the USA
Middletown, DE
02 June 2019